The Lives We Were Meant to Live

a novel

Pamela Hull

First Edition

PAGE PUBLISHING
Conneaut Lake, PA

First originally published by Page Publishing 2023

ISBN 979-8-88793-666-6 (pbk)
ISBN 979-8-88793-674-1 (digital)

Printed in the United States of America

Other Books by Pamela Hull

Nonfiction

Where's My Bride?

SAY YES! Flying Solo After Sixty

Moments that Mattered

Fiction, Short Stories

What Love Looks Like

A Novel

The Lives We Were Meant to Live

Then, now and tomorrow

Paul

Geri and Bobby
Neal and Jennifer
Josie
Peter
Evan

Burt

Thank you, Joelle Sander

This is our fifth book together, author and editor, a tribute to our enduring patience and friendship.

Keep your face to the sunshine and you cannot see the shadow. It's what sunflowers do.

—Helen Keller

Contents

Chapter 1

Waiting for his burger at the diner on the Lower East Side in New York City, Gavin could tell the difference the moment he saw her. Girls from the city, and he had known plenty, just didn't look like her - sweet-faced, country fresh, no makeup, pretty as could be with light auburn hair carelessly pinned, idle strands escaping. Her eyes were soft and dreamy, as if all she saw had magic around it, not the tired, disappointed gaze acquired by young women way too soon after they had moved here.

Gavin kept his book open on the table, a possible launch for conversation. Smiling politely while noting that his curly brown hair matched his shiny brown eyes, she set down his hamburger deluxe and glanced at the worksheets.

"Careful with the ketchup," she advised. "Don't want to mess up your pages."

"Are you a student too?" he started. In this part of the city, near the university, many undergraduates had part-time jobs.

"Why do you ask? Can't you see I'm a waitress?" she answered coyly, not sarcastically.

"Waitresses generally aren't concerned with the books and papers their customers are reading," Gavin replied.

She leaned over, wiped a leftover streak off the table, refilled his water glass.

Gavin was tempted to touch a loose curl, to sweep it back. He reached out his hand but then pulled back.

"Well, yes, I *am* going to college here. New York University. This job helps my folks back in Iowa who are borrowing from the bank to pay for it."

I knew it, Gavin thought, *no innocent face like that had been living long in this city.* "New York University!" Gavin said. "Me too! But I only live two hours away. Why have you come so far to go to school, if you don't mind my asking?"

"Same answer any gal from Iowa would give. I wanted to see the big city. Doesn't everyone?" she answered, smiling as if he would understand, as if he *should* understand, being a lifelong resident.

Orders were piling up on the counter behind her.

"By the way, my name is Gavin," he said.

"Mine is Ellie," she answered.

He laid his hand over his heart to dull its wild thumping. Could she hear its beat, see it pounding and thrusting beneath his shirt?

Gavin began to eat at the diner at least three nights a week. Pushing open its front door, he was greeted by the kitchen's welcome warmth and the smoky aroma of grilled meat. As soon as he saw Ellie's lovely face, he felt he had left the chaotic madness of the city and entered a private, precious space. He often arrived as her shift was ending so they could hang out and talk over a cup of coffee and a piece of pie, whatever remained in the glass case. Sitting in a back corner, they did their assignments together. Almost immediately, they began to name various items "ours." *Our* booth in the right rear under the clock. *Our* favorite coffee flavor, Original Grogg Decaf, no milk, no sugar. *Our* favorite dessert, pecan brownie pie, the house specialty.

When she first set down his burger, Gavin had fallen in love, but he was mindful of being too assertive. He sought to woo her but not to scare her, to make her feel attractive but without pressure. Like a friend, a steady presence, he would pursue her quietly but persistently. As they sat together in the back booth, he began to notice more details about her. For one, she always tied her hair back when she studied so it wouldn't fall over her starry eyes. He could then see the yellow flecks right in the center of the gray and the startled look of surprise, and yes, pleasure when she lifted her head and found him there. Keeping a pitcher of coffee on the table nearby, she was always mindful that his cup was topped off. When she said his name, she drew out the two syllables - Gav-een - French-sounding as if it were important, not an ordinary name. And he nearly fainted on the day he made her laugh with a joke about his cat Buffy, and she covered his hand with hers.

Ellie, he repeated to himself, *Ellie.*

Although Gavin would marry her this very day, Ellie was not keen to give up school or the adventure of living in the city. Not at twenty she wasn't. Not after her folks back home were scrimping to send her to college.

On her days off, they took long walks in the great city parks or on the promenades along the mighty Hudson and East Rivers that encircled Manhattan. They attended the cinema or a museum when it was a rare two-for-one night, discovering the city on foot, enjoying the many free things going on at every hour - parades, outdoor concerts, street fairs where they would ravenously consume spicy sausages with onions. Many evenings were spent in the apartments of fellow students sharing potluck dinners and drinking cheap wine out of plastic cups.

"Gavin," she said, "isn't this a wonderful city? Do you think we'll ever run out of things to do?"

On their strolls, Ellie now held his hand, but he was careful not to squeeze too hard, lest he frighten her off.

When you are young and falling in love, the world is without boundaries, Gavin thought. There were never enough words to whisper at each disclosure about themselves. Each confidence begat ten others. Could life at this age, in this time, be more delectable? Sitting in the back of the diner, though their books were open, in fact, they rarely studied seriously. Rather, they spent their time quietly murmuring about their lives, their families, sharing impressions about the city, looking up frequently, staring at each other. Their hearts thrumming and pulsing, suspended in that riveting sensation of the body being transformed.

On a ferocious winter day, when the streets were buried in snow and heavy tree branches bent low in the wind, public transportation was halted, and vehicles were abandoned. Stumbling and heaving in the freezing blizzard, Gavin made his way to Ellie's room - to help her prepare for an imminent test in abnormal psych, he would say. But the real reason for showing up was simply to be with her. In her disbelief and delight at finding him at her door, shaking, pale and numb, and covered with ice crystals, his hair frozen stiff and standing straight up like toothpicks, she fell into his arms.

"I love you, Gavin," she breathed into his shoulder.

From that moment, they both knew their fortunes would be irrevocably joined.

However, Gavin and Ellie also nurtured private dreams they chose not to share, believing it was the right thing to do. They were too young to realize the serious impact that unfulfilled longings, stewing below the surface of their lives, might have on their regard for each other, that secrets shape and alter relationships.

Gavin had always longed to become a painter. As young as four, he walked around the house with a crayon, drawing images of his cat, the neighbor's dog, the details of various dwellings. He was especially taken with doorways and often drew them flung open with mysterious elements beyond. His mother, thinking his interest a passing fancy, left pieces of paper scattered about for his use.

"Isn't Gavin adorable?" she remarked to her husband, smiling indulgently.

But the passion of the artist grew to be integral to Gavin's soul. As he grew older, he knew that he didn't have to go to New York University to be a painter, but his loving though misguided parents insisted he find in college a satisfying way to earn a living. They were counting on it, slightly alarmed that his thirst for drawing had not dwindled. Anxious to quell the desire, they wrapped their objections in a shroud of shame, of weakness.

"A frivolous pastime, not the work of a lifetime," his mother noted.

"Doodling," she had said repeatedly, "won't amount to anything. Some of these pictures are quite good. But how will they earn you any money? What if you get married? Have children? You think a picture will pay the bills? And how many would you have to sell to buy your children shoes?"

"Gavin, not going to college would be a big mistake," his father added. "You need to find a profession that provides a reliable source of income."

Gavin blanched at their muddled assumptions. *Studying texts and data, anyone can become an accountant,* he reflected, *or an engineer, but how many of us can conjure up an original aesthetic entirely out of our minds, our fingers?*

And so Gavin buried his wishes, his creative instincts. Diligently, he scanned major areas of study offered in the college catalog, a long list of wildly diverse departments. Surely he would find something of interest. And when he met Ellie, he finally took his folks' admonishments seriously. A man in a committed relationship was compelled to provide.

Besides, what girl would marry a man who painted pictures? Most girls he knew wanted a house, cars, a dependable domestic situation. Feisty Ellie, who came from a farm where the relentless work was never done, and after only a few hours' sleep, it was time to do the milking again; from a determined family in which each member was obligated to complete required tasks essential to keep the whole operation moving along. She deserved better. She deserved comfort. Above all, she deserved reliability.

And yet despite Gavin's sampling of disparate subjects, nothing but art history held the slightest allure. Sociology, anthropology, chemistry, French literature - dreary, grim choices. He needed to *create* something, not study it. Sitting in a dark auditorium while the fine arts lecturer clicked through slides of great historical achievements, Gavin bristled with envy, despair, self-loathing. There now on the screen was his idea of perfection - a hunk of marble and Bernini's *Apollo and Daphne* and his *Bust of Pope Paul V*. Another snap, and Raphael's superb painting *Madonna in the Meadow* appeared, and he was only twenty-two at the time of its execution, almost the same age as Gavin. And what had he produced as even a beginning of something, of anything? To exist merely on the far fringes of art seemed an unattainable dream. So Gavin put the thought away, stuffed it far down in his gut, and kept running his finger down the pages of the college directory - math, biology, colonial history, economics…

Lauren Bacall. Ellie wanted to get inside the sultry look of Lauren Bacall, to let her words spill out like a feathery invitation, to flip her hair, lift her eyes so that men would jump in front of a train or leave their wife, all because she had lured them to such endings. Ellie never told Gavin that she wanted to be an actress. All it took for such an ambition was attending a Debbie Reynolds musical with her friend Julie when she was in high school. She decided then, right on the spot, that acting before an audience in roles of the imagination was a glamorous notion, far removed from the daily tedium of milking cows and planting corn.

When she blurted out this notion to her parents, they were aghast.

"An actress?" they cried. "Living that loose life with no promise of steady work and cavorting with all kinds of characters? Actors never stay in one place, and besides, they live make-believe lives, preening and pretending and doing terrible things to gain advantage."

It was a formidable reckoning. She cowered before them, powerless to argue with their positions. She understood they feared for her well-being, but still, couldn't they allow her to take a chance at her young age? It was beyond her youthful grasp to comprehend why, in her parents' minds, being both a person of moral integrity and an actress would be automatically incompatible.

"Oh, no, young lady. A smart girl like you? You're going to college to make something decent of yourself. Why, you can be a teacher or a nurse. Maybe even a doctor! We don't want to hear another word about this acting nonsense."

When Ellie decided to attend New York University, she was surprised they allowed her to go to a school in the heart of the theater world. But in fact, living in Midwest Iowa, her parents were not tuned into what goes on in big cities far off. They never watched television or read newspapers, always exhausted, plumb worn-out.

How could she tell Gavin? If her own parents thought her dreams implied a lesser moral standing, what would Gavin think? Would he also consider her capricious and unrealistic, not a person of substance? So like him, she kept her dreams hidden. Out of his presence, she scanned issues of *Backstage* and *Show Business* for listings to auditions, checked postings at actors' hangouts - coffee shops, stage doors, producers' offices. The search often left her dejected. So few applied to her, an ingenue with no experience. Often, she was the wrong something of an infinite number of essential elements.

As she rushed around on buses and subways in snowstorms and downpours, Ellie wondered if she would ever find an announcement for an appropriate role for her age, sex, physical appearance, experience. And when she finally spied a reasonable request and showed up, so did hundreds of others. Even arriving hours early with a sandwich and a thermos, dozens of pretty girls would already be waiting on line. Often, she was forced to miss class.

Ellie assumed the others, although fidgety and impatient, would be helpful, a sorority of female peers with shared ambitions. But it was the opposite. Competing for the same role, they regarded her as a rival, each privately wishing failure for the other. They were a closed, fierce bunch of zealous, grasping young women aiming for stardom. As they waited down the block and around the corner, a few with pretty voices practiced singing, humming low. Others tap-danced in place, reminding her that she had never had a singing or dancing lesson, never touched a musical instrument. Woefully unprepared and naive, never had she considered the possibility of such indifference and isolation.

She shared these feelings only with her roommate, Jody, who was majoring in communications and found the whole process quite glamorous.

"Sometimes, Ellie, there are hardships on the way to the Oscars!" she gushed.

Month after month, in all kinds of weather and personal disappointment, Ellie continued to check things out, to show up, to stand on line.

After a long year of continuing desperation and failing to find her way in, Ellie lost her cheerful optimism and fell into an intractable melancholy. She pulled back from the competition, from the long parade of hopefuls, from the scowls on other girls' faces, from the terrible rejection time after time of failing to approach the stage door. She was used to feeding chickens in the snow and bringing in the cows under a grueling sun, all to a purposeful end, but here, she waited uselessly in one place, her legs and hands numb with cold or dripping with sweat just so she finally might have a *chance* to read, if the role was not assigned before she had the luck to try out. Occasionally, an usher appeared on the sidewalk and called someone's name. A squeal of joy as that gal was brought inside, and Ellie slowly realized that an opening in this business might require a personal connection. Alas, she had none. And there was this - if she failed to maintain her grades, her folks might suspect her attention was elsewhere.

In spring semester, she signed up for Shakespeare and the Art of the Bard and Theater in Colonial America. Gavin registered for Frescoes in Renaissance Italy and the History of the Medicis. Still, those selections served no purpose in furthering their goals. Rather, the courses reminded them of stagnating, of marking time with their personal ambitions. Poor substitutes for their diminished aspirations, they were merely secondhand experiences, peripheral to the real world of active participation in which they longed to engage.

On a rainy fall afternoon, when Ellie stood wet and damp on an audition line, which only lessened by five people every hour, she began an honest assessment of her situation. What benefit was she gaining from both her academic work and these rare tryouts from which she never received a call back? What value was she accruing for the burdensome bills sent to her parents? Why remain in college dabbling at this and that? Hoping to find a suitable direction now seemed an illusory goal.

Into this confusion and despair, Ellie's attitude began to change. She began to dream of home, for the pleasures of long sunsets, open skies, cornfields planted in neat rows that grew and blossomed from the farmer's diligent toil. Work to be done, action to be taken, a result that fed the family and paid the bills - so had she been raised. Her younger brother Tim wrote letters that he missed her. She fell into doubt, rethinking her parents' rebuke that acting was an ignoble pursuit. After all, who knew her better?

And so, after two years, ready to admit defeat, the uncertainty of her future came to rest on Gavin's shoulders. She had one reasonable choice. With Gavin, she would have an uncomplicated, endearing domestic life.

By the first semester of her junior year, Ellie decided to move back home. Iowa wasn't New York, but it might offer its own acting opportunities. After all, she had never looked into it.

Would Gavin leave the east and go back with her? There wasn't a foreign film cinema within two hundred miles. No one had ever heard of hot pastrami or pretzels dipped in mustard. There wouldn't be any of the things he loved - tall buildings, neon lights, elevators to the sky. What would he do on a farm?

"Gavin," she asked, "would you go back with me to Iowa?"

He kissed her on the nose and replied, "Of course! Let's get married!" he cried.

Gavin had also sought a reason to leave the classroom. Did it matter to his future well-being whether or not the Medicis were the patrons of Michelangelo? Or that the world was shocked at the master's revelations of glorious nudity on the ceiling of the Sistine Chapel? Perhaps in the vast spaces of Iowa, his eyes would find clarity, peel away their blurry film, allow him somehow to engage with his beloved brushes and paints. He hadn't found himself in New York. Maybe Iowa would surprise him.

In the jewelry section of the campus bookstore, Gavin brushed aside watches with faces of the bell tower, purple pins imprinted with a white torch (the school's logo), men's ties stamped with tiny bobcats (the campus mascot). There, at the end of the case was a small tray of simple gold bands.

The next night, Gavin beckoned over Ellie's fellow workers in the diner to form a half circle around their table. Nearby customers perked up. Then Gavin eased out sideways from the red leather booth and bent on one knee on the gray tile floor sprinkled with pie crumbs, a baby's pacifier, a crumbled napkin, and asked, "My darling Ellie, will you marry me?" As the customers cheered and Ellie laid her right hand over her heart, Gavin slipped a gold ring on the fourth finger of her left hand.

And so, the young couple began to make plans.

Gavin and Ellie took a train to his home in Elmhurst, an hour north of the city. His father, Martin, a skillful manager without a college degree, had just been promoted to foreman of a sprawling hardware store. Gavin asked to bring a friend and hoped to announce his engagement. In his eagerness to introduce Ellie to his parents, he was less mindful of their possible reaction to his decision to leave school.

Theirs was a comfortable home. Martin was happy to hang out with his black lab, Bodie; his wife, Grace; and Gavin's two brothers in middle school. Grace baked and cleaned and kept a garden. Occasionally, she babysat some of the neighbors' kids. Their life together was amiable and suited them both, though occasionally, each quietly wondered what their life would have been like if they had read and understood great books, if they had gone to college like their son and lifted themselves out of the working middle class. But these were thoughts not brought up very often. Why belabor regret?

Martin and Grace offered a warm welcome, smiling graciously when Gavin introduced Ellie. He could see approval on his mother's face, pride on his father's. There were home-baked blueberry scones on the coffee table. Bodie ambled up to Ellie and put his nose in her lap. Then Gavin, fidgeting like a kid about to open a present, burst out with, "Ellie and I want to leave school before graduation and marry right away. We're planning on moving to Iowa."

Martin jumped up. Grace put her hand to her throat. Both sputtered and fussed.

Is she pregnant? Grace wondered.

Gavin was immediately taken over with remorse. *I was too abrupt. I should have eased them into our news. Why did I say three things at once? Leaving school, getting married, moving away.* He doubted if his mother could even find Iowa on a map.

"Are you serious?" his father asked. "After we saved every nickel to send you to college? Do you want to work in a hardware store like me?"

"And of all places, to *Iowa*?" Grace managed, angry and disappointed, reaching for a tissue.

Bodie knocked a scone to the floor and started nibbling. The young couple sat close together, dismissing the parents' pleas. Gavin's mother lifted the coffeepot to pour. His father wrung his hands, over, under, as if scrubbing away dirt. Martin and Grace's shoulders slumped; their heads bowed. They had no leverage to mount a successful response.

When they returned to the city, Ellie called her parents while Gavin paced before her.

"Mom, can you ask Dad to pick up the extension?"

She could hear murmurs, shifting, something falling on the floor.

And then her father was on the phone. "Hi, honey, what's up?" he asked.

"I'm coming home, guys, and I'm bringing someone with me. His name is Gavin. We're getting married."

"What? Are you serious? Drop out of school?"

But Gavin and Ellie's bold decision was final. Neither possessed the maturity of an adult's long look back at repercussions for making hasty choices.

They prepared to leave the city in which they had hoped for beginnings, not endings, the city that piqued Gavin's artistic imagination but stymied his personal dreams. It was not quite a fulsome leave-taking. Ellie was sad at leaving her classmates and Jody. She regretted abandoning her aspirations to the windy and crowded streets. Had she put in enough effort? Occasionally, Gavin had a fleeting thought about completing his degree rather than becoming a college dropout. Leaving now, he would never be more than a high school graduate.

For the last time, they revisited their favorite places. At the bank of the Hudson River, Ellie threw a penny into the waters and made a wish. "To our happiness," she said, turning to Gavin, who was right then impressing upon his mind how the mist rose from the water and settled on the New Jersey cliffs across the way, how those walls of stone showed shades of lavender and blue through the haze when in reality they were mere rock, gray and brown. They stopped in for a last look at the Museum of Modern Art to view Picasso's disturbing masterpiece *Guernica*, both of them unsettled by those interlocking angles and broken circles, those chopped-up forms that conveyed intense emotional and physical suffering. Nevertheless, the man was a genius - they agreed - outrageously original.

The final meal before their departure was hamburgers at the diner. They sat in their familiar corner at the right back while the owner Dirk and Ellie's coworkers placed a whole pecan brownie pie before them.

"Hugs, hugs," they cried, crowding around. "Good luck, keep in touch!" In truth, it was a beginning but a beginning composed of failed dreams and a future about which they were not entirely honest with each other—a launch both dubious and ambivalent. Ellie and Gavin each quietly hoped this decision would somehow bring them closer to their personal ambitions.

To a rented car, they attached a U-Haul loaded with their personal belongings - secondhand furniture and bookshelves that had been left on the sidewalks - and began driving to Iowa. The trip was to last two weeks. Ellie and Gavin each had his and her own choices at which places they would stop. For Gavin, it was Frank Lloyd Wright's famous commission for the Kaufmann family, the magnificent *Fallingwater*, seventy miles from Pittsburgh. Poised over thundering waterfalls, would a painter go mad with the splendor of living inside those glass walls? And for Ellie, the Renaissance Theatre in Mansfield, Ohio, a place in which she could picture herself strutting the stage as Shakespeare's Cordelia uttering the lines, "Unhappy that I am, I cannot heave my heart into my mouth." And above her head in the majestic hall, the famous crystal chandelier weighing three thousand pounds that hung from the grand baroque ceiling.

Both of them were pretending they were merely sightseeing.

As they crossed state lines, first Pennsylvania, then Ohio to Indiana to Illinois and finally into Iowa, the landscape slowly changed from urban to suburban to bucolic to agrarian. Every now and then, a town suddenly popped up, almost sprouting out of the very fields. *It is a complete, tiny village,* Gavin thought, *like a miniature stage set.* Buildings were low - the library, the stores, even city hall - four stories at most. In less than five minutes, they had driven right through.

Ellie explained, "The land is mostly planted for agriculture. There! See those immaculate rows of low leafy bushes? Do you know what they are? You have no idea? Well, they're soybeans. Most of the fancy green pods go to feed the livestock for meat and dairy products. The rest go into consumer products."

"I've had tofu and soy milk," Gavin replied. "And I've seen soy flour in that bodega near your dorm, but I've never thought about where soybeans come from."

"Gavin, look" - Ellie pointed - "here comes the corn. You'll see such fields now all the way home. The stalks aren't that high yet, but they'll be flying their silks very soon, when summer arrives."

"Corn I understand," Gavin answered.

In the distance, they frequently caught sight of silos and red barns.

"We're passing through Amish country," Ellie said. "Kalona and Bloomfield and Hazelton, all Amish." She nodded to her right.

"Look at those decorations on the barns. Aren't they beautiful? Those designs are thought to protect the animals inside from all sorts of bad luck - fire, sickness, lightning, even demons and evil spirits. They're also believed to increase fertility of the livestock and encourage rain and sun for a successful crop. Most people think they're just Amish folk art."

Gavin slowed the car, trying to make out the intricate patterns. They were a bit far off, but he promised himself to check them out - intriguing backgrounds for a painting or two. Someday, perhaps.

"We have tons of cattle ranchers," Ellie said, "and dairy farmers. My folks raise corn and a few dairy cows but mostly corn and, of course, all the vegetables that the household requires. And you can't see them from here, but the hog farmers are back there somewhere. Those farmers love their hogs. Some even give them names like Lulu and Big Boy."

By the time Ellie drew another breath, they were pulling off the highway onto an unmarked road that cut right through cornfields on either side and ended before a neat white two-story farmhouse with a wrap-around porch. Running out to meet them were Ellie's parents, Pat and Sam.

Pat whispered to her husband, "Sam, praise the Almighty, at least she's done with that acting stuff." Then she turned to her daughter. "Your dad took a few hours off to greet you," said Pat as Sam walked over to the U-Haul, offering to unhitch the back end.

"Oh, leave all that for now," Pat said to him as they hugged and walked back together into the homey kitchen. Jars of canned peaches and plums filled the shelves, their ochres and purples glistening with color as the sun poured through the windows. On either side of the glass hung red gingham curtains stamped with roosters and chickens. The floors were unevenly wood-planked and worn; most of the boards were at least a foot wide.

Pat brought out her freshly baked cinnamon rolls, and they sat around the kitchen table, asking questions, sharing news.

"Now you understand," Sam said, growing serious, "that Pat and I are not really approving of this decision of yours to quit school.

But you're here now. As long as you've decided, and no one can change your mind, well, we want you to know that we'll help you however we can."

And with that, Ellie and Gavin were married in the open field beside the barn when the maple and oak trees offered up their bounty of early fall brilliance - scarlets, golds, the shock of orange. Gauzy swaths of white muslin billowed from the branches for their ceremonial enclosure. The sun shone bright, and the hay just harvested stood far off tied up in neat bundles, waiting, like guests on their best behavior. Horses nearby whinnied and snorted in happiness for their beloved Ellie and her Gavin, whose family had flown out from New York. Gavin's younger brothers thought it a great adventure to sleep in the lofts of house and barn while the parents squeezed into a small bedroom in the attic of the main house.

Despite both families opposing Gavin and Ellie leaving school and marrying so young, they kept their objections to themselves. No one wanted to begrudge the joyful couple and create unhappiness. So it was a grand day, a beautiful day, if only Ellie and Gavin had released their secret longings to each other.

A smaller version of Pat and Sam's farmhouse sat primly on the far end of the family property. A hundred years ago, the original landowners lived within its humble shelter. Now it was just an abandoned outpost until the young couple made it their home. Barely visible from the family house, it was private and cozy. Ellie and Gavin painted and scrubbed. Ellie hung pale blue curtains bordered with tiny red apples, hooked a rug for the one main room in colors of spring - apple green, yellow, pink. Gavin painted their battered furniture various bright colors and drew simple flowers scattered over surfaces and sides. From one of the many dogs on the farm, they adopted a golden retriever they named Lucky, for the dozen times a day Ellie and Gavin said to each other, "Aren't we lucky?" Alongside the house stood a grove of magnolia trees whose scented pink and white flowers, along with the bright-yellow forsythia, were Iowa's first colors of spring.

Besides caring for the property and his new bride, Gavin worked long hours at his new position as a school bus driver. The previous worker had moved to Illinois, and Gavin had fallen right into his job. *A pleasure,* he thought, *for a beginning.* All along his route were marvelous open spaces, and inside the bus, the kids were taken up with singing and cheering. As he drove along the country roads in his lumbering, dusty vehicle, he arranged in his mind the sights of rural life. On his break, he made quick sketches of such scenes as a fruit tree or a farm animal, birds flying south, a road disappearing into the woods. After learning the names of the children on his route, he would hand one of these small drawings to one of his special riders - for example, Susie because of her dimples or Troy because his father had died young.

Ellie volunteered to put on a school play for the kindergarteners in the local school, thrilled to hold a script in her hand, even if it did involve only fairies and princesses.

Over supper, she told Gavin stories about her day with her young thespians, explained how she was teaching them to act, describing the structure of a play, its scenes, its particular vocabulary - a*udience, comedy, dialogue, encore.* She was adamant that they memorize simple lines. Teasing, Gavin reminded her that these were four-year-olds. They were not performing a tragedy by Aeschylus, a comedy by Aristophanes.

"Silly you." She smiled with her eyes shut as Gavin carried her up the old staircase to their bedroom.

And so Ellie and Gavin began their married life.

Chapter 2

In those early days, Gavin reflected dreamily as he drove his bus along the rutted road; there was easy loving and unforgettable days and nights when everything was colored pink and sunny, and no feelings were clouded by confusion or blame.

After the house was fixed up, they slowly unpacked their books, handling them with reverence, all the more so for the regret they felt in abandoning them. All the while, they spoke fondly of Ms. Jamison who taught them to love poetry. At this moment, a line from the poet Andrew Marvell's "To His Coy Mistress" seemed perfectly suited for their mood - both buoyant and bittersweet together: "Thus, though we cannot make our sun stand still, yet we will make him run."

On a rainy September evening, Gavin remembered his lovely young wife reached behind the sofa and pulled down a book of poetry. She loved to read out loud. If more than one person was in the same poem, she would assume a different voice and tone for each character. He would rest by her side with his eyes closed, leaning back on the sofa with her head on his lap, his fingers gently playing with her curls. Ellie's voice grew soft as she tried to find the perfect rhythm, holding the small volume aloft.

> *You become. It takes a long time. That's why it doesn't happen often to people who break easily or have sharp edges or who have to be carefully kept. Generally, by the time you are Real, most of your hair has been loved off and your eyes drop out and you get loose in the joints and very shabby.*

> *But these things don't matter at all, because once you are Real you can't be ugly, except to people who don't understand.*

"From *The Velveteen Rabbit* by Margery Williams," she said softly as she closed the book, "in case you're not familiar with the book or author."

They caught their breaths, and then they both cried, holding each other.

After that special evening, they began reading poetry aloud every night after dinner. It suited them - the singsong tempos they both loved, the brevity of each poem yet every one replete with laughter and sadness.

Most poems, they soon realized, were about loss, separation, unrequited passion, aging, disloyalty. They often searched for works that ended happily forevermore, but there were few of those. Was life really true to that script of sorrow and loss? Not them, of course - or did the writer simply find a tragic ending made for a more interesting and complex poem. In the end, it didn't matter. Their love was brave, fearless, invincible.

Rupert Brooke in "The Hill" wrote this:

> *Breathless, we flung us on the windy hill,*
> *Laughed in the sun and kissed the lovely grass.*
> *You said: "Through glory and ecstasy we pass:*
> *Wind, sun, and earth remain, the birds sing still,*
> *When we are old, are old... And when we die*
> *All's over that is ours.*

"We will never grow old," they promised each other.

Ellie recalled browsing in the college bookstore two years earlier and coming upon Edgar Lee Masters's visionary and inventive *Spoon River Anthology*. It had been her last purchase before leaving New York. Now she noticed it on the shelf and reached for it as they settled themselves into the sofa cushions and each other.

"Gavin, honey, let me tell you this author's personal story," she began.

"Masters had grown up in a small Midwestern town. This book took place in a similar setting. Devising a unique approach, he wrote narrative poems of each character's life, told in his own words. But the stories did not portray the reader's usual assumption regarding congenial, hometown folks. Rather, he destroyed the myth of small-town America as the bastion of American virtue and portrayed churchgoing, principled middle-class Americans living among the corrupt, the abusive, the failed, and the discontented beneath a veneer of moral goodness. There were only a few untainted characters like Lucinda Matlock who lived righteously and gratefully to old age."

Gavin listened attentively. *What a fine teacher Ellie would make,* he thought.

From the graveyard, each resident told his own story. Gavin felt uneasy whenever Ellie revealed a character in which he saw himself, in which Masters likely also saw himself, such as in the person described in his poem, *Margaret Fuller Slack*:

> *I would have been as great as George Eliot*
> *But for an untoward fate.*
> *For look at the photograph of me made by Peniwit…*
> *But there was the old, old problem.*
> *Should it be celibacy, matrimony or unchastity?*
> *Then John Slack, the rich druggist, wooed me,*
> *Luring me with the promise of leisure for my novel,*
> *And I married him, giving birth to eight children,*
> *And had no time to write…*

Emma continued. "From his early years, Masters wanted to be a writer, but his father, a lawyer, pressured him to study law. And so he did, after which, he moved to Chicago and became a partner of the famed Clarence Darrow."

With a jolt of insight, Gavin realized that Masters's and his own plight were the same - Masters, a writer in his soul, a lawyer in life; Gavin, a painter in his soul, a bus driver in life.

As they made each book, each poem, their own, they moved it to a special shelf in the living room. First, *The Velveteen Rabbit* stood alone. But before long, there were others - Rupert Brooke, Edgar Lee Masters, Pablo Neruda. As Ellie read from William Wordsworth's Lucy Poems, Gavin recalled how she looked when he first saw her.

When she I loved looked every day
Fresh as a rose in June,
I to her cottage bent my way,
Beneath an evening moon.

When Ellie recited those famous lines from John Donne's splendid, *Death Be Not Proud*, "Die not, poor Death, nor yet canst thou kill me," they pledged never to die and be parted.

"Gavin," Ellie would say, and his hand would briefly stop stroking her hair, "was it destiny that you were in the diner that night?"

"Of course!" he assured her. "But if not there, I would have found you somewhere else."

Every other Saturday, they drove into town to visit Haley Max's dry-goods shop. In the back, dozens of books, especially poetry, a selection that spanned centuries, were stacked high and arranged in neat categories. Haley brewed his special coffee for them, black as the licorice sitting by the register.

"My old army recipe," he said, laughing, and left them to savor their discoveries. And there they relaxed in a pair of worn armchairs, volumes piled in their laps, opening up one book after the other, reading bits to each other, choosing, eliminating, vowing to purchase only three at a time.

When Haley took some small amount off the marked price, Ellie whispered, "Gavin, I'm not sure how many farm folks actually buy poetry books, but I'm grateful anyway!"

At home, they memorized random lines and spoke them to each other during the day.

"Fresh as a rose in June," he might breathe as he passed Ellie outside taking up her seeds and trowel.

Or as she hugged him goodbye, she might lower his cheek to hers and murmur, "I love your hair when the strands enmesh your kisses against my face," tugging at his curls.

In summer, evening drew down late, and they sat long hours on the porch swing, rocking, rocking, Ellie reading, and Gavin by her side.

Life was easy, mellow, unruffled. Nothing was unfinished, at least the parts they shared.

And as summer's warmth gave way to the chill of fall and the leaves on the maple trees turned blazing red, little Jack was growing in Ellie's belly, a sweet time, like planting your first garden of tomatoes and tulips. Something they had created, beginning to thrive but could hardly imagine coming into full bloom. Yet when fully ripe and mature, little Jack would emerge from his place of nurture and growth, full out into the loving light.

On a damp spring day, misty with drizzle, just as the purple crocuses began to nudge their heads through the winter soil, Gavin drove Ellie to the hospital. His parents flew in from New York. Pat and Sam rushed over after feeding the chickens. Younger brother Tim, clumsy and awkward, paced the halls. Gavin sat at the head of the bed, smoothing Ellie's hair, attempting to bestow comfort as her hands clutched fistfuls of the sheet. But even in the midst of this drama, Gavin gathered details for a sketch he would make later - the blur of nurses rushing in and out, the bright lights overhead, walls a pale-green color, Ellie's mound in his direct vision, a window. Outside, a tree.

Ellie finally delivered a hefty eight-pound star. The families were cooing, hugging and fussing around the edges, snapping photos, and Tim saying, over and over, "Hey, I'm an uncle! How about that?"

The new parents were overcome at the breadth to which love could expand.

Gavin stood by the window holding his infant son in his arms. He bent his head, whispering, "Jack, look. See how bright green the leaves are as they begin to unfurl." *How remarkable,* Gavin thought, *that just yesterday Ellie and I only existed as a couple. And now our lives are moving on this mysterious course, and who knows where that will lead?* He prayed for all good things, even as he described the color and shape of the leaves and noticed that Jack's tiny fingers quivered as he spoke, as if reaching toward the window. Was it the father breathing into his son's soul to observe closely a world waiting to be painted? Gavin held his child close, filled with such thoughts and musings. As Jack's murmurings continued, he chose to believe that the fluttering of his hands did indeed indicate leanings toward him becoming a man with unique sensibilities.

No longer, and never more, will Ellie and I be carefree and private, Gavin realized. *From now on, every gesture, choice, and movement would be complicated and mindful.*

Two together could make an exceptional pair, but the addition of a third lifted the coupling into a more exalted world.

Chapter 3

Ellie's younger brother, Tim, was elated that Gavin and Ellie had returned home to Iowa. And now here was Jack, another celebrated arrival. The proud uncle and little Jack instantly became inseparable, carrying on like two young pups, laughing, tickling, playing on the rug for hours.

As a teenager, Tim was growing out at all angles, his arms too long for his torso, his feet fitting into a size 12 shoe. He already measured out at 6'3" with a skinny neck, like a root stem, but in another couple of years, all would straighten out and match up. His sweet smile spread over his face when he looked at Jack, you'd think he had baked it in sugar just for him.

Girls also loved Tim's smile - direct, without guile or cunning. For this, they overlooked his gawkiness. He had many friends, and Ellie and Gavin were surprised that he wanted to spend all his free time with his little nephew. But Ellie was grateful for his help. It enabled her to lie down for an hour, weed her garden, fold the laundry. As she easily fell into motherhood, she especially loved watching this close relationship develop between her son and brother. At the same time, as she constantly met Jack's relentless demands, he kept offering up the superb rewards of infancy - his first laugh, his reaching out when Gavin approached, turning over, sitting up, and the entire parade of that first astounding year.

Still while rocking on the porch with Jack in her arms, singing a Broadway tune, and looking out on the fields of corn with the low hills in the distance, Ellie occasionally felt a nub of unease, a slight ruffling of distress, as if she were not comfortable in her chair. It came to her, the same thought, *What happened to my resolve to pursue acting? To accomplish something serious, something of my own?*

Her second pregnancy ended such thinking.

Those nine months were far too involving for further reflection or regret. In fact, they also ended the spare time she and Gavin had previously spent together, even washing the supper dishes side by side. Ellie bought plastic plates. After one use, she tossed them in the trash. Always exhausted, she did what chores she could, when she could. Whatever was left to do, well, Gavin finished up what remained. When their reading poetry together finally became unmanageable, however, Gavin persisted, not ready to discard this happy pastime. Instead of gathering nightly, he brought down a book once a week while Ellie offered excuses - "Too tired," "Not up to it," "We've outgrown it, don't you think?" Yet he took it upon himself to read aloud as she dozed on the sofa with her swollen feet propped on the ottoman.

But it wasn't the same. Gavin didn't have the voice, the modulations, the fervor. Nor did Ellie any longer lay her head on his lap, trusting, willing, while he stroked her hair. She was anxious to be upstairs, readying for bed. One week of making this attempt became two, then three, until one day, Jack, a toddler, was found swaying in front of the bookcase, reaching for a bright-red binding that had caught his eye. Gavin thought the book might be by the American poet E. E. Cummings, and with a sad and heavy heart, he recalled, *You shall above all things be glad and young.* Then he recalled another verse, *All in green went my love riding.* Suddenly, Jack's little fingers got caught in a tight space. Pushing and probing, he caused the books to topple.

Ellie came running. Was he hurt? No, he was happily tearing out pages, drooling on covers, and looking up at his mother with the delight of discovery. Ellie carefully gathered up their special collection and stored them in the attic with their college texts. Then she filled the shelves with Jack's toys.

Gavin left their bed before daybreak. An hour later, when the sun began to rise, Ellie was feeding Jack his oatmeal. The day was long. In the evening, after her maternal duties and chores, volunteer time with the kindergartners and their childish productions, while waddling around with a big belly, she collapsed in bed right after she put Jack down for the night. Gavin arrived home to find the house dark and quiet. If he wanted something to eat, he made himself a grilled cheese sandwich. The first few nights, he felt bereft, lonely. Yet slowly, the abandoned room became a kind of refuge. Time and space entirely his own felt like a gift. As he sat with his simple meal, he made drawings of incidents that happened on his bus run, a visual diary of his daily life - seven-year-old Shawn's dismay as he dropped his lunch; first-grader Joanie in her blue pinafore kissing her baby brother goodbye; shy little Maxine handing him a daisy. There was no help for it. His hand wouldn't stop unless he put a cast on it. Would he store the pictures in the attic? Or on the top of the bookcase where no one ever dusted?

From time to time, testing her reaction, he showed a few to Ellie. She hardly glanced at them.

"Oh, Gavin, if you have time to draw, I wish you would take Jack instead and help me out," she lamented.

So softly had they shown up neither Ellie nor Gavin were aware of the changes occurring between them. Perhaps because they seemed such a natural progression. After all, wasn't their household evolving and expanding? Weren't alterations and accommodations and reassessments part of their journey? Disappointments along with the pleasures? In four short years, they had come to this - a growing family, piles of bills, the slow fading of youthful romance. He missed certain loving moments, but it was easy to make excuses and look aside. Besides, there simply was too much he couldn't do about the accruing losses. In the end, Gavin came to resignation and decided that for all its benefits, marriage and children also had the ability to dampen the spirit, to wear one down, thereby deterring any consideration of taking risks.

When Ellie's labor started, Gavin again drove his wife to the hospital. This time, it was winter. A gloomy gray scrim covered the sky, hid the sun. Gavin's folks flew into Iowa from New York. Ellie's folks rushed over after they brought in the horses. Tim was now helpful and handy, skipping school to stay home with Jack. Again, Gavin sat at the head of the bed, whispering to Ellie, laying cold cloths on her brow. And when newborn Danny finally decided to make his appearance, Gavin called Tim with the news.

"An uncle, twice! Hey, Jackie boy, you have a little brother!" he shouted as he set Jack on his shoulders and danced around the kitchen.

Both parents in the hospital room hugged and took photos.

When the nurses had wiped Danny down and wrapped him in a blanket, Gavin held his second son and walked over to the window. Would his hands flutter like Jack's had? Indications of a dream taking root in his brain? Gavin had come to believe in such omens, in fated coincidences. His senses were constantly alert to life unfolding in fortuitous ways. Was that not a more comforting attitude than feeling one's life was buffeted by random acts? Outside, the air remained murky. Trees were bare. Branches thrust like bony fingers into the leaden air. With a powerful love, Gavin looked down at little Danny, but without thoughts of grandeur as the tiny hands lay still, folded demurely over his chest.

Tim had news.

"I've decided," he told them. "I'm going to move in here. You're going to need some help, and I'll do what I can after school. I can live without basketball."

And so from two, their family grew to five. It was a crowded, boisterous household. Gavin was promoted to overseer of the area bus system. He would remain in a fixed spot, stationed at the main depot with pencil and clipboard. No more driving on the road. No more colorful scenes to stir his imagination. The additional pay was welcome, but was it worth giving up the freedom of moving through the seasonal landscape with its luminously shifting sights? Worth the denial of chatting pleasurably with the kids?

Gavin bided his time. While making his sketches, his old dream had resurfaced. Someday, he would be a painter. But right now, he had a family for whom he was responsible. He would manage the bus depot and wait for a break. And then, somehow, life would change course. There would be a favorable opening, and picking up his paintbrush, he would begin his real life.

And so the family carried on.

Until one day, their lives were suddenly recast.

Pat was babysitting on the day that Ellie got the news. She was working with her kindergarten kids on a simple version of *Snow White and the Seven Dwarfs* when the school's full-time drama teacher, Ms. Gann, married a gym instructor from Sioux City and abruptly resigned. Ellie was summoned to the principal's office. There, Mr. Evan Pierce gestured to a chair in front of his old oak desk, messy with papers.

"Ms. Ellie, would you mind filling in and taking Ms. Gann's position for a few weeks? Finish up her production of *Peter Pan* until we find a permanent replacement?"

Instantly, Ellie's dormant dreams shot up so fiercely; it was as if they had never been put to sleep. Was this her answer to her musings in New York? An approach to acting from another venue? *Whoa,* she thought, *stop! This offer is only for a limited time.* No matter, she would make contacts with other schools, with the parents, the community. The newspaper would even print her name! Maybe post her picture?

She had to act quickly and jump right in. Ms. Gann's play was in final rehearsals. The performance was in three weeks.

That evening, she fed the children early and made them busy in the playpen with puzzles and toys.

When Gavin came home expecting to find the kitchen dark, dinner was on the table, and the sink was clean. Ellie had baked corn muffins to accompany the meatloaf. He didn't know what to think, but he suspected the news would be challenging. Tim? The pickup? He hung his jacket on a wall peg, kissed his wife, and waited.

"Gavin," she started sweetly, after he had buttered his biscuit and taken a first bite, "something exciting happened today."

They listened to the childish chatter in the other room. There was a bird on the windowsill looking at them, pecking on the glass. A drip from the faucet was insistent.

"Mr. Pierce asked me to be the full-time drama teacher today," Ellie blurted out. "Oh, just temporarily," she quickly added, "for a few weeks. Ms. Gann quit in the middle of *Peter Pan*."

Gavin's first thought was of her, even as he knew the responsibility for the children would fall more heavily on his shoulders.

"Honey, this sounds promising. Maybe an opportunity for change, something new?"

. When he thought later about his reaction, he was proud that what had not initially crossed his mind was a lament - but what about me? It was only in the night while he was trying to sleep and staring at the ceiling's black void, Ellie snoring softly beside him, that he was overcome with anger and self-pity. His wife was moving ahead while he was mired in domestic clay that was slowly hardening around his ankles.

In the darkness of his bedroom, he fancied sharing his concerns with Ellie, imagined her response.

A silly, impractical notion, this painting business, she might say.

Hardly a frivolous notion, he would reply. *My passion clings like a parasite to my bleeding heart.*

What if she laughed? Told him he couldn't possibly be serious?

This is how it began. How alienation usually begins, with small things that innocently spring up but are often overlooked or underestimated, unexamined. New opportunities might seem welcome, but their repercussions may well be negative and have a gnawing grasp on your mind, your soul. One or the other partner has been refashioned, but both or only one may have felt the shift. In any case, problems arise when the one left behind fails to keep up.

The play was a success, and Ellie was given full credit even though Ms. Gann did most of the work and Ellie had mainly tidied up and tweaked bits here and there, added a song, a dance. But when the youngsters took their second bows and the parents were cheering, Ms. Gann was entirely forgotten. For one heroic evening, Ellie was the center of swarming, adoring fans. A week later, she returned to her kindergarten class, assuming her usual duties. But as it turned out, there was to be another production after *Peter Pan* that required a director. And then another. Ellie kept directing, as Mr. Pierce seemed lax in interviewing candidates for the permanent job of drama teacher.

Jack and Danny, just past the toddler stage, and with help, could actually sit a pony, help bring the cows in for milking. And running on their wobbly little legs, they scattered feed to the chickens. The spaces for their games became vast, boundless expanses. After his stint at the shop, Gavin occasionally wandered the fields looking for the boys. It was an easy find. They were either hiding among the corn, teasing poor old Belle, their decrepit horse, or romping with the collies. Dusty but happy, their hands scraped, a band-aid on their forehead, their shin. Gavin was always concerned about injury. He kept thinking of Jack as a newborn, the way his tiny hands had fluttered when he held him at the window pointing out the various greens of the leaves. What if one or both his children inherited his artistic skill? What if some creative flame burned unlit? Gavin rubbed salve into their palms after their bath to prevent their rough skin from becoming hardened, hindering the fine touch needed to wield a paintbrush, a pen, a scalpel.

The farm life is for the hardworking, but not for the gifted, Gavin thought. If he couldn't have that rarefied life for himself, perhaps the boys could?

For several years, frustration had been festering inside Gavin like a tumor. How had he not realized that life on a farm valued different skills from those he himself possessed? How could he have understood the relentless insensitivity of this rough life if not experienced before taking it on? And he worried about presenting an alternative to farm life to his children. He was rarely alone with either of them. The family hovered, sharing meals, picnics, recreation. A loving presence, Pat and Sam, Ellie too, but an inadequate one, incomplete, so he thought.

Yet Gavin was determined that things be different. When he occasionally managed to steal the boys away for a short time, he would pull out his oil pastels, smooth a sheet of paper in front of them, and teach them how to draw - a horse, a bus, even their own hand. Lay the left out flat and draw with the right, he instructed.

"Fingers are difficult to draw," Gavin said. "So rather than draw the shape directly, draw the space around the fingers. That way, you'll automatically get the hand. That concept is called *negative space*, the same as any space around any object." He smiled as Jack eagerly held up a baseball mitt and wiggled his fingers between those of the padded glove. While Danny, whistling, paid no attention, watching two rabbits scamper into the bushes. Gavin showed them how to carefully smudge lines of color with a finger to achieve a shaded effect. But his efforts were usually cut short. Someone - Pat or Sam, usually - would bounce on over, take a look at the boys' papers, sticks of color sprawled everywhere, and remark, "Gavin, why don't you help the boys lift a saddle on the horses?"

One evening, he and Ellie were sitting in the kitchen with cups of clover tea, her shoes flung to the side, her collar unbuttoned. As she spoke of exposing her young students to an adolescent adaptation of *Romeo and Juliet*, she asked, "Gavin, do you know young Howie Simpson, Jerry Simpson's kid? Well, I've been working on his shyness and finally got him to read in front of the others. Maybe because I played Juliet to his Romeo! The kids thought that was hilarious. 'Ms. Ellie,' they said, 'someday you'll be a famous actress or movie star!'"

"Oh, don't I wish!" I responded.

As Ellie was telling Gavin this story, little Jack ran in waving a piece of paper. Gavin reached for the sheet, giving Jack his full attention. He had drawn a family grouping and saw right away that the forms were not the usual stick figures kids make. These shapes had depth, dimension. An attempt was made to draw a stomach on the man, curvy hips on the woman. There were shoes, a left foot and a right foot, even eyelashes!

Ellie, her Juliet story interrupted, answered curtly, "Jack, honey, can't you see I'm talking to Daddy?"

Jack's face squeezed shut, holding back tears. Gavin's heart tightened, then hardened. He breathed deeply, looking from his wife to his son. Whose story mattered more at this moment?

He waited until the boys had gone to bed and Ellie had poured herself a second cup of tea.

"Ellie, look here," Gavin began as he spread out Jack's picture in front of her. "Can't you see this drawing is special? It isn't just some silly childish picture. The woman has hips; the man, a belly and eyelashes! What little kid notices eyelashes? He's seeing details, important details, that others miss entirely. He is *looking* and *seeing*. And it is those two elements, plus the ability to draw what he sees in an interesting way that makes Jack different, and special."

Chastened, Ellie sat back. Gavin had never scolded her before. But now she paused, considered what he had said. *Perhaps he's right,* she decided. *Perhaps I've overlooked Jack's talent.* She glanced down again at the paper. Well, the people *did* have eyelashes, and the woman *certainly* had ample hips, but it still looked like a kid's drawing to her. However, she would pay more attention if her husband, a man who seemed to have artistic inclinations, thought it had merit.

That night in bed, Gavin and Ellie laid back to back. Gavin turned on his side and took his wife in his arms.

"Remember, Ellie," he said, "that when you took on the extra kindergarten class, then Ms. Gann's *Peter Pan* production, I supported you however I could. Well, now Jack needs you. Don't worry about him. He doesn't have to know how a tractor works at this age. But he *does* have to discover how far his imagination can take him."

Once again, Ellie was summoned to the office of Principal Evan Pierce.

"Young lady," he started. "I was in the audience for your *Peter Pan* performance and the two after that. Let me congratulate you on a job well done. Based on your direction of these three plays and recommendations from past years, I would now like to offer you the position of full-time high school drama coach. The faculty and

I agree. You'll have a much wider range to teach and produce shows with older kids who can do things like *Macbeth* or *Winesburg, Ohio*."

Stunned, Ellie sat mute. Unprepared, she yet quickly came up with an idea. Dare she make such a request? At this moment, she might have some leverage. *Take a chance,* she told herself.

"Mr. Pierce, I'm honored," she started. "I would love to accept your offer, but I have a favor to ask. In addition to my official school duties, I'd like to present a brief work once a year with a major female role and star in it myself - a one-woman show of sorts. Perhaps I can stage it in the evening, after school hours?"

Mr. Evan Pierce was quiet for a moment, coughed into his fist, swiveled in his chair. Then he replied, "Such a thing has never been done before. But you know, I don't see why we can't give it a try. As long as you fulfill your required work and take this on in your spare time. Or, how about this? Something to think about. Perhaps we can even have a faculty show of some kind. Let me consider the various possibilities, especially if we are going to lend you the use of school space."

Ellie shuffled her ankles, crossed them gently, to recoup the strength in her legs. Then a bit wobbly, she walked to the door and smiled as she closed it behind her.

"Are you all right, Ms. Ellie?" asked Ms. Whittaker, the school secretary. "You look a bit unsettled. Can I get you anything?"

Ellie, now composed, smoothed her skirt.

"Thank you, Ms. Whittaker, but I'm fine," she answered, flying down the hall and out to the soccer field, dancing on the grass while whooping aloud and throwing her keys into the air, not caring who saw her.

Of course she said yes to Mr. Pierce. Of course she was allowed to make her own schedule, three afternoons a week. Of course between her mother and Tim, she need not worry about the children. Of course she bought a few new outfits on sale at Miss Maddie's, the only shop in town that sold dresses as well as pants. Ellie momentarily felt she might be doing wrong by Tim, but he seemed eager to help, so she let her doubts float off. And Gavin? Maybe Gavin could get dinner going.

With her family's help, the schedule would work out well. Pat and Sam now saw the boys regularly. Pat was a gentle lady, slender, with long gray hair pinned up in a comb and hands that were always busy. Her husband was affectionate toward her, calling her honey in a soft tone, his clear blue eyes resting gently on her shoulders. Their farmhouse, a field away, was always neat and inviting. Danny had his favorite chair, the plaid one that swiveled, and Jack claimed a favorite cross-stitched embroidery that hung on the wall, proclaiming "God Bless This House." Pat loved to bake, the smell of crusty bread or oatmeal cookies lingering all day, an aroma that kept the boys close to her hip with their hands outstretched.

Too excited to wait for Gavin to come home, Ellie rushed over to the bus depot.

"Let's go to *Pepe's* right now," she suggested. "Are you almost done?"

And in fifteen minutes, they were having strawberry margaritas and listening to "Bésame Mucho" over and over on the jukebox, an old man in the corner feeding coins nonstop into the machine, tears running down his cheeks as he listened to the song's lyrics, and the voice filled with despair and longing. "Invisible tears in my eyes, incredible pain in my heart…"

They held hands across the table as she told him her news. Gavin watched her beautiful face, those gray eyes with their yellow flecks growing more animated as the details of her story expanded and swelled. At the same time, he at last saw an opening for himself. This was her chance, but also his. Why couldn't they do this together? An exciting relaunch of their lives? She with the acting; he with his painting.

But as the chip bowl emptied, he understood that things were not going to work out his way. She hadn't sought his opinion. She had accepted the proposal without checking with him. It was apparent that Ellie had moved beyond need of him. Still, it didn't alter his proposal.

"Ellie," he started, thinking it was the right time, together or not. "I'm glad for you. I see you've already accepted the job. But I've been thinking for a long while about doing something myself. Now seems the perfect moment, now that you have this wonderful opportunity."

Ellie suddenly closed her mouth, set her hands in her lap, and waited. *She has no idea what I'm going to say,* he realized, *none at all.*

"I'm going to give up being manager of the depot," he began. "Instead, I'm going inside to a desk job of checking the schedules and routes. It's only part-time, and I'll have some free hours to paint. But you'll be earning real money now, so I think we can manage."

Ellie was so still Gavin could hear the plink of the coins dropping into the jukebox. "Bésame Mucho." Again. "Improbable, I will forget," the song lamented.

He sat patiently.

"So what kind of painting?" she finally asked, lifting her head, the dark blond curls swaying as she moved.

"Canvases that hang on walls."

Ellie put her drink to her lips, scooped up the remaining salsa on her chip, turned to the man in the corner. "Indelible memories of sweet lovable you," the song wailed. *Was he once sitting at a table just like we are now,* she wondered, *reliving the past, predicting the future, and thinking about what part is real and what is gone?*

She stared at Gavin. He was serious. What could she say? He had obviously been thinking of this for some time, coming up with a response so quickly when she had shared her news.

"I guess if I'm doing what I want," she answered with some reluctance, trailed by doubt, "you should do what you want, as long as we have enough money to take care of the kids and the house."

A practical response but a sad reality, he realized. He had just dropped an amazing revelation on the table, and although she agreed to his plan, she expressed little enthusiasm. Didn't wish him good luck. Didn't tease that he might paint her future sets, her portrait.

Didn't say she was eager to see what kind of paintings he would produce.

Does she truly understand? Does she not know that painting a picture has equal merit with acting out publicly words written by a great writer? He signaled the waiter, ordered two more margaritas, then took her hand and leaned forward.

"Ellie, let me explain. Painting is all I've ever wanted to do in my life. It was my mistake not to say this to you ages ago, in the beginning, but honestly, I was intimidated by what you might think. You might not have considered it a serious endeavor - like my parents, who had tried to drum the artistic energy out of me my whole childhood.

"But try to understand. Painting is a creative pursuit, just like acting and directing and just as consuming. Why should one be any less worthy than the other?"

Ellie's face softened. He wondered if he had made his argument, if she would support his efforts. She licked the salt off the rim of her glass, then licked her lips, looking at his face, thinking of her own parents' rejection. Concern was all over his face; surprise, all over hers. *He is right,* she realized. *Who knows where his pursuit will take him, and for that matter, where mine will take me. If he wants to do this as earnestly and sincerely as I want to be on the stage, then he has to give it a try. He can always drive a bus.*

Ellie squeezed Gavin's fingers, smiling at this man she thought she had known well, this man with whom she had spent over a dozen intimate years but grievously, now discovered she hardly knew at all. Yet even with that unfortunate awareness, there was also the pleasurable prospect that they would now learn exciting new things about each other. Gavin dropped a few dollars on the table, and they left without saying anything further. As they walked to the car, Ellie took her husband's hand.

Chapter 4

The next day, Gavin was distracted, not only by the announcement of Ellie's new job but by her easy acceptance of his own intentions. He had longed for her recognition and approval, but he needed time to think, to make arrangements, and the days kept moving ahead.

In the evenings, he hovered around his boys. Checking their schoolwork, he searched for a unique idea, a sign of an original mind, precocious thinking. Danny usually lost his papers or threw them away, or they lay crumpled in his backpack, smeared with peanut butter. Careless and uncaring, he had nothing to show.

"Oh, Dad, it was a stupid assignment, to draw a picture of the teacher. That's what she told us to do! For heaven's sake, she was standing right there! Everyone could see what she looked like."

"Danny, did the teacher explain what a portrait is?"

"Dad, can we talk about this later? I want to go out with Lucky and help Grandpa bring in the cows."

Jack diligently saved his papers, smoothed them out on the counter so his father could have a good look. He even asked for a folder to keep his work neatly organized. Gavin looked down on his son's pages and saw what his own mother called doodling. She had no idea then what she was looking at, could not extract the exceptional from the mundane. But both his and Jack's handiwork were a lot more than mere childish scribbles. Here were Jack's crude but perfectly drawn renderings of their farm - a cow with four feet and spotted hide, the cow even with a stalk of grass hanging out of his mouth, a barn with a weather vane whose arrow had a sharp point, cornstalks tall in the background, a little boy hiding among them.

"Jack," Gavin commented, "these are strong drawings."

"Thanks, Dad," Jack answered. "Next, I want to make a drawing of Lucky chasing his tail."

"Ah, that's a tough one. Motion is difficult to capture. Let's first try a portrait of Lucky at rest until you get the knack of painting an animal. And a pencil is better than a crayon for such a subject - it makes a thinner line and will portray the details better. Plus, you can erase. With the basic anatomy down, you can then overlay the fur. Would you like me to help start you off?"

Ellie held her tongue and continued wiping down the kitchen counters. Although she accepted Gavin's plans, she still had not abandoned the hope that both boys would take over the farm. Occasionally, she succumbed to her doubts and required a bit more of a convincing argument such as on a lovely sunny afternoon such as when father and son sat on the porch rockers working over their sketchpads and she was planting begonias.

"Jack," Gavin said, "your technique is becoming quite sophisticated."

"Oh, Gavin," Ellie murmured, "enough!"

Startled, Jack looked up. Gavin asked him to please fetch him a beer. When Jack was gone, he turned to Ellie and said, "Ellie, is teaching drama useful?" Gavin asked. "Or essential? It's in your heart, something you love to do. For Jack, it may be the same."

"It's not the same, Gavin. I work in a school. It's a *job*, not a hobby, not a personal activity."

"There are jobs for people who draw, you know," he answered, "even professions. He could be a teacher, like you."

"Perhaps you're right," she answered cautiously. "It just seems that painting pictures provides at best a dubious livelihood."

Jack and Danny returned and started to play marbles while Gavin packed up their supplies. The two boys looked at their parents with curiosity - a rare instance of discord in a usually calm household. But then, even as they looked, their mother relaxed, smiled at their dad, and everything seemed fine once again.

One day, as Gavin's truck pulled up at the end of a work day, Danny came running up to his father.

"Daddy, Daddy!" he screamed. "I can't find Jack!"

"Well, he couldn't have gone far. Let's go find him," Gavin said as he took Danny's hand and tried to appear unconcerned. What kind of accident could befall a child on a farm? There were a thousand dire possibilities - a sharp tool recklessly left in the grass, something with the animals, a fall from the hayloft.

Behind the barn was a small machine powered by blades similar to those of a windmill. As they rounded a corner and checked behind a stone wall, there was Jack sitting quietly, staring at the generator. Wheels and gears were going round and round, and he fumbling with a piece of paper, trying to fold it like origami to somehow capture the idea of rotation, paper pleated this way, then turned, and folded the other way but awkwardly, inexpertly, with a child's hand. Startled, he looked up, his face pinched in frustration. "I'm trying to catch the movement, like Lucky chasing his tail," he cried. "I wanted to draw it, but I didn't have a pencil."

At that moment, Gavin knew that his son's inclinations were extraordinary, that Jack's eyes saw a world including the farm but far beyond it. He walked back to his truck and pulled out some paper, took out a pencil from his back pocket, and handed them over to Jack, still earnestly tucking and pinching, patting him on his shoulder. Then he took Danny's hand and led him away, leaving Jack sitting on the grass with his pencil and paper, focused on the generator, trying somehow to capture the whirring and circling.

That was the day that the shifting of familial relationships became apparent, each family member now going his or her own way.

The drama class took over Ellie completely as she was about to present an important show at the civic auditorium - *The Wizard of Oz*, a full production with costumes, sets, songs, and dances. There had been an unforeseen gap in its calendar, and the director of the local theater group decided to call the school to fill in as a community outreach gesture. Would the drama teacher consider putting on her show in a municipal building rather than on school premises? The local television station would cover it on the nightly news. Ellie was asked for a special interview. There were days she didn't come home until after dinner. She received phone calls from new voices. Her helpers, she explained to Gavin, on loan from the theater staff.

"Hi, Ellie, this is Luke."

"Head of props," she said.

"Lo, Ellie, it's me, Craig. Call me."

"In charge of lighting," she said to Gavin.

And another. "You know the name, call me back," the unknown voice said.

"Dean, the guy who handles publicity," she explained.

Danny was also fully engaged, practically growing up by himself. After school, he and Tim crossed the fields to help out with the farm animals and crops. Or they would happily throw baseballs together, kick a soccer ball into the net they had set up over by the creek. He asked for nothing but to romp his way through life. And if his father hovered more over his brother than him, it didn't seem to matter. His grandparents' and Tim's attentions fell cheerfully and sufficiently on his shoulders.

Gavin was now taken up with teaching Jack the elements of drawing - line, form, space, shape. Although these components were crucial to master before anything else, Jack was eager to move on to color, especially with Gavin's enticing words - "Jack, remember color. It's at the heart of every painting. Color sets the tone for how the viewer feels."

And yet each of them now pursuing their own interests did not seem to draw him and Ellie together. Sacrifices were made, losses accrued, consuming all their energies as they each inched forward into their own interests. There was nothing the four of them did together anymore, not even the most ordinary things such as dinner or breakfast or visits to Pat and Sam. Ellie and Gavin hardly had a moment to speak as they passed from one room to another on their way to someplace else. Despite their talk at Pepe's, growing apart somehow crept up on them as their lives unfolded. And meanwhile, Gavin was waiting for spring, when he would put forward his scheme and begin his creative life.

It was opening night, and Ellie, overcome with anxiety, was sitting at a table in her bedroom fluffing her hair. She didn't answer Danny's questions or hear Jack's requests. She ignored Gavin's offers of assistance. Images of her failing in front of the whole community loomed larger than any possible success. Had she taken on something too extravagant, *The Wizard of Oz*, with its oddly assembled characters and strange munchkins, the scary wizard? Why didn't she choose something simpler like *Beauty and the Beast*? A smaller cast, a more manageable script. She would be okay if the audience knew the story - didn't everyone? But if they didn't, certain aspects might appear weird.

She had to do a lot of reassuring to the little kids who played Jinjur and Kiki Aru and Isomere and the rest of the munchkins. This one's costume was scratchy; that one couldn't remember the munchkin song. And Joey Bennett always marched in the wrong direction - was he dyslexic? The local paper would send a reporter and photographer. *This is my breakout moment,* Ellie thought, and she had to rely on so many others for her success. She wished she were alone or with a small adult ensemble, going out on the stage to play the lead in Virginia Woolf's *A Room of One's Own*, for example. Boy, could she turn that into a personal triumph. But a whole group of elementary school kids? Who could predict the outcome with this irrepressible bunch? Sheila Dwyer had to go to the bathroom every two minutes, even when she *wasn't* nervous!

The scenic backdrops were also concerning. The set designer had come up with what Ellie considered acceptable screens of the yellow brick road and the Emerald City, but when Gavin had picked her up one day after rehearsals, he said he could paint them more imaginatively. His comment cast a pall over her anticipation and put her in a pouty mood.

Were Kyle's sets mediocre? Could Gavin really do better? I haven't really seen any of his work. Could a man working part-time at a bus depot really be a talented artist as well? Maybe next time I would have him paint a sample backdrop, check if he could do better than Kyle.

As Ellie tried to put those thoughts aside to focus on her makeup, she continued to wonder *how* would *Gavin have painted the scenery?* She took another sip of the wine he had left next to her hairbrush. Finally, she walked downstairs to find her two boys, husband, parents, and brother all scrubbed up, neat, and quiet, ready to go.

They were about to step out as a family.

It was because of the overwhelming applause that she knew the reporter would write a glowing review, the audience waving and cheering and handing her red roses as she came out on stage at the finale. And all those elements she worried about? Well, they happened just as she had feared. Lucy scratched her neck the whole time, even sat right down on the stage in frustration until Isomere pulled her up. And Joey Bennett marched in the wrong direction despite his pal Jamie grabbing his pants to turn him around. Sheila Dwyer ran offstage twice seeking a bathroom, but each time she returned, she stepped into the exact right spot in the munchkin line. Ellie never accounted for the audience's reaction, that they would find these flaws and mistakes utterly charming. But they did, adding to the winsomeness of the performance. These mismatched, mischievous young kids helped give her a hit play.

At last, spring arrived, along with the warm weather. Gavin then pulled back his own curtain and stepped into the life he was born for.

Except, from the beginning, it was all wrong.

Chapter 5

There was an old chicken coop - a shack, really - on Pat and Sam's property. This was to be Gavin's studio. He spent a long weekend scrubbing and sweeping, nailing up three shelves for supplies, laying a floor, and finally, placing a crude table in a corner with two easels propped against its legs. A couple of small windows provided a limited amount of light. The whole forlorn structure, thin and ramshackle, would function in the stifling summer months primarily as storage. But no matter, he preferred to work outdoors. In the freezing Iowan winters, it would not be feasible to paint either indoors or out, but Gavin need not worry about that for six months.

This old chicken coop embodied Gavin's dream - a place to paint, time of his own, solitude. But so far, the beginnings were difficult. Despite his grueling efforts, the shack was still a dump, smelling faintly of chicken shit. Maybe in two weeks, he hoped, the place would air out. *At least I've told Ellie the truth,* Gavin thought, *and thankfully, she didn't offer any serious objection.*

Sitting in the old wicker chair, he looked around at a landscape he had seen a thousand times. And even though each new season brought forth dramatic changes, transformations one could paint, its familiarity rendered it utterly uninspiring. A slight unease took root in his spirit.

Still, this was what he had been waiting for, so he laid out his paints.

The first few weeks, he made sketches of hills and trees on cloudy days, on sunny days, when the mist hung low over the valley, when Blackie grew restless in the corral, and when the sun set in a blaze of orange on the roof of Pat and Sam's farmhouse. Sketches became finished paintings that he stacked inside the shack. Yet after a few months, Gavin grew restless. The scenes he painted *en plein air*, outdoors, were tedious. *Nature is change,* he thought, *and water is motion, but the creek, the wildflowers on my canvases are inert, lifeless.* The lack of vigor sat heavy on his brush. Would his expectations be fulfilled in this particular place?

Gavin longed for newness; for other rivers and other gullies; for mountains, not just hills - images that would excite his eyes, make his hands twitch with anticipation, and lift the relentless monotony. His gait from house to shack became a plodding trek, like a pregnant cow. He worried about his growing apathy.

The best part of his day was when his children came home from school. Danny would run to the dogs, but Jack would race through the meadow and sit next to his father, eager to draw. One day, he surprised them both by adding wings onto the back of a cow. Both of them laughed, and Jack grew bolder. Next was an apple tree that grew watermelons. And cornstalks that danced with one another. *They are not silly nonsense as it might first appear, but an eye toying with fanciful concepts,* Gavin thought. *Clever. Exceedingly clever, certainly more imaginative than anything flitting over* my *brain.* These were the best times, for there was no end in the little boy's hunger to learn new things.

At dinner one night, Ellie had asked "How's it going?" but got up for the mashed potatoes before anyone could answer.

In this way, time disappeared.

With hardly a flutter, everyone was almost ten years older.

As Ellie continued to direct school productions, her old students moved on, and new ones arrived. Tim was always around to help. Jack and Danny were teenagers, hardy and strong from the outdoor life. Both were tall and lanky, but Jack threw off a romantic aura with his brooding eyes and, at their centers, dark pools of mysterious perceptions. He moved cautiously, like a cat. Danny too was handsome, with unruly brown hair like Gavin's and an impish grin, but his personality was open to all, much like Lucky as a pup.

He played varsity football, and his enthusiasm grew as the game got rougher. Although girls hovered and giggled around them both, neither was actually dating or had a girlfriend. They tended to do things in groups, which suited Gavin and Ellie just fine.

And Gavin continued to paint, struggling to find his personal vision, pushing far down in his soul doubts and fears that longed for air, refusing to think of his work as barren or, heaven forbid, futile.

What an unexpected pleasure that Lucy Gordon came into my life, thought Ellie as she waited for her friend on a bench outside the gym. "My best friend," she told Gavin. That exuberant head of dark tresses blowing around her face in the breeze - nothing else about her was listless either - her blue eyes darting left and right, fingers tapping on the table. Not yet thirty, Lucy taught fifth-grade social studies and had already had two husbands. *I love that she comes to my rehearsals,* Ellie reflected, *and after, when we hang around chatting like two teenagers. When was the last time I had a real girl friend? Best of all are the times we stop in at* Pepe's *for margaritas.*

This particular day, both had an extra hour's free time, and they hunkered down in one of the restaurant's ample booths.

When her drink was half empty, Lucy began.

"You want to hear what that lousy Rob did one night when I stayed late for teacher conferences?" Lucy asked.

"What, for heaven's sake!" Ellie answered, dying to know, thinking, something salacious about husband number 2.

"Well, he sold Beloved, my beautiful Appaloosa with his spotted coat, like you painted black dots on a white sheet. My daddy bought him for me when he was born. He was mighty stubborn but playful and smart too. Whenever he saw me, he'd come trotting over with that black streak running down his nose like someone drew it with a pen. Behind my back, that weasel Rob sold him to pay off his gambling debts."

Poor Lucy choked up, grabbed the soggy napkin from under her drink to wipe her eyes, streaking her mascara.

"The bastard. I could have killed him, but all I could do was divorce him."

While Lucy and Ellie were exchanging confidences at Pepe's, Gavin was picking up some sugar and flour in Haley Max's store. He wandered over to the books in the back, thinking, *It's been years since Ellie and I browsed through the poetry section. Had Haley sold any of these books all this time?* Gavin took his old seat in the corner and was quickly immersed in a volume by Emily Dickinson. He could hear Haley chatting with Liz Bailey about her sick husband, then with Brad Downing about his new job. He could hear the growl of Earl Stoddard's German shepherd and the screen door slam, but Gavin didn't lift his head.

How will Ellie respond if I buy her this particular Dickinson volume, wrapped with a red ribbon and left on the kitchen table? Skimming through, he read:

I hide myself within my flower,
That wearing on your breast,
You, unsuspecting, wear me too
And angels know the rest.

I hide myself within my flower,
That, fading from your vase,
You, unsuspecting, feel for me
Almost a loneliness.

Is this too sentimental? wondered Gavin. *Or will she be taken with nostalgia and receive these words with kindness? Maybe kickstart the marriage a bit? I'll give it a try,* he decided.

Then he noticed a pamphlet tossed on a side table. Idly, he picked it up.

Suddenly, the vessels of his heart exploded. As dangerous a moment as if he had fallen to his knees in front of a feral Blackie with eyes wild as he rose up high on his hind legs. Gavin looked again. The cover painting of the brochure depicted a crazy, mysterious image - spills and splatters of black ink, red slashes here and there, a tiny blue circle in the lower right corner. They were forms that immediately conjured up recent dreams he experienced of stones thrown randomly into the snow and a deer brought down by a hunter that left drops of blood on the trail.

"Jackson Pollock, the artist," it said across the page. His breath seemed blocked, shut down, then slowly relaxed, as if he were at the end of running a race.

And Gavin instantly forgot about the poems of Emily Dickinson as he clutched the Pollack circular that would change his life.

He began to read.

"An announcement of a show of abstract expressionists in New York City. This historically transformative art movement had been going on from the late forties into the early sixties," it stated. How could he not have been aware of this? Was he that isolated in Iowa from these seismic shifts in the art world? Seemed so. Driving a bus, two kids, a farm, all tiring work that left little spare time beyond those constraints. But here, now, Gavin felt as if he had stepped into a world of possibilities, and no one, not even himself, knew what lay beyond. The only surety was that now he was confident of an artistic future. It was like being baptized in the sea. He would be cleansed and renewed, and nothing less than a complete change of style, of vision, and of technique would follow. First, an awakening of his mind, then his brush. Just like that. Just from scanning that neglected brochure.

At that moment, Gavin knew he would burst out of the limitations of realism and become an abstract artist.

Eagerly, he unfolded the remaining pages. There were photos of paintings by Hans Hofmann, Franz Kline, and others, samplings of this inventive movement. He was especially attracted to those works by Mark Rothko and Helen Frankenthaler with their gorgeous depiction of color in a muted, easy manner as opposed to the harshness and angularity of others. But all were impassioned expressions of paint. And all broke ground from the past in major and original ways.

Emotions he couldn't name filled his mind and heart with discovery and peace. At last, a shift. *Not to paint what he saw but to paint what he felt.* Here was definition, clarification for his past frustrations when his pain and grievance had no place to go. It was almost impossible to absorb this new phenomenon. No longer would he paint a lake or a field, striving for accurate details. He would leave representational painting behind as if he were just now discovering light.

Gavin now realized that in college, his art history courses ended with the earlier Victorian era, that he had never studied contemporary art movements. Of course he had seen Picasso's *Guernica* at the Museum of Modern Art, certainly au courant and thoroughly modern, and he recognized its genius and political statement about Franco's fascism, but he didn't want to paint in that cubist style - a gored horse, a dead baby, a bull, screaming women - cubism and realism together that made a jarring vision, visible forms broken down in pieces like a mathematical equation. Besides, he was a kid, not paying attention, enraptured with Ellie. However, a friend had said he hasn't lived until he views Picasso's monumental work. Neither he nor Ellie was emotionally moved except to horror. Quickly, they fled uptown to the Met, lucky to catch their Wednesday two-for-one night.

There, Ellie happily strolled through rooms of the Impressionists. She loved Monet's flowers and Renoir's ladies. Gavin appreciated them as an observer of artistic technique, how to paint light as it drifts over the natural world. But in truth, he found the paintings overly dreamy and dewy-eyed. Anyway, during their courtship, he paid little attention to the Impressionists, the Abstract Expressionists, or anything else.

Haley's face showed concern as he walked toward Gavin, trembling and distracted. Handing him a cup of black coffee, he asked, "Gavin, are you okay, man? You look a little pale. Here, drink up."

"Haley, my friend, thanks, but I'm quite fine. This little brochure here on the table - can I borrow it for a while?"

"Of course, my friend!" Haley exclaimed. "Take it, it's yours!"

Gavin's foot bore down hard on the pedal of his truck. When he pulled into the barren patch of land next to the shack, he leapt from the car and charged inside. Frantically looking through his piles of supplies, he found it - a roll of raw canvas. On the highest shelf, he took down his longest pieces of wood for stretcher bars, four feet by six feet. As he laid the pieces out on the floor, the air sizzled with energy, a wall-to-wall electrical field that followed him around the little room. He yanked and pulled and stapled and folded until he had a finished canvas ready for his brush.

Exhausted, he then went outside and sat in his old wicker chair, staring out at the hills and feeling a restless hunger for action, for the passion his paintings would now express. Overwhelmed, he sobbed with relief for at last finding his direction as an artist, praying for the courage to explore where it would take him.

When Ellie heard the screeching of Gavin's truck bounding onto the property like a leopard after a deer, she ran to the window. Down the path she raced to find him slumped in his chair, his cries subsiding. He handed her the pamphlet from Haley's. Glancing at the cover, she thought, *What is this? An ugly picture with heavy black marks scrawled all over. A few red splotches. I've never seen anything like this before. It looks like nonsense.* She noticed the title, "Abstract Expressionists in Manhattan." *Is this supposed to be* art? she wondered. *What is abstract expressionism?*

But in Gavin's red eyes, she saw excitement, not concern - happy tears. *Thank goodness, nothing untoward,* she thought with relief, *not fear, not dismay but rather the fire of joy and somewhere in there, of reprieve.* A gigantic white canvas was propped against the wall, waiting. What to do? She could not remember when her husband ever cried except in the early days of their marriage when they read poetry together, and that was so long ago.

"Gavin, what?" she awkwardly began, dropping to the ground, putting out her hand. In the background, they could hear the wild mustang snorting, see the sweat drip off his shiny black flanks as he scratched in the dirt.

"Ellie, right now I don't understand it myself. I want to try out some new styles, some unusual techniques."

"Should I be afraid?" she asked. "Worried?"

"Why should you be afraid? Nothing to worry about."

Ellie was reluctant to leave. She flipped through the brochure. *Are these actual paintings?* she wondered. *Why, yes, they are,* she decided after she read they were by painters who apparently were successful and acclaimed. "Connoisseurs of this type of art compete to purchase a Philip Guston, a Robert Rauschenberg," it said.

She suddenly understood that Gavin could be taken up with these paintings in a way that might change all their lives. Nostalgically, she recalled the charms of the Impressionists like Degas and his ballerinas, the pretty scenes of gardens and boat rides, parasols and lace. She also recalled how disinterested Gavin was, wandering off. She had to call him back time and again. The circular in her hands was nothing like those. In fact, Ellie felt the paintings were just the opposite - strident, abrasive. Were they supposed to make the viewer angry, happy? Contemplative? Except for this pretty one here by a woman, what's her name? Let's see, Helen someone, who painted a pretty flower - I think it's a flower - on this background of jumbled colors and shapes. At least the colors are soft, not grating except for that slash of dark purple in the corner. Why is that purple there? At least those plum-colored strokes aren't all over. The artist seems to be creating a mood. But moody upset or moody serene? Perhaps the pleasant background is meant to portray a meadow - that is, if that yellow stroke was really a flower, Maybe a meadow in which you could dream away a summer's day? Ellie didn't know how to make sense of it.

Gavin turned to his wife and saw only confusion.

"Ellie, let me explain. I'm just discovering this myself. The painters in this pamphlet. See, they weren't painting *things*, not a house or a dog or anything you would actually name as an object. Instead, they were painting their *feelings, their reactions.* Color can express those in ways simply drawing a real object cannot always do. But you will surely know that the result makes you feel some profound emotion. Now if you see a painted house, you can say, 'It's pretty,' or 'I like it,' or 'I don't like it.' But if you *feel s*omething without actually putting a name to it, that feeling can be a hundred different things to a hundred different people.

"Do you understand?"

Ellie looked at her husband's earnest face, then at the folder in her hand. She heard his words. She understood what he was saying. But honestly, she didn't experience nearly the same pleasure as Gavin when she looked at those pictures. Didn't he say the viewer was supposed to have his own emotional reaction? Was dislike a feeling she was allowed to have?

She would just have to wait and see what kind of paintings Gavin would produce. Meanwhile, it was obvious that Gavin was keen to explore and experiment however that turned out. So she held her tongue, ruffled his hair, and walked slowly back to the house. He looked tired as well as jubilant, and she fervently hoped she would look favorably upon his work. If she did, fine. If not, somehow, she would try to figure that out at the proper time.

Then again, did it even matter if she liked his paintings? It was his vision, not hers. *Hopefully,* she decided, *I will be a strong enough person to provide Gavin with emotional support however I feel - despite the ugliness of those black squiggles with the blue dot at the bottom.*

Gavin anchored the large canvas to his easel and set to work.

On the following days, Jack or Danny or Pat or Tim, whoever was around, made his lunch and silently left a plate on the old wicker chair. Gavin would rummage around for food with his left hand while continuing to work with his right, sending off a vague wave of thanks with his brush raised high, as if a ghost had come and gone.

Chapter 6

Thank goodness Lucy was at rehearsals the day Ellie's car broke down, and she offered to drive her home. They were both feeling lighthearted, even bubbly. Neither of them had experienced a single problem with any student the entire day. As head of the drama department, Ellie had begun to set in place the methods and ploys that would be used in their projects, and it had been a challenging but rewarding afternoon. Even Mandy in the second row behaved herself as she refrained from flipping rubber bands at her seatmate, George. And to top it off, as he passed them whistling in the hall, two spirited young women with their arms linked, the principal, Mr. Pierce, smiled and said, "Good day for you, ladies?"

So who could know that this day would be one of alchemy - transformation, creation, recombination for her, for her boys, above all, for Gavin.

From her last divorce, Lucy snagged a Chevy convertible with whitewall tires, a spiffy car she treated like an adored pet, attentive to its every whim. The two young women hopped in and peeled back the canvas roof while passing students yelled out, "Wayta go, Ms. Ellie, Ms. Lucy!" Tucking in their skirts, they settled themselves for a joyride, straight on home in style, rolling onto Ellie's property like a pair of movie stars, brakes squealing, horn tooting. Happy and invincible, they jumped out of the car. Gavin lifted his head and gave them a wave with his paintbrush before turning back to his work. Ellie glimpsed the large canvas propped on the easel, a huge rectangular form entirely covered with color - reds, mostly - that at best looked messy and haphazard. Did those explosive eruptions of color represent some mysterious, obscure image? After barely a glance, she quickly turned away. An uncomfortable feeling of displacement sprang up - the sense of being an outsider in Gavin's life, not a true part of its private workings. As she took Lucy's arm, they strolled up the path for some of Ellie's strawberry lemonade, complaining about their messy hairdos and laughing together.

"Are the boys home?" Lucy asked. "It's been ages since I've seen them."

"Not yet, but soon," Ellie answered.

"Good, I'll wait," Lucy replied as she took off her shoes and put her feet up on a kitchen chair, cracking ice cubes between her teeth.

Suddenly, Lucy jumped up.

"Hey! You're always talking about that secretive husband of yours. Know what? I'm going out there right now and see what he's doing. He never told *me* to stay away, did he?"

Before Ellie could sputter an objection, Lucy was marching briskly across the field, right into Gavin's space. She walked round and round his easel, her dark hair lifting with the soft breezes. Surely Gavin was surprised, even bewildered, by Lucy's presence, her high spirits. However, their conversation seemed animated and cordial. More talk at one time than Gavin and she had enjoyed in quite a while. Lucy pointed, tilted her head, looked away. After a few minutes, she leaned over to kiss his cheek, then strolled slowly back to the house.

"Ellie," she started, stepping onto the porch where Ellie sat waiting. "Your husband is a genius. His work is amazing. I've never seen anything like it. I felt transported in some way but had no idea why. I was so overcome I cried. Imagine a painting doing that! If something can make me feel like that, it has a certain magnificence. Wouldn't you agree?"

Ellie was shocked at her buoyant reaction. And Lucy so particular about her likes and dislikes.

"Why do I have to understand it if I feel it?" she added.

"*What...what* are you talking about?" Ellie stammered. "Your words - *overcome, magnificent* - and you don't even know what the painting was about? Sorry, I can't be more sympathetic, but Gavin told me to stay away until he was ready to show me something. So far, I've not been invited."

"Well, you better get yourself the hell out there and take a look."

Reluctantly, Ellie followed Lucy back across the field, nervous as a hen in a pig pen. Was she being presumptuous? Shouldn't she have waited until he sent for her? Yet here she was, shy with her own husband. But she couldn't turn back. Lucy held firm, guiding her forward.

Ellie crept up slowly, uneasy at what awaited, fearful as to the man her husband would become, perhaps had already become. *Will these new ideas of his change our relationship, our accommodations toward each other?*

Suddenly, there it was before her, a meteor exploding into fiery shards, a mass of released energy that blotted out the fields, the horizon beyond. Ellie heard herself gasp, put her hand to her throat to quell the quivering.

Reds.

An abounding assortment of reds, light and dark and shades in-between. Light red like her pink hat, dark red like her winter coat. Reds from the palest coral blush to the deepest cerise as in the unfolding of a peony. Even a wizard could not conjure up another shade of red. Lines intersected and careened in all directions though they didn't feel random or angry. But not relaxing, either, like the flower, if it was a flower, by that lady in the brochure. Here and there were splotches of bright blue, streaks of yellow. And over in the center top, a lime-green circle all by itself that hung suspended like the moon and a smaller one in the center bottom.

It was the strangest thing she'd ever seen. Unlike Lucy's reaction, hers was one of confusion and disturbance. *Is it* art*? Is it even* painting*?* For a moment, she had the feeling that this is what their future would look like - confused and disturbing, something she could not understand, something that aroused anxiety and felt like fear. *What will Jack think of this?* Ellie wondered.

No one had spoken. Ellie sat down on the grass while Gavin turned and scooped up on his palette knife, all together, three shades of red - one like a tomato; another of deep burgundy, like Sam's favorite wine; and the third a raspberry hue like that new ice cream at Matt's Drugs. Swiping the blade across the canvas, he turned the knife this way and that, smoothing down some surfaces, raising others up in thick globs. He stepped back, took a look, went forward again. This time, he took up a wide brush, feathered out corners and angles. Then the knife again, dipping into ultramarine and cerulean blue and pouncing with the knife's broad side, then turning to its sharp edge. Rather randomly, it seemed to her, but she imagined he worked with a plan. What was it? She was not taken up with enough curiosity to read about those Abstract Expressionists nor inclined to continue sitting on the ground watching her husband paint in what she considered an alien manner. When his knife began to descend on cadmium green, she brushed the loose grass off her pants and walked back to the house. It felt like a retreat, the walk of the defeated. Lucy, however, had more things to say and remained behind.

At the kitchen table, Ellie sat rigid as a post.

"Wasn't it marvelous?" Lucy asked, bouncing in the door. "You must have been overwhelmed since you didn't say a word!"

"Lucy, everything seemed so bizarre - the painting, his technique, his intense focus. I don't know what to say to him."

"Oh, honey, you'll figure it out," she replied. "Maybe he'll try to explain it, though I myself find that the work speaks for itself. Give yourself some time. You'll get used to it. This is something new. Anyway, gotta go. It's getting late. Time to do the lesson plans, right?" And off she went, scrambling into her car and giving the horn a smack. Gavin turned with a smile - a smile - and waved her off.

That day when Ellie's car battery blew and her best friend, Lucy, gave her a ride home was the day Lucy also moved in on Ellie's marriage. It happened that very moment when Lucy marched boldly over the fields, greeting Blackie with sugar cubes from her strawberry lemonade and going right up to Gavin demanding to see his work, showing a dogged interest, exactly what Ellie should have done. As his wife, she should have felt the desire to share Gavin's dream. Lucy had implied as much. *But that's unfair,* she told herself. She hadn't even known about his dream until a short while ago. And he had told her to wait until she was invited. So what should she have done? Forced herself on him when he wasn't ready? Then pretended to be enamored of his work?

Lucy started showing up unexpectedly.

On a Saturday - "Just passing on my way to the market at Hudson Farm." Or occasionally on a weekday afternoon - "Brought some yummy peaches from Carver's. Looks like Gavin is stretching another canvas." Sometimes this - a note tacked to the big maple when she knew Ellie was at rehearsal - "Stopped by to see if you wanted to run over to that new dress shop by the highway. Sorry I missed you. Looks like Gavin has put down some color."

After Lucy's comments, and Ellie's first foray out to the shack followed by her insights into being distant from Gavin's new venture, you would think she had learned she should talk to her husband about his involvement with this new style, his goals for this purposeful effort. But she hadn't. What if he asked if she liked it? If she felt something, anything that was emotionally moving? What if he said he hadn't anything specific in mind, that he just painted a mood, a feeling, and how did she feel about that? Befuddled she was as to exactly what those reds conveyed. And what *feeling* was intended by the bright green ball on the top and bottom, dangling? Could she say that his style didn't please her? That the whole thing made her restless and despairing? So they both pretended Ellie had never been out to the shack and seen the canvas of reds, raging and howling.

When Jack heard about Lucy's visits to the shack, he decided not to wait for an invitation. A few of his long strides, and in short order, he was next to his father. Ellie watched from the kitchen window - hand gestures, pacing back and forth, but it was difficult to determine if it was a positive experience or one in which Jack pulled back in horror. At last, he returned, stomping his feet, his eyes flashing wildly with surprise.

"Mom, my father is clearly brilliant," he cried, taking the stairs two at a time without another word.

I'll look again soon, Ellie decided. *Maybe I'm missing something.*

Only after Ellie stopped by the shack a few more times did she finally conclude that she still disliked what Lucy and Jack both adored. Trusting their judgment in other matters, she now felt insecure about her own opinions. Truth was, she was nervous, almost afraid of being there, like a mouse scurrying around to check on dinner and finding the cheese was not where he had left it. Who had taken it?

What is expected of me? she asked herself. *Is it my failure to grasp or his to clarify?*

Gavin's work seemed to speak directly to Lucy's personal needs. She brought a folding stool and sat nearby. Neither spoke. Mostly, she watched as Gavin's hands moved, his brush flew. But occasionally, rarely, he would set down the charcoal or his pencil or his rags, and he and Lucy would chat out there in public view, yet Ellie well knew that a change in sentiment, in empathy, could be as strong an emotional bond as any other.

Gavin was chattier at supper these days. He no longer fidgeted. His impatience and anxiety had diminished. Ellie could feel his growing confidence. Was his assurance because of Lucy's support or because he had been painting for almost a year? Full-time now, with no outside jobs. The bus business had ended six months earlier. Even in their bed, rather barren and devoid of affection in the recent past, both of them rolling over to their separate sides. Gavin was becoming more mindful even though nothing between them had actually changed. The more Ellie thought about it, the more she decided that his good mood was Lucy's doing. Likely Ellie was now his obligation while Lucy was his muse, his confidante, and he displaced his need for Lucy on their intimate moments together.

Surprisingly, Ellie was only mildly jealous, moderately angry. Did she have sleepless nights? Tears? More than she wanted, but not as much as she expected. The truth was, she was now involved in a new circle of friends and colleagues, old hands from *The Wizard of Oz* production visiting her rehearsals, bringing her lunch. They also brought backstage stories, gossip of goings-on with shows and plays both local and distant, talk of Broadway and their hopes to move on from Iowa and take their chances in the big city. There were endless questions - what was it like living there, right in the middle of Manhattan, and waiting on line in the snow for a slim chance to audition? And why would she ever return to Iowa?

Ellie's life had spun off into two segments, home and work. And the one she had away from home began to interest her more. Within the latter, she was the pivot point, not the outsider. But she was married, existing in a strange state of suspended commitments and needs. An occasional thought of indulgence with one of the guys hanging about on the fringes had crossed her mind, but truthfully, an occasional fling was not for her. And being divorced like Lucy sure didn't look attractive either. Lucy didn't have kids, but she had two wonderful boys who adored their father, especially now that they had both seen his work. Jack thought him a hero, a truly original artist. Even Danny was in awe - "Gee, Dad, how the heck did you think of doing that? Wow. What a mind thing you have going on there."

When Ellie wasn't home on one of Lucy's visits, one of the boys would mention it in passing.

"Mom, Lucy stopped by today. I think she brought Dad some fresh fruit."

"Mom, Lucy came looking for you, but you were at the theater. She said to tell you she says hi, see you at school. She checked on Dad."

Enough, Ellie thought.

She reviewed her objections and options, and it was clear. No matter what happened between Gavin and her, Lucy had no right to hang around her home and husband, even her kids, when she was not there.

Ellie waited for the day she and Lucy shared playground monitoring, the kids whooping with abandon and arranging themselves into cliquish groups - the girls showing off their nail polish, the boys doing pushups.

"Lucy," Ellie started, "don't you think you're visiting Gavin just a little too often? Especially when I'm not around?"

"Ellie! For heaven's sake, I'm just giving the man a word of encouragement. He's all alone out there working hard, doing his thing. He doesn't even notice me."

"Lucy, give me a break. You cannot say no one knows when *you're* around."

"Why, thank you! I'm flattered! But it's true. I just watch, silent as a tree. You should try it sometime. Really fascinating how he decides what stroke to put down and where. A swipe comes out of nowhere, and the whole thing changes."

"I don't need advice how to deal with my own husband, thank you."

They didn't speak again directly, not even when they were directing the kids back to their rooms. And that was also the end of their after-work drinks at Pepe's. But knowing Lucy was in many ways irreplaceable, Ellie mourned the loss of her best friend.

She thought Lucy was done with her visits to Gavin, but a couple of months after their talk, she showed up at the shack when Ellie lingered after school. And then again, two weeks later. Not as often as before, but often enough. *Nervy,* Ellie thought. *Should we have another confrontation?* Inexplicably, Ellie let it pass. Preoccupied as she was with her own concerns and new friends from the local theater group, she was less involved with Gavin's. But she always knew when Lucy had been around. On those days, Gavin sang his way across the field for supper, entering the house to the last strains of the Beatles' "Here Comes the Sun." The boys and Ellie would stop whatever they were doing and look up. Embarrassed, Gavin would ask, "What? Something wrong here?"

The man had been hungry for praise, for recognition, and Lucy for a steady guy. Something meaningful was building between them, something Ellie could not give him. And she let it happen.

And just like that, everyone's role shifted.

Ellie was finding professional satisfaction in the plays she presented, gratification in the skills with which her kids were performing. There was a pleasant rhythm to her days, a pleasing plateau of contentment.

And then, in the midst of just such a harmonious day, two older women with slacks and blazers walked into rehearsal.

"Ms. Ellie, I'm Maidy Forbes. This gal with me is Penny Lawler. We're from the repertory theater group over in Tylersville. We have a proposition for you."

Ellie told the group to rehearse the dance routine in act 2 while she offered the women seats.

Maidy began.

"A few of our members heard of your success here in the school's drama productions as well as your experience back east. We have also heard that the parents love you, and two are on the theater group's board of directors."

"Would you be interested in playing the leading woman's role in two or three of our productions?" she rushed on. "Parts such as Susan B. Anthony in *The Agitators*? Or Bella in *Lost in Yonkers*? We're putting on a woman's festival in a few months. You can keep your job here and spend your evenings and weekends with us," Penny concluded.

Ellie stared in disbelief at the ladies seated in her tiny orchestra pit, looking up at her standing at the edge of the stage.

Her first reaction was relief. She would no longer have to appeal to Mr. Pierce for the use of the auditorium on an occasional Saturday night. Her second, was the thrilling sense of destiny that a significant theatrical experience was offered without her waiting for hours in the rain and snow. Her third was that her family would be deprived of their mother.

Still, she accepted.

Ellie played Bella. Ellie played Susan B. Anthony. Her performances were favorably covered by statewide media. Photos of her appeared regularly on television, in the newspapers. Many a week, she found herself sitting under lights advising community groups, schools, churches, and clubs on putting together amateur shows and telling amusing stories of her high school group taking on Molière and Chekhov. "If you give young people a challenge," she said, "they will meet it." And so, Ellie's name became known for hundreds of miles around.

Except there were times when she felt as if she had fallen into a patch of stinging nettles, those plants whose hairy stems and leaves were like hollow needles filled with acid. Her own particular nettles were those loathsome age lines accruing around her eyes and mouth that makeup did not conceal and that were apparent on the TV screen. The stress of her alienation from Gavin was showing up right there on camera. She told the producer to have the guys shoot from far back, but inevitably, they disregarded her wishes and zoomed right in.

At their monthly staff meeting, Ellie examined Lucy closely. They were the same age. Was she also sprouting those nascent lines? Or did her cheeks bloom, her eyes sparkle?

Chapter 7

On an ordinary Tuesday afternoon, an agent from Chicago showed up waving a card in front of Ellie's face just as she was trying valiantly to coax a sterling performance out of Sarabeth Atkins in the *Diary of Anne Frank*. She had just decided she had had it with serious plays. The next production would be lighthearted and hopeful. She was thinking of *Aladdin*, a musical. For a change, the kids would sing and dance. She would call in Stephanie Jenks from glee club and Joe Dunsmore from orchestra. Maybe if all of them contributed their skills, she could pull it off.

The agent said that Ellie had been seen playing Shakespeare's Claudia by a member of his staff, that another had heard about her production of *The Wizard of Oz*.

"No, I personally don't know where or when," he replied when she asked. "The bosses don't tell me that, but they want you to audition for a summer production of *Spoon River Anthology*. Ever heard of it? We're trying something new - one woman to play several different women in the book. Think you're up for that?"

Did she ever hear of Spoon River*?* Tearful, Ellie turned away. The poor man wondered what he had said wrong. He thought he had just made a special offer, but Ellie was remembering when she and Gavin were newlyweds reading aloud *Spoon River* to each other. Now she wasn't even sure where she had stored her copy.

"Why me? That description sounds like a heavy acting load," Ellie said.

"Ms. Ellie, our reps and directors can always spot talent. Believe me, they know just what they're looking for."

Ellie called a pause with Sarabeth.

"It's not the big stage, not like Broadway, you realize, but a well-known venue nevertheless - the Hastings Community Playhouse. And it's in Chicago. Should this play be a success, there could be no limit to possibilities."

And did he say summer? When I'm on vacation?

"My orders are to stick around until you give me an answer. I'll be in town for two days with my cameraman. If you say yes, we'll just film a little reading from the book and send it in for final approval. How does that sound?"

Two days. Two days to talk to Gavin whom she hardly saw anymore except at supper. She lamented the loss of Lucy's friendship. Lucy surely would have told her to absolutely, positively go for it. Longings for her old friend nagged at her like a chronic ear infection. If she said yes and was absent for a summer, she knew it might strengthen Gavin and Lucy's relationship. Was she ready for that? On the other hand, was this invitation meant as a nudge to move on? The intervention of God's hand?

Gavin walked in for dinner, surprised to find his favorite meal of roast chicken and fried potatoes waiting, hot and savory.

"This is a surprise. A nice one. What's going on?" he asked.

"Gavin, a man came to see me today," she started.

"Ah, a man. A new man?" he asked, with a wink, laying down his fork.

"It's not what you think."

Ellie thought it was a positive sign that he could still tease her. Flirt with her.

"He's from a community playhouse and wants me to spend the summer in Chicago performing in *Spoon River* and playing a few of the female parts with multiple costume changes and different sets and…" she ran on, racing to get the words out before she faltered.

When she had finished, Gavin spoke directly.

"Ellie, I think you should go. This is what you've been working toward for years. The boys are away in school. And I'll do what I always do - paint."

"By the way, I had already heard about the offer this afternoon while you were still at rehearsal. This guy pulled into the driveway and asked for Ms. Ellie's husband.

"He thought I might help convince you to say yes. And then an extraordinary thing happened. He took one look at my roiling reds painting and went absolutely dead still."

"This your work?" he asked.

"Yes, it's mine. Do you see anyone else around here with a paintbrush?"

"Do you mind if I snap a picture and send it round to a gallery owner friend of mine who shows stuff like this? Don't understand it myself. I prefer looking at pictures of lakes and mountains, even people, you know. But each to his own taste, right?"

So on an afternoon when the appearance of a stranger turned an ordinary day into something extraordinary, husband and wife began to plan how the next months would work out logistically and emotionally. Ellie had a school contract for a summer production, but contracts could be renegotiated or broken. She was surprised that Gavin was so agreeable to her going away, but after all, why not? Why would he say no? Always a generous and considerate man.

Suddenly, they were shy with each other. They hadn't said so many words together in a long time. Just hearing the sound of their voices in an extended conversation seemed a strange occurrence. And this was not your usual everyday talk but words that would change their life's trajectory, words that moved them closer to their individual dreams.

Well, wasn't that what Ellie wanted?

Wasn't that what Gavin wanted?

But like this? Apart?

Was he thinking of Lucy?

"It's only for a summer," Ellie said. "The weeks will go by in a flash, and you'll be able to paint as much as you want with the long hours of daylight."

Ellie served the chicken. They picked up their forks and began to eat, their heads swirling with private thoughts of cherished possibilities.

The next day, the photographer found a shady spot on the school grounds to film Ellie's reading from *Spoon River*. She chose her favorite character, Lucinda Matlock. When she was finished, the hardened cameraman put up his fist and raised his thumb. Both men knew instantly that this was a done deal. Within twenty-four hours, the clip had been sent, reviewed, and approved.

Ellie bought two suitcases at the big box store and set them on the beds in the boys' room.

Neither Gavin nor Ellie took much notice of the wildflowers as they began to make their spring appearance - purple geraniums, red columbine, and those bluebells with their curly edges, mingling together under the trees, in the fields, aside the porch. A fluffy spray of goldenrod clustered at the base of the paddock posts, and Blackie with his nose in the bunch.

It was an unusually luxuriant spring; the mild rains and sunny days brought forth lush fields of daffodils and tulips. But the wonders of the season were ignored as Ellie and Gavin rushed by, their days tinged with melancholy and uncertainty. Come fall, would their lives have been altered? Couples often outgrow each other as they pursue different goals. And who knew if they would find success. It was a time of ambivalence. Neither had really known any other home but theirs together. They hoped to manage the separation without regrets. It was a shame that no one coming and going at their house reached down to pluck a few bluebells for the table.

Ellie was always making notes, checking off lists, scouring through references on *Spoon River* for insights that would enrich the characters' personalities. She spent half a day in the attic until she found their old edition in the box under the window, beneath the small stack of volumes by Wordsworth, Brooke, and Donne. Walking from bedroom to living room, porch to barn, she read aloud various passages involving the female characters. Almost half the book! How was she going to manage such an assignment? Even for an accomplished actress, this was a formidable role. Her clothes were flung carelessly about - Jack's bed for those items she was taking; Danny's for the discards. Every few days, she changed her mind and rearranged the piles.

With the agent's card tacked to a post in the shack, Gavin tried to step up his painting. Not that he would be rushed, one of his primary pleasures being to paint at leisure, but he upped it just a notch should this unknown gallery owner in Chicago wish to display a canvas or two. Even more important, he asked Lucy not to come around anymore. He needed to give 100 percent attention to his work.

Tim filled in. He shopped and weeded, mowed and watered. He played ball with the boys and washed the dishes, delighted for a reprieve from cows and corn. Jack and Danny made guesses, devised scenarios, speculated. Their dad's art could bring him fame. They might be rich. Their own mother might become famous like Greta Garbo or Bette Davis or, gasp, the sultry Lauren Bacall. Between semesters, they ran errands for their folks and romped around the house like spirited young colts, taken up by the high emotion circling around.

"I refuse to be nervous," Ellie kept telling herself. "I'm ready for this. I was chosen by scouts who came looking specifically for me. And *Spoon River* is as familiar to me as any work they could have chosen. Imagine acting the role of several disparate women! It's an opportunity to be angry, remorseful, grateful, revengeful; be young, old, defeated, victorious. Everywoman! And such an original idea. The critics will notice."

"Be determined," Gavin said to himself. "Paint your vision. No distractions, including Lucy. Keep your brush on the canvas as long as sun lights the sky. A man from Chicago saw your work and knows there's a gallery beyond Iowa in which paintings like yours are sold."

The day of Ellie's departure was unusually warm, like the middle of summer rather than its cooler beginnings. Ellie wondered if Chicago would be hotter than Iowa because of its population density or cooler because of the breezes coming off Lake Michigan. The boys were restless, hopping around like human frogs. Danny stowed her luggage in the truck; Jack handed her the briefcase containing *Spoon River*. She ran her hands over the leather, held it to her chest, sighed, and looked around at everyone. The kitchen was neat, not a single dish out of the cupboard or on the drainboard. *Good,* she thought, *it's always a good thing for a woman to leave a clean kitchen.*

Over an hour's ride away, there had been discussions of who would take Ellie to the airport. The boys said they would sit in the back of the pickup and not make a sound. Pat and Sam asked if they could take their van so they could all go. Finally, Ellie quelled the commotion.

"Gavin and I are going alone. And I'm driving, so that's that," she said firmly. "We'll say our goodbyes right here at the house. Then you boys can start right off on your hike. And you, Mom and Dad, won't have to sit in tight quarters." Everyone hugged one another. Pat was teary. Sam was sniffling. And with that, Ellie walked out to the truck.

On the highway, Ellie and Gavin thought of a thousand things to say, but where to start? With the past, the future? Who wanted to pick up with crackling issues just as they were about to be separated? Leave-takings always raise grievance or sorrow or melancholy. Besides, with distance, old concerns might seem somehow sweeter - in memory, recall often rises to the good. So they discussed directions, Gavin's hand on her knee. A few miles off, the signage appeared - Huntsman Regional Airport - arrows pointing. And then Ellie was turning onto the road leading to the massive round-roofed terminal.

"A new addition," Gavin remarked, "that roof. I read about it in the papers."

"Yes," she added, "I like it. Very fancy for Iowa. Belongs in New York, don't you think?" she asked, smiling wistfully.

Gavin set the luggage on the curb and beckoned for a porter. He sensed Ellie's impatience - that she would rather be alone now. It would be awkward sitting inside with hundreds of others, looking out the windows, watching folks say their goodbyes, their hellos. They stood shyly together on the sidewalk, holding hands. The porter loaded the suitcases and waited patiently. A tight hug, Gavin's feathered kiss on her cheek, and Ellie turned and followed her baggage into the terminal.

Waiting to board, she pulled out her copy of *Spoon River*. All around her were folks crying out greetings or bidding farewell, talking, talking, weeping, laughing. She decided to take her own advice to her budding thespians - memorize the words, then rehearse, and rehearse again, then let it go. "Overkill makes your work seem worn and stale. Besides, I have no idea what the director's plan really is for this production," she said to herself. "Better to read a magazine or doze and leave the rest for when I'm on site."

Shortly, her plane landed in Chicago, and she was in a cab on the way to the theater. The city resembled Manhattan, but it was not as high and slightly less dense. Still, with masses of people in a hurry everywhere. Behind every window and door were endless choices for pleasure and commerce.

"Unlimited possibilities," as the agent had said to her.

But then, those were also her thoughts when she went off to New York years ago with hopes for new beginnings. Well, her acting dreams failed, but she was accepting and married. She thought of Gavin painting in a shack on a farm. She thought that her fortuitous moment right now could not be more distant from his. She tried to make sense of the disparities, the contradictions, but before she could settle into her thoughts, her taxi was at the theater door.

Greeted backstage by Old Man Otto, as the actors and employees lovingly called him, she smiled at the watchman who had been there longer than most of them had been alive.

"Oh, you're the new gal!" he bellowed enthusiastically, showing two missing teeth. "Welcome aboard, the gang's waitin' on yuh. Gimme your luggage and go say hullo."

A middle-aged man in yellow sneakers and spiky gray hair, his round red spectacles reflecting the glitter in his sparkling eyes, appeared mysteriously from behind a curtain. Ellie was immediately reminded of the Ronald McDonald character. Was this a friendly omen?

"Ms. Ellie Taylor I presume? Welcome, welcome! Take a look around at your new home. We're so pleased to have you. What a Cordelia you were, my dear! I'm the director. You may call me Marlon!"

A flurry of cast and staff appeared. Introductions were made; hands were shaken; hugs bestowed. All were deferential, as if she were already a star. She felt misplaced, mistaken for someone else. What did any of them know of her?

Someone named Pete whisked her and her luggage down the street to a tiny studio apartment reserved for the lead of the summer production. A second-story walk-up, it resembled a garret in Paris. There was a slanted ceiling, a single window overlooking waves of rooftops, pigeons on ledges. A microwave and a hotplate stood on the only sliver of countertop. *As far from Iowa as possible,* she mused, opening her suitcase on the small bed while Pete waited, casually slouched in the single chair - brown leather, cracks on the arms. She shook out a few dresses, then they returned to the theater. Marlon handed her a script. The players gathered round, and holding a tuna sandwich that had been thrust into her palm, they began.

After seeing Ellie off, Gavin drove home by a slower route, savoring his physical surroundings - the sunny day, the cloudless blue sky - the emotional solitude. This time right now struck him as being both rare and precious for its quiet isolation. No human was in view, and there was peace over the fields abundant with okra and lettuce. *So lovely,* he thought, *a refreshing pause from my mind usually afire with invention.*

Suddenly, there was a shift in the road. There was a hill steep enough on its upward climb to show nothing but sky. Gavin pressed hard on the pedal. Up, up, up before an abrupt descent onto a flat straightaway and then a sight so astonishing he imagined it was a mirage. Like the Emerald City of illusory splendor in *The Wizard of Oz,* where all things were seen as green through colored lenses. Here Gavin viewed a similarly spectacular world but of golds and yellows, from pale lemon to deep ochre depending on where the sun shone.

A field of sunflowers.

He was staring at endless meadows of sunflowers as far as the eye could travel. Not a farmhouse to be seen, as if these wonders of nature just miraculously sprang up by themselves. "Oh, such beauty," Gavin cried out. He pulled the car over on the shoulder and parked. "I'll be darned," he muttered to himself. "Would you take a look at this fantastic sight?"

Could he paint what *fantastic* felt like?

As he sat by the field, he remembered that when he was a kid, posters of Van Gogh's famous sunflower fields hung on the wall of his dentist's office. He wondered at the time if in reality there really were such places, or they were conceived from the painter's imagination. Much later, he learned something far more useful and interesting - that Van Gogh used a technique called impasto, the thick application of paint with a palette knife, to create the sense of a third-dimension. Hence, to awaken the spirit of the painting. Without consciously realizing it, he had just painted reds using a similar approach.

But now, here he was over an hour away from his farm, sitting by the side of a road bewitched by fields of sunflowers swaying and drifting in the middle of nowhere. They just *existed*, a presence belonging to no one but nature. Alongside a common highway. Beyond these fields, there would be nothing but corn all the way home. Gavin gazed at these beauties and imagined the sunflowers growing from seed, inch by inch, reaching for the sun to become as tall as a man or taller, seeking, striving for their full glory. There was strength and courage in these gigantic flowers that grew on rough, hairy stalks, their heads large as plates, yellow petals trembling slightly in the breeze. He had heard that their faces looked east in the morning and kept turning toward the sun all day as the earth revolved. As he sat, Gavin could almost feel the subtle movement occurring, as if the flowers had a brain that reacted to the tremors of God. *But no,* thought Gavin, *this phenomenon is better than having a brain, an organ which is always getting in man's way, offering impediments. But instinctively, without obstacles, the sunflowers know where to go for growth and sustenance.*

From one of their poetry readings, it came back to him. He thought it strange then, but not now, a remark about sunflowers from Helen Keller, who was deaf and blind, "Keep your face to the sunshine, and you cannot see the shadow. It's what sunflowers do."

He already knew that he would paint this scene in thick swaths of yellow, great free strokes with his palette knife, here and there, touches of green earth and blue sky, deep purple for their black centers. Perhaps no viewer would know his intent or his source, but Gavin was sure it would be a great painting.

One pickup truck, then another, stopped and offered help. He waved them on and continued to sit. When the sun began to lose its heat, he finished the drive home, pulling into the worn plot of land they used as a driveway. He rushed to his easel and adjusted its height to accommodate an immense canvas he had readied just last week for his next, until this moment, unknown project. Rummaging around in his tubes of paint, he squeezed onto his palette a hefty dose of Naples yellow and cadmium yellow. Then a measure of yellow ochre and lemon yellow. Scrambling around further, he pulled out ultramarine blue and burnt sienna, mixing a bit of each into the phthalo and viridian greens to depict stems, leaves.

Then taking up his palette knife, Gavin dipped it into the yellow ochre, into the Naples yellow. Generously loaded with paint, he slowly, thoughtfully, approached the canvas.

In odd moments, Gavin and Ellie thought about each other. Mainly at night in the brief time before they fell asleep, taking a few minutes to review the successes and shortcomings of the day. They were generous in their thinking, gratified each was progressing nicely with their respective pursuits.

"Gavin, let me tell you about Old Man Otto."

"Ellie, do you know of Iowa's sunflower fields?

After the call, but before she closed her eyes, her last thought was that he hadn't mentioned Lucy.

Gavin hoped to make it to Chicago for Ellie's opening night of *Spoon River*, but it didn't happen. Shedding his messy painter's pants, setting down his brushes for the seven hours required for driving each way, plus the two days' stay required was too much of a sacrifice.

No way would he leave his work now. Who knew if he would recapture this stupendous momentum? He couldn't risk it.

Instead, the boys set out joyfully with Pat and Sam packed into the back seat. The radio blared out songs from the Beach Boys' *Greatest Hits*, one after the other - "California Girls," "Do It Again," "Catch a Wave." The car was rockin'. Even the older folks in the back seat were snapping their fingers.

"Hey, boy! Watch the road!" Sam cried out as Jack suddenly turned his head.

"Look, everyone! Hurry, look!" Jack yelled, unable to slow the car with automobiles behind him. A meadow of sunflowers ran alongside the road. Thousands rose together, thickly clustered, yellow bonnets circling black faces. Busy fiddling with the radio, Danny didn't bother to look or stop singing. His grandparents were gazing down at their lap, cleaning their glasses, missing the splendor completely. But Jack kept his neck turned until the flowering fields abruptly ended. Determined they were, those sunflowers, not only to flourish, but to reign, put there by a mighty hand to catch you up, to startle you, to make you realize that this world is not a humdrum place.

And then, they were gone.

Jack drove slowly, in thrall to a vision. Did his father pass this field on his way from the airport? He could hardly wait to ask him. His head once again filled up with images of those showy round heads bravely atop stalks strong as rods, tiny black seedpods clustered in their centers. Would he ever forget their dignified generosity?

There was a free day before Ellie's performance. How would they fill it? After checking their bags in a flat one floor below Ellie's - special accommodations for her family - Jack would find the Blue Moon and Richard Norton Galleries. Both featured work of the Abstract Expressionists. He would take a close look at why their influence had remade their father's art. With its splendid view of Lake Michigan, Danny was off to Jackson Park for a pickup game of basketball. Pat and Sam were comfortably settled on a bench in view of the court. A vendor was selling hot sausages on a roll. There was a breeze off the lake, and the grandparents thought this spot one step away from heaven.

The next evening, Ellie's small family gathered in the front row. For the first time, Jack proudly wore his black jacket with the Nehru collar, a stand-up collar with no lapels, no fastenings. It was a birthday gift from his father. The lights, the glitter, the hum of the audience, musicians tuning up - Jack lamented his father's absence for missing this gaiety on their mother's behalf. As well, that he would not see his son this night in his new outfit.

Jack had first seen a picture of this jacket in the school library, not on a real person, but in a celebrity magazine that showed a painting by an artist who designed posters for rock stars. Her name was Bonnie MacLean, the only female artist in the sixties working in this genre. Her style was driven by psychedelic motifs, swirling lines and raucous colors, suitably hip and outrageous at the time for the world of rock and roll. The poster Jack had come upon was done for a Pink Floyd concert, and the group were wearing Nehru jackets. On the bottom, a note that the poster had been in a show at Manhattan's Museum of Modern Art. *Dad would like that,* Jack thought.

The look was sensational and original, and Jack desired a similar image. Quite funky, but so what? His parents where not shocked by unconventional clothes. Hadn't they lived in New York where everyday folks on the street wore outlandish ensembles? On the other hand, that was almost twenty years ago, and they had, after all, lived in Iowa most of their adult lives.

"Dad, I really like this jacket," Jack began, handing over the magazine. "Can I get one? We'd probably have to send away for it. I'm sure McGuire's won't stock it!"

In two weeks, Jack will be nineteen, Gavin thought. *It makes a good birthday present, something he desperately wants. Why deny him?* Gavin understood Jack's artistic sensibility, his preference for clothes other than the farm's reliable outfit - T-shirts and jeans. And besides, Gavin himself was blown away by the poster's style. *Gorgeously drawn,* he thought, *clever and riveting.* So he bought the jacket - black, an elegant color, nothing garish. When it arrived and Jack slipped it on,

Gavin was not only startled and charmed to see Jack wearing such a sophisticated garment, but also pleased to know his son's head was thrumming with the imaginative artistry of Bonnie MacLean.

Now tonight, Jack wore it for his mother's Chicago debut while Danny dressed in black jeans, a white T-shirt, and a corduroy sports jacket of Gavin's. When they came round to Ellie before the show to wish her luck, she looked at her two boys and could see the men they were becoming, even the slant of the paths they might each choose, typified by their dress. Both were pearls of manhood, dear, good creatures.

Pat cried throughout the play, whispering, "My girl, that's my baby," with no recall of her disdain for Ellie's acting dreams all those years ago. Sam kept patting her knee, dabbing his eyes. At the end, the boys were on their feet, whistling through their fingers and calling, "Bravo, way to go!"

They ran to Ellie with open arms, swinging her in the air and heaping compliments on her shoulders. Ellie tried to hold back her sobs - such an arduous, complex performance she had just given - her makeup pooling and smearing from her eyelashes to her chin.

Early the next morning, everyone bundled into the car while Ellie was having an early breakfast with Marlon, tweaking the glitches for that evening's performance.

On the way home, Danny couldn't stop chatting about the young blond girl sitting next to him. "She has her own horse named Chuckles. Isn't that cute?"

And Sam, repeating to Pat, "Dang, woman. How about that? Our Ellie will be famous!"

Jack was quiet, thrilled with an insight that suddenly came to him as he stared at himself in the mirror wearing his Nehru-collared jacket - his own particular direction that popped out at him with the force of a bullet.

All came clear. At once, he was relieved and elated. He didn't have to paint lakes and mountains and fields like his father had. And much as he admired his dad's current abstract style, that approach didn't sit well with him either. It seemed too laborious, taking days, often weeks, to finish one canvas. Also, there were no visual elements of reality in his father's work now, components that still attracted Jack but in a different way. That drawing of Pink Floyd, for example. There was no doubt who it was. But then the artist had taken his painting of Floyd and stuck it in what seemed like an electric socket. And it became Pink Floyd charged up! Why couldn't he do that? Until now, Jack had been confused, unsure about his own artistic destiny. Until he skimmed through a magazine and found Bonnie MacLean, a woman who showed him how to be inspired and nimble in an entirely new way. When she used neon colors, it was expressive of just how he felt - pumped up, on fire! Imagine earning a living by creating posters for rock stars! For the Beach Boys!

When Jack turned into the family driveway, his father walked out to meet them. Everyone talked at once, sharing the good news about Ellie's outstanding performance, the havoc of success. Three curtain calls! Jack was impatient to get his father alone. He had an important vision to share.

Chapter 8

Impressive offers arrived for Ellie by mail, by phone.

Not from Broadway, the major player, but still, overtures from places such as Boston, Los Angeles, Miami, well-known venues. Ellie was pleased. She hadn't really expected Broadway to come calling, but there was beginning to be a buzz about her, and she could build on that.

Chicago had been her launch. Forty-eight performances as Everywoman in *Spoon River*, an exhausting feat that impressed both audiences and producers; the latter astonished at her hard work. It was time to go home and decide what to do next. In the quiet Iowa peace, her mind could rest, and the path forward would become apparent. However, boarding the plane for the flight home, she knew too well that there were risks involved in making choices.

At the airport, Gavin and the boys welcomed her with a gigantic banner spanning six feet.

"Our Leading Lady!" The letters swirled like waves. Ellie's face sketched by Jack in iridescent hot pink, green, and purple. She had never seen anything like it, so radically chic. A sign Ellie would hang like a painting over the living room fireplace. Passersby circled around the boys to get a better look.

On the drive home, she stared out the car window. Cornfields, silos, barns, cows, horses, more corn, more cows, farmhouses painted white with wraparound porches set back from the road. Almost immediately, the reality of her old everyday life returned - always shaking off the dirt from one's boots, never wearing high heels or makeup. Her mind staggered and lurched at the possible loss of these elements she had grown to love. And here she was, not even home yet but already thinking about leaving again. How obligated emotionally was she to stay?

The truth was, and she knew it, that she had outgrown Iowa. She had outgrown teaching, being a director, a manager. With the little ones, there were constant behavior and attention issues. With the high schoolers, the headaches were bigger - showing off, wanting their own way, laughing at private jokes, sneaking outside for a cigarette. She had enjoyed it at the time, but her stint in Chicago took her far from her past. Gavin was prescient when he sent her off with the words, "I hope, Ellie, that you don't grow beyond us." Her Gavin, unerringly insightful and noble, letting her go even if her ambitions would take her elsewhere.

"Gavin, honey," Ellie asked as they drove along, "aren't the sunflower fields somewhere around here? You said you'd show me."

"Ellie, summer's over. The fields are barren. The sunflowers are done. In the spring, the farmers will plant again."

They both sat quietly, melancholy at thinking how life sweeps one up in its inexorable march of time, of those glorious beauties once seeking the sun, now just a heap of drooping petals and withered stalks, sad creatures awaiting the plow.

The boys were impatient to be done with college. "Little more to gain," they said, complaining they felt just like Blackie when they first brought him home, restless, fretful, tugging at his ropes, pawing the ground. It was a sure bet that Danny would marry a girl from town and take over the farm. Jack would enter a world no one could imagine, but not a soul doubted it would be far from Iowa. And Gavin? As a pair, he and Ellie were quite amiable, loving as parents and friends, but it was evident now their individual ambitions would separate them. Did they still have a true marriage? Could they remain close in a platonic way? Regaining their personal intimacy seemed difficult to recapture. Besides, in Chicago, Ellie had begun to think she didn't want such a return. Her mind had moved to another place, and it wasn't in Iowa. And Iowa was where Gavin was.

It didn't occur to either of them that if Ellie chose to leave, Gavin could accompany her. A painter could work anywhere. But Gavin confined in an apartment with his substantial canvases and supplies? Never. He belonged to open spaces, the air, the sky. So Gavin became an *issue*, a heavy burden of how and where to fit into Ellie's life.

By the time they had driven into the yard and braked the truck, Ellie had almost made up her mind. She would look closely at the offers, but Boston was the most enticing. A great city with a unique history, dozens of universities, an abundance of live theaters. Also, theater folks from Manhattan followed closely what went on in Boston.

As she walked past the shack, she noticed Gavin's easel and idly wondered what he was working on, what he had produced throughout the long summer. But it was only a fleeting thought. She wasn't curious enough to stop and peek or check out what finished works were in storage. Rather, her mind was on the clothes she would need if she indeed went to Boston or to any of those other cities. Owning only rough farm wear, she would have to do some serious shopping. And it was flair she would be after.

With us being separated for almost three months, her lack of interest is painfully obvious, Gavin thought. Resentment stung like a wasp, the swelling starting to rise. Would he ever show her his wonderful sunflower painting? It was the finest thing he had ever done. He had no doubt that someday an enraptured buyer would love it madly and want to own it. Oddly, her indifference calmed him down as he realized it was sadness he felt; that this was how things were now.

The boys twirled Ellie around the kitchen, bumping into chairs, knocking over a basket.

"Hey, Mom, told yuh! Another Lauren Bacall!" Danny shouted.

"Boy, Mom, a star is born!" Jack cried, passing her from one pair of hands to another and adding a deep curtsy, like in a waltz.

Gavin realized that he hadn't missed Lucy's presence. Somehow, she had slid without fuss into becoming part of his past, remembered with fond nostalgia. When he was insecure and wavering, Lucy was generous with her support, and he was genuinely appreciative. But now, assured of his own powers, he was glad for feeling detached, relieved. Now was not the time to become further anchored to Iowa, just the opposite. He knew that his red painting, the sunflowers, and several others recently completed were remarkable. And like Ellie, he had earned the right for his talent to consider wide-ranging possibilities.

He would leave Iowa. Perhaps he should head toward an edgy city like San Francisco or London, where contemporary artists were dabbling in experimental, uneasy creations. His new style and technique might be welcome in such an environment. Their appeal, however, seemed to hinge on trends and fads, and Gavin sought a more elevated, rarified atmosphere in which to work, a place that was both settled and new at the same time. Would he find the "new" in Italy? And yet, could any place compare to Italy's grandeur, its thousands of painters and craftsmen throughout history bringing magnificence to the world?

He had no idea how his work would find acceptance in such a traditional country, but it is to Italy he would go.

Pat prepared a lavish coming-home dinner. No one could remember the last time the entire family had all sat down together. There were steaks, green beans, corn, and of course, three kinds of pies - apple, strawberry, blueberry, all the fruit plucked from bushes encircling the house. With the exception of Pat and Sam, everyone at the table was on the cusp of taking a large step into an unknown future, and the meal was raucous, a cacophony of sounds and wishes - sentimental and wistful, loving and hopeful.

When it was quiet at last and they were in their own bed, Gavin and Ellie talked into the darkness, gently, cautiously testing, treading carefully, posing possibilities.

"I've an offer from Boston," she murmured.

"Yes? Do you want to go?"

"It sounds exciting."

"What if I leave the farm also?" he asked.

"Leave the farm? The boys? Where would you go?"

"Does it matter? Leaving the farm means away."

"And Tim? I imagine he'll marry someone from town and work with Danny," Ellie said.

Questions thrown out into the dark.

"Can we manage financially?"

"Do we give Danny the house? What then for Jack?"

Though their talk was kind, the concerns were boundless. Each one raised brought new considerations, none of which were resolved. They began to feel drowsy from the sweetness of the wine, the excitement of the day. So after a few nods of yes, maybe, why not, they shut down the conversation. Eventually, the assorted issues would work themselves out. Their whispers grew softer until finally the stars came out, and they fell asleep holding hands, Ellie dreaming of Boston, Gavin of Tuscany.

They slid easily into making their decisions, then into the logistics of shifting course.

Arrangements for Ellie took no time at all. A subdued meeting with her principal and her contract was easily vacated. They would miss her but would she give them two weeks to train her replacement Ms. Olson, the librarian who often read stories to her charges in after-school daycare? A letter and three phone calls to Boston discussed arrangements, terms (not generous but adequate), and it was done. No assigned roles as yet, of course, but they were aware of her talents, and she need not worry. Within walking distance, a small state college offered rooms at a special rate for their theater company. She would like it there with young people all around. Meal plan and laundry service were offered. Should they reserve for her? And last, notification to her home theater group - a farewell dinner at a Chinese restaurant carried off like an improv performance, lots of laughs and good wishes reading imaginary messages contained in the fortune cookies.

Her high school actors from spring term held an impromptu reading of *Spoon River* in the gym. Students and faculty packed the bleachers to celebrate her future while also lamenting the imminent loss of her presence. A group of eight stood in a circle, each holding a copy of the book as they wrung a heap of emotion from those pages, just like she had taught them. When it was over, the girl who read Lucinda Matlock, Jodie Barnes, her long hair in a single braid - *like Lucinda might have worn,* Ellie thought - draped a necklace of wild daisies around Ellie's neck. They were flowers Lucinda might have collected. *I will miss these kids,* she thought sadly. The principal gave a brief talk of how, because of Ellie, Iowa must now live up to its auspicious beginnings in the drama department. "Watch out world," she said, "Riverton High's name will soon give Chicago a run for its money!"

With tears on her cheeks, Ellie played the diva's part, throwing kisses in all directions, sweeping from the room to a whole lot of hootin' and hollerin'.

Jack advised his father to check out certain magazines in the public library, so Gavin drove over for a quiet afternoon of research. It seemed like much of the town was also there, engaged in some activity or another. Middle schoolers were being tutored. Adults were taking a computer class. A new librarian was being trained. Gavin gathered up a handful of publications and made his way to the rear of the great room. Under a domed skylight, he found a comfortable chair and settled in.

On a side table, he set down his bounty of arts and travel magazines. In the back pages were advertisements and announcements for every taste and inclination - requests for roommates, rentals, purchases, exchanges for castles and cottages in Capri, southern France, Sweden, Old Prague, New Prague, lakeside cabins in Norway.

It was a distracting business, easy to get caught up in the lure of the articles themselves. He kept reminding himself to stay with his mission, although despite the glamorous choices, he really had decided - only Tuscany.

After three days, he found it - a charming bungalow set among gentle hills and fields of wildflowers on land owned by a monastery. Nearby was a picturesque, historic village. The photo showed the tiny house almost buried by Tuscan poppies in a season when these "stunning, vivid red beauties covered the countryside," the article said. The ad was placed on behalf of a seventeenth-century monastery inhabited by an order of monks, a hospitable sect that rejected vows of silence. It even owned a vineyard, produced and sold its own wine on premises. He continued to read:

> *One cozy bedroom, a modest living room adjoining a large alcove full of light for a writer or painter. A garden.*

Gavin again studied the photographs of the cottage. Ivy grew over the snug facade with its window boxes of red roses. There was a narrow stone path to the front door.

> *In early spring, Tuscany is covered with Alpine pansies and primroses. In June, poppies smother the hills and valleys. And in summer, it is time for the majestic golden sunflowers at nearby Val d' Orcia and Pian d'Alma, especially around the town of Maremma. The sunflowers had originated in America but had somehow settled in Italy. No one could explain how they came to this country.*

Sunflowers?

Born in America? The seeds then drifting on the winds to drop in Maremma? Surely, this is an omen. Surely, this is an indication, Gavin thought, *of where I am meant to go.*

He hurried to the map section on the second floor. The town was close to Florence and not far from an international airport. An American contact number was listed. Quickly, he rushed to the library basement and put some coins into a pay phone. Punching in the number, he exchanged information and made his commitment. He then went back inside and continued to read like a man famished with untold hungers.

> *Unforgettable, magical views.*

All that remained was to book his flight. It was that simple to effect a seismic shift. Gavin packed up his canvases and emptied the shack. He had never heard from the Chicago guy who waved his card in front of his nose, but who cared now? He had produced a small stock of finished works thanks to the man's promise of possibility. Likely the fellow had cooked up the scheme as a ruse to lure Ellie.

Standing now in the empty chicken coop, held up by a few weathered boards, his head was reeling with prospects, his heart beholden to memories. Just past his fortieth birthday, it was later than most to be making a breakout career move. One might think Gavin would shake his fist at the forlorn little shack and think, good riddance. This was an unholy place to bring forth creative talent. But in fact, he was grateful. It was here in this humble spot that he discovered his flamboyant modernist style, honed his ability to focus, clarified his purpose. And now, with all his supplies arranged and ready, he was at his moment of reckoning.

As the days of departure approached, Pat kept twisting her apron; Sam kept spilling his lemonade. They had received the news of Ellie's and Gavin's plans at almost the same time. Boston! Pat trembled. How far away was Boston? Certainly farther than a car ride to Chicago. And Jack gone who knows where, as well. Now, Gavin to Italy. It was too much, all at once.

Danny sat beside them on the floor, took both their hands in his.

"Hey, guys, not to worry. I'm not going anywhere. I'll get married, and before you know it, you'll have a whole bunch of great-grandkids running around getting in your way."

Somewhat mollified, they stopped sniffling and gave a big sigh - after all, children were entitled to their own lives. Being farmers, they knew for sure life was unpredictable every day you got up. Whether the news with the crops, the kids, the bank, the weather would be good or bad was up to the Almighty.

"Do you already have a girl in mind?" they asked hopefully.

Danny laughed and said, "Whoa, guys, gimme a break. I just graduated from college. I have to look around a bit, don't you think?"

They made Ellie promise she would return for visits at least twice a year.

"Of course! And how about if I fly you out to Boston after I settle in?" she asked.

We're way too old for such trips, her parents thought, but just being asked was comfort enough.

In any case, it was done.

Weary and subdued, Pat and Sam got up from their chairs and started buzzing about, getting supper ready.

Chapter 9

This sure ain't Iowa, Gavin thought as he sat at a small Italian café in the cozy plaza having his morning *caffè*. Gazing beyond the local shops to the rows of olive trees climbing the hillsides, he once again considered how, almost overnight, his life had gone from the mundane to the splendid, from despair to renewal. Could he ever have imagined such a turnaround? Still, dark musings followed. If he could capture light from dark, the opposite could occur just as unexpectedly, a descent from his present contented state into the morbid, into deprivation of this incandescent, translucent Tuscan light.

Gavin - forty-two years old and lanky, his frame hard and taut, as artists living meagerly are often formed - harbored such notions as he drank his cappuccino. His sharp brown eyes focused on the shadow created by a leaf blown onto the table, on scattered pastry crumbs, on a pigeon's fluttering wing. Very few visual details escaped his discerning eye. There, across the way, an old woman was tending her vegetable cart. Behind her, Gregorio, the gelato vendor, was folding back the shutters of his shop. Gavin watched closely, fitting his observations into a future painting that would express the notion of pulsating, purposeful activity.

And yet if one were thoughtful and observant, life here seemed fixed, eternal - the men still laboring in old ways in the vineyards, the women still shopping daily from outdoor peddlers for their *spaghetti alla carbonara.* Francesco, the café owner, had used a mortar and pestle, not an electric blender to grind his coffee beans. It was clear that the natural world was ephemeral even amid this ageless setting, a juxtaposition of elements that Gavin loved. Yet suddenly, an inexplicable sadness darkened Gavin's cheerful mood.

With his long white apron wrapped around his ample middle, Francesco was attending to seats for an enthusiastic family of six, serving them platters of *bomboloni*, deep-fried doughnuts that caused the children to shriek with delight. Next, a plate of *castagnole*, lightly crisped dough filled with chocolate. Gavin decided to put away his melancholy reflections and think happily of his work and the discoveries he had made since his arrival. And he would dip into the joy around him.

In Iowa, Gavin had lived mostly a solitary life without noteworthy visual stimulation, but not here. In Tuscany, everything one viewed was touched by an artistic sensibility - the carvings on the church door, Francesco's *biscotti* in a handwoven basket, a shopkeeper's window with plants arranged like an outdoor garden. Gavin could spend a lifetime studying the architectural details alone of the monastery's cloisters and frescoes and intricate milled panels.

Painters of the past had captured that sense of Italian timelessness, which the whole world cherished - art that was exacting and laborious, faithful in great detail to its subject. There were no vague, drifting strokes to be found, set down with wide brushes as was Gavin's preference. Paintings were detailed portrayals made with small brushes, faithful to authenticity. Note the gorgeous, intricate particulars of Filippo Lippi's fifteenth-century *Madonna and Child.* Then compare that work with the dazzling, tumultuous representation of another female figure painted five hundred years later by the contemporary master Willem de Kooning with his *Woman* painting. One could not conceive of painting the other's pictures, yet both men could have had coffee in this very town square.

The children at the next table were now singing Italian folk songs while Gavin continued to sip his coffee and ponder the truth of history with the reality of contemporary life.

He loved to think about such things.

He really should consider putting away his acrylics even though they well suited his technique, an impetuous approach to putting down color. But their essential quality of drying quickly, enabling easy paint overs, was irresistible. Made of fast-drying plastics, acrylics were products of the modern age, but they lacked the history and integrity of oil paint. They offered no opportunity for layering, with the top color virtually eradicating the previous one. And that is how one should paint scenes in Italy, layering on a rich surface that more appropriately conveyed a sense of history and evolution. But his style was now, not then. Besides, although he was ashamed to say it out loud, he loved working with acrylics, despite the venerable art supply store on the corner's refusal to even consider stocking them. Thus far, he had purchased them by mail, but it was becoming tiresome to wait for the post. He supposed he could shop for them in Florence, if he could find an heretical art shop in some hidden alley that sold such products.

The old and the new - both together comprised past dreams and future ambitions.

In no rush, Gavin could take his time, be inventive with every new canvas. Just as an experiment, he might even go so far as to put up a small test canvas and give oil painting another try. While musing on this, he noticed that the child who had come over to him earlier with a pastry now had a dab of chocolate smack in the center of a dimple on her left cheek.

Just then, a strong hand gripped his shoulder.

"*Buongiorno,*" a friendly greeter bellowed. "*Buongiorno, come stai?*" Antonio repeated. "How are you this morning, my dear American friend?" Gavin's new pal, a master at harvesting the grape, was here to exchange morning regards before starting his day.

With a small cry of relief, Gavin pulled up another chair, giving quiet thanks for the interruption. He was about to turn his thoughts to a difficult subject, missing his family.

Stay in the present, he told himself. *Don't belabor your decisions. Stay with what your gut tells you. If you can do that* - Gavin reminded himself - *the leisure of Tuscany will unfurl like the opening of a gift, allowing friendship and dreams to enter and grow.*

While Gavin was having his morning coffee, Ellie was on the Boston stage reprising *Spoon River* yet again. She had hoped for an exciting new play, but the director, Hank, had been filled in on her Chicago performance and was thrilled to be reminded of that often-forgotten play by the genius Edgar Lee Masters. So pleased was he, in fact, that he scheduled it for the fall season and made Ellie his assistant director.

When she looked uneasy, Hank added, "Don't worry. You can also be in the performance. But not all the female parts this time. There are too many other aspiring actors who want their chance. However, you can have first dibs on choosing your characters.

"Two," he said, "you can choose two."

Right away, she chose the character of Rebecca Wasson, confessing her pure and poignant reality:

Spring and Summer, Fall, and Winter and Spring
After each other drifting, past my window drifting,
And I lay so many years watching them drift and counting
The years till a terror came in my heart at times.
My hundredth year was reached! and still I lay
Hearing the tick of the clock, and the low of cattle…

And Ellie's other choice? The lines of Jenny McGrew and their mysterious unraveling:

Not, where the stairway turns in the dark,
A hooded figure, shriveled under a flowing cloak!
Not yellow eyes in the room at night,
Staring out from a surface of cobweb gray!
And not the flap of a condor wing,
When the roar of life in your ears begins
As a sound heard never before!
But on a sunny afternoon,
By a country road…

There, she thought, *with these two, I can create acceptance, despair, joy. Hank is placing me at the beginning and the end. Good. I'll wake up the audience with Rebecca, and when they sense that the play is about to end, I'll send them out of the theater with Jenny, dazzled and celebratory. Always leave them on an emotional high, right? Downhearted or elated, either one, so long as their feelings run strong.*

Most of the men and women in the company were single and chose to live, as she had, in the college dormitory annex. It was an attached facility, not a separate building as she had assumed. Therefore, their rooms were a close part of the undergraduate scene, a delightful surprise. Twice the age of the students, Ellie loved their exuberance, the chatter and activity hovering around them. Most of the girls harbored secret dreams of becoming actresses, even the math and physics majors, so Ellie was held in high esteem. Someone, girl or guy, was always coming up to her asking questions. "How did you get started in this business?" Most were eager for advice. Even those who feigned indifference listened closely.

The attention puffed up her ego. *Be careful,* she told herself. *Think of how well your colleague Julie is playing Lucinda Matlock.*

Ellie pined for her family more than she expected - her boys the same age as the students; this one reminding her of Danny with his casual slouch and rugged hands, that one of Jack with his serious gaze, his T-shirts with the slogans "Paint to Live" and "Relax, Pick Up a Brush."

She didn't speak to Gavin very often. Calls abroad were expensive, and besides, the time difference hardly ever worked in their favor. When he called, she was often asleep. When she called, he was almost always painting with his phone turned off. "If there is an emergency," he had said, "call the number at the monastery, and they will send someone to fetch me."

Neither anticipated such a need.

Danny was back home along with his college chum Brett. Between the two, they put in long days managing the crops and animals and the grandparents' weekly errands' run to town. While Pat and Sam shopped, the boys scoped out the town for pretty girls. If you were a young thing eager for a cute date, you made sure you were hanging around Haywood's Mercantile on Wednesday afternoon when Danny dropped off the folks.

And Jack? A buddy from college had visited the farm and was dazzled by Jack's banner of Ellie above the fireplace. He told Jack about a company in his Chicago hometown that might have a job for someone who likes to draw pictures, especially if he was into creating funky, oddball illustrations. Essentially an advertising company, it was big-time in the commercial graphics world.

Jack sent off a few samples to the firm, including a Pink Floyd drawing in the style of Bonnie MacLean. Anything Floyd related was his good luck charm. Ten days later, he received an offer. And before the end of the month, he packed a trunk, hugged the family, and made his way east. As Pat and Sam sat in their rockers talking after supper, they marveled again and again, "Can you believe our Jack could be drawing pictures that would someday be seen on television?"

"Our work here is a collaborative process," Jack's boss told him. "You have to account to me, then to Mr. Briggs, my superior. There are specific assignments rather than each individual employee drafting his on individual schemes. Money is our end game."

Jack was concerned. He had never worked in a group, but at least he took comfort that he was only trying it out, that he could quit anytime. Besides, it was exciting to work in a tall building with glass windows looking out on the city and its waterways. And on the first day, he met two young men in the publicity department looking for a third roommate.

The first week passed as expected, meeting people, organizing his desk, checking out the company's rooms and machines. But almost immediately, he bumped up against a diverse pack of moral dilemmas.

For his housemates and many of his coworkers, their social lives revolved around parties - giving them, going to them, social drinking before and after. Or they threw potluck dinners in their apartments where pretty, flirty girls showed up. Jack didn't know where they came from. Some faces were repeats; some were new. To a farm boy, the constant sociability made him feel awkward. Besides, he was ambitious. In his free time, he preferred experimenting with his own designs, taking an office project one step further than was assigned.

As a youngster, he sat by his father while he worked, Gavin was a determined, ambitious, purposeful man. Would he think Jack's new job frivolous? Or would he think it was nifty, stylish, even cool? Yes, it was commercial advertising, but he was still drawing, putting out original work. And if Jack shared his experiences, what would be Gavin's opinion on his rollicking colleagues? In any case, when father and son spoke intermittently on the phone, the calls were rushed, breathy. Each lived in widely disparate worlds. Neither was prone to letter writing. And Gavin didn't ask specific questions, letting Jack parcel out his news however he chose. Naturally, he spoke of his visits to the Chicago Art Institute, the Navy Pier's Shakespeare Theater. On another call, he described the Shedd Aquarium right on the lake, a gorgeous building displaying sea creatures he had never known existed.

Was one waiting for the other to venture out first into their respective personal lives?

A year passed.

It was a full year of seasons around the world. Hot summers everywhere with fierce humidity in Boston, followed by a brilliant fall to revive its people's spirits. Corn and soybeans in summer, but a cold, snowy winter in Iowa, though nothing compared to the deep freeze of Chicago. And a sublimely lovely Tuscan spring, winter, fall, and especially summer, the land glorious with the scents and colors of sunflowers, poppies, and roses, and never was there a day not gracefully bestowed.

It was a seminal year in which dramatic changes occurred, but so slowly and naturally that no one noticed. Gavin finished several paintings. Danny had a girlfriend. Jack disliked his job but nevertheless was assembling an impressive portfolio. While Ellie was waiting for the role that would make her famous, she directed her first play.

One day following the next.

Danny was dating Maryann, a girl he had known in high school. A sweet thing, she particularly took to Sam, doing little things for him before he had a chance to realize the task was no longer in his ability to manage, such as bending over to sweep up a dustpan of broken glass.

Pat taught her to sew. When Maryann finished her first project, an apron of blue gingham, she gifted it back to Pat as a thank-you for being her teacher. Danny was not such a rugged, outdoorsy guy that he didn't notice these thoughtful gestures. At such moments, he grew tender with Maryann, smoothing her hair, peeling her an orange.

Jack had been given a promotion, and with it, two exclusive accounts. Thankfully, he now had his own apartment. His rooms on the eighteenth floor with a tiny balcony overlooked Montrose Beach on Lake Michigan. Not a balcony big enough to sit out on, but with the doors open, Jack could look down every morning on the beautiful view and guess which jacket would be most appropriate for the day's weather. He was often wrong. High up, looking down, it was always cool and windy, the air having a sharp bite. But when he got to street level, it could feel like the lift of spring.

Some of his submissions were discarded, others were accepted or modified. It rankled him that his boss was less creative than he, more of an overseer than an artist. However, although Jack never had the satisfaction of being the complete owner of any one thing, he did achieve a unique victory when a guy in the music department added a catchy jingle to one of his creations. Regularly seen on television in thirty-second spots, the particular image of two dolphins with human faces became a popular and beloved image in the current culture. No one outside the company knew Jack's name, but he received a generous bonus, and everyone in the department gave him high-fives for a whole month. And Pat and Sam laughed and cried every time they saw it on their television screen.

Jack took a week off and flew to a beach in Florida where he lay in the sun and evaluated his professional life. *What's next? More of the same?* When he thought of the elegant halls surrounding his office, his concerns intensified. On its walls hung huge paintings of dramatic motion, often spanning eight to ten feet. They could have come from his father's hand. Each one had a wall of its own with directed ceiling lights helping the colors jump and sing, all by the same artist, comprising quite a valuable collection.

Francine Holzman. Hers was a talent that was shared with the world in the most intimate way. This woman could make any observer stand absolutely still and think of nothing but past mistakes and future dreams, old regrets, and celebrations to come. How could his puny, kitschy drawings, in and out of fashion, with no specific artist attribution, begin to compare?

Jack continued to swim in the ocean. Riding the waves, watching the circling gulls, he thought further of his situation. *I don't really want a reclusive life like my father's. I don't want to paint single canvases. In fact, I like the type of work I do. If I could only manage to get just one big commission either at my company or from work done on my own time, I could settle into something really special.*

Confused, Jack returned to Chicago.

There had been a scheduling error on the company's docket, and a month's time had become available. Ellie discovered a piece by an unknown writer about a mother who, as she lay dying, gave up her only child to a whore.

She pleaded with Hank. "It's brilliant, Hank. We have to do it even though the story is a bit unconventional. Did anyone think that *Fiddler on the Roof* or *The Producers* or certainly *Cats* would be successful?"

"Why not?" Hank replied, his red glasses trembling. "Theater is all about trying something new."

He well knew any original theater production was risky, but he was a guy who believed in long shots. After the opening, Hank's belief in Ellie's career soared. He sent a bouquet of dahlias to her dressing room.

"Bravo to the director," the critics wrote.

"A quiet gem," the headline said.

"That gal's trajectory is up, up, up."

Ellie bought multiple copies of the reviews and sent them to Gavin and the boys. In a week, Danny responded, "Way to go, Mom! Will you take me to the Academy Awards? I showed it to Grandma, and she cried. Asked when you are coming to visit."

In two weeks, Jack responded, "I'm real proud of you, Mom, finally hitting your stride."

In a month, she received a note from Gavin, "Hey, Ellie, good for you. I knew you had it in you. May your many talents take you to high places."

After she received Gavin's note, she put them all away in a green lacquer box and cried pitiably into the night. She didn't understand why; she simply couldn't stop.

In that first year, from the Brothers in the monastery, Gavin learned to differentiate between various wines and their vintages. And when he volunteered his time in the wine shop, he began to meet his Italian neighbors who warmly embraced him. The DiGiornios, who ran the monastery's vineyards and had eleven children, all of whom worked in the fields. There was Francesco, the café owner; his wife, Lola, a superb baker; and their five *bambini*, three of whom attended school. The two youngest skipped around his table as he drank his morning cappuccino, teaching him simple Italian words in singsong voices. His faithful pal, Antonio, cheered him every morning with a hug and unflagging optimism, happy to sit and schmooze despite having a sick wife at home. The Lattazzas rented several precious acres of the Brothers' land containing the flourishing olive groves. Piero Lattazza ground the olives and extracted their oil the old way from large millstones.

He told Gavin stories about the olives, as if they were a sacred trust.

"Legend tells us the ancient Greek goddess Athena had actually created the olives," he began. ""Homer called the olives 'liquid gold.' King David considered them so choice that he hired guards to protect Israel's olive groves and storerooms."

That afternoon, after he heard Piero's story of the olives, Gavin picked up his brush, and in gray, black, and brown, he attempted to honor Piero's tales with a painting of heroic significance. A week later, when he had finished, he worried that his colors might indicate doom or death, even though he was after just the opposite idea, a purposeful subject with historical continuity and a living legacy. So to ensure life, he added a few touches of well-placed red and lime green, sparingly.

Aha! Now he had captured its compelling glory.

Gavin was painting profusely, as if a torrent of blood was released from a wound. And still, more came. Occasionally, the monks wandered in for a look. Their faces were puzzled, concerned; their comments mere murmurs. "Ah, my friend, we see you are hard at work," then leaving quietly, shaking their bald heads, hands concealed in the pockets of their robes. The youngest, Father Bianchi, with the looks of a boy, was always the last to leave. He stared, his eyes popping, fingers fiddling with the string tied at his waist. His mouth open, he seemed about to speak, but instead, he sighed and followed the other monks from the room.

Piero Lattazza stopped by to see Gavin's painting inspired by the olives.

"Ah, Gavin, magnificent! I don't understand what you are doing, but I love it! I love it!"

After Piero's visit, Gavin decided he it was time to try selling his paintings in Florence.

Chapter 10

Gavin purposely had not yet ventured into Florence. His plan was to step into the city not as a sightseer but as an observer with the most delicate and appreciative mind. It was only now, after a year, that he felt ready to take into his soul its glorious offerings, its inexhaustible treasures. And in return, he would offer something of himself - his paintings.

The American writer Mark Twain called Florence the "city of dreams."

An independent republic of incalculable wealth at the time, it was in fifteenth-century Florence that the Italian Renaissance was born, transforming the Middle Ages to modernity in a spectacular fashion. Geniuses walked its streets and, through their work, altered the entire world.

This golden domed city rested in a basin along the River Arno, cradled and embraced by the rolling Chianti hills. Not a single aspect of life and thought then was untouched by astonishing, unsurpassed accomplishment. And not just by the hands of masterful sculptors and painters but by skilled unknowns, the talented stonecutters, masons, glass makers, craftsmen who toiled in obscurity but brilliantly fulfilled their masters' visions.

And to bring the world into this new age, Florence birthed far more than artists such as Leonardo da Vinci and Michelangelo, Donatello, and Masaccio; dazzling philosophers as well - Erasmus, Machiavelli; intellectual titans; eminent scientists - Galileo; and writers. Together, they crafted new concepts of heaven and earth, proposed original theories that unearthed and honed human thought, and wrote epic poems for the masses as well as for royalty. Dante Alighieri lived at this time. Along with Petrarch and Boccaccio, the trio are known as the *tre corone*, or three crowns, of Italian literature.

All sponsored, of course, primarily by the fabulously wealthy Medici family, but also by other prominent families and institutions. The Catholic Church was essential to the building of splendid cathedrals and religious institutions that enriched its own innumerable and diverse aspects. Producing a high quality of work during the Renaissance required expensive materials and extensive workshops. The greatest artists did not work on their own but on commission - Ghiberti's bronze baptistery doors, Giotto's Bell Tower; the spectacularly inventive architect Filippo Brunelleschi whose astonishing dome crowns Santa Maria del Fiore and looms majestically over the entire city. Only royalty and dukedoms, religious establishments, and princely organizations could afford to fund such luxury.

The towns tucked just outside the city - Fiesole, Bellosguardo, Settignano - were also noteworthy with their winding roads and dense forests, splendid churches, and archeologically significant town centers. Another day or month or year, and Gavin would hike through their splendid realms. But for now, it was time for him to step into the city that was to him like no other on earth.

His lodgings in Florence were taken care of by Brother Silvio, who described an ancient building that belonged to their sect, tucked behind a consulate from a small African nation and the Basilica di Santa Croce. Already in their possession, he told Gavin, was a letter of praise from the Brothers on the mountains relating accounts of how Gavin volunteered his time in the wine store, the vegetable gardens.

"Would you like to stay there?" he asked. "Our Brother Amato would take good care of you. We have only to send word and a room is yours."

"Of course, I'd be most grateful," Gavin answered, and word was immediately dispatched.

Upon hearing of their guest's imminent arrival, Brother Amato scurried off to change the sheets and sweep out the dust.

Gavin packed up two sample paintings and photographs of others. Then he began the short trek down the hillside to the bus station. Halfway there, he took an unfortunate misstep while adjusting his unwieldy load. His shoe found a crack, and he fell, hard. Sprawled on the ground, he rethought his decision. Perhaps he should turn around and return to his cottage. The act of entering Florence with two small canvases on his back seemed preposterous. Utterly foolish was the notion of walking into a gallery and expecting a stranger to look at his paintings, marketing himself like a peasant peddling his wares, an itinerant vendor.

Yet hadn't Ellie done just that, parlayed herself from a small-town drama teacher into an upcoming star in a Boston theater company? *Perhaps I can speak with her, just to boost my nerves.* Then Gavin thought again. *Ask her advice regarding paintings that only confused her? What if she hesitated even slightly? No. I stand by my work. Someone will notice.* He stood, rearranged the bundle on his back. Focusing on his feet and the loose stones, he continued on his way. And at last, with sweaty brow and clammy hands, he waited in front of Francesco's café for the bus that would deliver him into his future.

On and on, past farms and vineyards, humble dwellings and medieval castles, the bus carried him closer until he saw, springing up out of the air like a mirage, the reddish bricks of a cathedral's dome, the towers of distinguished palazzos, spires of ancient churches. And then, there it was - Florence, a city of luster and grace coming into splendid view.

Gavin strolled along the lively streets. The crowds were enjoying a gaiety akin to a national holiday. Busy cafés were bedecked with flower boxes. Italian flags flew from rooftops. Eager shoppers swarmed the boutiques. The quality and abundance of elegant goods - leather, enamel, jewelry - was not to be seen even in New York. Vendors sold exquisite watercolors to tourists for a few dollars. Gavin's heart swelled. People were buying things. Might they have money to spend on art? Wandering musicians played Neapolitan love songs. Pouring from elaborate fountains, water flowed from the mouths of stony Greek gods. Gavin recalled the stories the Brothers had told him about the famous fountains of Florence - the Fontana del Nettuno by Giambologna, depicting the all-powerful marine god Neptune, its proud demeanor similar to that of the fountain's benefactor, Cosimo de' Medici; Fontana dei Mostri Marini by Marinelli with its mythical sea creatures. And nearby his lodgings, one that Gavin would see that very day, the fountain in the Piazza Santa Croce with the city's flower, the lily, at its crown.

Everyday life lived like a festival.

Surrounding this array of exuberant humanity stood, like giant colossi, one after the other, Florence's heroic Renaissance buildings. Of stone and marble, pillar and arch, elaborate iron gates led into their hidden, exclusive domains. All, fit for kings and princes, were now housing museums, elegant offices, and cultural institutes as well as aristocrats, the wealthy, the eminent, and a fair number of remaining princes.

Gavin's eye lingered on carvings of stone, decorative motifs, statuary, putti swirling into shadow, out into light. He had hardly walked two blocks when he knew he must extend his stay. As urgent as was his peddler's task, it was not as compelling as discovering what lay beyond those gates. Before he attended to business, therefore, he would explore and discover in honor of the municipal jewel before him.

For almost a week, ten to twelve hours a day, Gavin wandered. Yet not a single gallery or shop did he see that might buy his work and likely not even take on consignment. Were there paintings anywhere from the last hundred years not done in a traditional style? It was apparent that in all things, Florence was fully conceived in the fourteenth-century and, ever after, remained intact. Here was a serene city, burnished golds and coppers, siennas and taupes, a gentle, aged scrim laid over its timeless beauty. It bestowed a reticent but beneficent cordiality to visitors, magnificence following one's every step.

But could his paintings ever belong here?

The Vasari Corridor, so said the tidy sign, was closed for renovations. Nevertheless, for Gavin, the Brothers had arranged a private tour with three papal nuncios, an unheard-of privilege for a common tourist. Many visitors to the acclaimed Ufizzi, housing its discreet entrance, did not even know of its existence with its cache of priceless treasures. A clever piece of architecture enabling royalty to walk undisturbed above the heads of the common folk below, the elevated Corridor was built by Giorgio Vasari in five months in 1564 as an enclosed bridge directly above the busy, commercial Ponte Vecchio. Its entirety spanned the Arno River, linking the Palazzo Pitti, a Medici residence, to the Palazzo Vecchio, attached to the Ufizzi and housing the state offices.

On its walls hung one of the most complete and precious collections of artists' self-portraits in all Europe, including the largest collection of works by women artists - Angelica Kauffman, Rosa Bonheur in the eighteenth and nineteenth centuries, Lavinia Fontana as early as the fifteenth century. The Medicis began accumulating portraits very early on, said the guide. As Gavin walked respectfully behind the clerics, the air was so still he could hear the sound of his shoes pattering on the stone floor.

Peering closely at the superb line of portraits, looking directly into the eyes of Andrea del Sarto, Rembrandt, Velazquez, Delacroix, he overheard the guide mention that recent masters such as Chagall were beginning to appear on its walls. Chagall! Gavin's breath grew uneven - modernists in this venerable Florentine gallery? An image of himself sprang up. He would paint a self-portrait also, he decided. And not like these brooding geniuses on black backgrounds wearing dark coats from which the face luminously beamed. Rather, his would have green hair and blue hands, perhaps a rim of deep purple around the eyes. He kept walking, looking, planning.

The Corridor was one kilometer long, shorter than a mile, but not by much. The small group arrived at its end to emerge into sunlight bringing them directly to the Medici dynasty's grand Palazzo Pitti and its magnificent grounds, the Boboli Gardens. The latter he would explore another time, all eleven acres displaying renowned sculptures and structures. But now, he would turn to the Pitti itself, containing one of the most spectacular collections of art in all the world. The scope of priceless works was almost unimaginable. The Palatine Room alone displayed the largest group anywhere of known works by Raphael. And the principal rooms had remained unchanged, exactly as the last Medici had left them.

"The Boboli Gardens were opened to the public in 1776, but the palace was not opened to public viewing until 1928," our attendant said as we parted, pointing to a discreet sign naming the four museums now contained within its walls: Treasury of the Grand Dukes, Palatine Gallery and Imperial Apartments, Gallery of Modern Art, and Museum of Costume and Fashion.

Modern Art! Gavin's head exploded with flashing colors, spatters of hope. Ignoring the surrounding glories, he ran up the stone steps until - there! Carved out from the former sumptuous residential spaces of the Grand Dukes of Habsburg-Lorraine was the grand opening into the Gallery of Modern Art. But the paintings represented modernism as defined by the Italians but not by him. Disheartened, he dropped onto a bench and scanned works from eighteenth-century Neoclassicism until almost the 1900s. All were somber, dark, bucolic, courtly, religious, framed ornately in gold, and hanging one next to the other, almost touching.

That night, Gavin seriously reconsidered his position. It seemed likely that Florence might not be the place where he would be accepted. Rome, perhaps? A larger, more inclusive city willing to incorporate contemporary works into its history.

One more day of wandering, and then he would take the bus back to his mountain.

Almost at the final moment, he came upon it - his stake in the days to come.

At the end of a short alleyway was a glittering gallery lit with a hundred bulbs. *Sofia's Place*, the sign said in English with block letters printed in capitals, done in royal blue with the *S* and *P* in bright yellow. Happily snug between two adjoining ateliers, the three shops together were hewn from a single cave. The massive rock enclosed them in a wide embrace. The gallery's glass facade offered a dazzling view into the interior where a dozen contemporary paintings hung on its walls - huge, unframed, each placed like a treasured masterwork. Gavin stared, disbelieving.

On its right, Gavin peered into a shop whose front door stood open. An old man with an ancient tool was pounding holes into a briefcase, its rich leather smells drifting into the street. On its left was a young girl whose space was illuminated by a dozen thick pillar candles. He glimpsed her in a back room pouring candle wax into molds shaped like stars. Scents of lavender, jasmine, and sandalwood mingled with smoky, tarry leathers.

And between them, exploding like fireworks, the gorgeous abstract paintings that told his heart, someone else is aware.

Gavin pulled on the sleek door handles, long rods of stainless steel. Inside, he turned round and round, alone in the silence with radiant colors that glowed from the walls, each emitting an energy that the canvas could hardly contain. Into the hush, there was the swish of a curtain, and a woman appeared in a far corner.

"May I help you? My name is Sofia."

She was as much of a shock as the paintings. Approaching forty? That mellow age when some women, at least this one - or all Italian women? - had acquired the confidence of a full female sensibility. Assured that her femininity was a gift, something to behold yet something she had grown into and took for granted. Thick, strong hair, brown like a chestnut with strands melting into lighter hues of bronze and copper, dropped to her shoulders with sable eyes to match. Pale-blue silk fell gently to her knees.

Gavin stood rooted. He wouldn't allow it, to be drawn to her. Silently, his eyes fixed on her face.

"May I show you some examples of my work?" he somehow managed to say.

As he unwrapped his package, she asked, smiling, "And your name, sir, is?"

"Gavin," he said, "Gavin Taylor."

Abruptly, she turned back to the curtain, whisked out a bottle of Baldassarre Tuscan blend red, and set two glasses on the tiny bistro table flanked by metal folding chairs.

"*Sedere*, sit." She pointed, pouring the wine while keeping her eyes on his samples, two small copies, eighteen-by-twenty-four inches of his larger works, roiling reds and sunflowers, now fully exposed, leaning against the walls.

After a long sip - *delicious,* he thought - he found his voice.

And their stories unfolded.

First, hers.

Then, his.

"You seem surprised by my gallery," she began. "In my youth" - saying *in my youth* as if she were an old woman reminiscing of bygone years, though her words sang in her throat with a sweet young timbre and, of course, with that indescribably enchanting element of a beautiful Italian woman speaking his language with her native accent - "I attended school in New York. Have you ever been to Manhattan? Do you know the Cooper Union in the East Village?

"Yes?"

He nodded. "Yes."

"I returned home with the intent of opening a gallery for modern art. There was nothing like it in Florence. But no landlord would rent me space. No museum or organization would intercede on my behalf. After all, they said, if people wanted to look at pictures like those I proposed, they could go to New York's Chelsea area or London with those quirky galleries such as the Cob or the Proud or the Tate Modern. But Florence is far older and more protective of its artistic heritage, they added smugly.

"My father is an overseer at the Bargello National Museum, primarily of the Donatello Room. When I told him my plans, he was aghast. I had gone to Cooper Union for an architecture degree, you see. But I finally convinced him to offer his help. And so, here we are," she gestured, sweeping her arm around the room.

"Mainly, I have two types of buyers, and there are few of them, at that. Wealthy young people with a taste for the avant-garde.

And also, a small handful of investors who hang traditional work on their walls and store purchases from Sofia's in vaults, expecting them to appreciate in value. Oh, an occasional tourist, if they find us. Japanese, mostly.

"So far, it has provided enough to stay open, though barely. Knowing that I provide a venue for painters like yourself keeps me going."

Gavin heard her words with joy in his heart and a very dry throat, a parched man who had toiled alone for years. Until now.

Slowly, he took out photographs of his artistic output. Sofia pulled her chair closer. He was confident that this woman would see through the plastic and paper to the soul of his work. While he was arranging his offerings, he described his beginnings in Manhattan and the many years following in Iowa, with its farms and flying corn silks, holding back on describing the chicken coop, his boys, and his marriage.

Later, reliving their meeting, his sample paintings resting like a third presence in the room and Sofia unable to stop staring at them, he thought she had sighed, "Oh, Gavin," but he couldn't be sure.

"I love them both," she said, "but I must see the larger works. If my intuition is correct, we will hang this one first," she remarked, pointing to the sunflower's yellows. "The other, I will hold in reserve."

"Hang first?" he said aloud. The words echoed in Gavin's brain, dangling. *There will be more?*

"Is that agreeable to you?"

Was that agreeable *to him?* he asked himself, astonished.

"Space is carefully assigned," she continued, mistakenly thinking he was put out by her promise to display only one work at a time. "Look around. We have many wonderful artists."

Gavin had never known colleagues with similarly congenial artistic tastes or inclinations. He had been an isolated soul, his creative world severely limited. He was surprised to know that of the five artists Sofia was currently exhibiting, three were women. Why was he surprised? He had just seen the amazing collection by female artists in the Vasari Corridor.

"Sofia's Salon," he was to learn how her devoted followers called her gallery.

Privately, they called her Sofia, the Savior. As he was also now inclined to do.

Gavin looked over at his two smaller copies of his massive paintings back in his mountaintop cottage, seeing them through her eyes. The fiery yellows were ablaze like a desert sun. There was a glorious feeling of abandon, of cheer, yet not from flowers you could specifically name, not from a meadow either or a garden or any other particular place but simply from an exuberance that conveyed nourishment and sustenance.

"No one will exactly understand what they are seeing, Gavin, but your beautiful painting brings to mind the dazzling physical aspects of an Italian summer. Or it does so for me. Someone will purchase this extraordinary painting *if* the large ones show the same promise," she added. "Go home and bring me back the real canvases."

He picked up the very next bus out of the city, passing the proud, noble bridges that led onto the bumpy roads. The stone of the city receded, and the green Tuscan landscape appeared with its purple tulips and yellow buttercups. A week ago, he was in despair that no one would even look at his samples or photos. But now? *One must believe in himself,* he thought with enormous relief. *Where there is hope, the mind can rest.*

After some time, the driver pulled into the tiny plaza of his village. *I must tell Francesco,* Gavin thought. He hugged his friend, ordered a coffee, told him of his luck in Florence.

"Too soon to talk more about it," he said. "Only a beginning, after all."

Francesco slapped him on the back, removed the coffee, and set down two glasses of Chianti.

"A toast, my friend! Today, it's on the house."

Before vespers, Gavin stopped in at the monastery. He conveyed to the Brothers the same message he had given Francesco, thanking them for arranging his lodgings and promising to be more attentive in the future to the needs of the vegetable garden. With his right hand, Brother Silvio made the sign of the cross over Gavin's head and murmured a blessing.

That night, Gavin packed up the two paintings Sofia had requested, and in the morning, he took the first bus back to Florence.

When the sunflower painting was placed in the proper setting with a few feet of blank space on either side and spotlights directed at its heart, the yellows seemed to be swaying as if, somewhere, a soft wind was blowing on its surface.

Gavin and Sofia stood back. Sofia spoke of its virtues in terms of human qualities. "Alive. Vibrant. Mysterious," she said.

"Gavin, did you ever see sunflowers in Iowa?" Sofia eventually asked.

"Once," he said, pausing as he remembered his melancholy at having just seen Ellie off on a plane for the first time in their marriage. But Sofia, mistaking the slight faltering for a reluctance to share, didn't follow up, and Gavin didn't offer any further particulars.

"Gavin, if the first person who walks in that door doesn't buy your painting, I don't know my business," Sofia remarked as they remained standing, still assessing.

"Ever since I was a child," Gavin said to her, "I've wanted to be a painter. But I never dreamed of ending up in a gallery as spectacular as yours. And in Florence! The aura of the greatest artists who have ever lived hovers over this very shop. Yet you're showing a painting I made on an Iowa farm. It's truly remarkable." Gavin bowed his head and wept.

Sofia gently touched his arm. Her voice was hoarse, thickened by her own sense of beauty.

"Gavin, I can only suppose how you must feel, how wonderful it must be to love something so much."

When Sofia mentioned it could be so, that a client would walk in and immediately buy his painting, Gavin thought she must be joking. In fact, it happened just as she had said while they stood in the middle of the room debating whether the painting was hung to its best advantage on the long wall opposite the entrance, or should be moved to the short wall by the corner curtain.

"Gianni, how good to see you!" Sofia exclaimed to the tall man who had just entered through the glass doors.

At the sight of her, he smiled widely, this debonair, middle-aged man with black hair whose gray strands gleamed under the strong lights.

Bestowing a flirty grin, she kissed him first on one cheek, then on the other.

"My dear, dear Sofia. How have you been? You look ravishing, as usual."

Almost immediately, he noticed the painting.

"Well, what have we here?" he said, walking up to Gavin's sunflowers, standing close, then stepping back, forward again, then back again. "Doesn't it seem as if the sun is pouring through the skylight?" he asked Sofia. "And look! It is actually one of Florence's rare cloudy days.

"This is a marvelous piece. Simply *meravigliosa*! I must have it. *Quanto costa*?" What is the price? "It reminds me of those sunflower fields over in the Maremma region, especially around Castiglione della Pescaia. You know I have a small house there overlooking the coast, nearby the medieval fortress on the hill, adjacent to the lovely Natural Reserve Diaccia Botrona with its herons and flamingos."

Gavin trembled in the corner, pretending to be examining a painting in blues, grays, and purples by a woman named Elena Morelli. He hovered there, unmoving. Sofia had not consulted with him about a price, yet she calmly stated an outrageous amount. *Thirty thousand dollars! Could that be correct*? His breathing was irregular; his forehead suddenly wet. Discreetly, he reached for his handkerchief. Sofia winked at him.

She and Gianni proceeded to a black lacquered table from which she drew a purchase agreement and made some notations. When the papers were signed, she and Gianni threw kisses at the painting. "*Congratulazioni!*" said Sofia, "you chose a real beauty this time, Gianni. And now, my dear man," she began, rising from the desk and looping her arm through his, "let's shake things up a bit. It makes no sense to store this sensational painting. Why not hang this in the front hall of your Pescaia house? Facing the flowers at Maremma? Or perhaps in the conservatory of your villa here in the hills. It will be the rage of Florence. Think of it! You'll be admired for your foresight and courage. Besides, it's time. I was told that self-portraits by the likes of Chagall will soon hang in the Vasari Corridor. And if Chagall, who knows how many other contemporaries? A trendsetter, Gianni. You can't keep brilliance like this in the dark forever."

"Maybe you're right, Sofia. I'd love to greet this painting every morning rather than visit it in a storage room. Now will you have dinner with me?"

Ignoring his request, she smiled coyly and raised her hand, beckoned Gavin.

"Gianni, here is your artist. Gavin Taylor, an American."

The man turned, surprised to see Gavin almost at his elbow. His dark eyes were appraising. Mr. Amatucci had no artistic talent but admired greatly those who were so gifted. He extended his hand. The two men smiled cordially, taking each other's measure. But the relationship was apparent. Each had his own power. Neither could do without the other.

"So, my dear fellow, is Sofia here hiding anything else you've done? She usually keeps a spare picture tucked away."

Her heels tapping behind the curtain, Sofia brought out Gavin's roiling-reds painting. If the great strokes of yellow reminded Gianni of sunflowers, Gavin hoped this one would prompt him to thoughts of the orange-red poppies that were everywhere in the month of May, especially between the hill towns of Pienza and Montepulciano.

"*Fantastico!*" Gianni exclaimed. "I'll have that one too. My dearest Sofia, are we speaking of a price similar to the other? Perhaps a small discount for the purchase of two paintings?"

Sofia found a mysterious smile.

"Dear Gianni, this is Gavin's first public exhibit. He's hardly had a chance to be seen, but surely his paintings would be scooped up immediately, as you have done. Consider it special that you are the first to view - and purchase - these exceptional pieces."

Sighing, he turned to Gavin.

"Young man, you will learn soon enough that this beautiful woman favors her artists more than her clients!"

What happened here? Gavin wondered. *Did I sell both paintings for thirty-thousand dollars each? And all in ten minutes?*

"My dear Sofia," Gianni continued, as if he had just bought some goods for pennies, "what do you think of this? I'll hang both of these in the conservatory of my villa. Across from each other, as if they are having a conversation. And between them, in the center of the room, I'll place a dozen of those wild butterfly orchids. Or perhaps the Ophrys speculum. Both species grow in the Chianti area, in the provinces of Florence, Siena, Arezzo. The arrangement will be an interior replica of the real Tuscany that is just outside the door. How spectacular would that be!"

Forsaking Sofia without waiting for her answer and giving Gavin his full attention, he began. "So what do you say, young man? *Posso chiederlie*, may I ask? Have you ever been north to Castelluccio in early spring and seen the poppy fields there? *Belissima*! Or any specific spot that might have inspired these two paintings?"

Should I tell the truth? Gavin wondered.

That they were both done during a hot Iowa summer outside a chicken coop, on a farm with little physical beauty but for some distant hills whose peaks at sunset were tinged with purple. That for weeks, they had been stacked against the walls of a crumbling, weathered old shack. That he had only once had a brief sighting of a sunflower field. That for the other work, he had only a desire to see how many hues of red would interact with a vigor that engaged him. That at the time, Tuscany was hardly a jot on that part of his brain that guides his brush.

Gavin paused for a moment, then smiled at Gianni Amatucci and replied, "Everything inspires me, sir."

Chapter 11

As the bus with Gavin aboard entered the SITA station in Florence, Ellie was having dinner with David Tompkins, the visiting director of a theater company in New Orleans. He arrived a day early, and Hank had asked if she would mind keeping him company.

"He's an engaging fellow, full of gossip about this crazy world of ours," he added.

It was a dinner like many she had with powerful men who bestowed favors on aspiring actresses. *Not much different,* she thought grimly, *from other worlds, Jack in corporate, Gavin competing for artistic hegemony. Even Joyce in the nearby dorm, knocking on my door with a story about her inappropriate math professor. And how many friends speak of conflicts while auditioning before lecherous directors?* Thankfully, Ellie was not in that position, but she did occasionally wonder why she was so hesitant regarding a casual liaison. Neither she nor Gavin had yet asked for a divorce, but they were literally living worlds apart. Would it hurt if she partook of some intimate affection from time to time? Did he? Likely it was her Iowa roots that restrained her. Anyway, she was not willing to compromise herself for a brief connection. What if, for example, an intimate evening with this David Tompkins resulted in an unforeseen outcome? He had the power of authority. She could as easily be brought down as raised up.

Yet despite her working consistently, Ellie felt her professional life had recently become a bit of a slog, especially when she remembered her early days in New York. For every available role, there were a hundred young women ready to push her aside should the opportunity arise. Not much had changed. Furthermore, she was now twice the age of her colleagues. Just the other day, Hank mentioned a role for her as an older woman. "A college girl's unmarried aunt," he had said. *Well, it might be feasible someday,* she thought, *but not just yet. Certainly not yet.*

"So, my dear, what is your pleasure tonight?" David asked in the darkened bistro, candlelight glittering off the silver, flickering onto her shoulders.

"Um, let's see," she replied, unnerved by his steady gaze and the flames dancing around his handsome face. "Perhaps the red snapper," she ventured, her voice tentative. Did this David Tompkins notice? Not interested in attracting intimate overtures, nevertheless she felt a slight pull toward being flirtatious. He was so darn good-looking.

But whenever she leaned close into her companion, any companion, the same feeling - missing her family - always showed up. If those moments were intended to act as her personal barrier to further involvement, they always worked, briefly. But by dessert, she had once again summoned up her usual good humor. And by the time the check arrived, such considerations had almost entirely vanished.

Besides, right now, as she scooped up the last bite of fish, something important was on her mind. Tomorrow, she was doing a special reading for Hank. So taken was he with the enormous success of *Spoon River* that he decided to mount a similar play, Thornton Wilder's *Our Town*, also taking place in a small place called Grover's Corners. The main character, the stage manager, was both narrator and commentator of the actual theater in which the play is being performed. A fair amount of finesse was required to pull it off, and traditionally, the part was played by a man. Its themes were as relevant for a contemporary stage as for any in history - the worth of a simple life - to appreciate its value while living it, to value friendship and love above all. There would be almost no props but for what the actors would be able to make the audience imagine with their gestures and dialogue. Hank had surprised Ellie when he asked, "Would you like to play the part of stage manager?"

"Yes, sure, of course!" she cried. She would have to work on lowering her voice, but that was manageable. The men in the company were not too pleased. When Hank assigned roles, everyone grew covetous of each other, endangering friendships and putting goodwill at risk.

At the beginning of act 3, Ellie would deliver a monologue on an almost empty stage. Even while David was lifting his glass, even when he set it down close to her hand resting on the white tablecloth, the lines were running through her head:

> *We all know that something is eternal. And it ain't houses, and it ain't names, and it ain't earth, and it ain't even the stars…everybody knows in their bones that something is eternal, and that something has to do with human beings. All the greatest people ever lived have been telling us that for five thousand years, and yet you'd be surprised how people are always losing hold of it. There's something way down deep that's eternal about every human being.*

As David helped her on with her coat, before he even asked if he could see her tomorrow, she knew she would decline.

Ellie wandered along the Emerald Necklace, a pedestrian path running alongside the Charles River that linked a series of parks and waterways. When the snows melted, many folks in Boston were to be found here - strolling, pushing carriages, bicycling, skateboarding. She loved to sit on a bench and watch the boats, letting her mind drift. Boston winters were long and frigid. People rushed about without lingering. But come spring's thaw, everyone came out, and friends saw each other again. Boston's landscape burst forth like the reveal of The Emerald City, becoming a luscious green, a brilliant green covering earth, shrubs, and trees. Spring's annual reckoning. Nature's gift to people hunkered down for months in their houses. How different it was from spring in Iowa where its first showing was tiny wildflowers starting to pop, the land emerging in patchy greens and browns.

Today, Ellie thought, sitting on a bench under a warm spring sun; nature did indeed sparkle like clusters of emeralds. The Emerald Necklace - who bestowed such a perfect name? At first, Ellie assumed it was a homesick Irishman who missed his homeland until she learned that it was named by Frederick Law Olmsted, its famous landscape designer. The planned "chain" appears to hang from the "neck" of the Boston peninsula, he thought, and so there you have it. The Emerald Necklace - both versions had a poetic aspect that she thought Gavin would appreciate.

I bet Gavin could capture the feeling of this stunning place, Ellie reflected, startling herself by even thinking of such a notion. She remembered his first breakthrough painting, all those roiling reds. She never realized that red could be so many wonderful shades, from the richness of a cardinal's cape to the soft pink lining a bunny's ear. Despite her lack of understanding, those turbulent reds held an allure she wouldn't or couldn't, admit at the time. Now her heart thundered with regret at the drama of it, at her laziness of disregard. In the first instant of looking, she had thought of so many things - lipstick like Marilyn Monroe, a shiny Mackintosh apple, a wounded bird lying in its own blood. But she had been dismissive. Why?

If he had a palette of greens, Ellie wondered, *would Gavin capture what I'm feeling right now? Is that what he was trying to make me understand - the emotion of beauty without a single leaf or tree depicted?*

Moody and pensive, Ellie continued to sit. When had she ever considered Gavin's work in a positive way? She had been wrong! Wrong! She had simply not appreciated what he was working to convey in his own way, not hers. And worse, she had barely tried to understand, tossing off his intent as mere whimsy.

On the opposite side of the river, renowned academic institutions hugged the grassy bank. Spires and bell towers from the universities thrust their elegance skyward, just like sand castles drizzled into shape by children at the beach, reaching ever higher, much like Gavin constructed his paintings, stroke by stroke. In their racing boats, crews swiftly glided along the water reminding her of Blackie when he was let out of the paddock, running gracefully and evenly with the wind, his mane flying.

Have I been here too long in Boston? Ellie wondered. Despite the positive reviews of *Our Town*, important offers from other venues had simply not materialized. And now this slow awareness had taken hold that the lure of Broadway had lost its appeal, simply upped and disappeared. She hardly thought about it anymore. That burn in her gut was now barely on simmer. Maybe it was a blinding flash once, but it seemed to have depleted its own energy. From loneliness? From a slow erosion of enthusiasm? From a nub of doubt that living without family was something she was no longer willing to accept? Ellie couldn't shake the feeling that something imminent in the future would be decisive to her thinking.

And she had broken her promise. She had not yet been back to Iowa to see her family. Word from Danny was that Pat and Sam now directed the boys from their rocking chairs on the porch. That Pat made a robust lunch and dinner only on Thursdays and Sundays. That dinner on the other nights was light, like lunch.

She thought herself down, down, down into a negative dark hole. Her thrumming heart slammed against her ribs. Gasping, she struggled to breathe. A young jogger - perhaps around eighteen? - stopped and offered help, running in place. "No, no thanks," Ellie replied, but not before she noticed the girl was beautiful, that there were always dozens like her outside the theater doors. But once again, her mood shifted to the good as she turned her head to the masses of red tulips nearby. So what if the acting life has lost its luster? What could come next? In the past, she had loved teaching. Perhaps doing so again would provide a suitable pivot, a reliable income, fellowship with both professors and students. Age and experience were positive factors in her favor. And Boston *did* have a glut of schools with drama departments.

Thoughts of home and aging, time as ephemeral and hazy, were then dropped full on into her fantasies about Tuscany, about loss and nostalgia and possibilities. Suddenly, she was not thinking of the endlessly flat lands of Iowa's cornfields or of the fascinating urban density of Boston, not even of her far-flung family, but rather of the poppies and sunflowers scattered exuberantly over a rolling landscape peppered with vineyards and wineries and stone farmhouses.

Jack had an appointment that brought him to Boston while his mother was performing in *Our Town*. When she recited her monologue about how humans squander time's precious and fleeting nature, he couldn't help wiping away tears. Everyone around him was also dabbing their eyes. *Mom is really special,* he thought. *Were her emotions purposeful acting or were they feelings of being a continent away from my father? If she doesn't bring it up, I won't ask,* he decided. He raved to Ellie how marvelous she was, then mother and son had a late dinner at Durgin-Park. He eagerly attacked a slab of their famous roast beef while she took her fork to a shrimp dish, sauce on the side. He needed to talk seriously with her about Julia, but he never found the appropriate moment. At dinner, waiters hovered, and there was a noisy buzz in the room. Besides, he felt like a child. He was long an adult living away from home and should be able to solve his own problems.

She kept mum about Gavin, and he about Julia, and the next day, he flew back to Chicago.

What was he going to do about Julia?

She held an important position as head of publicity on the floor below his, a valued executive on the corporate team. But also one of the frisky girls who went out for a beer after work. Slender and dark, she dressed for the office in beautifully tailored clothes, her hair pulled tightly back in a neat chignon. But after hours, she took out the combs and fastenings and put on her short skirts and tight sweaters. Jack was enamored of her, but he didn't love her. Julia wondered if she loved him, but she wasn't sure she liked him. Right from the beginning, Jack sensed he shouldn't sleep with her. There was a cunning about her that was worrisome. But when he sought to end the relationship, she wouldn't hear of it and became a hoverer, a stalker.

None of his friends believed him.

"Julia," they said, rolling their eyes, "the babe downstairs? C'mon, Jack, you can handle her."

Discreetly, Jack met with Julia's boss and stammered out a complaint.

The man looked at him in disbelief. "Are you sure? Our Julia shadowing you? Do you have proof? She's an important member of our team."

And so Jack resentfully sidled out of the office, now seeing validated first hand, that people either don't believe you, lie to themselves, or cover up the offense.

Julia followed him, as quiet harassers do, noiselessly and unseen, but with a constant presence, keeping watch. Was he in danger? What if she made an untoward move? For a young man raised on a farm, he was at a loss about what to do next. Skilled in using a gun, yes, but Chicago was not a farm.

At this same time, Jack had created images for at least three jingles. His name was becoming known in the advertising world. Folks in the street were whistling the tunes, a phenomenon that translated into company profit. His superiors were pleased. He should have been enjoying his growing success, not become mired in relationship issues. How was his boss thinking about this situation? And in the darkened corners, Julia continued her frightening ways, present in the most ordinary places - at the movies, a bar, a night out with the guys. He felt her aura like a neatly coiled snake waiting under a rock.

Should he give up his promising job in Chicago and move to Boston near his mother? It was a possibility, but when they had been together at dinner, she had seemed uneasy. What was bothering her? Did she have plans of her own?

Danny mailed out three notes on pale-blue stationery to Boston, Chicago, and Italy:

> *I am marrying my Maryann in five months' time, when spring arrives and the magnolias are in full flower, their petals covering the path leading to the*

altar beside the creek. Make your plans now. Mark it - third week in April!

Gavin computed costs and expenses. With the sale of his paintings, there would be more than enough for a ticket home, more than enough to give Danny and Maryann a generous present, even enough to reroof the barn as well as buy Ellie something special.

And that was the way life stood for the Taylors when Danny sent out his wedding invitations.

Gavin relayed the news to Sofia.

"I'm returning to Iowa for a wedding. I'll be back in a week."

Chapter 12

The corn was still growing, and it would keep on reaching for the sky until it got higher than a man in a top hat. But on this special day, it seemed even the corn felt the excitement of celebration, its rising silks flying aloft in the gentle breeze as folks started pouring in. Sensing upheaval and the parade of visitors, Blackie was restless in his paddock, snorting and whinnying and pawing the ground. Lowering his head to be petted by all, he eagerly accepted the cubes of sugar presented. Upon seeing Gavin, he nuzzled his face in the palm of his hand, sniffing his fingers for the odor of paint.

Jack arrived first, eager for the safety of home. Wearing gray slacks and a cashmere sweater, he felt overdressed when Danny picked him up at the airport wearing jeans, T-shirt, and a cowboy hat.

"Hey, dude," Danny greeted. "Pretty spiffy there!"

Jack grinned sheepishly. "Sorry, bro, work clothes. Got my jeans rolled up in my suitcase."

Driving home, they reminisced about the time they dropped a cat in the chicken coop and another time when they stashed a badger under the bed until it gnawed its way out of the shoebox. Laughing, slapping their knees, still, Danny felt some restraint hovering around his brother.

"Hey, Jack. What's up? Something bothering you?"

"I'm okay, not to worry. Really," he answered.

When Ellie rolled in, the family was sitting on the porch drinking Maryann's lemonade. Stepping out of the car in a rust suede skirt and flat ballet shoes, a brown and orange batik scarf tied around her head, she looked quite the spirit of the theater. Jack was immediately reminded of the dancer, Isadora Duncan.

When he said as much, Danny said, "Isadora who?"

"Oh, just some dancer," Jack answered. *Well, of course, she would look glamorous. She's on the stage almost every night,* Jack thought. He wondered if she had jeans and a T-shirt packed in her suitcase.

Gavin arrived late in the day. He was full of apologies as he sprang from his rental car.

"Sorry, gang, so sorry. My changeover in Amsterdam was delayed three hours. But hey, I still made my connection!"

Ellie noticed that Gavin's look of despair, of watchfulness, was gone. The boys thought their father looked upbeat and self-assured as he sprinted over with hearty hugs and kisses.

Gavin looks cute, thought Maryann. *Maybe Danny will look like that in twenty years.*

Before supper, the family made their way down to the creek, chatting and laughing, buoyant at being together. The magnolias were generously offering themselves up. Their branches were thick with blossoms, yet dropping enough petals to carpet the ground for the wedding procession.

"We've been praying for days," Maryann observed, "that there'd be no wind or rain to bring down those flowers - looks good for tomorrow!"

Ellie thought Maryann looked radiant and so pretty, her dark curls flouncy around her face. Her petite, trim figure bounced and twirled with happiness. And when her lustrous black eyes rested on Danny, they were gentle as a dove's.

Instructions were given for the procession and the ceremony, then a run-through of protocols before and after the vows. Everyone was bustling about and teasing the engaged couple. Starlings settled in the trees. Rabbits scampered into the bushes. Blackie was nickering with pleasure.

But beyond the good cheer, Ellie felt a sense of forced gaiety. Jack with Julia on his mind, she and Gavin tentative at being together. It was good that the happy commotion disguised some of the unease.

The guest list was shared. "Pretty much the whole town," said Danny, smiling, contrite. "Who would you leave out?"

During dinner, a pleasant bedlam floated over the table. No one asking a question waited for an answer. Everyone talked over one another, telling stories. The whole time, from the tomato soup straight through to the apple pie, his hearing in the left ear almost gone, Sam kept asking, "Hey, Ellie, hey, Jack, what did you say? Huh?"

The next morning, the sun shone bright but not hot, in a cloudless, radiantly blue sky. Guests from all over the county arrived one after the other. Pickup trucks were haphazardly scattered over the fields as if they had all run out of gas. The townspeople were dressed in their best going-to-church outfits. Creamy white blooms fell lightly on their hair, pooled at their feet. Most of the guests had known the couple their entire childhood and throughout their courtship and were thrilled that two of their own were staying around.

The crowd waited eagerly when suddenly, as soft as a fiddle could get, Johnny Jenkins began to play "Can't Help Falling in Love with You" by Elvis Presley. The bride walked slowly toward her Danny. Everyone thought Maryann was the perfect bride, oh so lovely holding her bouquet of lilies of the valley from Pat's garden and a matching sprig in her hair. Ms. Nancy, seated near the front as an honored guest, was pleased that after sewing for two months, the wedding dress had turned out just right. Ellie and Gavin patted the dampness from their eyes but held back on letting out any tears. The crowd sniffled and blew their noses, and Jack, standing at Danny's side, squeezed his brother's shoulder. A slight breeze caused the magnolia petals to sway, like an orchestra leader hoisting his baton. The bride's veil lifted with a flutter, then fell softly, as faint as a bird opening and closing its wings. Maryann kept walking, her eyes on her Danny, and when at last she reached her beloved, Pastor Dan took over.

Generous trays of foodstuffs had been set out on barn tables covered with lavender cloths. Each was centered with a china pitcher stuffed with flowers, also from Pat's garden. Jack recognized roses, daisies, and marigolds but could not name the pink one with ruffled edges. Tucked randomly around the sides were philodendron leaves cut from plants Pat had begun to grow as soon as the engagement was announced. The women had been cooking for days, bringing specially requested favorites - Joanie Bishop's turkey chili, Donna Silver's heirloom tomato pies. Water raced fast and gurgling in the creek, and Johnny Jenkins - part-time musician, full-time hog farmer - played a lively fiddle. Children chased frogs while their parents admonished them not to dirty their good clothes.

After the second toast, the more adventuresome guests bounced up to dance to Johnny's sprightly rhythms, his foot tapping, his eyes rolling around in his head. Marge Clancy, who styled the hair of many of the women, called out, "Hey, Johnny, how about 'The Devil Went Down to Georgia'?" The less daring remained in their seats, remarking that Johnny was sure to become another great fiddler like Charlie Daniels or Bobby Hicks. And wasn't he just working that instrument for all its worth?

Jack and Ellie wandered off together. Ellie felt her son's unrest as his eyes darted nervously from Blackie to the creek, then to the shack, on which they lingered. *An unfamiliar gesture,* she thought, rubbing his hands as if washing and washing, then clasping them behind his back.

"Jack, honey, tell me about your life in Chicago," she said, carefully but directly.

And that request was all Jack needed to blurt out his problems with Julia, as if a full confession was his only choice.

"I thought of moving away," he finished. "Getting another job isn't a problem, but where would I go? Boston, maybe?"

Ellie flinched. Jack recoiled. Did she think him an intrusion in her life? Ellie touched her son's arm.

"Honey, it has nothing to do with you. I'm not sure of my own situation at the moment. What if you move to Boston, and then I leave?"

Since Jack told her his story, it was only fair that she be honest with him, especially since the possibility of a move was on his mind. Slowly, she shared her feelings of confusion and vulnerability as she sat on that bench along the Emerald Necklace. Shocked, Jack had thought his mother was thriving in a world of her choosing. Always, she had been bold and confident. To hear her speak this way made him fearful, a sturdy post against which to lean, now wobbly. The truth was that people deny or hide reality for a thousand different reasons. *Look at myself,* he thought, *and the situation with Julia.* So how does one ever truly understand another? Even when love is strong?

Watching the newlyweds, Jack and Ellie felt confident Maryann and Danny had shared their hopes, laid out their plans - the farm life, fixing up the barn, adding a room to the house, having babies. Jack fervently hoped neither of them harbored dark longings. *Look where having secrets got my folks,* he thought, *the inchworms had turned into moths and then flown off to their separate lives.*

Jack put his arm around his mother's shoulder. He had hoped to find comfort for himself, but instead, he gave her his full measure. They sat in silence while the birds trilled, and the frogs grunted, and Johnny fiddled with the energy of a bull. Then suddenly, with the next song, his fiddle grew plaintive with "Cowboy Take Me Away." The audience grew quiet, listening with nostalgia for their youth, for love, for old dreams; more than a few guests envied Danny and Maryann for being at their beginnings. When the notes faded away, Ellie and Jack walked back to the party holding hands. They agreed to speak of these topics again later.

Jack moved over to his dad, their chairs unsteady on the grass. They were far enough off so they could speak without the interference of noisy celebrants.

"So, Jack, how's the career going in Chicago? Doing any drawing?" Gavin started.

Yes, he understood it was a job in graphic design, and that's fine. The skills he learned as a child would be put to good use. But did he get the chance to paint? Jack was such a talented young artist. One needs to work at it constantly, honing one's abilities, practicing, refining, learning.

"No, I haven't painted at all," Jack mumbled. "I have very little spare time. Also, my colleagues are always after me to join in after-hours fun. I have to participate once in a while."

Gavin turned his face, but Jack had already seen the slight look of dismay. That his son had a good job, even an interesting one, was reassuring to Gavin, and Jack was grateful for that. But that his father considered that he was possessed of talent that lay dormant and unexplored was painful to him.

Again, the fiddle picked up, bouncy and frisky. They watched as Danny spun his bride around, her dress lifting and twirling.

"A man named Gianni Amatucci was the first person to buy one of my paintings," Gavin said. "The sunflowers. Do you remember when I painted it? So audacious at the time! And you beside me commenting, 'But, Dad, that doesn't look like sunflowers.'"

Jack took his father's hand and whispered, "Yes, I remember. How could I ever forget?"

Gavin sat quietly with his son, but soon enough, his mind turned to Italy and his generous benefactor. Gianni would soon return from a business trip to London, desirous of taking a look at more of Gavin's work. He had mentioned starting a "collection of works by Gavin Taylor." This comment gave Gavin considerable pause. Such acquisitions would limit his exposure to the mainstream art world, and that was now Gavin's hope, to have his work known and owned by many.

All this, he refrained from sharing with Jack, feeling selfish to be thinking of himself with one son by his side, the other happily dancing now with Ms. Nancy, the dressmaker.

"And by the way, Jack, I'll only be returning to the States occasionally. Living in Italy has become a serious love affair for me. But perhaps you'd like to visit?"

Visit Tuscany? Jack was incredulous. Was that a sincere offer or merely a gratuitous one? Although the monastery and grounds were substantial and vast, Jack thought it might have been an empty gesture knowing his father lived in a modest cottage. When he looked up the name of the religious order involved, there were photos of a sprawling twelfth-century complex spread over an entire mountaintop, turrets and walls, a medieval fortress. And covering the surrounding hillsides were thriving vineyards. It was almost inconceivable that his father had made his way from a chicken coop, still standing right now twenty yards away from where they sat, to such favorable circumstances.

So far, his own path had been made easy by the intervention of a friend who set him up with his first job. It required no personal ambition on his part. Rewards had accrued if you measure success in dollars, but is this what he wants to be doing ten years from now? What happened to his ambition of creating rock poster art in the style of Bonnie MacLean? He thought he might have failed himself by making easy choices.

After Danny and Maryann drove off to the mountains, Ellie and Gavin were shy together, as if meeting for the first time. They were unsure how to speak of their present lives, complicated as they were. Each wanted to present a positive image. Each would be careful that their conversation not be loaded with hints and innuendo or misrepresentations and misinterpretations as to intent or goals. The question that hovered was, would they divorce? But at the moment, both of their lives were in flux, dead center of dramatic shifts and movements, a shaky basis for making irrevocable decisions. Besides, no one was in a hurry. Perhaps they would feel more certain in another year. So they avoided personal discussions and talked about the wedding. Wasn't the bride beautiful? And wasn't Johnny Jenkins something special with that fiddle of his?

Looking around at the expanse of lawn and house, both felt proud of what they had produced. The result of their youth and subsequent years together was right here in front of them - two fine sons; a flourishing farm with its crops and animals; the books and poetry by Yeats, Brooke, and Masters stored in the attic but still on the premises.

The family gathered on the porch under the stars. Pat and Sam sat in their rocking chairs, Pat snoring lightly. Content and relieved that the wedding had gone off well under a clear blue sky, they reviewed the afternoon's events - too much dill in Mrs. Buckley's potato salad, Mr. Hayworth's sudden attack of the gout, Dougie proposing to Millie just as Maryann was walking down the path toward Danny. Still, Jack seemed distracted. Ellie longed to assuage his worries - the girl, the job. Gavin shifted restlessly against the railing, considering whether or not he should take Ellie's hand. After all, their Danny had just been married.

In the end, Ellie didn't provide Jack with the solace of easy solutions, and Gavin never reached for her hand. Ellie settled her parents in their bedroom upstairs and didn't come down again, washing up and changing into a pair of Pat's pajamas. Jack and Gavin finished their beers, exchanged a hug, and climbed on up to bed. When Gavin entered the bedroom, Ellie was already asleep. Her last thought had been how comfortable and right it felt being home again. Gavin fell into bed beside her wearing his good shirt and the jeans he had changed into when cleaning up. *Here's my family,* Gavin thought gratefully, *but there's my Tuscany.* He and Ellie slept straight through until morning, but before Ellie had set her feet on the floor, Gavin was on his way to the chicken coop.

He slouched down in the battered wicker chair outside the shack and tried to recapture that time when he was obsessed with the importance of art, with creating works from his imagination rather than from only his eyes. But all he could bring to mind were the beautiful hills of Tuscany and how, at this very moment, its riotous spring flowers were about to start their show. And here he sat in Iowa, pining to see them unfold.

Ellie crept downstairs to start the coffee. Looking around the kitchen, she observed that nothing had changed - the same table, same chairs. No one had even moved the toaster or rehung the photographs she had taken of the Lower East Side. She wandered into the living room and ran her hand over the top shelf. Yes! Here it was - the *Veleveteen Rabbit* - the first book she and Gavin read to each other. She had kept it here specifically to read aloud to the boys. She wiped the dust from the cover and opened its pages:

> *You become. It takes a long time. That's why it doesn't happen often to people who break easily or have sharp edges or who have to be carefully kept.*

She had once cried at these words without understanding their full meaning. *What a shame,* she now thought, *that wisdom never seems to make itself known before the need arises.*

You become. But what had she *become*? A woman who left home, her husband, her children, her parents, and flew off by herself because she had a dream for success in a world unavailable if she stayed. Had she *become* what she had hoped?

Because she now had doubts about these original plans, did that mean she breaks easily, has sharp edges, has to be carefully kept? Why not consider herself strong and courageous for making difficult choices with no guarantee of success, no idea how things would turn out? Ellie had a lot to think about as she sat at the table with her coffee. Robins perched on the windowsill, pecking at cake crumbs. The faucet was dripping again.

Jack walked into the kitchen. Now they could continue yesterday's conversation. Like in the old days, Ellie rose and started to scramble some eggs. Years ago, Jack had shed the habit of eating breakfast, but he wouldn't refuse his mother's sweet gesture. In the few minutes it took her to place the eggs on the table and the pan in the sink, Pat had joined them, ending their hopes for any serious discussion.

The last two days of their visit passed uneventfully. Except for Jack and Ellie's chat, no one had gone deeper into their thoughts about each other and themselves. It was as if they had all taken a silent vote and decided, "Okay, next time. We'll talk next time."

Ellie left first, then Gavin, then Jack.

As she walked to the car, Ellie glanced at the shack, berating herself once again. Where was her head years ago when she decided Gavin's paintings were without merit? Why had she refrained from talking to him about his artistic vision then, in the beginning? She blanched at her early cavalier attitude, her contemptuous disregard. Knowing of his present success, she was bewildered and angry at the colossal miscalculations she had made in her youth - speaking to him of possible failure and misplaced dreams, opinions he never raised regarding her own aspirations. How she had underestimated this dear man who had always treated her kindly, lovingly!

She must decide whether or not to remain in Boston. Then whether to become a drama teacher, pull back from the stage, and assume the role of a mentor. Would that resolve her career concerns and make her happy? Or, inevitably, should she begin to assume the roles of older women? *Think Ingrid Bergman, Helen Mirren,* she told herself. *Think Vanessa Redgrave.* But when she did, images of them in their senior years were not an agreeable sight. Yes, she was that vain.

As Jack hugged his father goodbye, he waited to hear if Gavin would again mention visiting him in Italy. Or were his words simply an offhand statement made in haste to dispel an indelicate moment?

"Take care of yourself, Jack," Gavin said as he walked toward the car. "Try to find some spare time to paint a picture and remember what I said about coming to Italy."

Gavin put his foot on the pedal, leaving the chicken coop and his family behind. Who could have imagined such shifts in their individual destinies? He prized his family dearly and would, if he could, have scooped them up and whisked them to the top of his mountain. There they would know what he now knew - that he was an accomplished painter, understanding at last how life had changed his heart in ways that were good and nurturing.

Chapter 12

Although Jack stayed another day to postpone his return to Chicago, the entire family had finally dispersed. The rooms were empty. The robins flew off. One could hear the echo of footsteps on the creaky stairs.

Pat and Sam rocked on the porch and murmured to each other, "A lovely wedding, but wasn't it a short visit, dear? When do you think we'll see the children again?"

Fortunately, they didn't have long to wait. Danny and Maryann soon returned from their honeymoon and showed them photos of lakes and forests. They bought Sam a cowboy hat and Pat an apron with roomy pockets.

The next morning, the newlyweds rose early, put on their work clothes and took up their chores.

Chapter 13

On his return flight, Gavin reflected on Danny, happy and settled, and on Jack, mysteriously gloomy and unsettled. And Ellie? She looked well, but she seemed restless. He expected her to be pleased with her accomplishments. Hadn't she just directed her first play? Yet there was something tentative about her. If she had remorse at their separation, it was regretful, but he saw no way they could reconcile. If she had other troubles, the physical distance between them made any firsthand support impossible.

Gavin accepted a glass of Chardonnay from the flight attendant and turned his mind from family matters. He decided that he would give the Italian language a stronger focus, the better to speak easily with his new friends. Sofia introduced him to three of her artists who lived in Florence, and with these pals - two men, one woman - he took long hikes up and down the valleys, lunching in small towns, peeking in local galleries. On those gallery walls were various artworks of pastoral scenes, local cathedrals, famous landmarks. Occasionally, Lorenzo, the most outlandish of the four, would pull out a small drawing from his pocket, something with lines and circles and intersecting planes and thrust it in front of the proprietor. Always, the owner would frown and say, "*Che sciocchezza è questa?* What nonsense is this?" As the playful quartet left the shop howling with laughter, Lorenzo would shout, "*Pazzo*, madman, *ignorante*!" as the group made their way to the nearest café.

On the second lap of his flight, Gavin began to consider ideas for his next painting. A modernist's memory of a farm wedding?

The frenzy of folks dancing to a fiddle? He thought yet again of why someone was drawn to a painting. It was almost as personal an attraction as selecting a spouse. Were the colors, the lines, irresistible? Were they soothing? Did they make the blood race? Was there something mysterious in the way the colors had been put together? An approach that the viewer had never imagined? All was speculation he concluded, nevertheless thrilled that every painting held different meanings for every pair of eyes.

As Gavin began to recline his seat, his fingers suddenly began to quiver. Staring out the window, he clicked his seat upright again and pulled out his sketch pad, a few crayons. Just outside the glass, passing like a dream that he could almost reach out and touch were puffy clouds in the softest shades of pale yellow, pink, and lavender. Like a gust of wind, a fleeting jot of an ethereal substance, they appeared, then disappeared quicker than the eye could hold them. With a few marks on paper, he mentally stored the visual information, assured of the specific *sense* of what he had seen. This image would be his next painting.

The microphone crackled. The stewardess in the trim blue outfit called out, "Please fasten your seat belts. We'll be landing in ten minutes."

Unlike Gavin, Ellie did not have to cross an ocean and part of a continent to get back home. Yet traversing a great sweep of the Midwest and New England was not a short trip. Too restless to pull out the script Hank had thrust at her several days earlier, she settled in for a nap. However, she knew that failing to scan its pages before their meeting tomorrow would be a mistake. In the past, she was always prepared, but lately, she worried about slacking off a bit. She had better find the cause of this inertia before getting embroiled in the coming season. If she lost the joy, she would perform subpar, causing the critics to pounce on her performance.

Her thoughts turned toward Gavin and his newly burnished confidence. He no longer turned to others for approval. Small gestures became alluring, such as his pointing to the mashed potatoes and asking for the *patata*. His manners, also. He was no longer switching the fork from left to right hand after cutting his food but keeping the fork in his left, as Europeans do. And his curly brown hair covering his neck - he had let it grow. Now his appearance was as provocative as that of a gypsy wanderer. Yet this seductive man was no longer her lover, her husband. In fact, he acted like a brother.

She often wondered why she didn't seek out engaging men involved in the theater world. Not necessarily actors, often an unreliable and vain lot, but directors, producers, investors. Might it not be worthwhile to reassess? Might a good look provide the means to a new awakening? People form various attachments throughout their lives, often multiple times. Look at the glamorous life Gavin has fashioned for himself.

Just as she began to speculate on whether Gavin might have taken up with someone, the public address system boomed that the plane was now circling over Boston Harbor. In minutes, they would land at Logan Airport.

On the plane, hunched over by the window, Jack wondered if, in his brief absence, Julia had lost her maniacal interest in him. If she had, he would go off with his friends Ryan and Jim and get drunk. If she hadn't, he would complain to his boss a second time. Having put aside an adequate amount of money, he wasn't worried about losing his job.

He looked far down to the tiny strip of elegant Lake Shore Drive running along lovely Lake Michigan. He was surprised to feel a slight ache at seeing its beauty, as one feels when arriving home. If it weren't for Julia, he might love this town. With a slight dip of the plane, the peak of Willis Tower came into view. He preferred its old name, Sears Tower. *Whenever something changes hands,* he mused, *its old personality disappears, and it gets a new name. Just try saying Sears Tower to the natives, and they will look at you as if you are from a foreign country.*

The tumult of O'Hare International greeted him like a physical assault. Suitcases and carriages rolled past in all directions. Huge crowds, rushing and impatient, frustrated him to the point of despair. He forgot about Tuscany. He forgot about Boston. Everything was wiped from his mind but the hordes of people and the grotesque image of Julia, raising familiar fears that surged through his pores and settled on his skin like a colony of fire ants.

It had been no surprise that Gavin was attracted to Sofia. He had been painting in seclusion for a long time now. Naturally, he would crave an intimate connection. And Sofia was not only gorgeous but warm and generous as well. She alone had made a new life possible for him.

Yet with all his feelings for her, Gavin chose not to pursue her romantically, not even ask her out for dinner without a third person in tow lest he wander from his resolve. An intimate relationship might put her sponsorship in jeopardy. One never knows how something like this will turn out. What if she felt slighted or rebuffed? Would Sofia, a supportive woman, like most women, become unpredictable? It was she who occasionally rested her arm on his while expressing an opinion or lingered over a kiss on the cheek. Was she making a forward gesture of her own?

Gavin was doubly fearful of showing too much interest or not enough.

What I need, he decided, *is the will of a lion and the wisdom of Freud.*

Gavin knew almost nothing about Sofia's personal life. Parents, yes, her father helping her out with the gallery. Yes, the family owned a flat nearby the Piazza della Signoria. But did she live with them? He knew of her discovering abstract art while she was studying in Manhattan. But was it her idea to open her own gallery, or was it the suggestion of an American lover?

As an expat living in Italy, Gavin reflected, *Did his Italian friends wonder about the details of* his *life?* He never mentioned, for example, that when coming to Italy, he had separated from a wife and grown children. No one ever questioned him. It seemed to be the Italian way, granting friends their individual privacy. And yet, they spent much time in cafés chatting and gossiping. Until he better understood the Italian mind, Gavin decided he would be cautious. For all the exuberant welcomes, he was a stranger in a strange culture. A dazzling culture, but still, it crossed his mind that others might be talking about him when they reverted from English to Italian in his presence. Mostly, he waived off such concerns, but occasionally, every now and then…still, his wasn't a disreputable past, but one mutually acceptable to Ellie and himself.

So why should he be concerned?

Behind the curtain at the far end of the gallery, Sofia stretched out on the couch daydreaming about Gavin. She loved to recall her first sighting of him rigid on the cobblestones outside, his eyes disbelieving as he stared through the glass facade like a kid spotting a shiny red bike with silver spokes and a horn shaped like a megaphone.

An American, or perhaps an Englishman, she had thought, but who expected one to wander in on a slow weekday afternoon? Was this stranger attracted or repelled by the art on the walls? Could he be a potential buyer?

He wore fitted jeans that flattered his long legs and a black unstructured jacket that hung loose and casual over his shoulders. Lanky and somewhat craggy, he was not particularly distinctive or remarkable, but to her, beguiling, nevertheless. As she emerged from behind the curtain and he turned toward her, his face had no time to compose itself. She saw it all - shock, surprise, pleasure, a man with a rising flush on his cheeks. They shook hands, and when he extended his arm, Sofia saw a dab of red paint on his right wrist. *Ah, a painter.*

And then he was silently unwrapping his package and leaning its contents against the wall.

His brown curls exactly matched his brown eyes. And there was this - the deliberation and mindfulness with which he handled his canvases. It was so unlike the Italian men, almost universally swarthy with black hair, assertive with their hands, assured in placing things about.

Who can define the qualities one finds attractive in another? She was charmed, intrigued.

And something more - his paintings were shocking in their exceptionalism.

Under Sofia's auspices, in little over a year, Gavin had now sold four paintings to Gianni Amatucci. The three had become good friends. After each sale, they strolled over to nearby Matteo's café for a celebratory supper. There, they raised a few toasts and stayed for hours over a leisurely dinner.

During these occasions, Gavin would attempt to coax from her discreet bits of information about her personal life. He finally learned that she lived alone in an *appartamento* on the top - seventh - floor of her building.

"I have a splendid view of the river and beyond of the trees in the Boboli Gardens."

She told humorous stories of how she had cajoled her landlord into installing ceiling lights in a seventeenth-century flat. He had agreed to her request in exchange for an "occasional bowl of your *spaghetti aglio e olio*, easy on the spicy *peperoncino rosso, per favore*."

Gavin thought surely the man was in love with her.

"I have only a single painting on each wall, usually the second one the artist has left on reserve. When I sell the first, I bring the spare into the gallery. Since I'm constantly rotating works in and out, I don't allow myself to get attached to any in particular. Although, Gavin," she added, touching his arm and leaning in close, "I was crazy about your painting of those magnificent yellows, the work Gianni bought so quickly that I hardly had time to enjoy it."

Gavin began to notice that in her individual habits, Sofia acted similarly wary and elusive.

At Matteo's, he always ordered the same meal. As soon as Matteo spied him at the door, he cried, "Aha, signor! *Mamma* in the back has already started your *cacio e pepe* with extra *grana padano* and a pinch of black pepper, just the way you like it." But at each visit, Sofia asked for a menu, slowly looking it over as if she had never seen it before. Gavin was sure she could have recited every listing, as could he, though he never ordered anything but the *cacio e pepe*. It was a small gesture on her part, but to his mind, it was curious, odd. Was this ritual part of maintaining her public mystique, taking her time every visit to peruse the same choices?

Then Gavin realized that other than sharing his emotions about his painting life, he had confided very little in her as well. He had never uttered the name Ellie. As Gavin dug heartily into his *cacio e pepe*, he wondered how much even good friends truly knew about each other. And if many were reluctant to open up, did this flaw affect their lives as it obviously had his, having learned that secrets did no one any good?

Sofia was waiting for an appointment with Tommaso, the youngest of her flock. A fine painter, he also crafted exquisite jewelry.

"Gorgeous gold pieces fit for the Medicis," he urged. "Are you willing to sell them along with your paintings?"

Considering her decision brought Sofia back to the nature of her business and how she might be caught in her own image. Her status of being unattached was part of the gallery's cachet. Artists and patrons both loved flirting with her, the better to receive her favors. If she had a husband or child, she would not be the glamorous diva she presented to the world. A husband at home, *bambini* underfoot, didn't conform to anyone's fantasy. *A partner will* diminish *me,* she thought. Starting up with Gavin, for example, would raise only complications. Yes, she found him attractive, but it would be an impossible arrangement. For one reason, just to start, he loved his solitude, and she thrived on sociability.

What mattered to her success was the dramatic aura of the shop itself. And that ambiance relied on her as its mistress, emerging from behind the curtain in high heels and silk dresses to set its rooms aglow. In human form, she was similar to the works presented on her walls - unique, unable to be reproduced. If she wanted a permanent relationship, she could have one. Long lines of suitors awaited, but in truth, this arrangement suited her.

Perhaps one case of jewelry will *bring in the wealthy Florentine women,* she decided. *And I'll wear his pieces myself, adornment as advertisement.* For one, Elena Ricci, the elegant aristocrat who had purchased Gavin's painting of the clouds, would certainly covet Tommaso's splendid rings and necklaces.

She recalled the afternoon Ms. Ricci purchased the cloud painting.

"*Lo adoro,*" I love it, she had cried. "I will redo the main salon in my Fiesole villa to showcase this spectacular work."

"Everything will be *bianca,*" she said to Gavin and Sofia, "white, pale as the clouds themselves. Upon entering the room, one's world will become one of utter serenity. A glass of good wine from the Montalcino Vineyards and you will long to stay there forever."

Sofia's smile was buoyant. A frisson of exhilaration ran through Gavin. His work entered another realm of acceptance. Gianni's intent, now Elena Ricci's, was not only to hang his paintings but to create settings exclusively for them.

Gavin approached the Brothers for permission to build a studio adjacent to the cottage.

"I must have high ceilings," he explained.

"We presume something behind the copse of pines. Will it be a bit modest, not to disturb the land?" they inquired. "Oh, glass skylights, you say, and the whole north side to be glass also? Not exactly what we expected."

Gavin waited for their answer as Brothers Silvio and Antonio exchanged meaningful glances, likely reflecting on Gavin's contribution to the upkeep of the monastery's vegetable garden, to the installation of its watering mechanism, to the wire fence keeping small animals at bay. Silently, they nodded their agreement.

Gavin and Ellie spoke on the phone. She was now dating a theatrical producer who had taken her to Broadway for a week of shows - musicals, tragedies, comedies. Every night, they attended a different presentation. Gavin wondered if that whirlwind trip was the beginning of a courtship.

Maryann was about to deliver her and Danny's first child. And twins, it would be.

Jack was resentful, the stinging words of his boss still echoing unfairly.

"Sorry, Jack, too volatile a situation for us. You know how these things are."

Cleaning out his desk, Jack decided to ask his father if he meant what he had said at Danny's wedding, that he could come over to Italy for a visit.

Chapter 14

Gavin's phone rarely rang, so its harsh sound screeched ominously in a room silent but for birds twittering through an open window. He quickly set down his brush and wiped his hands of paint. Holding a clean rag, he reached for the receiver. Jack was calling from Chicago.

"Dad?" he began.

A tentative, cautious hello, Gavin thought. *When did we last speak? A month, six weeks ago?*

"Er, uh, how are you doing over there?"

"I'm doing fine, Jack. Painting constantly, as usual, but you know me - work, work, work. What's up? How are things with you?"

"Well," he said and then a long pause. Gavin found a chair.

"I'm changing jobs right now and have a little break." There was another lull. "And I was wondering if you meant it at Danny's wedding when you asked me to come visit you in Italy," he spit out before he lost his nerve.

There. It was said.

Startled, Gavin tried to recall words he had spoken at the wedding with its incessant festivities. Never mind the numerous toasts with local wines pledging fealty to a long marriage. Never mind the sharpened emotions involved in reuniting a divided family.

Jack's voice sounded wobbly - was he in trouble? Assessing his small quarters, a dozen difficulties arose in Gavin's mind, including the possibility of an extended visit. Didn't Jack say he was between jobs?

Before Gavin could answer, Jack added, "Dad, I've already booked a flight."

He sputtered out the information - time, date, airlines, five days hence.

Gavin tried to manage his concerns. There was the reality of Jack's shaky condition, as yet unknown. Issues at hand amounted to a list of deprivations and inconveniences, and none of them inconsequential: relinquishing his privacy; forsaking an occasional urge to paint at all hours not five feet from where Jack would be sleeping; postponing suppers with Gianni, with Sofia; canceling day trips with his artist companions. What about morning coffee at Francesco's? He had only recently begun sharing that routine with his new friend, Mia, the pretty young woman who now ran the art supply shop, the young woman who would move into his arms if he gave her the slightest encouragement.

Nevertheless, he set about putting his few modest rooms in order: gathering his scattered materials and placing them in neat piles next to his easel; emptying drawers, and making up the spare bed, really a cot pushed against the wall on which he usually tossed his clothes; lastly, checking the cupboard for coffee, sugar, bread. Then he stepped outside to pick a bunch of wild irises for the low table beside his son' s bed. Only when he completed his preparations did he walk down the path to the monastery and stand before Brothers Silvio and Antonio.

"My son Jack will be visiting in a few days. I'm not sure how long he'll stay," he started. As always, the Brothers initially refrained from speaking, their arms tucked into the loose sleeves of their robes. Would they refuse accommodation? Gavin thought of Jack with his suitcase packed, about to leave Chicago only to be told that he was forbidden refuge. Gavin knew these Brothers were a hospitable sect, yet would they welcome another visitor? After a moment, they both offered up a similarly cryptic smile. *What kind of signals did they send each other?* Gavin wondered.

And then Brother Silvio declared, "Fine, Gavin. We know your son will respect our premises, just as you do." Both men nodded, made the sign of the cross in Gavin's direction. On slippered feet, they left the room.

Chapter 14

Gavin waited in the international arrivals area of Amerigo Vespucci Airport watching one plane after another circling round and then sweeping down onto the runway. At last, an alluring voice with a sweet lilt, first in Italian, then in English, announced the arrival of flight 594 from Chicago, USA. As the plane rolled up to the gate, Gavin idly wondered what the woman actually looked like, the one who had just purred like a song Jack's arrival over the public address system.

When Gavin last saw his son at Danny's wedding, Jack was a fit and hardy young man, dressed - if he recalled correctly - in neat khaki pants and a fancy sweater. He worked at a job he enjoyed and at which he was successful. Nothing had seemed amiss. He had a few private moments with his mother by the creek, but otherwise, nothing untoward occurred, no hushed, furtive confidences of which he was aware. Yet Gavin was instantly alarmed at the Jack who walked into the terminal. He was the exact opposite of the Jack he remembered. Disheveled, scruffy, his hair was tousled, his shirt was missing a button, his jeans were faded. His eyes were red, and he carried a single gym bag, hardly enough for a long visit.

They managed only a brief, awkward embrace. After Gavin's initial greeting of "how was your trip?" and Jack's reply, "it was a trip, no big deal," they both grew quiet.

On the drive back to the mountain, Gavin kept glancing at his son, waiting for him to speak. But Jack was silent, even refusing to look out the window at the wildly beautiful Tuscan valleys and villages, the famous landscape through which the world longs to take just this drive. Every glance offered a sight of monumental beauty - vineyards, lakes, tall cypress trees running along roads and cemeteries. There were vast olive groves, heavy with growth. It was impossible to believe that anyone, no matter his troubles, would not pivot his shoulders a few inches to take it all in.

The straight road began to curve, winding up, up, all the way to the top of the mountain where the great medieval monastery awaited like a fortress, spread out like a dragon over the rocky dips and falls. Only heaven reached higher. Outrageously lush roses in pink and crimson put on a splendid show sprawling across the roof and walls of the cottage.

"I'm pretty tuckered out," Jack said. "Do you mind if I lie down for a while?"

And with that, he fell asleep for ten hours on the cot, covered with a duvet embroidered with sunflowers by nuns from the convent in Maremma.

What exactly is my parental responsibility if my child is a grown man? Gavin wondered. Meanwhile, he napped fitfully in the garden, trying in vain to push dire thoughts from his mind, inhaling the scent of the roses, waiting, waiting, to hear whatever his son would soon tell him.

When he finally heard the rip of the duffel zipper, Gavin went into the kitchen and started putting up the coffee, peeling fresh mangoes, laying out a hunk of Asiago Mezzano cheese, tiny pots of pear jam and fig mustard. Jack stumbled about, rubbing his eyes, patting down his hair. His face was awash with a sheepish look, likely recalling the indifference with which he had only yesterday greeted his father.

The aroma of Gavin's favorite brew, Lavazza Gusto Ground, filled the cozy room. They each took a cup, then faced each other across one of the Brothers' castoffs, an old planked refectory table, which Gavin prized. After a few long sips and a deep sigh, Jack stood and gave his father a full embrace.

"I'm sorry about yesterday. Just a bit out of sorts after a long trip," Jack said.

Then he again lapsed into silence. A few more gulps, another sigh, another glance at his father.

"I had some trouble, Dad," he started, at last.

And then he opened up with his woeful story regarding this girl Julia; the stalking; his fear of being harmed; his friends doubtful, disbelieving; the police; filing complaints; interrogations in dank rooms; his company doubtful, firing him. It was so humiliating, and through no fault of his own.

"After the police took care of Julia with orders of restraint, you'd think I'd get out of town as soon as possible, wouldn't you?" he then asked his father, lifting his head, meeting Gavin's eyes. "Instead, I hid in my apartment and didn't shave for a month. And then I thought of your invitation."

He voiced concerns about his mother. That he told her he was thinking of relocating to Boston, her hesitation at his interest. "I'm worried about her," Jack said. "I thought she'd be glad to have me nearby. Isn't she happy up there with her theater group? Wasn't that what she wanted?"

Gavin tried to imagine Jack's feelings of fear and rejection, his life in mortal danger. In his late twenties, Jack was no child. Still, he was an Iowa farm boy, gone off unprepared to live in Chicago. Was it his and Ellie's fault that he had little instruction in navigating a big city?

Gavin suddenly felt sad to recall the young boy racing through the fields eager for instruction from a father he thought the most wonderful man alive. In turn, the father had trained him to take on any creative challenge. But perhaps not to take on life off the farm. Now this child stood before him, bigger and taller than himself with a short beard and even some shots of gray in that beard.

Troubled, Gavin began to make an accounting of his family's woes, of the hesitation Ellie conveyed to Jack. Could age be unsettling her? He must call her and have a long talk. Then Danny and Maryann's wonderful news of the pregnancy was tempered by concerns of having twins, petite little thing that she was. Would she be able to carry two babies to term, petite little thing that she was?

Jack wandered out to the garden, but Gavin remained seated, thinking, taken up with the fragility of life and his helplessness in keeping it from unraveling. He picked at the cheese, cut off an edge, put a dab of fig jam on the top, then tossed it back onto the plate.

He thought of Sofia. With Jack's presence, things between them might change. But how? Surely there would be a dramatic shift in their delicate balance, almost as if she had married. It grieved him to think of it. Theirs was a precious emotional bond held together by the flutter of a heron's wing. Art was the glue. Despite his cautionary approach, their connection had nudged both their creative efforts up a notch. How reductive they would become should either of them give in to the vicissitudes of an ordinary romance. Would Jack's presence be this kind of diversion?

And then there was Mia, a pretty young woman who had shown up one day for tea and now sat by Gavin's side every morning. What was he supposed to do with Mia?

Gavin could not imagine any type of work here suitable for Jack's skills. And the impediment to a long stay was his ignorance of the Italian language. With Gavin leading the life of a recluse, the language issue had not posed a serious problem. But it would be different for Jack, a sociable young man who, from the start, had functioned only in the corporate world of peers and colleagues - talk, talk, talk, all day long.

In hindsight, Jack had regrets that he hadn't told his mother he was flying to Italy. She might have found comfort knowing that if he was unhappy, he would be with his father. But *he* thought she might be jealous he had not come to *her*. After all, his original idea was to move to Boston.

One day, Ellie found herself sitting in an empty theater watching the company on stage rev up for a new production. Hunkered down in the back, the house dark, she was grateful for the anonymity. The actors were rehearsing a new play about three sisters in their twenties, all with different mothers, same father. Looking over the scene, she suddenly grew sweaty and feverish. Dread alighted on her shoulders, digging in. *Don't cry out,* she told herself. *Don't. Everyone will come running and make a big fuss.* Holding firm to the armrests, she waited, face to the floor, until she could breathe evenly again. A panic attack - that's what it was, like the one she experienced before, the one at the Emerald Necklace - an attack brought on by the thundering insight she refused to confront, that those young women on stage were the same age as she was when she met Gavin. Double that number and that's how old she was now. Double, almost exactly, and then a tad more.

As she rubbed her chest, waiting for a steady heartbeat, she inadvertently drove the distress in deeper. Even in her late forties, the encroachment of age on her face, neck, and hands was apparent, a stealthy assault that was relentless.

And yet again, the realization she was no longer interested in acting.

The whole thing was puzzling. Why her attraction had peaked, she had no idea, but it did. She felt quite alone, far from Danny and Maryann; far from her parents; far from Gavin, still her husband yet a stranger. This sense of displacement, of personal loss, had been creeping up for some time. Now it had arrived.

And further, the theater itself had simply flown out of control. Producers and directors had banished from their rosters, classic dramas such as *Spoon River* and *Our Town*. Even this current show with the three sisters, *Don't Look Back*, was now considered too traditional, too tame. After its run, it would be eliminated from the repertoire. Hardly any company was presenting towering female characters such as the great Amanda from the *Glass Menagerie* or Ranevskaya in the *Cherry Orchard* and oh, the marvelous Mrs. Alving in *Ghosts*. The company was now committed to taking on daring theatrical events by untried, emerging writers. Hank was readying scripts that involved demons and shadows and futuristic worlds, relying on wildly abstract sets and rock music and special effects like smoke and magic, which contemporary audiences demanded. Those titanic female roles that commanded the play, causing the viewer to *think*, were simply not being staged. An *event* rather than a *play* best described this change.

The whole situation gave her a headache.

Ellie slunk away, back to the college annex in which she lived. Students gathered in the halls, on the walkways, purposefully making plans, arranging their futures. Some stopped to chat. Almost everyone waved. Suddenly, she despised them all. Everything about her dreams, her spirit, her body seemed old. It was shameful, a middle-aged woman living in a college dorm. No one cared that she had grown up on a farm, married, taught high school drama, and was the mother of two adult men.

In Boston, freezing cold patrician Boston, Hank had found a whole handful of younger women he now favored more than her. *Oh,* she thought, *the fecklessness of this business, its conceit, affectation, arrogance, narcissism.* The words poured from her mouth as she paced her small room. In fact, now that she was thinking about hubris and bluster, she concluded that the whole city had an outrageously high opinion of itself with colleges and universities on every block, an entitlement to a superior life. On the other hand, perhaps she actually *would* find teaching a rewarding notion. Imagine - living in a proper apartment, having a real address with a mailbox, mingling with mature folks of accomplishment! But would the allure hold amidst the arrogance of Boston's elitism?

She had no idea, but she might look into it and find out.

At her request, Hank had given her a few days off. So easily did he grant them that she suspected he was relieved at her absence. She spent them in her dorm room, locked away. But in truth, at this moment, in her mood, the small space turned out to be for the best. The free time forced her to lay down on her thin mattress made for bodies twenty-five years younger and think about her life.

At one time, she and Gavin did what young people do best - dream, plan, strive, manage, love. But they had kept secrets from each other. The resultant frustrations had been tamped down and left to fester until over time, years later, they erupted. The shock of revelation changed everything. There were accusations of betrayal. She and Gavin had at last come to an understanding, but she pledged never to be dishonest with herself again.

Leave the company she would, but then what? She had grown beyond Iowa and even beyond Gavin in Italy. Last time she had heard from him - two months ago? - he had sold an important painting, something about clouds and a rich lady who would hang it in her villa in the Fiesole hills.

And to think that for love of me, he would have stayed in that darn chicken coop forever making paintings, she reflected. *Because, really, he had never mentioned leaving Iowa until I went to Chicago and then got the Boston offer. And he now lived as he wanted, painting whatever suited his fancy, while I remain dependent on the favors and whims of others - directors, producers, the perfect script - to help me inch my way to minor triumphs.*

Yes, she would leave the company. Turning in her skimpy bed, Ellie wept.

Gavin was about to confront his initial concerns over Jack's arrival as he began to share his life with his son.

First, to Francesco's café, to introduce his friends to a grown child, a man no one knew existed.

Slowly, they made their way down the trail. The hillsides were covered with purple cornflower. Sweet alyssum fragrant with dew clustered between stony slabs along the path. Was his erratic heartbeat similar to Ellie's stage fright?

At the edge of the small plaza, Gavin abruptly stopped for Jack to absorb the grace of this enchanting space - snug together, charming shops of limestone with tiny mullioned windows. Raised in Iowa, working in Chicago, what did Jack know of this noble culture? Flowers everywhere, lush in window boxes, lush around doorways, lush in patches here and there. At Francesco's lively café, a few old folks were already sitting with their espresso, playing checkers. And vendors filled the main square with chatter and goods; baskets of lilies, or *giaggiolo*, hung from old lampposts. He must not forget to tell Jack the tale of the lily, the symbol of Florence, its culture and sports, for over a thousand years. All this, Gavin felt as he waited to enter the plaza with Jack. All these years, he had similarly hesitated whenever he arrived, as if to honor the space he was about to enter.

They finally stepped onto the cobblestones and found seats at one of Francesco's tables. Mia was crossing the square, waving, smiling. As she drew near, she noticed he was not alone. Covetous of her brief minutes with Gavin, a frown formed across her brow. Even now as she walked toward him, she was sweetly plotting how to tear him away from this stranger. Then she noticed their smiles took on the same curve of the lips, a similar tilt of the head. Why did Gavin have his arm over the younger man's shoulder?

Gavin rose and introduced them. Jack put out his hand and then blushed as Mia gently pushed it away. Relieved and pleased he was when she kissed him on one cheek, then the other.

"*Ciao, ciao,* everyone," she said.

"Mia, Francesco, Antonio, this is my son Jack," Gavin offered.

Francesco ambled over, blurting out, "Your son a grown man! Gavin, you never told us!" taking up Jack in a clumsy squeeze.

Then Antonio with his lusty, "*Buongiorno,* my friend! I see you have a visitor!"

As their numbers grew, Francesco added another table. Soon there were china cups of cappuccino, bountiful plates of *cornetti* and *biscotti*. And small ramekins of homemade blueberry yogurt served with tiny gelato, or *palettina*, spoons.

Jack smiled and sat quietly, taken aback by the warm welcome of strangers, the abiding appeal of site, food, people, café. Everyone talked at once, jumbling their Italian and English.

"Gavin, what a handsome young man! *Bello, bello*!"

"Gavin, you *vecchio sciocco*, you old fool, where have you been hiding this boy?"

"Gavin, you with a *figlio*, a son, this age?"

"Gavin, what are your plans, *i vostri piani*, for the boy? Or should I say, this young gentleman? *Cosi,* so?"

Since he had arrived in Italy, except for his first trip into Florence, never had Gavin arranged his time more than a day in advance. Just last week, he was laughing with these same people, holding hands with Mia, and now he was introducing them to his son. How could one plan? Suddenly, he noticed that Mia was smoothing her hair, playing with her earring, staring shyly at Jack. His heart ached with the knowledge that simple things might become gravely complex.

A daylong hike in the hills. We'll start with that, Gavin thought. *The ravishing landscape will go a long way toward bringing peace to any heart.*

But first, he and Jack stopped at the monastery to greet Brothers Silvio and Antonio.

"So glad to meet you," the Brothers chorused. "You're even taller than your father! Gavin is such a boon to our little enclave here, always helping out in the shop, the gardens. Gavin," they said, turning toward him, "please pick out a bottle of wine for your dinner. Let it be our little gift."

Jack and Gavin then visited the wine shop in a low sandstone building that looked as if it had grown out of the landscape. Surrounded by oak trees hundreds of years old whose branches overhung the red clay roofs, they sheltered open arches of a sweeping loggia that faced the vineyards and hills below. For the customers' viewing pleasure, the Brothers had set out a row of rocking chairs. As they meandered among the counters and cabinets filled with bottles from the Brothers' own vineyards, Gavin explained how the grapes were harvested, how the wine was made. He chose a bottle of the monastery's best white, dry and fruity with a faint flavor of peach.

On their walk, neighbors and local vintners frequently crossed their path. Barely could they travel a kilometer without stopping to chat. The DiGiornios waved Gavin over while keeping track of five of their eleven children playing hide and seek among the grapes. The two youngest clung to Jack, obliging him to give them rides on his back. After a few words of good cheer and some hearty sips of a local Chianti red, they continued on their trek. Soon, another turn, and there was Piero Lattazza with his crew, ladders propped against the gnarled olive trees. Piero launched into stories with Jack about Gavin, his *padre meraviglioso*, wonderful father, such a dedicated artist who makes beautiful paintings and a fierce checker player to boot. And Jack nodding his head, yes, yes, a marvelous man, a superb painter, trying to understand the emotions without language as Piero grinned and slapped Gavin on the back. Yes, a *padre* what? A dedicated painter, but also a *fierce* what? Checkers? Of course!

After they shared a lunch of Bagoss cheese - Jack detected a hint of chestnuts - on brown bread, Gavin and Jack continued their walk. Gavin picked up his stories of Tuscan history: that opera was born here in the late 1500s by a group of artists named the Florentine Camerata whose objective was to recreate the Greek storytelling through music; that the black plague of 1348 wiped out seventy percent of Tuscany within one year; that Tuscany was first in all of Europe to pave its roads; that there are several other smaller towers - church bell towers - that lean other than the Leaning Tower of Pisa. As they walked along, they waved to the drivers on their way to market, their wagons filled with plums and pears. Strolling by medieval churches with the locals streaming in for mass, they passed an abandoned quarry, and just beyond, a dozen nuns in full habit were working in a convent's flower garden. *A dazzling way to greet Italy,* Gavin thought. Jack was in full stride, relaxed, smiling. Throughout the day, he grew more confident, even bold. In time, he heartily returned the greetings of passersby with a booming, "*Ciao! Ciao, come stai?*" Hello! How are you?

The land and people were joyously radiant, and Jack had no choice but to love them back. It was a good first day, and Gavin hoped that by week's end, Jack's spirit would know peace.

The next morning, Jack appeared, showered and dressed, looking for his father and his morning coffee. Gavin noticed that he stood straighter. His eyes were bright. *Yesterday's jaunt was a test that had gone well,* he thought. Now he had a more ambitious trek in mind, a scheme to bring Jack fully back into his life.

Nevertheless, Gavin couldn't help but hear a small voice in his head reminding him that he was not priming his canvas for his next project, which he had planned to start as soon as the sun rose the very morning of Jack's arrival.

Chapter 15

Gavin and Jack planned to be gone for a week.

No itinerary, no reservations, just two willing souls eager to roam and replenish their spirits. For all Gavin's trekking with his artist friends, he had never ventured farther than where they could reach on foot in a single afternoon. But now, he and Jack would randomly hop on trains and hitchhike like two kids running away from home. Both men carried pens and sketchbooks to record scenes large and small - farmhouses and cathedrals, the texture of stone, the grain of wood.

Gavin hoped to return with fresh impressions for his work, but in fact, he was somewhat dubious. Expressing in paint on a flat, two-dimensional surface impressions of a journey that would encompass mind and body seemed a daunting prospect.

No matter. Best of all, he was with his son, and the two of them would fall in love with each other all over again.

At the Santa Maria Novella station in Florence, they caught the first train that pulled into the terminal. An hour southeast of Florence, they jumped off at Arezzo, an ancient Etruscan city, later a strategic Roman outpost. They wandered into the somber Basilica of San Domenico and found themselves standing almost alone before the thirteenth-century painter Cimabue's masterpiece, the *Crucifix*. It was an ordinary occurrence that would happen again and again, to simply stroll into a local building or church and find historical treasures and precious artworks entirely unguarded and unprotected.

A priest was lingering before the Cimabue. His expression, contemplative. He asked them if they knew what this painting represented.

"No," they answered, "is it particularly significant?"

"This is the painting that represented the dividing line between the old [stylized, flat] and new [humanistic, realistic] traditions in Western European painting," he replied casually, as if his statement was just an ordinary observation and didn't represent a monumental shift in the history of art.

Gavin and Jack looked at each other. This iconic painting hung here in a church in the town of Arezzo and not a caretaker present to guard against mischief. No elaborate description other than a sign with names of the work and the artist, modestly displayed to the side.

They next happened upon the Arezzo Cathedral at the highest point of town. Gavin was reminded of how the people named their land - *hill towns* - spectacularly built on top of hills or into sides of mountains or cliffs, all having splendid views of valleys or seas or villages below.

Featured in the cathedral were painted vaulted ceilings and a fifteenth-century fresco of Mary Magdalene by Piero della Francesca who lived two hundred years after Cimabue. Next, down the hill-side and in the nearby Basilica of San Francesco were Piero della Francesca's stunning frescoes - *Legends of the True Cross*. Known as an Old Master in Early Renaissance art, Francesca was a mathematician, a specialist in geometry. As a pioneer of painting techniques such as linear perspective and foreshortening, he made the shift from flat representations of the Middle Ages to a more naturalistic, less stylized approach. Gavin and Jack were again astounded at the fact that here in this church they discovered the artist foremost in formulating perspective and foreshortening, elements essential to all painters since the Renaissance. It occurred to Gavin that by simply moving from one town to the next, they could trace the history of western civilization.

Dozens of candles flickered unattended on the altar rails. Breezes wafted through open doors. It seemed easy for an idle flame to go astray and create a conflagration. Gavin recalled that on one occasion, he had entered the grand ballroom of a private villa, now a museum, that had belonged to a prince. On the walls were two paintings by Raphael with only one guard in the doorway, fast asleep.

The first train out of Arezzo traveled southeast for an hour to the splendid town of Pienza. Hungry, they immediately sat for lunch at a café in the main Piazza Centrale. As Gavin translated the menu, a man at the next table leaned over and asked, "You are visitors, yes? Americans, yes?" Eager to share the history of their lovely town, the man and his wife began a conversation.

"Ah, did you know that Pienza is a renaissance town built to embody the humanist vision of the ideal city? Enea Silvio Piccolomini - you might know him as Pope Pius II, no? - decided to redesign this small village of his birth and make it the embodiment of humanist architectural harmony and ideas. In fact, built in the mid-fifteenth-century, it was the first example of Renaissance architecture."

Astonished, Jack and Gavin sat mute. In the most ordinary circumstances, another monumental statement had been unleashed by the tongue of a stranger. And this time, they learned that not a singular work, but an entire town, had been designed as a work of art. It was a transformative work in a transformative era.

"Oh, *scusami*, so sorry. My name is Alberto. This is my wife, Angela. My English is okay?"

"Excellent. Please continue," Gavin replied, eager to learn more.

Alberto beckoned the waiter and ordered two bottles of wine.

"The pope gave the job to the architect Bernardo Rossellino and the great humanist Leon Battista Alberti. In only three years, they built everything you see around you. The stunning Piazza Centrale, in which we now sit, the Pienza Cathedral, the municipal palazzo, and the papal residence called Piccolomini Palace, in which Pope Pius spent his summers. Hence, the city of Pius, or *Pienza*. There are *affascinante*, charming alleyways along which to stroll and browse. And the views from the hilltops over the Orcia Valley? *Superbo*, superb! Have you climbed up to look?"

After their lunch, Alberto and Andrea hugged the two men and invited them for dinner should time permit. As they walked away, Gavin thought, *I bless the United States and all its people, but above all, I bless that I am now living in this exceptional place.*

After lunch, they wandered along the narrow streets of shops and cafés. The sight was numbing in its charm. Gavin divined an idea for a painting wherever he looked. At one pause, he examined closely the intricate brass design of a massive doorknob on the facade of the cathedral. *I can make this very handle into a mysterious and seductive painting of whorls and coils,* he mused, *and no one would ever guess what inspired me.*

Leaving town, they walked along country roads through small villages, witnessing the lives of farmers, vintners, a hundred different manner of folks at work and play. Strangers waved, called out *ciao* time and again from the fields, from doorways. After a few hours, a farmer driving a truckload of melons stopped alongside.

"*Dove stai andando*?" Where are you going? he asked, looking down from his seat, tires and engine belching and sputtering. "*Il mio nome è Tony*," he said, putting out his hand. "My name is Tony. I'm heading for *Castiglione della Pescaia* and its beaches - *Marze, Punta Ala, Rocchette.* Can I give you a ride?"

Southeast of Pienza, but not far, perhaps an hour's drive, Gavin calculated.

"The cafés along the water love my melons," Tony added.

When he dropped them off, he invited them to stop in and meet his children if they ever found themselves in nearby Grosseto.

Gavin and Jack stood on the sand and gazed out to sea at the grand vista before them. To a distant point, left and right, were dazzling beaches of white sand; their coastal zones flanked by enchanting towns. If they stayed for a dozen years, it would not be nearly enough time to embrace these people, to take in both the natural beauty and that which they had created from their own hands.

They found a cheap *pensione* for the night - an accommodation in which an Italian family rents out a room or two in their house. Since few of their hosts spoke English, Gavin conversed in Italian while Jack sat silently, smiling and nodding as grandchildren ran around the kitchen. Once, they slept in a monastery - spartan, immaculate, two single beds, a table, a hard chair. Another night, they bunked at an *agriturismo*, a farm, with stables partitioned into four rough sections with a common bath. The divisions were the old stalls, swept out and re-floored. So tired were they that even a stranger's snores could not disturb them.

Heading home, traveling northwest now, they stopped in *San Gimignano*, another famous Italian hill town. Enclosed by thirteenth-century walls, its center was lined with fourteen medieval houses attached to looming towers; in the fifteenth century, there were seventy-three that once served as military lookout stations. Those towers, the town's most distinctive feature, had but few openings, mere slits, to protect the occupants in the old days from well-aimed arrows. Other cities such as Florence had their towers destroyed by war or catastrophe, but *San Gimignano* managed to preserve a few. Seven centuries and still intact! Gavin and Jack tread carefully, realizing they were walking through a country that measured time in centuries.

Pulling out their notebooks, they sketched those particular structures jutting skyward, especially the impressive *Torre Grossa*, built in 1310 and housing a bell tower, now a symbol of civic pride. If one climbed to the top of its 218 steps, the viewer was rewarded with astonishing views. Work on that particular tower, they learned, was started four months after Dante Alighieri, the great writer of the *Divine Comedy*, had visited.

Only one day more of their trip as they strolled by the Chianti vineyards between Florence and Siena. The air was refreshing and brisk; these particular hills cooled by the famous mountain air that made for a distinguished yield of grape. Thousands of vines extended to the horizon, reminding them in a certain manner of the cornfields in Iowa. Both were similarly planted in precise rows, like military regiments lined up for inspection. Yet the two differed greatly. In

Tuscany, the plantings were dotted with churches and monasteries. Or a stone winery, approached by a winding allée of tall, narrow cypress trees, which were a lovely blue-green and seen everywhere. It was well-known that these trees grew three feet a year and often lived to be over a thousand years old. The vineyards were integral to the life around them. In Iowa, the cornfields stood alone. Only crops and sky could be seen, a view seemingly untended and serene with its own particular form of beauty - pure and bountiful.

"My friends always bought cheap Chianti wine - that red stuff with the straw wrapped around the bottle," Jack said. "Is this where that wine comes from?"

"Not quite," said Gavin, smiling. "Look at the vineyards reaching all the way to the next valley. Aren't they beautiful? This is the *Sangiovese* grape," said Gavin. "There's nothing ordinary about this wine. Let's go over to the main building and have a taste of their *Chianti Classico*. Then you tell me if you've ever tasted this at your parties in Chicago."

The two wanderers made their way to the tasting room. After a few slow sips, Jack grinned and offered a princely thumbs-up.

Jack was dressed early, long before the Italians awakened. Soon, they would leave for Florence. Gavin planned to explain the history and significance of every sight they passed and end the day in Sofia's gallery. But first, a morning *cappuccino* and *cornetto* at Francesco's. Jack had developed a taste for that pastry the Italians nicknamed "little horn," similar to but softer than a croissant. And Francesco made his special by adding marzipan in its center. Then the bus ride down from the mountain through hills and valleys covered with poppies and purple irises. Finally, the grand approach to the city, its noble architecture slowly revealing itself against a sleepy blue Mediterranean sky. Gavin watched Jack's rapt attention all the way.

On the walk to Sofia's Place, Gavin pointed fingers and told stories. Passing the Accademia di Firenze, he spoke of "Michelangelo's original *David* standing tall just inside this very building, at the end of a long, classically elegant space. His four monumental unfinished

Prisoners or *Slaves* sculptures are on either side. Jack, here is genius… we'll stop in on another day.

"So many great *palazzi*," said Gavin as they turned a corner. "This one, the Palazzo Strozzi, begun in the fifteenth century by a rival of the Medicis. And there, Dante's home. And now, this is one of the greatest of the great cathedrals, Santa Maria del Fiore, called Il Duomo. Its dome was the first ever built without a supporting structure. At the time, it created a sensation throughout Europe."

"The Duomo has a remarkable history. I'll tell you a little as we stand here in front of it. The architect, Filippo Brunelleschi, in the fifteenth century, originally a goldsmith and sculptor, won a tough competition for this assignment. There were bitter disputes by cathedral architects, Brunelleschi not being an architect by trade. But as it turned out, he was a marvel with engineering and found unique solutions for the many problems that arose. Cosimo Medici, by the way, paid for everything. Two geniuses, the designer and his patron.

"His solution for its permanent durability? Two domes, one built within the other to counteract the various opposing forces of stress and collapse. He invented techniques and devices that he largely kept secret such as machines that could move enormous weights and lift them to considerable heights. And bricks laid in certain patterns that reinforced the walls. It's a complicated story. One more sensation in this amazing city where on a simple daily stroll one can witness achievements that transformed the world."

When they arrived at the river Arno, they rested on a bench, gazing along its length at two bridges built in the fourteenth century. "The famous *Ponte Vecchio*," Gavin said, "by the architect Taddeo Gaddi, and farther down, the *Ponte alle Grazie* by Lapo Tedesco, who also built the *Bargello Museum*. These were built in the thirteenth and fourteenth centuries, Jack. Isn't that something?"

Jack was enormously impressed with Gavin's ongoing descriptions. This from the same man who years before had sat outside a chicken coop all summer painting those baffling canvases.

And himself? What had he ever done that was bold? When had he ever taken a chance that involved sacrifice or invention? He knew little about the world's cultural history as if he had been living under a rock. His father had done it all, knew it all.

In late afternoon, they appeared on the short street with the three shops built into a cave. Gavin paused outside, allowing Jack to absorb the ingenious design of the leather and candle ateliers flanking *Sofia's Place*. The gallery itself was lit up like a birthday cake with spotlights directed toward the brilliant paintings on the walls.

"Jack, see how these shops were carved out of boulders and then embraced by them." Gavin paused, then pulled on the great steel handles. Inside he pointed. "Look there! My latest work."

Jack turned toward a massive painting in raw umber, sepia, and gold, reminding him of that very day's walk through a city dusted with just those colors. *How magnificent,* Jack thought. His father had perfectly captured the sense of Firenze. This work was far finer than those that hung in solitary splendor along the corridors of his company in Chicago. A painting he would be honored to buy himself, even if it took the rest of his life to pay for it. He squeezed his father's fingers.

A curtain fluttered in the far corner. Sofia emerged, looking particularly beautiful in a silk dress the color of spring grass. As she walked toward them, the fabric swayed softly, as if a swarm of butterflies were accompanying her. The upper part was tightly fitted, the hemline loose, sewn with a loopy stitch to create a twirl flaring from her knees.

Where does she find these exquisite garments? Gavin wondered. *And surely that necklace of heavy gold links was plucked from Tommaso's glass case now displayed along one side of the gallery.* As Tommaso had promised, his pieces were indeed fit for a Medici. He found he could have conducted his business entirely through custom orders, but he was faithful to Sofia. She had sold his paintings before anyone else and continued to do so. His loyalty never wavered.

Sofia smiled broadly, not realizing that the two were together.

"Sofia, this is my son Jack," Gavin said.

Stunned, she glanced from one to the other. *Gavin with a grown son*? She looked for the resemblance, and there it was - both tall and slender, with curly brown hair, Jack's thicker and darker but still the same texture. There was a similar intensity of focus in both of their dark, coffee-colored eyes. The sense of them in their dignified demeanor was alike. *Is this boy an artist too?* she wondered. Quickly, she composed herself, reclaimed her face with its usual congenial aspect.

"*Bene, bene,* good, good," she cried as she brought out three glasses and a bottle of Chianti, pointing to the chairs and the round table.

"So tell me all about yourself, Jack," she urged.

How should I answer? he wondered. What could he say that would compare to the vivid week just passed under his father's tutelage? It seemed as if his whole life had been lived in a state of mediocrity waiting for the clouds to part, for the sun to shine through. He recrossed his legs, tasted the wine, swallowed slowly, and glanced at his father.

"You must know, I grew up in Iowa," he started. Sofia was leaning toward him. "Then I moved to Chicago where I worked as a graphic designer for an advertising firm creating offbeat, funky images" - stopping again, looking from his father to Sofia; they both sat, waiting comfortably - "and I managed to create a few that appeared on television," he finished shyly.

After a moment, Sofia asked, "How long do you plan to stay?"

She looked at Gavin.

"Did you know that Gianni has a department of graphic design in his company? Should Jack talk to him?"

Gavin paled, and instantly, Sofia knew she had made a mistake. The room grew quiet, as if the wine were now water, without warmth. Had she overstepped her bounds? She knew nothing of the relationship between the two.

Just then, Tommaso walked through the doors.

"*Buon pomeriggio*, good afternoon one and all!" he cried.

Sofia jumped up and ran over to greet him as if he were an angel come to forgive her lapse.

Gavin greeted Tommaso, then kissed Sofia goodbye. "We'll speak tomorrow."

The Brothers had once again offered the hospitality of their sect's lodgings in town.

"Would you like that?" Gavin asked as they deposited their bags in the modest room. "To work for the man who is a patron of mine? He seems to be a generous man, but I have no idea what it would be like to be in his employ."

"Might it be worth a try?" Jack asked. "Just to see what kind of graphics they produce in such a place."

Gavin recalled how this past week, Jack's excitement had grown at the sight of every flower and stone. As well, his eyes flared with enthusiasm when he looked at Mia and Sofia. Just this morning, Mia had hovered over Jack's coffee at Francesco's, her long legs gracefully crossed in her short skirt. With coquettish aplomb, she demonstrated how the Italian fixed their *cappuccino*, twirling a spoon, stirring the sugar while pushing her hair back, fiddling with her necklace. Jack had listened raptly to her Italian-accented English as if she were a film star.

"Do you think I should meet this Mr. Gianni fellow?" Jack asked again.

This Mr. Gianni fellow? Gavin thought. *You mean the first person who ever bought a painting of mine?* Sunflowers - *the one he hung in his dazzling conservatory along with roiling reds. You mean* that *Gianni fellow?*

"It's up to you," Gavin answered. "Just let me know, and I'll arrange it."

"Okay, let's give it a try," Jack replied.

"By the way, Gianni bought *Sunflowers*, the first painting I ever sold."

Covering his father's hand with his, he answered, "This Gianni must be an exceptional fellow."

Gianni was rich enough, thought Gavin, not to be obligated to anyone. On the other hand, he likely wouldn't be averse to granting a favor for one of his favorite artists. So Sofia contacted Gianni's office in central Florence. An appointment was arranged for the next morning.

While Jack was having his interview, Gavin strolled through an exhibition in the Uffizi Gallery entitled, "Da Vinci in Florence." *Exceptional brilliance lived in that man,* Gavin reflected. The world knows da Vinci mainly for his art, particularly the *Mona Lisa*, but paintings were only a small part of his output. As masterful and anatomically enlightening as his drawings and paintings were, equally outstanding were his engineering skills; his scientific inventions - the parachute, the helicopter, the calculator; his discoveries in anatomy, astronomy, and physics. Detailed diagrams and descriptions filled several rooms - an attempt to dam the Arno, a folding bridge to be used by soldiers. The popular phrase *the Renaissance Man* was coined for him. Ever after, it would be applied to someone of great versatility and accomplishment.

"Very fancy," said Jack, reporting to Gavin after his interview with Gianni. "The whole place is far more elegant than our headquarters in Chicago. Someone from their advertising section, a man named Edoardo, showed me around."

"Well, you know the Italians have a way with design, with making ordinary things beautiful," Gavin replied, "like the French, like all Europeans, actually."

"The only drawback," said Jack, "and it's a big one - is that everyone speaks only Italian. Two or three know English, but no one speaks it. Edoardo stayed by my side the whole visit to translate.

"Oh, and I was told I have to live nearby. Often, they work late. I was referred to a lady who lets rooms in her townhouse a half mile from their office."

Gavin wondered if that had been a deliberate act on Gianni's part, managing Jack's living accommodations in town for my convenience. If so, he was a more sensitive man than I had thought. *Well, no matter, all to the good. Jack would now be responsible for his own life - colleagues, friends, women - as it should be.*

They returned to the monastery on the mountain to gather Jack's things and to say farewell to the Brothers, then a stop at Francesco's, and another at the art supply store where Mia was pouty at hearing Jack would be living in Florence. Then, once again, they took the usual rutted bus ride through the countryside and into the city. Meandering through the streets looking for *71 Via dei Leoni* (*leoni* - live lions were indeed kept near here seven centuries earlier), they eventually came upon a seventeenth-century building of that address. The elegant Renaissance architecture, with its rounded pediment over the door and pilasters on either side, was worn but intact, like an aging diva who still lives but fails to stay fresh.

An ample but pleasant eighty-year-old widow, Mrs. Luisa Ferrucci, answered the bell.

"*Benvenuto!* Welcome! I was told to take good care of you. Do you like *gnocchi alla sorrento*?" Laughing at his confusion, she said to Jack, "Never mind. I'll put some meat on your bones." She kept talking as they climbed the stairs to Jack's room, passing heavenly creatures painted centuries earlier on the walls of the winding staircase.

"My darling husband, Fabio, had his final heart attack climbing these very stairs," she continued with a tired sigh. The occasional hitch of her slippers on the splintered stairs had Jack concerned; he steadied himself in case she should fall backward into his arms.

A dormer window opened to a distant sight of the Duomo. The room was immaculate and bright. A china flowerpot held purple violets. Three oranges were arranged on a blue plate. A quilted coverlet in rose cotton edged in exquisite cross-stitching covered the bed.

"The work of a young girl from the *orfanotrofio*, the orphanage," Mrs. Ferrucci explained, seeing Gavin's admiring gaze.

The men embraced. "Good luck, Jack. If you need me, Mrs. Ferrucci knows how to reach me."

"I'll be fine, Dad. Not to worry."

Once again, Gavin boarded the familiar bus, riding on the pitted roads alongside the fields of scattered wildflowers. The driver on this daytime route had long ago become a close companion. His name was Enzo.

"*Buongiorno*, Enzo! *Come stai oggi*! How are you today?" Gavin cried, patting Enzo on the shoulder, then sitting by his friend as they sang songs in Italian all the way home.

Gavin was so immersed in his work that he barely heard the birds sing in the garden. He couldn't work fast enough as the images of his travels with Jack raced from his brain to his fingers. Neglecting to weed the flowers, Gavin appealed to Brother Silvio, who sent down a novitiate with a trowel and spade.

Sofia dispatched two messages by post. "Are you well?"

Mia sent notes with Piero Lattazza, who slipped them under his door. "How are you doing? How is Jack getting along?"

Jack called. "Dad, would you like to meet in Florence for an afternoon?"

"No, no, no," Gavin replied to everyone. "I'm well, but I'm busy."

He was surprised when Jack showed up at his studio without advance notice but glad and relieved that he looked relaxed, at ease, exuberant, in fact.

They sat around the table with mugs of *Lavazza Gusto Ground.*

"A lot has been going on, Dad. First, about Mr. Amatucci. He's really a good guy, but his setup doesn't work for me. It's not what I do. Mainly, he needs mass marketing tools for publicizing distribution of product. And like Chicago, there are corporate bosses, a strict departmental structure."

Gavin brought to the table a box of cranberry biscotti that the novitiate had left on his back stoop.

"Talk flew all day like a flock of crows circling round my head," Jack said. "I had no idea what they were saying. I don't belong there. I'm not really interested in learning Italian. The good thing was my time off when I wandered around the city. I was thrilled with everything, especially the paintings in the Uffizi where I went a dozen times. And you know what I realized while seeing the sights?" Jack paused, knowing he was going to surprise his father with his news.

"I realized that I love what I do - my type of drawing. I'm great at it, thanks to you. It's incredibly fun and original, and it suits me. It's just that in Chicago, I was frustrated with being an employee. But if I'm the boss, well...so after a couple of weeks of serious thinking, I made a decision. This is a gorgeous country, a fabulous place. I can see why you love it. I can see why you are thriving here. But it's not for me. I miss the States. Here, I feel like a tourist. But that's not a bad thing because, guess what?" Jack asked, waiting for Gavin to guess.

Gavin sat quietly, dipped the biscotti into his coffee.

"Feeling like an outsider gave me the idea to call my friend Ryan. Ryan Sullivan. We worked together in Chicago. He also hated it there. He's a pretty talented guy. I asked him if he wanted to start up a two-man company of graphic design. Between us, we already have some good connections and lots of experience. He was ecstatic, hollering his head off. I could almost see him dancing around the room.

"And get this. He's from Boston. His family lives there. So we're going to start up in Boston! There are dozens of private schools in the city. Each of them has tons of clubs and activities that use the services of graphic designers. Plus, there are several art schools and great museums. We could teach on the side until we're up and running. Mom's there, and how terrific is that? But if for some reason she moves, we'd still be in a great location."

Gavin watched his son's face as his story unfolded. The visit was a fine success, after all, a pivotal experience. Jack looked fit and appeared healed. His mature thinking and decisive action augured well for his future. Gavin jumped up to grasp his son.

"It's a grand idea, Jack, a wonderful idea. I'm darn proud of how you've figured this all out. Let's go to Francesco's and have a fabulous dinner and a bottle of his best wine. What do you say?"

Jack collected his belongings from Mrs. Ferrucci and stayed on the mountain with his father for a few days. They walked and talked and sat beneath the roses telling stories of Iowa and the farm, of the family and the shack, of the field of sunflowers and how that particular painting had become the lodestar of the contemporary art world. This time, when Gavin drove him to the airport, Jack couldn't stop speaking about the beautiful countryside and the Italian people, the wondrous city of Florence, and how he would never forget this trip, not ever. Nor would he forget his father's bountiful heart, which made all his tomorrows possible.

At the departure gate, father and son hugged and wept. Gavin promised to send a small contribution toward his son's beginning effort. Jack promised to visit again as soon as he and Ryan were settled. And then, like Ellie leaving Gavin on the sidewalk and walking to the plane on her way to Chicago, so too did Jack step into his own future. Overcome with triumph and a small ache of longing, Gavin thoughtfully drove home to his own unique and spectacular present.

Chapter 16

Gavin looked at the clock. *Just after dinner in Boston. She might be available now.*

"Hello?"

Did she sound tired, energized, happy? For heaven's sake, Gavin scolded himself. *All she said was hello.*

"Ellie? It's me. Jack just spent a couple of months here," he began.

Silence. Were the wires disconnected?

Ellie was thinking. *How could members of a family be out of touch for a couple of months? Should she be upset at those weeks of silence or relieved that Jack was safe with his father? On the other hand,* she thought, *the phone works both ways. I could have easily called him as well. Oh heck, the days pass so fast that two months seem like two weeks.*

"Ellie?" He tried again.

"Hello, Gavin."

How much of her truth should she tell him?

"Gavin, tell me about Jack. When we talked at Danny's wedding, he was having trouble with a girl."

And then, just like that, Gavin and Ellie were parents again, concerned, protective.

Gavin spoke sparingly of Jack's difficult circumstances - his unhappiness with his job, the turmoil with Julia. Mostly, he focused on their adventures traveling around Italy together and Jack's return to his previous positive outlook.

"Ellie, and hear this. He plans to open a business with a friend named Ryan in Boston! He would love to be near you, of course, but he knows your plans aren't firm. Not to worry. Ryan has family in town. Jack will be fine."

"Gavin, you'll have to tell me more about Jack's plans with this Ryan boy, but if you think it's all a good idea, I'm sure it's fine. I knew at the wedding he was having some personal concerns, but we didn't go into it very deeply. We had planned to talk further, but with the wedding and all…" Had she fallen short with her son? *Thank goodness his father brought him back,* she thought gratefully.

"I was not much use to him at the time," she said sadly. "You know, Maryann is in the third trimester of pregnancy," Ellie continued. "She's simply enormous, such a tiny thing. It's very hard for her. The doctor thinks one baby is okay but isn't sure about the other. Maybe I should fly back to Iowa for a couple of weeks."

She had let one of her sons down, but she wouldn't do it again.

And then, they were done speaking of the children. Now they would speak about themselves.

"So, Ellie, what's going on with you?" Gavin continued.

Sharing her unease with an estranged husband who was thriving seemed a shameful confession. It had been her choice to leave home, and what had her dreams come to? As she did not want to appear needy, sharing only random incidentals that occasionally went static was the best she could do.

"I might be up for a change," she offered tentatively.

Surprised, Gavin waited for more, but that was all she offered.

"How are things going with you?" she asked.

There were so many lovely stories he could have told her but didn't - the peace of living on top of a mountain, his many friendships, the exquisite lifestyle of the Italians, and his painting successes. Nor did he speak of his relationships with wealthy clients who lived in gorgeous villas, not while she was struggling. Rather, he described the simplicity, even severity, of his daily life - solitary, reclusive, and how it suited him.

"I live with monks and paint constantly. I've had a bit of luck selling a few paintings through a gallery in Florence."

She considered asking if he had any personal attachments. Instead, she said, "It's good you managed to help Jack."

When they said their goodbyes, both felt incomplete. Gavin was unable to render effective comfort without knowing the cause of her unhappiness. And he failed to speak of other truths in his life. Ellie learned nothing of his private circumstances and kept mum about her professional conflicts.

Once again, they were left with the sense of feelings unshared. But this time, the scales were unequal. Gavin no longer had any emotional need that would be satisfied by her, and she had so much emotional need he couldn't cope with it. And honestly, did he really want to become involved with whatever was to blame for the lack of uplift in her voice?

"Mom, I need your help," Danny cried into the phone. "Something may be wrong with one of the babies. Maryann needs a specialist. They have one at the hospital in Cedar Rapids.

"She's been seeing Doc Miller in town, but all he can tell is that one of the heartbeats isn't as strong as it should be. And two days ago, Grandma broke her ankle falling down the porch steps, and Grandpa's hearing is gone in one ear, and I'm trying to get help with the farm so I can take Maryann to Cedar Rapids and stay with her for a while. Remember my friend Brett who helped me around here after college? Well, he got married and moved to Ohio, but he's going to see if he can break away for a while and come lend a hand. Everything's happened so fast. Thank God it's winter, and we're not bringing in a crop. But there's so much snow here. Mom, can you come?"

"Yes, honey, I'll come," she answered.

Ellie had a small part in a new play that was about to open. Their winter season was set. Hank reminded her as she stood in his office requesting time off, but if necessary, he supposed her understudy could take over.

"No problem, El. Do what you need to do."

Was Hank being understanding or indifferent? She couldn't tell. But as she looked around his office, someone's old dressing room with a three-way mirror on the vanity table and a folding screen in the corner, she realized it didn't matter. Her family needed her. As she packed her bag, she fretted over her sweet Danny. How could he manage his wife, his grandparents, the household, the farm? And now the concerning worry about his babies.

Ellie buckled her seat belt. Before the trip had even begun, she was frazzled. From its gloomy beginnings, this journey felt inauspicious, even menacing. There had been a five-hour delay because of a severe blizzard coming up from the south. In the terminal, hundreds were stretched out on the floor. Babies were wailing. Vendors had run out of food. When she finally boarded, the plane sat for two hours on the tarmac waiting for clearance to lift off. It was a bumpy flight all the way, with high winds. She had an hour's wait for a bus into town that dropped her off in front of Matt's Drugs where eighteen-inch icicles hung like daggers from the eaves over her head. She was about to go into Matt's to use the phone when Neal Bowman, a neighbor who raised hogs, came out the door.

"Neal, hey! Hi! Could you possibly drive me out to the farm? Name your price."

"Hey, there, Ellie. Good to see yuh! No price, it'd be my pleasure."

"Be right with you. Just have to call Danny and tell him the plane landed."

First, she heard the fear in her son's voice, then the relief.

Ellie climbed into Neal's frigid truck, shivering while the heat kicked in. She huddled against the seat as the snow piled up in towering drifts. If she couldn't see the road, how could Neal? As he crept along, she worried about Danny and Maryann driving to Cedar Rapids in this weather.

"No worries, Ellie, sometimes I've driven this road with my eyes shut!" he joked.

A turn off the main road, and finally Ellie saw wisps of smoke rising from the chimney. The snug white farmhouse was invisible against the storm until they were almost parked on the front porch. Tears of gratitude at arrival froze on her cheeks. Ellie stepped out of Neal's truck into a snowbank almost up to her thigh.

The house was cozy. Pat lounged in a chair with her crutches nearby. Sam was asleep in the rocker. Maryann leaned against the sink with her huge belly and eyes wide open, as if she had seen a bear. Danny came in right behind his mother, brushing off the snow and shouting, "Ma, thank heavens you're here!"

Danny's cries awakened the household. Pat reached for her crutches. Sam jumped up, adjusting his suspenders. Maryann gave a small peep, then drooped as Danny rushed to her side. Ellie, cold as a snowman, stood with her back to the fire, hoping to melt.

Danny put out leftovers of cold chicken and avocado mash and bean salad. Maryann remained on the sofa, her feet propped on an ottoman. They talked of the storm and getting to Cedar Rapids in the old pickup. Danny babbled nervously. "Mom, can you take care of Pat and Sam and also the house? Mom, are you sure you'll be okay?" And after a pause, added, "Thank goodness Neal was in town."

And Pat added, "Amen to that. I must remember to bake that man a pie."

At five in the morning, the skies were still dark. *Even the dead wake up if a ghost flies over their grave,* Ellie thought grimly as she was jolted into consciousness by the county's snow plows. Their gears were grinding and shifting, back and forth, as they cleared piles of snow high as a man's chest, now thankfully, no longer falling. Snowflakes soft as feathers blew aloft on the slightest wind, and ice crystals atop the gathering mounds glittered like crushed diamonds under the outdoor lights.

Danny and Maryann's door was ajar. Ellie tread lightly down the stairs. The young couple was anxiously sitting in the kitchen waiting for the plows to finish up. A suitcase stood near the door. Suddenly, the plows were quiet, and Danny stood to gather their coats. The three looked nervously at one another as if the hush would invite the spirit of good or the spirit of evil; they knew not which, to fill the void.

Danny hugged his mother, whispering, "I'll call when we get there."

Maryann leaned into him, and Ellie watched as they walked cautiously down the narrow path.

Danny looks like a young boy, his mother thought, *too young for such crushing responsibilities.*

She sat at the timbered table recalling how many meals she had shared with her family in this room. She thought of the play she directed in which the dying young mother gave away her daughter to a whore. *That writer could probably write up a similarly compelling drama on events occurring right this minute in this very kitchen,* she thought. Sighing, she got up and peeked out the window. Fading tire tracks from Danny's car were all she could see in a world as pristine as the day it was created. Ellie said a prayer that they would reach the hospital safely. Should she call Hank to tell him she had arrived in Iowa? Likely his mind was on other things. He might even have forgotten her. No. She would put aside for now the issue of dealing with Hank. First, she would refresh the fire, start the coffee, wash last night's dishes, put on some clothes.

And call Gavin.

"No, Gavin, don't come. The weather is terrible. I'm here, and Danny just called to say the drive took two extra hours, but they're finally at the hospital and getting Maryann settled. I'll keep in touch." Then almost bashfully, she added, "Gavin, we could be grandparents soon."

Gavin called the hospital in Cedar Rapids and located his son. "Danny, are you both all right? Should I speak with the doctor?"

"No, Dad, we're good now that Mom is here. The neonatologist keeps looking in on Maryann, and they found me a room for out-of-town relatives. I'll be here a week, at most, ten days. Check at the house for messages."

As Gavin hung up, he thought, *As long as children are alive, they need their parents.* He was here for Jack. Now Ellie was there for Danny. But what would happen with her work in Boston? Wasn't she scheduled to open in a new show? Despite what they both said, should he fly out?

Jack called.

"I'm coming, Mom. Don't argue."

Ellie was glad. In truth, it would be onerous to manage both the house and her parents, and she wasn't eager to worry all by herself. Besides, Jack could at least feed the animals and read aloud to Pat in the afternoons.

Jack arrived late that night. He swept into the kitchen like a young Hercules and immediately took over the heavy chores, even carrying his grandmother upstairs. He looked strong, and Ellie was grateful that Gavin brought him out of his troubles.

Right away, life settled into a routine of relentless tasks. Ellie had forgotten the energy required for such continuous chores. The meals alone were an unspeakable burden. It had been years since she made a small meal for herself. When Ellie finally fell into sleep after a long day, she was too tired even to dream.

Danny called daily. Gavin called right after for the updates. Ellie gave the report.

"Maryann is resting."

"Maryann is having contractions"

"Maryann is in full labor."

"Maryann just delivered two babies, a girl and a boy. They named the girl Emma; the boy, Ethan. Emma's doing fine, but little Ethan is having a rapid heartbeat and rapid breathing. The doctors are concerned."

"Something is wrong with Ethan's heart. It's a possible risk that can arise with twins," said the specialist. "The problem might go away as he grows. If not, there is a surgeon in Chicago who would handle his case. Amazing procedures exist these days for pediatric heart surgery. Meanwhile, we'd like to keep Ethan in the hospital at least another week until he's a bit stronger."

Finally, the doctors said, "Ethan has gained a pound. We think he's stable enough to take home. Make sure he sees your local doc every two weeks for two months. Then come see us."

So Danny and Maryann, Emma and Ethan made the long drive home. They had left the house as a pair and returned as a family.

When they walked in the house, each baby swaddled up tight against the cold, you would think the Lord himself made his entrance. Pat's eyes were glistening as she reached out her arms. Sam held out his, and for an hour, all was quiet as the babies slept in loving arms. Jack entered quietly and peered with wonder into their tiny faces. Ellie sat unnoticed, trying to absorb this epic new reality that two gorgeous lives had been brought into this world and that one would flourish and the other would thrive only by God's grace.

Gavin should see this, she thought to herself.

When asleep, both babies looked the same but for a pink cap and a blue cap. But when they woke up, you could tell. Emma howled for her bottle. Ethan mewled like a kitten.

Everything had changed but not as they had expected. Fear and joy stewed in the same pot. Maryann cried often, worried about her little boy and not feeling the power of God to make him as strong as his sister. Danny was plumb worn-out worrying how he could manage the care of the farm, his fearful wife, and now two babies - one prospering, as expected, the other, not.

They all knew there would be a pretty big ruckus with one newborn, but two turned their snug little farmhouse into cluttered chaos. Piled around the kitchen were bottles of formula, lotion, moisturizer, containers of cotton balls, baby powder, towelettes. Jammies and diapers were stacked on the dryer. In the corners, there were two portable cribs. In the pantry, a double stroller was kept ready, waiting for a clear day. Everyone but Pat and Sam took turns for night feedings - even Jack, who got the hang of things under his sister-in-law's instruction. Folks were running into one another on the stairs and in the kitchen as they scrambled in vain to make order out of the mayhem. When Danny and Maryann complained how many arms were needed for the twins' care, the older folks clucked and murmured, "Don't we know!"

In two weeks, Maryann and Danny took Ethan to see old Doc Miller. He read closely the notes from Dr. Matthews in Cedar Rapids. Then he leaned over the babies and listened long and hard with his stethoscope.

"Ethan's holding his own," he finally said. "Let's see him again in two weeks like Dr. Matthews recommended."

As they walked out of the office, Doc Miller's words echoed in the fluttering of their hearts. "He's holding his own." *And* how long *would he be able to* hold his own? they wondered. Those words seemed temporary, gratuitous. They each had that same thought but were fearful of saying it out loud. And so they left in silence.

Pat was now out of her cast and able to prepare the meals. Sam's sciatica was acting up, but he still accompanied Danny to the barn and helped scatter the feed. Danny's friend Brett was due any day, and together, they would manage the most burdensome tasks - repairing the paddock; mending the roof, the barn beams; remaking the porch steps, which had tripped up Pat. Jack, already in Iowa for three weeks, was readying to leave. He had tickets to fly to Boston. Ryan was waiting. Besides, too many bodies in a small house were causing ungodly havoc. One could hardly move from stove to sink.

In this way, weeks turned into months.

How much longer will my presence be needed here? Ellie wondered.

Maryann was holding herself together but barely. She had taken scrupulous care of her body during her pregnancy, but after all, as the mother, how could she not blame herself for Ethan's precarious condition? She had come to depend on the emotional support of her mother-in-law. Gavin now called every few days. It was decided that he would visit after the winter.

Meanwhile, Hank had not called Ellie to check on when she would return.

Danny and Maryann took Ethan regularly to see Doc Miller. He was eating and breathing with less vigor than his sister, but enough to develop in an acceptable fashion. "Holding his own," they were repeatedly told. The parents prepared to make the drive to Cedar Rapids. Winter was lifting, and Ellie would accompany them.

It was a quiet trip, both babies asleep and Danny driving carefully. After an easy turn off the highway, the large brick building appeared, and the nurses came running. They made a big fuss and cried how glad they were to see the children. Nurse Nancy cooed over Emma. Nurse Christy held Ethan, kissed his fingers. Everyone exclaimed how much the twins had grown and how well they looked.

Dr. Matthews appeared.

"Don't the babies look delicious!" the pediatrician remarked as Nurse Nancy undressed them. She began asking questions. Maryann would answer. Danny would elaborate. Ellie kept quiet. Stethoscopes were placed; babies were turned; legs were lifted; backs were tapped.

"Emma is doing just fine. She's gained four pounds. Ethan has gained two. Not as much as *we'd* like, but still, *we're* moving ahead. I'm going to add a supplement to his formula, but otherwise, just keep on as you are doing. We'll see you again in a few months."

Maryann wondered why doctors always said *we* in regard to their patients. Her OB did the same annoying thing.

"How are *we* today?"

"How is *our* weight today?"

For heaven's sake, it was not *we* but *I* and *me*. After all, the doctor wasn't pregnant; the doctor's baby didn't have a heart defect.

"It's too early to accurately predict how Ethan will progress," Dr. Matthews was saying. "He could possibly need surgery in the future. But he may not. He may just always be a little less active than his sister, but still live a good life."

As she turned to leave, she added, laughing. "Don't you have an artist or two in the family? It might be a good idea to put a brush in his hand rather than a soccer ball!"

On their way to the car, Danny and Maryann exchanged glances of hope and despair, but fear of calling down the evil eye restrained them from commenting on the fact that the doctor spoke of a future for Ethan, and rather nonchalantly at that.

In the spring, wildflowers covered the hills and fields.

For the rhythm and sound as well as for the instruction, Ellie sang out the names of the flowers as she pushed the twins in their stroller. "See the spiky purple prairie clover? The bright orange butterfly milkweed? There's the lemon mint and prairie sage! Isn't it all just so pretty? Oh, look, white wild indigo and gray-headed cornflower!"

Ellie loved to name things.

Gavin called. He was sorry, but he would have to postpone his trip for a couple of months. The lady in Fiesole who bought his cloud painting had commissioned him to paint a mural on the walls of her indoor conservatory. It must be completed for the garden tour in two months. Wasn't that simply grand? He'd have to work every minute to make the deadline.

"And oh, how are my beautiful grandbabies?"

Despite his eagerness to see the twins, a mural for Elena Ricci whose splendid soirees attracted the intelligentsia and the powerful, the talented poor and anyone of merit would enhance his career in an incalculable way. This was by far the most involving and important work he had ever undertaken. As soon as he finished the call, he turned to his preliminary sketches spread out over the floor.

Now they made the trip to Doc Miller every month rather than every two weeks, and the trip to Cedar Rapids every three months. Maryann could look at her babies and know almost exactly what the doctor would say. Hadn't she observed their progress in the most minute detail - the day Emma opened her eyes and looked directly at her mother; the day, three weeks later, when Ethan did the same; the minute Emma rolled over onto her tummy and back again; then when Ethan did the same, four weeks after that. Yet they still lived for Dr. Matthews's examination. They anticipated the visit with a prayer and hoped for a blessing on leaving. As expected, Emma was right on track. Ethan wasn't as swift, but he was running his own good race, and everyone hoped that was good enough.

Pat was suddenly beset with aging difficulties - arthritis in her hands, neuropathy in her toes. There was mending to do and laundry. And Sam now sitting mostly in the kitchen, reading the paper or doing a crossword, right in the middle of things.

Ellie called Hank weeks ago and told him she was uncertain when she would return.

"Okay, El. No worries. We're doing fine," he barked into the phone.

If his intent was to comfort, thought Ellie, *he had failed.* He spoke through a scrim of detachment, with a take-it-or-leave-it attitude in regard to her coming back. If this was to be her future, a growing indifference from those in whom she put her trust, she was not enticed. Occasionally, she missed the lively milieu of the young students, the showy exuberance of the Emerald Necklace. Life on the farm could hardly compare to the vital culture of Boston, yet she felt no strong inclination to make her way back. So how would she resolve this haunting restlessness?

First off, she would go into town and ask Lou at Matt's Drugs if he knew someone Danny could hire as a part-time helper. With the burden lifted from Maryann, she would reassess.

On a sunny spring morning, as Ellie was potting geraniums on the porch, a car turned off the highway and sailed on down the lane toward her. A navy Chevy sedan churned up dust. A man and a woman, in their forties she would guess, got out. Both were neatly dressed in pants suits - his gray, hers blue. The woman was wearing low heels. They looked like a matched pair. Did she know them? They smiled, extended their hands.

"Ms. Taylor, the actress! We're so pleased to meet you!"

Ellie wiped her messy hands on her apron. Her hair, in need of a wash, was pulled back with a ribbon. She wore old boots usually saved for the fields.

"We're from the repertory company over in Tylersville. Do you remember when you played Shakespeare's Claudia from *King Lear* there? Oh, many years ago now?"

Yes, she remembered.

"Come in, please," she offered, trying to recall if the babies were upstairs or asleep in their porta cribs in the kitchen, if the breakfast dishes had been washed, if Sam was sitting at the table in his undershirt and suspenders. She pulled off her boots, undid her apron, and like a queen, breezed through the cluttered but thankfully empty kitchen. Settling her guests in the living room, she then took the wing chair in the corner, crossed her ankles, folded her hands in her lap, and waited.

"This is Jim Rodman. I'm Linda Moore," the woman said. "Now as we started to say, we both saw your performance of Claudia from *King Lear*, when we were much younger, of course. Since your appearance, and it's been a few years, naturally, the company has maintained its high standards, but to be honest, it has not expanded the way we had hoped. So the board is looking to infuse it with a jolt of excellence, to bring it up a notch. When we heard you were back in Iowa, an actress of your caliber, we decided to make a call and see what your plans were."

And then Linda stopped, glancing at Jim. Had she said too much? She tended to be chatty.

"We are looking for a director," the man Jim said.

How would Ellie play this role in faded jeans and bare feet, her hair askew? And now Emma beginning to wake up whimpering small sounds that would soon become a hungry howl. Running through her mind was the notion that fate more than once had its part in determining her future. Was this proposition a timely intervention just as she was experiencing this implacable inner turmoil? If she said yes to their proposal, she would become the director of a regional theater, living nearby her family. She had no doubt she could whip the company up a few notches from being a mediocre venue to a superior operation. She had maintained her contacts with Chicago and now wondered if they could serve her in some way.

The director of a regional theater. She recrossed her legs, looked out the window - no robins but a bright blue sky.

"Would you be willing to direct a few plays for us?" Linda asked.

Ellie uncrossed her ankles, leaning forward as if listening intently, hesitating, leaving them briefly in suspense.

"Would I be able to choose the plays?" she finally asked.

Linda and Jim exchanged glances.

"Well, perhaps with the approval of the board, of course," Jim answered. "They're a reasonable bunch. I'm sure that won't present a problem."

"Would I be able to act myself from time to time?"

"Why don't we see how things are going first. Nothing is impossible."

Ellie's mind crossed several thresholds - a steady job, a reliable income, a position of authority, the possibility of acting as well as directing and choosing classic plays like *Our Town* that would attract older folks, yet adding a few with offbeat theatrics that would bring in the younger crowd.

Did the company have sufficient funds for props, special effects, staff?

As her mind tripped over these questions, her face remained composed, enigmatic. She would act aloof but not indifferent. Negotiate the conditions. They had come to her. She had the advantage.

"I assume the next step is a meeting with the board," she said.

Linda and Jim jumped up together. "Yes, of course!" How about a week from tomorrow? Would that work for you?"

"Yes, that would work just fine."

They left as they had come, extending their hands, smiling, in a spray of sand kicked up by the tires of their navy Chevy sedan.

Chapter 17

Jack called, breathless.

There was much news.

"Ryan's family has turned out to be an unexpected surprise. Wait till you hear."

Relieved, Ellie found a chair and made herself comfortable.

"First off, Ryan's family lives in Milton, a Boston suburb. His dad owns a couple of tire franchises as well as a small rental building in Cambridge. He'll rent us three small rooms for a hundred dollars a month for a year while we get started. How great is that, Mom? We already have it planned out. One room for our two desks, one for a studio, one for files and a bookkeeper. And right in Cambridge! That means half a dozen colleges nearby, plus another dozen private secondary schools. All of them will need posters and announcements. Young kids especially love our stuff.

"And Ryan has two cute sisters, especially the one who just graduated from Simmons. And guess what, Mom? She's an economics and accounting major and has agreed to work with us in the beginning. She could be a big help with figuring out the business end of things."

Ellie was smiling at his description. "Cute sisters," he had said.

"Mom, are you there?"

"Yes, sweetheart. It sounds so exciting."

"Of course, I'm sad that you're not here right now, but probably you'll come back, right? Anyway, I just want to tell you what's going on. How are the twins doing?"

"We're getting along. When you have a few minutes, I'll fill you in some other things that have come up. But nothing urgent. We'll talk again."

Ellie purposely avoided telling Jack that she would not be returning to Boston anytime soon. This call was about his news, not hers.

Dropping into one of her "thinking" moods, Ellie decided to walk out to the chicken coop or shack, as Gavin had called it. "*Shack* sounds slightly more upscale than chicken coop," he said, laughing. Purple crocuses and pink hyacinths were poking their colorful heads through the winter soil. The warm air whispered of spring. Here was the familiar row of forsythia bushes emerging into full bloom. The sight was always breathtaking and affirming. Year after year those glorious buds erupted out of sticks first thing in April as the earth was turning from gloom to glory. Right now, they were a wild, untamed eight feet high and an astounding fifty feet long; and still they kept growing.

She remembered racing out here as a little girl first thing every spring. In happy abandon, she would throw herself down on the grass and stare at the branches, willing them to come into full flower while she was watching them. At the time, Pat had told her there were many types of forsythia. This one on their property was called Meadowlark. How beautiful a name was that? Others, she said, had happy, fun names such as Magical Gold, Citrus Swizzle, Fiesta, and Sunrise. She thumbed through the encyclopedia searching for Meadowlark but found something else instead. A bird called a Meadowlark. She said it out loud, "Meadowlark," and thought it sounded like the beginning of a poem.

> ***Meadowlark*** - *"a melodious songbird with a brown or black back and bright yellow underbelly." Unlike other birds who only sing when perched, the meadowlark sings while flying.*

Imagine, a bird with a yellow throat singing and flying all at once! From then on, Ellie recalled, *I kept looking for meadowlarks. Sometimes I would spot one, but they were so far up in the sky, I couldn't hear anything. I even climbed a tree once to get higher to their sounds, but the thick branches dulled any singing I might have heard.* The encyclopedia said even more:

> *That the meadowlark symbolized cheerfulness, that we are obligated to find joy in our lives. Also, it represented abundance and impending harvest.*

How wonderful that a small bird is looking after my happiness. She went to bed that night wondering what kind of song meadowlarks actually sang. The book didn't tell her that.

Ever since Ellie read that, she vowed she would never forget to chase that song.

All this Ellie remembered as the sun came out, and she pulled Gavin's decrepit chair from the shack and looked around. Yes, shears still remained in place on the top shelf. Before she left, she would cut down armfuls of golden branches to fill pitchers for every room in the house.

Jack had sounded eager and optimistic, Ellie thought as she moved her chair to face the forsythia. That lift to his voice was reassuring. Gavin had trained him well, and now he would put his skills to work on his own behalf. Jack had a purposeful plan and a friend with whom to share his journey. Who knew where this step would take them? The beginning was in their favor.

And there was Jack's incipient fondness for Ryan's sister. Did he say her name? Was it Caitlin? The way he said it rang with sweetness. And then his offhand mentioning that he tried to call her "cat," and she had playfully swatted his arm.

In a way, it's similar to my own start, Ellie thought, *a comfortable job, a settling in, until one day, circumstances intervened and the agent from Chicago showed up with a proposition I couldn't refuse.*

And in doing so, she freed Gavin.

And in being healed by Gavin and taking the initiative, Jack made his own future and freed himself.

Ellie mused how easily people could pass by an apparent opportunity, giving it little regard from fear of failure or from not recognizing its potential, from minimizing possibility. But whether out of personal passion or an elusive dream, we three refused to let our special moment slip by even though, in truth, none of us could help ourselves.

"Do one scary thing every day." Someone famous had said that; who?

She understood why others failed to advance, remained stuck in place. Scary often presents as dangerous, not challenging, and playing safe is almost always the easier decision to take. But her family always chose the *scary thing*, even though she and Gavin paid the price of losing each other. Ellie sighed. Sometimes a loss was beyond recall. Still, they would choose the same way again. And Gavin made the most dramatic leap of all, flying thousands of miles away to another continent, to a country in which he was a stranger. Because he made a plan and hoped that this change was where he would make his mark.

Ellie watched Blackie slowly drag himself around the paddock. He was old now. Pat and Sam had him sire a young foal with Neal Bowman's mare Grace. Their offspring, who Danny named Sugar because he had white spots scattered over his nose, had grown into the spirited creature beside him, nudging his father, wanting to play.

And she was about to become a theater director.

Life turns and turns, but one thing is for sure. This family did not ignore clues for favorable prospects. Ellie was proud of that familial quality. Even Danny too focused on his own dream, to run the farm, marry, and have babies.

Gavin was coming at last. Ellie picked up the shears, snipping and plucking, anticipating how cheerful the forsythia branches would look around the house. A nice welcome for Gavin. As she was finishing up, she thought about her old friend Lucy who particularly loved the flowers of spring. Had she married again? Was she living in the area? Ellie had long grown thankful that Lucy encouraged Gavin when he was most needy. She did for him what his own wife had not, brought him into his true self.

Slowly and thoughtfully, she walked home, her arms full of yellow flowers.

Is Lucy still around? she wondered.

Ellie was considering her options. Should she wear jeans or a skirt? Which would give her an authoritative air yet not be so lofty for a modest town in Iowa? *This is not Manhattan,* she reminded herself. The recruiter Linda was dressed in a tailored pantsuit. Had Ellie ever owned such a garment? She was sure she hadn't, not her style. Jeans - she decided finally - her good pair of black jeans, a long gray silk tunic blouse, and a scarf in a turquoise and mauve print that she wrapped twice around her neck. *There,* she thought, *a bit of Iowa and a bit of Manhattan. That seemed right with the black Capezio flats.*

She was shown into an informal conference room where a long table composed of an old barn door was thrown over a pair of sawhorses. *Homey but not tacky. Appropriate,* Ellie thought. She was reassured that these folks might be amenable to unorthodox suggestions. Posters from previous shows adorned the walls. *Jack's work is much more creative,* she thought. *Maybe I can have him send them some samples.*

"Ellie, so good to see you again," said this one and that one. A half dozen men and women were each standing in turn, holding out his or her hand. Their faces were vaguely familiar but not definitively so.

"So good to see you as well!" she replied enthusiastically.

Jim Rodman, the recruiter, spoke.

"Ms. Taylor, may we call you Ellie? We're in need of a director. Peter Kahn, our local dentist and an amateur writer occasionally composes short pieces for our group. He saw your play about the dying whore when he was attending a medical conference, in Boston, as I recall. Anyway, he hasn't stopped talking about it since.

"On his recommendation, you may be just what this place needs. It's our good fortune that you came back home. Oh, and congratulations to your family on the birth of twins! We hope that won't keep you from finding time for us."

"Would any acting for myself be possible?" Ellie asked for the second time in a week.

"Why don't we see how things move along first?" Jim answered, the same reply as before. "We don't see why not, but we want to get the company in good shape first. What do you say?"

Ellie paused, as if she were seriously weighing her decision. But, in fact, she had already made up her mind and couldn't wait to get started.

"I accept," she replied, "and I'll give it my best shot."

They all stood, congratulating each other, as Linda took Ellie's elbow and guided her out to the front of the house where the actors were assembled, waiting to meet their new director.

On her way home, Ellie stopped at Matt's Drugs. If you wanted the latest gossip, Matt's was surely the place to find it. Folks lingered on stools at the soda fountain in back until, sooner or later, the counterman Lou would fill you in.

"Lucy Gordon? She was a good friend of yours at one time, wasn't she? Her last name is Powell now. Married this guy Marty who's a crane operator over at Western Equipment."

"She lives a couple of miles outta town where the highway turns off at Nathan's Produce. You know the spot?"

"What about this Marty fellow?"

"Well, he comes in early every morning before his shift starts, close to seven o'clock. He likes the cinnamon doughnuts. He had a kid before marrying Lucy, and then they had two of their own. After her bad divorce way back, she didn't seem like the marrying kind, but I guess he got her to change her mind. She's got her hands full, that girl."

Ellie decided to just spontaneously stop in. If she called ahead, Lucy would likely feel obliged to wash her hair, put on pressed slacks, apply full makeup. Why should she make her bother? Ellie had seen her a dozen times without help from cosmetics.

As soon as she drove into the yard and saw Lucy, she knew she had made a mistake. She had forgotten her old friend's vanity, always the one with shiny hair and neat clothes. And here she was, her house in the middle of nowhere, rosebushes dying by the front door, down on her knees by the kitchen steps putting in seeds for green beans and carrots. Daring Lucy had previously welcomed any outlandish challenge, but at this vulnerable moment, two former friends meeting again with a man shared between them, she might not have been pleased to be caught wearing old jeans and getting her fingernails dirty and Ellie with mascara and blush and lip gloss, having just come from her interview.

If it were possible, Ellie would have turned the car around, but once you made the turn at *Nathan's*, you were on Lucy's property. And if you happened to be working outside, why, you were stuck with an unannounced visitor. Ellie quickly snatched off her silk scarf, half-tucked in her shirt to make herself look a bit unkempt.

Lucy rose, shaded her eyes against the sun.

"Well, I'll be!" she cried. "Look what we have here. The big city actress come back to the farm. What the heck are you doing here, girl?"

In the kitchen, Lucy kicked aside three pairs of boots, two pairs of work gloves, a weary cowboy hat. While she placed unwashed glasses in the sink, Ellie looked around. The boots were a substantial men's size. Of course! With Danny and Jack in their twenties, her boys would at least be teenagers. On the windows were white lace curtains edged with pale-blue smocking. They could use a good wash and an iron, but would do. A clock on the wall was slow by half an hour, the battery likely needing to be replaced. A scruffy dishtowel was tossed across the counter. On the walls? A few crayon drawings by a child dated ten years earlier, hung with scotch tape.

They started right in, just the same as in school when they walked the halls arm in arm, sharing gossip.

"Tell me about New York."

"Tell me about this guy you married."

"I read in the papers about Gavin's paintings. How great!"

"You have a couple of kids?"

"Excuse the way I look. Did I expect a celebrity to drop in?"

"Puleeeze, I've been a nanny for months."

Lucy brought down a bottle of wine, and they laughed and told stories, and Ellie found out that Lucy married Marty because she got pregnant and thought it was time she had a baby. Lucy found out that Ellie didn't really miss acting so much and was excited about being a director. Lucy said that Marty had a kid from an earlier marriage, and the kid was okay - his name was Caleb - but with her two boys, it was a heckuva life, and she missed having a girlfriend. Ellie remarked that she wanted to start dating again, and Lucy kidded that she'd love to go out with some handsome actor, even a farmer, if he had blue eyes! And Ellie said, well, she couldn't get her a date, but maybe she *could* give her a small part in one of the plays, and did she think she could act? And never mind; she was such a dramatic character herself she would do just fine.

Ellie looked at her watch. Suppertime. Maryann would need help. She hugged Lucy, her best friend, all over again and scooted out the door before she had a chance to meet any of the men in Lucy's life.

"How you doing, Jack?" Gavin asked his son on the phone. "How's Boston treating you?"

"Great, Dad, just great. We have a neat little setup. And we got our first commission! Our office has two windows facing the street, and Caitlin, she's Ryan's sister, had the idea of attaching posters to the glass. So guess what? Two older guys came in and asked if we would design something for their event to distribute around town. They're from Rotary. Did you ever hear of Rotary? An organization devoted to social and humanitarian issues. They're having a fundraiser for underprivileged kids. Our posters should be a hit. I tell you, kids love us.

"Dad, when are you coming for a visit? Time to see the twins and all, and you could stop here first."

Astonished, Elena Riccci stood in the center of her elegant glass pavilion just outside Florence on a sunny afternoon and thought the room was on fire. Adjacent to the whiteness of her living room and its cloud painting, she felt as if she had walked into a fiery blast. The two rooms comprised entirely different passions of heat and serenity, and yet, somehow, they worked together, creating a mysterious, abiding sense of beauty and unfolding. *So astonishingly unalike,* she thought, *how did Gavin create this compatible dual effect?* She sat in the green swivel chair pushing and turning, her eyes probing and disbelieving until she felt she had encircled the earth, while Gavin stood quietly in the corner.

"It feels like a paradise, *un paradiso*, of earthly delights," she said to Gavin.

It was the only way she could begin to describe this room in ordinary words.

Gavin's spectacular mural developed from fearless swaths of deep purples, reds, pinks, whites, done with extra wide brushes. Elena had given him permission to furnish the room with plants and clustered strategically were flowers reflecting the colors in the mural - red gloxinias with white ruffled edges, amaryllis the color of claret wine, a few butterfly plants with burgundy-striped leaves. All these rested beneath four tall Madagascar palm trees, one in each corner, with white flowers atop their crowns. There were two sixteen-foot-high walls of mullioned glass. The other two were solid, painted by Gavin. All sides reached to a vaulted glass ceiling, the entire room shimmering with radiant light. "A purple, red, and pink sensation," professors at the university would enthuse, standing at their podiums, lecturing students about the complexities and nobility of modern art, writing of Gavin's mural in the newspapers as the exemplar of this style. *Yes, an unforgettable sight,* Ms. Ricci realized, *and right here in my own home.* She turned to Gavin with tears in her eyes.

"How did you do this? I don't understand, but I'm transported to…where, Gavin? Can you tell me?"

Gavin smiled. He had no idea to what fantasy she had been carried, but his intent was to create her dream.

"Wherever you are, Elena, is up to you, but I'm so pleased I've sent you there," he replied.

On the day Elena Ricci hosted the garden tour, it was another one of those perfect Italian days. Bright and warm, the air so delicious you could almost wrap it around your shoulders. As the guests gaped and gawked, even her friends were jealous at the praise and notoriety now heaped upon her.

They tried to be generous.

"Such an insightful woman, our Elena, so prescient, so forward-looking, and courageous. Imagine, having such a daring work painted on her own walls! How did she ever *think* of it?"

Gallery owners tried to lure Gavin from Sofia's Place with generous offers. Requests arrived for other mural commissions - one for a palazzo owner's expansive wine cellar, belonging to a Signor Stefano Amato. Another from a Venetian nobleman, a Signor Andrea Carraro, who had built a contemporary wing onto his grand residence - and wouldn't a mural by Mr. Taylor look *fantastico* as one entered the astonishing new structure, as Signor Carraro wrote to Gavin in his letter of request.

Not used to a crowd brushing against him with glory and acclaim, Gavin was ready after only an hour to return to his little cottage. On leaving, he passed a gilt mirror in Ms. Ricci's grand foyer and glanced at his image. A little grayer, but so far, his hair was still thick and curly. And due to his days of solitude, he remained lean despite the occasional splurge at Francesco's. Thinking of Jack, Gavin had bought a tailored black jacket with a Nehru collar and decided it would be just the right garment for this special day. And in deference to his beloved Danny, he wore black jeans and a white T-shirt under the jacket. *There,* he thought, looking at himself, *both my boys are with me on this remarkable day.*

As he walked home to his quarters on the hill, he thought of the various projects proffered. Should he accept the mural proposals? Enticing propositions, but did he want to live in Venice for a month or longer? Was his life moving too fast? The Ricci project had taken him away from painting individual canvases. Did it matter? Wasn't his goal simply to paint?

Gavin took deep breaths as he climbed higher up the mountain. All were astonishing choices, but needing a break, and this being an opportune time to pause, he would go to Iowa and meet his grandchildren.

He was greeted at Logan Airport in Boston by Jack, Ryan, and Caitlin. Looking at their sparkling faces, he experienced a wave of - was it regret or anxiety? - at their high-spirited energy. He felt old! He didn't feel that way with his Italian friends. But here? He would count numbers and pounds and wrinkles. *And why is that?* he pondered, as the cheerful group scooped him up.

On the short drive to their office in Cambridge, they passed one famous sight after another, pressing together like gifts waiting to be unwrapped.

Ryan narrated.

"That's the Charles River. There, right now Boston University's varsity crew is rowing. An eight-man boat today. See the school insignia on their shell? There's MIT, and a little way off is Harvard. Quick, quick, turn to the right! See the golden dome of the State House? Mass. General Hospital is right near there."

Gavin quickly became aware that this was no ordinary tour. This is where Ellie had lived. She knew well the sights Ryan was describing. By the look of it, Boston seemed a thrilling place, a hefty amount of cultural power compressed into a relatively small geographical area. One could walk from one end to the other. She hadn't told him about any of this. Hardly had he thought about her life outside her work. Most of their talk had been about the theater, company gossip. He had assumed she was closeted most of the day, returning to her dorm in the evening tired and hungry. Yet she had grown dissatisfied with living here. Perhaps tomorrow, Jack would accompany him to the theater district for a look-around.

On the opaque glass door, the name TheJackRyanStudios was painted in chartreuse green and copper by one of the boys, or both, with a great flourish of contemporary lettering. The first letters of each word - *T*, *J*, *R*, *S* - were huge, curling like a snail; the others, smaller, fit snugly inside.

"This is our office and studio," Jack said proudly. "My drawing table, and Ryan's. Caitlin's desk, the window where she taped the posters. A bathroom down the hall, drawing supplies against the wall, and a gift from Ryan's dad - that wide file cabinet to lay our drawings out flat."

There were computers and screens and 3D printers and other digital devices of which Gavin had no knowledge and no use. It was a state-of-the art, contemporary workshop. In this room belonging to his son, he felt embarrassed, a relic with outdated artistic notions. He had to remind himself he had just successfully painted a sensational mural that astounded art critics everywhere.

On the walls were samples of work the boys had done in Chicago, half-finished screens for ongoing projects, sketches for samples to be distributed. Gavin was taken back to the day when he had boarded the bus to Florence with those small canvases on his back, hopeful and almost defeated until Sofia opened her doors. That backpack he had carried now seemed a paltry thing beside the sheer possibility of momentum and monumentality here. Gavin could turn out one or two paintings a month that a limited number of people would view, but Jack could produce thousands of any one particular image. If it was of someone like Pink Floyd, even millions could view it, buy it.

Gavin studied the wall illustrations, calculating how Jack conceived of such imaginative projects.

"I'll be sure that our signature - TheJackRyanStudios - now at the bottom, will be visible," Jack explained. "Or maybe instead of our signature at the bottom, what do you think of this, Dad? Go with TheJackRyanStudios across the top, in big letters, like the movie studio *MGM* or a Broadway theater like *Gershwin Theater*." They were thinking about it - dare they?

Gavin knew that a photo reproduction could be made of any of his paintings. Printing companies had been doing that for years. He particularly remembered Van Gogh's *Sunflowers* from his childhood. But to him, it was just so much common paper. He had never liked the whole concept, that a great work of art could be copied and reduced to a flat sheet of paper with no life, no energy. Often, the colors were way off, the dimensions made to conform to poster size. No, he would never allow that. He was content with selling his paintings directly to clients with whom he became acquainted, viewing where his paintings would hang, often consulted as to where that should be. Anyone who bought a Gavin Taylor painting always asked him to dinner.

"And here's the presentation book we're compiling to show potential customers," Jack continued. "We just started it, and…hey, Dad" - sensing his father's attention about to stray - "enough about us. Why don't we have some lunch now? It's about a mile to Harvard Square, but it's an interesting walk. There are a zillion great cafés along the way. Are you interested in seeing the Fogg Museum or the Graduate School of Design? We can stop in."

On his third morning, the day before he was to leave for Iowa, Gavin and Jack took the trolley down to the theater district and got off halfway there. Gavin wanted to walk along the Emerald Necklace and see the beautiful Victorian and Edwardian townhouses along Commonwealth Avenue. As they strolled through the famous Boston Common, a huge civic park, the oldest in the country, Gavin was amused, realizing that in Italy, he was the guide, but here he was the tourist with Jack as the pilot. Eventually, they found their way to Ellie's old company theater with its facade of weatherworn brick, curlicue ornament, and peeling gold leaf. Old Otto with his toothless grin was reluctant to let them pass until Jack said, "Ellie Taylor is my mother," and he then smiled widely, pointing the way to where Hank was standing center stage, holding a script.

A harness was wrapped around the waist of a young girl, and red and blue lights were pulsating from above the third balcony. Clearly, they were disrupting him. Clearly, he was ill-disposed, the cable on the harness giving the propman some trouble.

"Yes, yes, yes," Hank started. "I'm Hank, and you're Ellie's family. How's the old girl doing? It seems we've lost touch. Tell her to give me a ring when she has a chance," waving them off into the dark rows of empty seating.

Jack and Gavin backed off. Had they expected a grieving Hank pleading for Ellie's return?

Looking around, Gavin didn't notice anything particularly noteworthy. Just an aging theater with charming architectural motifs in need of sprucing up. This was Ellie's dream? Here, in this very spot where the only thing to consider were those pages in her hand?

Perhaps at one time but apparently not anymore.

Ellie had already spent a couple of weeks with the repertory company before Danny drove out to meet his father's plane. Tylersville had built its citizens a modern new facility of glass with its white trim and black roof planted right in the center of downtown like a majestic white pelican spreading its regal black and white wings. Flashier and glitzier than the gloomy, crusty theater in Boston, even the small rehearsal rooms were awash with light. From the ceiling in the main performance center dangled enormous lighting fixtures that looked like planets orbiting the sun and were imported from Austria.

Ellie loved everything about her new position, from being the boss of the entire production to overseeing a play's most minute aspects. Hers was a broad vision - set design, music, props, actors, and almost the best part, choosing the program. No longer was her mental lens directed at one single character. She made new friends, and Lucy was nearby. Especially significant was meeting the young mayor, Jeff Richmond - everyone called him Mayor Jeff - a widower with a son and daughter about to enter college. He found the most unlikely of excuses to show up as her day was ending, always famished. And if she was hungry too, why would she like to go out to dinner?

Gavin really is coming tomorrow, Ellie thought as she pulled a tray of cinnamon coffee cakes out of the oven. She was glad. Face-to-face, she would finally know how they both regarded the future. The house was full to the attic. Where would he sleep? Too much living had separated them from being casually together. As well, the shadow of Mayor Jeff hovered nearby. What could be arranged? Ah, Pat in their bed, and she alongside on a cot. And in Pat and Sam's room, Gavin next to Sam in one of the twin beds. Yes, that would work. No one would complain.

The moment Gavin entered the kitchen, it was the whole of him that she took in. As always, he was slim and tall, not at all stooped from leaning over an easel. Nor did he yet have the need for eyeglasses even from working close to his canvases. Only a few facial lines embedded here and there - outward from the lips, the eyes, across the forehead, written across his skin from the Mediterranean sun. As her lines evolved over time and from caring for young children. She was told Gavin often painted in his garden. A lesion removed by a doctor had left a tiny scar on his chin. Creating separate new lives with experiences and challenges unknown to the other - here you had it, how Ellie and Gavin looked on that day they saw each other again. Barely fifty, those two, and not in bad shape, not at all, except for those lines. Then again, how concerned should Ellie even be about her own minor creases? Hadn't Mayor Jeff told her just the other day that she looked like a young starlet?

Still, there was an aspect to Gavin that she might call long-lived. The notion of time's passage is inescapably etched on the face and hands, and it is especially noticeable when you see someone only occasionally. Changes are clearly apparent, alterations that can be counted on, transitions that are reliable and visible.

As Gavin stood on the threshold, Ellie felt immense relief. She no longer felt drawn to him romantically, not even in that part buried deep inside that tugs and yearns. Amiable and comfortable she might say despite his keeping his hair long, curling around his neck. Perhaps wistful but nothing that could not be abolished in the face of new encounters. Likely Mayor Jeff had something to do with her attitude. But Gavin had been supportive of her as she had made her choices. How could she not feel anything other than gratitude toward him?

And Gavin regarded Ellie, still lovely, an essential part of his history, but no longer crucial to his well-being either. But since she was the beginning of his journey and the mother of his two boys, he could not feel anything but kind regards toward her. Now they had two beautiful grandchildren who belonged to them both and who they would share for the rest of their lives.

When Emma came toddling into the room, Ethan crawling behind, Gavin swept them up into his arms, examining toes, fingers, eyes. Both were pink-faced, gurgling, squealing in his loving embrace, and causing a great fuss. Gorgeous children. Perfect.

Gavin didn't think anything looked amiss. As twins, they were close in facial affect and complexion. But suddenly Emma reached for his face and giggled at his unshaven cheeks while Ethan barely lifted his hand, just stared in wonder at this new person in their midst. Emma laughed with delight at Gavin's silly sounds while Ethan merely smiled. And when he put them down, Emma took off running while Ethan dawdled behind.

Later that evening, the adults gathered before the fireplace, planning a second birthday party for the twin's first year, the one Gavin had missed for real. They were all chatting about balloons and cakes and Sam dressed as a clown when suddenly Maryann, close to tears, burst out, "The doctors are pleased that Ethan is holding his own. Dr. Matthews even talked about his future, as if he would have one."

The family stopped talking, fearful of her next words.

"She said Ethan may never need surgery, but we have to wait a few years to tell. He's likely to be physically slow all his life. But, Gavin, you won't believe what Dr. Matthews said at the end of one of our visits. I couldn't tell if she was kidding or serious. She said I should give Ethan a paintbrush instead of a soccer ball! Do you think that's a prediction of some kind?"

"What? The doctor said that?" Gavin replied. "Why?"

"Maybe she knew about you," Maryann said. "Why else? Or maybe she was looking into a crystal ball."

And as they all climbed the stairs to bed, Gavin thought, *What a peculiar thing for the doctor to say.*

Chapter 18

It's a fierce love grandparents have for their grandchildren, Gavin thought. All those who anticipate being in such a situation have been told this many times, but despite the warnings, you are completely unprepared for falling hopelessly in love. Giving yourself over fully, you immediately know that love has neither barriers nor boundaries.

Emma was at his feet, lying on her back and swinging her rag doll back and forth until it finally dropped from her hands, and she was asleep. Ethan was in Gavin's arms with his eyes closed, but still, his grandfather managed to lean down and put a pillow under his granddaughter's curly head.

His mind was working over his family's future. Ellie's new position over in Tylersville kept her out of the house all day. Danny ran the farm, more than enough work for any one man, but he was looking to hire permanent help year-round now. Jack, now settled in Boston, would be merely a long-distance uncle. *Who would help Maryann?* he pondered. Maybe Lou at Matt's Drugs knew someone who could work daytime hours. He would stop in tomorrow and ask. Ellie had mentioned something about that but said she hadn't gotten around to checking it out.

Concerning that odd comment from the doctor about Ethan picking up a paintbrush. What was her intent? She might have simply been offering a humorous, offhand comment of comfort. Or perhaps an actual, realistic suggestion for a career with little exertion. *If one must lead a still and quiet life,* Gavin thought, *one could be an accountant or a librarian, even a teacher. But to engage in the creative life, talent must be simmering, a zealous flame burning within, granted to only a few. Perhaps it was a throwaway remark, intended to amuse Ethan's parents.*

He remembered Jack's birth. His tiny fingers fluttering at the window. *Yes, an omen,* Gavin had thought. *A sign, but what kind?* Eventually, it became clear. It was in him, the drive to live in his imagination as his instincts sent him scurrying every day to his father's side. If Ethan had similar leanings, Gavin would be concerned. His parents, both farmers, might be insensitive to the needs of an artistically inclined young child.

Well, let's wait and see, Gavin thought, rocking Ethan in his arms. *Let our little tyke grow up a bit, see what he's made of.* The precious prince he was holding gave a hiccup, or a burp, or maybe a kiss in a dream, and Gavin began to whistle softly "You Are My Sunshine." Slowly, his grandson opened his eyes and gazed at his grandfather.

Gavin sat on a stool in the back of Matt's Drugs finishing up an ice cream soda. *This sure is delicious,* he thought, rummaging around in the bottom of the glass for the last drops of strawberry ice cream. He had never had a soda like this at the diner where he met Ellie. An ice cream soda was not fancy enough for a diner that aspired to higher cuisine. Peanut butter chocolate pie was its idea of a step toward the gourmet. And certainly there was nothing like it in Italy. No, this treat was pure Iowa. He sighed, turning to Lou who smiled with delight, having added an extra scoop of ice cream.

"So, Lou, what's new?" Gavin asked.

"You mean for the last dozen years what's new? Or what's new since this morning when Marty Powell stopped in for his cinnamon rolls new. You're the one with what's new, living over there in Italy with all those hot gals for so many years. You got any stories to tell me?"

"Lou, believe me. I'm not the most interesting guy. I live in a monastery and paint all day. Occasionally, I sell a painting. But I want to ask a favor. Maryann needs some help in the house now that Ellie is working over in Tylersville. Know anyone who can put in some time during the day?"

"Lemme think. Most everyone round here is doing one thing or another."

Late that afternoon, Lou called.

"Gavin, I'm sending over my niece from Red Bluffs. She's available. Been dawdling since she graduated from high school last June."

When he heard the car, Gavin looked out the window to see a childlike teenager stepping out of an old jeep. Carefully, she straightened her blouse, smoothed her skirt, and walked up the path. He opened the door to a neat young kid, smiling and relaxed. Her shiny brown hair was in a ponytail, her clothes clean and pressed. She wore saddle shoes with socks. As she put out her hand, she looked Gavin directly in the eye.

"My name is Susan," she said.

A promising start and endearing when she walked over to the cribs to peer at the twins and make small cooing noises. A half hour of small talk, and both mother and grandfather were satisfied. That settled, Gavin turned to thoughts of Ellie. Both were content to leave things as they were, and with Maryann's situation now manageable, he was free to go home.

A week after Susan's arrival, he left them all - Ellie and Maryann, Ethan and Emma, Danny, Pat and Sam - and flew back to Italy. Immediately on his return, he painted a baby gift for the twins. A lovely blend of colors that seemed designed in pairs - one part in reds and pinks, the other in greens and purples. Somewhere in the middle of the canvas, the colors blended and ran together. It was impossible to analyze as something one could understand, yet the viewer thought it was a beautiful thing with a heavenly aspect in how all the disparate colors and strokes worked together. He shipped it off as soon as the paint dried.

Sofia had now become a kind of entrepreneur for the gifted. Most evenings, she was busy hosting various soirees and receptions for her artists. The young girl who owned the candle shop next door had fled to Padua with her boyfriend, and Sofia had taken over the lease, naming the space, *Sofia's Annex*. Now there was additional space to sell the unique dresses that she herself wore, one of a kind garments for wealthy women.

The Antico Setificio Fiorentino, Florence's renowned silk factory, wove the fabrics and master seamstresses sewed them into beautiful dresses. In addition, up in the Fiesole hills, Sofia had hired three elderly women who created exquisite clothing from rare yarns and fibers on looms in their living rooms. Tommaso's cases had expanded to three, and Sofia hung a trio of his paintings above them. Her keen eye also saw an opportunity to market a product not widely produced - very small evening bags made of gorgeously dyed leathers in colors such as pink, crimson, or lime; fancy purses embellished with jewels and spangles by a gifted silversmith who had long toiled in anonymity but whose talent now saw the light. Such a bag would be held discreetly at a woman's side, a sign of affluence that a functional object could be sized so modestly. At *Sofia's Annex*, a woman of means could be outfitted for any occasion. And while they were on premises, clients were welcome to wander into the gallery next door and enjoy a glass of wine along with descriptions of the paintings by Sofia herself.

She appeared at the podiums of illustrious art schools and design ateliers in Milan and Rome, striding onstage with the glamorous cachet of a superstar. All this while Gavin happily remained by himself in his cottage, rising with the sun, rolling out of bed, and landing at his easel. The Brothers had allowed him to add a proper bedroom off the kitchen, and with that, Gavin now expected he would be a loner forever, an occupant of the cottage as long as he wished.

Still, he was not celibate. He did have a short-term affair now and then. Mia, first. But when she married, he didn't really miss her. A year later, the waitress at Francesco's. But when she returned home to Sicily, he didn't really miss her either. And there were a few others, but when the liaisons ended, none affected him deeply. He guessed that the women sensed he was not a long-term prospect and never fully relaxed into themselves. Besides, Gavin had emotional ties to his existing family, and with his many Italian friends, they completed his circle of personal need. It was enough.

Gianni and Sofia and Elena urged him to move into Florence proper.

"A flat that looks out on the domes and steeples," said Gianni.

"Gardens on the rooftops," urged Sofia.

"Along the Arno, facing the Uffizi?" asked Elena.

"No thank you," he answered. How could he paint without light and a garden, without birds on the studio roof? Or worse, live in one place and travel to a studio nearby? He had everything he needed - a mountain from which the hills and valleys seemed to go on forever.

Gavin did, however, indulge in a special pleasure - sending off monetary gifts. To Jack, for a larger studio and a second bookkeeper; to Danny for a permanent farmhand; to Maryann so Susan could live with them in the spare bedroom upstairs; even to Ellie, enabling her to rent a small house near the theater. At last, she would have the privacy befitting someone of her growing stature and a place where Mayor Jeff could visit.

"Dad?" Jack asked as Gavin picked up the phone. "I have a surprise." And then quickly said before he lost his nerve, "Caitlin and I were married yesterday. We didn't want a big wedding. You had just made a trip here, and Mom's new play was opening. A pastor friend conducted the service in a small grove of oak trees along the Charles. Dad? I hope you're not upset. At least you met Caitlin when you were here. Isn't she amazing?

"Dad?"

Gavin suddenly saw a little boy running eagerly across an open field, waving his pencils. His own inner rhythms of time's passage began churning and racing. But he quickly recouped.

"Jack, that's great. Caitlin is a delightful young woman. I send you both my deepest congratulations. And Jack? Just a word - make sure you grow together in your dreams and ambitions."

"What do you mean, Dad? We work together all the time."

"Just be sure she's happy with what she's doing and not doing it only for you."

"Our new apartment is an easy walk to the office with a view over the MIT campus. It has a renovated kitchen and bath. And there's something new that we both discovered together. Rowing!

Seriously! We've taken it up and are looking into joining a rowing club."

Gavin again lifted his brushes to pay tribute to a significant familial passage - a wedding present for his son and his bride. First, he laid down a continuous thick stripe of slate blue from left to right. Then he added swipes of green and pounces of black here and there. And in the foreground, dancing swags of red in a circle. Would they know that the strip of blue depicted the river? That those daubs of green were trees, and the random spatters of black their friends? Would they guess that the dancing swags of red were the newly married couple rejoicing in new beginnings?

With three of his paintings hanging in Sophia's gallery, Gavin now felt comfortable accepting commissions for murals that would take him off the mountain.

First was the wine cellar for the esteemed Stefano Conti. His palazzo stood almost adjacent to Giotto's revered Campanile tower and the Duomo Cathedral. As Gavin looked out the window of Signor Conti's piano nobile, the main salon on the upper floor, he was moved by the beauty of the view. Particularly alluring for the eyes of an artist were the intricate details of the Duomo, its sublime white marble facade embellished with pink, green, and red polychrome.

Somehow, he managed to pull himself away from the scene and descend into the dark recesses of a lower floor devoid of windows.

His plan was to paint directly on canvas cloth cut to the size of the walls and pinned in place. It would be directly affixed, but if need be, could be removed for portability. His eager patron offered him a suite in his mansion, but Gavin chose to live with the Brothers, invigorated by his walks to and from the site. Besides, he needed to clear his head from the wines' fruity smells embedded in the cracks of the old wooden tasting table.

The Brothers now kept a permanent room for him, a monk's cell, really, and in return, he left generous contributions on the donation plate. It suited him. He would not be tempted by Signor Conti's lavish meals nor the burden of being cordial and chatty. He was tired of being asked, "So how do you get your ideas?"

Although the wine cellar was well-lit with spotlights and sconces, still it was an underground room without natural light, moody and evocative. One would have expected Gavin to use bright colors - red like a chili pepper, yellow like lemons, blue like denim. But he chose exactly the opposite - sable like animal fur, chestnuts and rusts like decaying leaves, and deep ochre like saffron.

Sophisticated and elegant, the finished work was also highly original, devoid of the bottles and glasses usually seen when decorating such a room. Instead, there were whorls and eddies, loops and twirls, a feeling of liquids pouring and flowing. To wake up the somber palette, he added dollops of pale violet, judiciously placed. And when he unveiled his work, Gavin stood humbly with his head bowed, receiving Signor Conti's lavish praise.

While Gavin was laboring in his wine cellar, Ellie was getting dressed for opening night. She had fretted long hours over the many difficult hurdles. First, the choice of play. Should she revert to old classics like *Spoon River* or take on an oddball contemporary piece like *Kinky Boots*? There was much to consider - a Midwest audience, the limitations of the actors who were not trained singers or dancers, the budget allotted for props and scenery. An orchestra was out of the question, but a five-piece ensemble would be reasonable. Notices were placed in major state newspapers. Interviews by her or her publicity man had been conducted on local television stations. Everyone would be awaiting the results from the new director "straight from the theater worlds of Chicago and Boston." Ellie felt she had chosen well, but she knew audiences were notoriously fickle. You could never guess their reaction. If they loved you, you'd be on top of the world. If they didn't, there would be an empty house within the week.

She glanced again at the program laying on her dressing table:

The Secret Garden

Orphaned while living in India, ten-year-old Mary Lennox returns to a town in Minnesota to live with her embittered, reclusive uncle Archibald, whom she has never met. There, the ill-tempered and lonely

Mary meets Martha, Mr. Archibald's maid, who tells her of a secret garden that belonged to her aunt Lily before she died. Mary's search for the garden introduces her to a slew of other characters and a spirited robin that seems to be trying to talk to her.

The play was based on a famous novel of the same name. *I would guess many in the audience may have read it,* Ellie mused. *It was extra work, but if I do say so myself, it was clever of me to switch the locale from England to Minnesota.* The company was competent, but most weren't capable of mastering an authentic English accent. Simple props and testy behaviors, a bit of intrigue, and a stubborn older man, a troubled child, and a strong ending may well keep the audience engaged. Out of these disparate elements, a magical play would emerge, Ellie prayed.

She thought again of its major themes - a compelling tale of warring human emotions, forgiveness and redemption as well as people's cruelty toward those who are different, a theme with a sharp sting but popular with theatergoers. Courage to resist and prevail is essential, the play reveals, as is the battle to stay true to oneself. Everyone loves such titanic emotional struggles, Ellie thought. The moral, the human lesson that justifies the show, is that happiness results from thinking less about yourself and more about others. Although the ending might seem sentimental, the play isn't sappy or judgmental. Hopefully, when the curtain falls, the audience will be on its feet.

To me, a perfect work in all its aspects, Ellie decided, reaching for her shoes. As she gave her hair a final flip, she recalled the opening of her *Wizard of Oz* all those years ago when she knew so much less than now about the theater. She remembered how Gavin, to calm her nerves, had left a glass of wine next to this very hairbrush. Danny and Jack, little boys then, were dressed in their best clothes, waiting with their father to escort her to the theater. How delicious they looked, how earnest they were! Now they were all gone except for Jeff, who would be hovering in the wings. *This is a pivotal moment in my middle years,* she told herself. *The beginning of something new. Well, I love it. And I can do it. I will bring in a big hit for the Tylersville Repertory*

Company, and the directors will congratulate themselves on the wisdom of choosing me for their director.

And in reality, I'm not alone. I have a grand family, still. No one has forgotten. Hadn't everyone sent best wishes?

A telegram from Gavin: "Hey, Ms. Lady Director, go get 'em!"

A note from Danny and Maryann: "We'll be in the audience!"

A call the day before from Jack: "Hey, Mom! Guess what! I married Caitlin! I just told Dad. Cheers! Break a leg! We'll talk more tomorrow!"

And Jeff was waiting downstairs.

As Ellie moved out into the hall, she didn't know what to think about first - that Danny and Maryann would be in the audience, allowing themselves a rare night out? Or that Gavin still was mindful of her in some way. Perhaps that Jack had a successful business as well as a new wife. All good thoughts. Still, Ellie shook her head. *None of these notions are to be considered now. Focus on the evening ahead. Go out there and see about making a hit show.*

Chapter 19

It was sent by courier and brought to Gavin by one of the Brothers - a thick creamy envelope with a heraldic imprint sealing the closure.

With his name written in beautiful script, Gavin was reluctant to break the fastenings, turning it over and over, admiring the beauty of handmade paper, feeling its significant heft.

It was from the Venetian aristocrat who had previously extended to Gavin a unique commission to paint a mural in the vast lobby of a building adjoining his seventeenth-century palazzo. The space functioned as a regal setting for exhibitions of all kinds, for the arts, for events related to Venice, for anything the signor and signora deemed worthy. Change would be constant, displays rotating in and out.

Inside the envelope were photographs of the venue. But Gavin was hesitant. He had never undertaken anything of this scale.

The note attempted to persuade:

> *See how grand the site is, Signor Taylor! I give you my word not to interfere with any of your decisions. Venice is a glorious city of art and architecture. Its history is celebrated wherever you look. Oh, do come and give Venice the pleasure of your work.*

Gavin didn't reply for a week. He had reservations. Would a contemporary mural be worthy of living within such noble architecture? He thought of the Ricci and Conti projects, both executed in unusual and untried settings, both turning out superbly. But this location was far distant from his mountain. Despite the photographs, it was an architectural entity of unknown elements. Gavin wanted to stand in the center of a space before committing to its decoration.

However, the fee was princely. There was mention of a bonus upon completion. If he continued to live in his usual manner, the sum could last a lifetime. Besides, he had never traveled to Venice. Wasn't it acclaimed as one of the world's most astonishing cities?

Had he ever before turned from any artistic challenge? And so, he cautiously accepted.

The entire world knew that Venice was a city built on water, that it was composed of canals, not roads. Still, he was unprepared for the majesty of the sight when he emerged from the Venice train station. He likened it to seeing his grandchildren for the first time. Awesome. Spectacular. The scene was a ravishing blueprint that long ago had been implanted in the minds of men for the birth of a city. Upon this original plan were layered untold wealth and genius, hopes and prayers, until over the centuries, the city grew to its present eminence.

Gavin stepped into his patron's gondola and was immediately encircled by a romantic, enchanting fantasy, spun out of a thousand dreams and Venice's extraordinary maritime commerce. For hundreds of years, Venetians controlled the flow of luxury goods and spices between Asia and Europe, and Gavin now stared at the benefits reaped from such trade.

The gondolier paddled silently along the Grand Canal as Gavin looked right, left, right. Like all Italian cities, the colors were amber, gold, sienna. A glow of honey gently cloaked the palazzos with their balconies and flowerboxes, flags and porticoes and loggias—all thrusting skyward from foundations set into the water. Before each residence was a pier with *poli*, or mooring poles, used by boats for docking purposes. The tall round posts were painted with diagonal stripes whose colors represented those of the original families - aristocrats, nobility, royalty.

The boatman spoke reasonable English. Gavin had read ahead, and as they passed beneath a spectacular single-vaulted span with handsome arches marching across its length and two arcades of shops contained within, Gavin asked, "Would this be the famous Rialto Bridge? Wasn't this built in the sixteenth century, one of the finest architectural and engineering achievements of the Renaissance?"

The gondolier pounced. He loved to explain the story of Venice's beautiful bridges.

"Yes. The Rialto is the oldest, *il più antico*, of the four bridges - how you say, spanning? - yes, spanning the Grand Canal. Our lovely *Ponti di Rialto*." The boatman sighed. "*Bellissimo!* Venice has many names. Did you know? Yes? The City of Canals. The Floating City. The City of Bridges. Each bridge in Venice, some three hundred, is unique, *unica*. Oh, signor, and one hundred sixteen islands linked by one hundred fifty canals! Or one hundred seventy-seven canals, depending on how you count. And all in the lagoon between the mouths of the Po and Piave rivers.

"*Guarda qua*, look here. This one - the Bridge of Sighs over the Rio di Palazzo. See the stone bars across its windows? Inside, it has two passageways that split like scissors to reach different floors of *Il Palazzo Ducale*, or the Doge's Palace. One side goes directly into the new prison. The other goes to the interrogation rooms. Most who went in never came out. *Oh mio!*" (Oh my!)

While Gavin listened, enthralled, he saw no rolling vehicles nor heard the sound of horses' hooves or blaring horns. Only did he feel acutely the swirling waters under the pearl-laden haze that settled over the resplendent architecture. The buildings sat silently, built deep into the roiling waters upon which the city's commerce thrived. Thus it was. At all hours, the canals teemed with enterprise while the grand palazzos remained mysteriously still. The boatman - "My name is Vito," he said - wondered if he should continue. Was Gavin paying attention?

Yes, he decided. He would continue. This man had the same dreamy expression as all those others who viewed Venice for the first time.

"One of our bridges is called the *Toletta*, a small length between two very old buildings. Many of our bridges link building to building, not to public walkways. Do you know how the *Toletta* is named?

No? After *piccola tola*, a small wooden board once used as a removable bridge for the waterway underneath. Did you know there were no bridges until the tenth century? No? And then only steps up, then down, *su, poi giù*, over the water, no railings or parapets. Those weren't built till the eighteenth century. Do you know the painter Canaletto from that time? Ah, yes? A genius, a *genio*, don't you agree? Yes? Even we boatmen know this artist Canaletto. If you look at his paintings, you can see how the bridges looked in the eighteenth century."

As Vito continued to row, he turned away from the Grand Canal. Gavin reclined on pillows, indulging in the splendor of the journey. Not before him was the blocky, stolid heft of Florence but a gossamer delicacy so fragile that a child would think he had fallen into the exoticism of *The Arabian Nights* or *The Tale of Genji*, even *The Desert of Souls*. Canaletto's brush had surely captured its soul, especially how the light made the waters dance, how the ancient buildings shimmered in the song of the waves. And yet, although his paintings portrayed a serene contentment and an immortal beauty, there was another busy life behind its canals - winding waterways, cobbled courtyards, and little alleys called *calli*.

Vito himself, in the traditional gondolier's costume - black pants and black shoes, striped shirt, Vito's was blue - looked pleased as he paddled gently onward. The gondoliers were accustomed to the *turisti*, the tourists. One look, and they were bewitched. Some gondoliers wore a banded straw hat, a ribbon around the crown, but not all, not Vito. Perhaps he was too vain to cover his glossy black hair.

As Gavin sat back, he idly guessed what likely masterpieces were spread throughout these palatial rooms. A Veronese, maybe two. A Giorgione, for sure. Several. And the *boiserie*, or hand-carved paneling on the walls, rubbed with gold or silver. Ceilings painted with scenes of Venetian history. What had led Signor and Signora Carraro to think his work would have a place here? Were they mad? And how did this Signor Carraro arrange to build a glass museum in the rear of his palazzo? Surely Venice would object to such a thing. This new benefactor must be powerful indeed.

For this assignment, Gavin would have to stay in the palazzo itself.

"But not an upstairs bedroom, if you don't mind," he had requested, "something small, a servant's room."

When Vito at last paddled into Signor Carraro's *poli*, Gavin gazed up at one of the grandest palazzos on the Canal. Was it five floors? Seven? The bottom two were painted cream; the third, the most prominent with the tallest, widest windows, was painted a soft yellow. Italian flags, family flags, provincial flags flew from the balconies of this third floor. Window boxes that hung from ornate iron railings contained lavish plantings of red and white geraniums and green ivy, a patriotic display, the colors of the Italian flag.

An elegant man dressed in a tailored suit and silk tie greeted Gavin at the dock. Was he Signor Carraro himself? A business associate? A butler? The man bowed and said, "Seguimi, per favore" (Please follow me). *Ah, a butler.*

In the entrance hall, a Titian - Gavin was certain - hanging above a mahogany settee whose sides were carved with a graceful swan on both ends. Massive urns of black granite lush with white hydrangeas and ivory roses stood on stone pedestals ten feet high. Gavin was engulfed in a sumptuously adorned space in which every surface was either painted or sculpted, carved or gilded. There were marble floors in complex patterns, its stone chiseled from the quarries in the Apuan Alps. Gavin's seatmate on the train had pointed out those mines, which also sourced the marble for the great sculptors Antonio Gambello and Tullio Lombardo. He looked up at ornate ceilings that took years to paint by a dozen artists lying on their backs. On the antique walls, eighteen-foot-high tapestries woven on looms found at only a few select workshops in Europe.

Following the attendant, Gavin continued up a wide staircase whose balusters were embellished with gold gilt turnings. He entered a study with grand proportions and fittings. A man of superb style immediately stood up to a height well over six feet. Signor Andrea

Carraro. He extended his hand over a desk of inlaid marquetry edged with bronze and cried out, "*Benvenuto,* my dear Gavin Taylor! *Hai fatto un buon viaggio?* Did you have a good trip?"

At that moment of reaching across the desk and shaking hands, Gavin thought of the ramshackle chicken coop on his Iowa farm. Next, he looked down at his rumpled khaki pants. And then, after noticing a second Titian on the wall behind his patron, he was assaulted by the frightful awareness that he might not belong here.

As he had requested, he was given a spare room below the main salon. But hardly was it servant's quarters with its dove-gray paneling of swags and bows. Signor Carraro left him on his own for a few days to absorb the sense of the city and to browse through the space in which he would paint his mural.

The butler led him around the palazzo to a new building so cleverly molded into the abutting walls that he hardly noticed it. A discreet approach, not a looming structure seen from afar. The design made sense if one wanted to build something new in a city as ancient as Venice, the city fathers likely keeping a close watch. Gavin smiled to think what they would say when confronted with enormous swaths of brilliant color washed over Signor Carraro's walls. And there would be nothing restful or discreet about it.

The designated space began below ground and grew into a glass-roofed structure thrusting its way into the first level, much like I. M. Pei's Pyramid annex to the Louvre in Paris. The portions in public view did not intrude in any way on the surrounding area. In fact, they were hardly visible. Gavin's charge was to paint the entire lower area, the light from above filling the space below with a natural radiance.

Still, standing now in the vast expanse, he grew wary once again.

Did he have the verve, the flair, to pull off such a monumental project? This particular palazzo had a far reach. It was often photographed for international publications. Renowned talents, exceptional minds, and the spectacularly rich frequently visited. Ms. Ricci's commission had garnered Gavin popular acclaim, but if he were successful here, there would be major consequences such as fame, tributes, honors.

Almost immediately, Gavin made his decision.

He would paint Venezia itself, but with a stark twist - an abstract representation of the watery landscape, the bridges, palazzos. His execution would be in a style no one had seen before. Deciding that right off was a comfort, restoring his confidence.

Yet would his enduring passion be compromised? That of painting for the pure love of the act itself? His precious solitude might be invaded. So he would consciously avoid the invasion of celebrity to paint within his own context his own fancies without his patron's scrutiny or his approval. After all, it was always the unexpected that gained Gavin his devoted following.

Stop worrying, he said to himself. *Carry on. If all goes well - and why shouldn't it? - these concerns will seem foolish.*

Gavin sat in the palazzo's sunny inner courtyard, pencil and paper across his knees. Pale-pink dahlias and peonies were planted in random pockets of paving, tumbling over onto the stone paths. Soaring fig trees were placed on each side of the three entrances. After a long initial glance of admiration, Gavin looked no more. Despite the gurgling sounds of the famous fountain of Daphne, he kept his head down and began to sketch. Despite the sun's rays flashing on the water spilling from Daphne's fingers. Despite the buzz of the bumblebees happily humming around the flowers tucked around Daphne's base.

Suddenly, a shadow fell across his drawings. He looked up, his gaze rising from her expensive black leather shoes to her expensive black slacks to her expensive black sweater with royal-blue trim at the neck and cuffs. Gold hoop earrings appeared from tangles of black hair flying loosely about her head and shoulders. Finally, the face of a man's dreams emerged - olive skin, oval eyes keen to engage, moist, plush lips.

He stood quickly, scattering his papers over the dahlias, over the stones.

She laughed at the disarray. But seductively, knowing his discomfort was because of her.

"I'm Signora Carraro," she murmured in a husky, breathy song, yet bell-like, like a meadowlark. "Please call me Cecilia."

For only the second time in twenty-five years, Gavin fell madly in love.

Surging with lust, he was miserably embarrassed. He had never become instantly inflamed in this particular way from looking at a woman's shoes, slacks, face.

"I'm sorry I was not here to greet you, Signor Taylor," she murmured.

What a relief, he thought, *that she spoke first, giving me a moment to compose myself, to find the nerve to look up.*

She continued. "Welcome to Venezia. Please call me Cecilia. My husband and I are eager for you to paint the lobby of our new exhibition space. Do you foresee any problems?"

Problems? Gavin saw dozens. He hadn't yet formulated his composition and was still apprehensive of the excellence required. And now, this woman. What was he to do about her?

Cecilia. Is that what he should call her rather than Signora Carraro?

Did she love her husband?

"No problems," he offered. "I'm just now trying to work on various ideas for this spectacular space. I hope the result will please you."

"Oh, I'm sure it will," she replied. "I saw your mural for Signora Ricci's conservatory garden and could hardly find my breath. Really. *Straordinario*, extraordinary. I was taken away, *portato via*. I'm sure you will do at least as much for us here."

Then she turned and drifted off in her expensive leather shoes, so expensive they hardly made a sound.

Gavin collected his papers. He wasn't sure what had just happened. *Why did she make those comments to a stranger about not being able to catch her breath? Why didn't she just pay a simple compliment, mention that my mural for Ms. Ricci was remarkable, but without the sexual innuendo, the personal intimations? How am I to think about that?*

After examining Sofia and Ellie dispassionately for many years, he knew that women didn't always say what they meant. In fact, they rarely did. Underneath their words were layers of churning emotions that presented constant conflicts, obscure decisions. Yes or no. Now or later. Too much or too little.

In any case, it made life puzzling for men who attempted to differentiate between truth, innuendo, and flirtation.

After a week of planning, Gavin was ready to begin.

Venice was a city floating on water, so that was where he would start. Visitors walking directly into the building would feel no disruption of transition. Walls of blues and greens, darker where there is no sun, lighter and sparkling where it touches the surface. An active scene with the gondolas plying back and forth. And not recognizable as boats but as moving colors. There would be suggestions of this very palazzo with Italian flags drifting around the edges. But not painted as flags, only bands of reds and greens and whites, commingling. And a bridge, maybe two or three that would span the openings of entrance and exit. Of course, the viewer would not consciously *know* or *see* any of this. Nothing would be named or recognized. What a viewer would have were *emotions*, an *awareness*, of familiarity, but from the unique perspective of outside to inside, feeling comfortable in either space.

A small crew had set out his supplies, including ladders, brooms, and mops, the last two experimental devices that Gavin would try out. Buckets, rags, and paints waited like tools on a surgeon's tray. Floors were inlaid in a simple pattern of taupe and cream terrazzo. Not decorative enough to distract but still revealing an extravagantly costly treatment, tiny rectangular shapes inserted in corners and seams. At the moment, they were covered with heavy cloths.

Gavin had asked that no one enter the area when he was working.

"As you wish." Signor Carraro laughed, with a small bow and a wave of his hand.

As always, before he took brush to canvas, Gavin deliberated, recalling the shack in Iowa. The magical epiphany he underwent in Haley Max's general store. The transformative power of a brochure carelessly tossed on a table. The frenzied excitement with which he had raced home and painted "roiling reds." Such reflection of his humble past was like prayer. It centered him. After a moment, he put away such thoughts and turned to the task at hand. He could do this, he told himself, and do it well.

He would start with the eternal flow of water, the moving life force of the city. He scanned his tools - his usual brushes could not begin to show the truth of it. And so, like a surgeon picks up his scalpel, Gavin picked up the broom.

Just as he was about to dip into the waiting buckets of paint, a voice holding a slight quiver asked, "Signor Taylor, do you mind if I watch now and then?"

Cecilia. He was instantly annoyed. Hadn't he asked her husband that no one be admitted? He became distracted, off-balance. And her first word? His name, sexually arousing, painfully intimate.

"May I call you Gavin?"

Turning, he stared into her oval eyes.

"Signora Carraro?" he asked.

"Cecilia, please," she answered. And she asked again, "Do you mind if I stop in now and then?"

This woman and her husband are my employers, Gavin reminded himself. *How do wealthy Venetians regard this type of patronage relationship?* His mood swung from anxiety to outrage that she put him in this position, walking in here, expecting him to stop and chat, answer her questions. He would take a chance and risk her goodwill.

"Signora Carraro, *mi scusi.* Excuse me, Cecilia," he muttered, correcting his error and feeling like a peasant. She could perceive his righting her name as either a sweet mistake or a fawning attempt to fit in. After all, he was living in her house as her guest. She might think him a dumb rube sounding foolishly inauthentic. Yet despite her insistence, addressing her as Cecilia seemed inexcusably rude. It then crossed his mind that her intent was to discover how he managed, with brush and paint, *to take her breath away*.

"I would prefer to be alone," he answered. "Another's presence disturbs my concentration."

She smiled cryptically. Was she wistful? Or annoyed? He hoped he had quelled any possible anger. She turned softly and walked off, wearing another pair of expensive shoes, this time olive like her skin.

Gavin sat down and opened a thermos of coffee. He could not proceed until his heart stopped thrumming, and he dismissed those eyes and the urge to touch that tawny-toned skin born of the Mediterranean. He had to restrain himself from covering the walls with a thousand pairs of olive eyes.

His eagerness for an ambitious start had evaporated. Would it return? Or would another hire be asked to complete this assignment?

Gavin tore off his smock and left the palazzo. It seemed always to be spring here. And always the same components of life - water, flowers, bridges, stately palazzos. Gondoliers greeting fellow gondoliers. But actually, it was always seen anew as the sun shone, the water moved, the exquisite light reflected off the water's rippling peaks like handfuls of rhinestones.

He found himself under the Bridge of Sighs and looked up, knowing now that prisoners who walked across that bridge were never seen again. What could that last walk of freedom have been like, glancing out the small windows covered with bars at the luminosity of Venice?

Gavin sighed with relief. He was free, living outside those bars. Inviting gratitude to fill his heart, he turned around.

As he entered the palazzo, he noticed the heraldic coat of arms above the entrance, complete with shield, motto, crest, lions. He assumed that since the moorings, the *poli*, were of the original family colors, this plaque would claim similar ownership. He would ask Signor Carraro at dinner. Italians loved to talk about their history.

Returning to that brilliant space with its massive glass trapezoid, Gavin's could think only of the silver-colored tips of the water. Of its wobbly reflections of palazzos and flowers, of the *poli* shimmering like dancing rainbows. How the sun bleached the ochre on a building to pale yellow, a light blue to almost white. Every single detail - shadow, light, adornment, and embellishment.

Remember it all, he told himself. *Paint it.*

With those images spinning in his brain, he again put on his smock and picked up the broom.

Cecilia respected Gavin's request and stayed away, but it was difficult to expunge her presence from his thoughts. They had dinner together every night, occasions that were distracting and mysterious. Sometimes Signor Carraro was present; sometimes, not. Yet Cecilia never missed a meal. Often, there were guests. This was most favorable since then he need not look directly at her. But when only the three dined, they used the spectacular but smaller breakfast room. He was forced to be aware of her nearness and tried desperately to focus on the room's architecture. Framing its octagonal shape, doorway and moldings were antiqued white with threads of silver, rubbed down to the softest luster of themselves. Designed like an aviary with trompe l'oeil murals on walls and ceiling, birds flew among the clouds and the trees, behind trellises and into fountains. It was a serene and ordered world, an ageless fluttering of nature.

The lobby of Gavin's creation would convey just the opposite - contemporary, abstract, active. Only movement, no peace. Its throbbing walls would leap into the viewer's arms, his portrayal of nature's antithesis to serenity - its other aspect, the one of turmoil, the one in which passion lives.

How to describe these meals? Ambivalent and seductive together.

Nightly, Gavin sat close to this woman Cecilia. What were her thoughts? Her words "take my breath away" haunted him as he watched her fork enter her food, then move up to her luscious mouth. She was so near, two arms' lengths away. Mad with desire, he could hardly swallow the exotic foods on gorgeous plates set before him by their servant, Lilly. The tiny lobsters surrounding the caviar canapés. Something orange and red - vegetables? - on a plate that was sauced with a gold leaf purée. When the meal was over, he could not remember a single thing he had eaten or a single thing they had discussed. All he recalled was the bow of her lips, the charm of her Italian and English sprinkled together, the urgent need to lay his hand against her cheek. When he returned to his room, he was lonely for her.

Cecilia encouraged his interest with small gestures - a turn of her head; a lowering of her eyes; a smile directed at him, not at her husband, who sat at the table like a benevolent monarch. Always gracious to Gavin, the signor seemed not to notice any of these quivers. Gavin was puzzled by their relationship. Cecilia continued to toss provocative questions in Gavin's direction.

"Were you always so passionate about painting? So…fervent about your work?"

Occasionally, she would place her hand on his arm or cover his hand with her own. Coyly but without hesitation, as Sofia often did. The lightest touch, a mere pulse, like the wing of a dove. Was Signor Carraro aware that Gavin's limbs were burning, howling? Cecilia was calm and elusive, the aroused reaction on Gavin's face apparently sufficient to please her.

Six weeks of such dinners. For every one, Cecilia dressed exquisitely, not in slacks, not with flat black shoes, but in designs by the finest Venetian dressmakers - the style of clothes Sofia would wear whenever she dressed up. Elegant garments in silks and satins, tiny jewels adorning hems, framing necklines.

After being isolated in his glass structure for many weeks, Gavin's work on the mural was finally done. Arrangements were made for the grand opening. A few days before the celebration, he would privately show the completed room to Signor and Signora Carraro. He was immensely grateful and, frankly, surprised that despite his warnings to stay away, the signor had not asked to see his progress, not even toward the end. Suddenly, he was alarmed. What if the unveiling was unacceptable? Would they simply paint over everything? Restore the space to the anonymity of whiteness?

Gavin's supplies were packed; the floor cloths, lifted. He stood alone in the center of the room and appraised the space, a whirling fantasy of color and motion. Not a speck of surface was untouched by brush or broom. *If I never paint another thing,* he decided, *and this work remains, the result will have justified my life as an artist - from modest beginnings to a palazzo in Venice. Unimaginable.*

Yes, I'm absolutely content with what I produced. Let them have their opening. There will be critics. But let my patrons, because of me, consider their home a masterpiece of the noble past and a glorious future.

Signor Carraro had urgent business in Milan. He would return the next day, and the three of them would then view the mural together. Cecilia and Gavin dined alone in the breakfast room under the wings of the painted birds. There was awkwardness and halting conversation. He excused himself early, hoping his withdrawal did not cause offense.

The surprise of it nearly stopped his heart.

In the dark of night, his door opened gently. It was Cecilia, her slippers muffled on the floor. Her hair was loose and free, framed by a shadow from the hall's half-light. Gavin's body erupted with longing as she threw off her robe and fell naked onto his body in that narrow bed with the pale-blue walls of swags and garlands. There were few words and many murmurs, deep sighs, pivots, and turnings. At one point, she cried, kissing his face, his fingers, purring words of devotion. He promised her a world beyond the one they now knew. And there she stayed until the bronze light of dawn began to show between the curtains.

His body was sore, used up. That next morning, he would not have breakfast beneath the Italian swallows and the red-throated loon. He would remain in his room and weep until his heart dried up like that of a dead man. Despite last night's ineffable joy, despite their whispered pleas, he knew such pleasure would never happen again.

When Signor returned, the three walked down to the new wing. Signor smiled expectantly and, with a grand gesture, threw open the massive double doors. All gasped, even Gavin; this was only his second viewing after completion. Surely with the sun pouring down on the watery walls that swayed under the light and the hundreds of strokes and swirls applied with rags and brooms and brushes, the vast space was not merely a mural painted by Gavin Taylor but a revelation designed on the last day of Creation. Surely an extra day would be needed to produce a scene as breathtaking as this. Both Carraros burst into tears. Signor reached for Gavin's hand, his lips to Gavin's palm.

"My dear Gavin," he sputtered, his words mangled in his throat, "when I come to my senses, we will talk."

He thought Signora whispered, *You stop my breath. You have my soul,* but he wasn't sure if she referred to the mural or to their evening together. Or even if she had said it at all.

The day of the grand unveiling of the new Carraro family wing, streamers and banners flew across the facade of the palazzo. Locals and tourists, curiosity seekers, museum lovers - all swarmed through its glass doors. Critics gathered in corners with their notebooks, pens scribbling, praising, cheering. Now and then, one would put his nose close to the wall attempting to capture a detail, but at that point, so close, everything dissolved into a colorful mist.

"The wonder of our times."

"Another Picasso."

"Better."

"Original, mystical, a work for the ages."

Almost everyone loved the splendid sight, all except those few whose imaginations remained bolted to earth - "What is this work about?" they pressed. Signor and Signora Carraro eagerly accepted extravagant praise from their guests. Dressed in his black Nehru jacket and black jeans, Gavin shook hands and answered questions. In his breast pocket was a bonus check from Signor Carraro. The number was astonishing.

Soon, Gavin grew impatient, a wanderer anxious to return to his cottage on the mountain. Just as the work no longer belonged to him, so he himself no longer belonged here. After a respectable time, he slipped away, promising Signor Carraro he would return for a donor reception, a talk at the university, a dinner for the board. The two men kissed each other on both cheeks, the great patron of modern art patting his eyes with a white linen square.

Where had Cecilia gone?

The butler carried his bags to the *poli*, where Vito awaited. The gondolier held out his hand and helped Gavin into the gilded boat for the brief ride to the train station. When he was seated against the pillows, Gavin looked up at the tall windows on the third floor, framed by stone carvings of angels who looked down on the scene. Would his damaged heart manage to carry him home?

"Signor?" Vito asked, concerned.

Beyond the window, there was a slight flutter of curtains, a clutch of dark hair, and like the angels, Cecilia kept a close watch.

Chapter 20

Backstage, Ellie listened to the audience's rapturous cheers and whistles.

Everything went off perfectly. She smiled at recalling her first production of *The Wizard* years earlier with dyslexic Joey Bennett confused about directions and little Sheila Dwyer always running to the bathroom. She had learned a valuable lesson then that sometimes mistakes can be to your benefit. You just have be receptive, stay loose, don't clamp down on any one thing. At any rate, tonight's company performed like true stars and deserved to do a little preening. And the cast was grateful that Ellie had pulled out of them the best they could give.

When the theater had emptied, the performers and staff gathered on stage in jeans and T-shirts, settling in a large circle and telling stories about themselves, the show, what happens next. A couple of cases of cold beer were set down. A dozen pizzas showed up. Tonight, they were family. Mayor Jeff joined them, rolling up his sleeves and sitting beside Danny and Maryann.

Danny put his arm around Ellie and whispered, "Mom, you're amazing, the best. I hope Emma's just like you."

Suddenly, Christy Jenkins, the young woman who played Mary Lennox, jumped up and raised her arms. "Quiet, everyone. Toast! Toast!" Facing Ellie, she cried, "To our wonderful director, Ellie Taylor, who made us all heroes tonight. How can we thank you for this marvelous experience!" And she did a deep curtsy as if she were paying homage to royalty.

At that same moment, Ellie wanted to thank the crew for what they had done for *her*. Ever since her panic attack on that bench along the Charles River, certain crucial issues had been living in her head. The birth of the babies had put them on hold. But now, here was the truth, right on this stage.

Yes, she had many years of small victories, toiling in hot, damp theaters, but her successes had been sporadic. If she were truthful, she would say she was just another name on a list of producers' possibilities. Wasn't it a fact that she had never been approached by a major theater in Manhattan? This show, here tonight, made her realize she loved directing, controlling the *whole thing*, being the one who is panned or praised, having the thrill of choosing the work itself. Why, she was on top, the one to whom all deferred, and mighty thankful to have been given this chance. Managing an entire production, not only the cast, but all the creative details involved, required a constantly inventive spirit. And when the curtain came down, she realized it wasn't solely acting to which she was devoted - it was the *theater.*

She turned to the sounds of raucous laughter. Tommy Hyland, who played Uncle Archibald, was reprising lines from the play with Nora Gibbons, who had the part of Martha, Uncle Archibald's maid. The two were dancing together flirtatiously, and Ellie was happy. She had no further aspirations beyond being right here. If she remained the director, this theater would thrive and become known throughout the state. People would travel far to see its performances. And Jeff was beside her with his sweet support, a constant, undemanding presence. She had forgotten how much she missed that loving boost from a good man. Tall and slender like Gavin, but with straight blond hair that was slowly going white, and soft hazel eyes that changed color with the sun, he dressed like a fancy cowboy in jeans or chinos rather than suits. *Cute, not hokey,* she thought, pleased that she had shed the last of her uppity eastern aspirations.

And she wanted to be a real grandmother, one who was present and useful. Ethan might always require a helpful hand, and she could be of benefit. If he was inclined to paint, she would see to it that he was nurtured artistically. If not, perhaps she could provide him with work in the theater. A quiet, behind-the-scenes job where he could experience its excitement yet still live a calm existence like managing the accounts, the bookings, and oversee inventory. She would wait and see where his interests lie. *Just let him live*, Ellie prayed.

And so on this grand evening, Ellie's future was settled. She would not live in rooms that were temporary or belonged to someone else nor be distant from her family. She would not spend a single day without a garden. She wanted to see the forsythia unfurl in spring. She wanted to walk in the fields listening for the meadowlark. Home. Here she was loved, wanted, needed. And here she would stay and prosper.

Every morning, Maryann woke up with dread coiled inside her gut. She knew what she would see as soon as she heard little chirps from their bedroom. Emma standing up in her crib with one foot over the top of the railing trying to climb out. Ethan lingering, lying flat, kicking the mobile with his foot and watching it spin around. Then turning to look at his mother as if waiting for permission to start moving. When Maryann saw this, her heart lost its beat. Did she really expect that one morning he would awake with as much vigor as his sister?

Keeping busy, she managed to stave off taking personal blame during her waking hours. Everyone had talked to her about this, even the doctor. Ethan's condition was not her fault. But at night, when the house was quiet and everyone was asleep, she couldn't help crying tears of sadness. Knowing Danny fell asleep exhausted and would wake up just before dawn, she tried to stay silent, but he always heard her and laid a warm hand of comfort on her back or belly. But he too felt the sorrow. Truth be told, neither of them could say whether Ethan's situation was bringing them closer or driving them apart. They just didn't talk about it anymore. The doctor said time would tell. So they were waiting, but for what, neither had any idea.

Ryan and Jack were turning out wildly imaginative posters for half a dozen disparate groups. Their finished works were rarely similar. Some portrayed quirky futuristic images, others a modern take on a traditional theme. Fantasy and reality were juxtaposed with just enough of the latter to remind the viewer of the importance of attending or supporting whatever event was promoted. But all were done with an original panache that became known as the particular style of TheJackRyanStudios. If you were seeking some product not seen before that would lure the eye, folks in Boston knew where to go.

Caitlin had turned out to be far more useful than an ordinary bookkeeper and business manager. A crackerjack go-getter with her leggy good looks and clear blue eyes, she had the idea to go directly to sources. Without an appointment, she would walk into offices and boldly ask, "Do you want to greatly increase your outreach?" She then laid out samples from TheJackRyanStudios, and soon thereafter, walked out with a commission. Her successes enabled her and Jack to move from their starter apartment to a large loft with a view of the Charles and a distant sighting of the Weld boathouse. Their new place, with its marble floors, fifteenth-story balcony and sliding glass doors, was not a home for children.

But they had decided. There would be no children. Neither felt so inclined. Weekdays, their lives consisted of long hours, creative enterprise, and tense deadlines. On weekends, they rowed and worked out in the boathouse. Children wouldn't fit in, at least not for a long time. Maybe in a few years, and who knew if even then.

Jack and Caitlin now spent every weekend at their rowing club. On their initial sighting of the Charles River, they had immediately fallen in love with the grand architectural designs of the boathouses scattered along its length. Harvard's Weld, opened in 1906, and the slightly older Newell, built in 1889, were revered by Harvard students and faculty for their historic character. Both formed the core of buildings designated as part of the Charles River Basin Historic District.

In the beginning, with members of their club shouting instructions, Caitlin and Jack paddled their way up and down short sections of the Charles. Working in slow increments to build up strength and skill, they could barely make it from one landmark to another. First, the Eliot Bridge, then a pass by Newell Boathouse. Next, Anderson Bridge and past Weld. Farther along, Weeks Bridge, then Western

Avenue Bridge. Following was a killer stretch, a powerhouse length of one mile, no pausing, to the River Street Bridge, past Riverside Boat Club to the BU Bridge and BU's DeWolfe Boathouse. It took months before Caitlin and Jack were able to do even a portion of this route in any respectable time, but they kept at it as intensely as they did their work at the office.

The rigor and discipline, the rewards and the glamour - all of it thrilled them both - and yes, the prestige. And also something unexpected. Their rowing experience became the genesis of two weighty projects. First, Jack conceived of doing a series of fantastical colored drawings of all the boathouses, casting a mystical aura over a representational subject, a daunting prospect. The bridges would be included; were there six or seven? No one would think of taking the revered Weld Boathouse and redesigning it as an imaginary vision for the next century. His task would be to transform on paper something traditional into something futuristic, slightly altered yet still recognizable. He didn't know how he would manage to do this, but he had to be careful. He didn't want to mimic a venerable Harvard entity like the *Lampoon*, Harvard's undergraduate humor magazine, often did. It was not his intent to be sarcastic or ironic. After all, Harvard's customs were sacred. One had to reshape and amend with great finesse that the original be respected. If there was offense, *TheJackRyanStudios* would suffer.

These works, he decided, would be promoted as singles or as a folio. Thousands would covet them, not only current students and faculty, but alums and townies as well, and rowers from around the world. His drawings would hang on the walls of devotees everywhere.

The full morning sun was just rising in the east when the second idea occurred simultaneously to both Caitlin and Jack. They were rubbing their hands from the cold, turning up their collars, and carrying their shell down the ramp when they shouted, "Yes, the Head of the Charles! Let's do it. Let's try to qualify!"

The largest three-day regatta in the world. Held in late October when the fall foliage was in full glory, eleven thousand athletes rowed in almost two thousand boats in sixty-one events. The final race, three miles from Boston University's DeWolfe to just past the Eliot Bridge with thousands more hysterical, cheering fans along the route. It was a weekend of extraordinary endurance and athleticism, the mood as festive as the Fourth of July. Booths representing universities and private clubs were scattered along the riverbanks. Families whooped and hollered as their favored boat passed by, the rowers heaving and pulling. Alums wore sweatshirts adorned with their school's logos. The heads of infants were covered with wool caps embroidered with Yale, UCLA, or Oxford. It would take at least a year to qualify, but they were eager to take up the challenge.

Meanwhile, Ryan now had a serious girlfriend, Meghan, a grad student in Irish history.

Everyone thrived. They thought it would last forever.

Ellie was bold in running off to Chicago. She was bold to star in a unique and demanding role. She was bold in moving to Boston where she knew no one. But now she was about to make one of her boldest moves of all.

She would visit Gavin in Italy.

"Now that the kinks of the show have been worked out and the assistant director can take over, I'm going to take a break," Ellie decided. "It's been an exhausting time with the twins and now the theater."

Jeff had suggested taking a special trip. "Anywhere you'd like," he said. So to Italy, they would go. Doesn't everyone want to see Italy? Now, she had only to present Jeff with her wishes.

Ellie reviewed her decision, not to overlook any consideration.

Since she had rented her own place, talk had begun about her and Jeff. One couldn't hide much in small towns. Charlotte Miller next door spent half the day rocking on her porch and waving to Mayor Jeff whenever he pulled up. She was a nice old lady but a gossip. Neither Jeff nor Ellie had an enemy that they know of, but people speculated - how did it look to the children, a widower carrying on with a married woman? And their mayor, after all, was not just anyone like Troy down at Troy's Stables or Fred from Fred's Ice Cream Treats. Folks wanted to look up to their leader.

Jeff hasn't asked me to marry him, but I'm not interested in marriage, Ellie thought. *He has two children, almost grown, and I have a large family. It all gets rather complicated. But I think two adults who are dating would be more acceptable to the community if one is legally separated and the other is divorced. Yes, a legal separation makes sense. And a gradual transition to divorce if ever comes to that.*

Ellie reflected little on whether Gavin would even want to see her. She wasn't showing up to get in his way. The question of a separation would take but a few minutes. *Of course, he'll have to meet Jeff, but I can tell him over the phone that I've been seeing someone, and we're coming over together. Likely he already knows about Jeff. I'm not the only one from around here with whom he keeps in touch. Anyway, I've never been abroad. And who wouldn't be curious to see your famous painter almost ex-husband living on a mountaintop?*

All this Ellie pondered as she lounged in her garden thinking the roses needed pruning. Yes, it seemed a good plan. She would tell Jeff tonight. But as she turned back to the house to fetch her rose clippers, she suddenly lost her breath and sank to the ground. Taken by fear of imminent calamity, she murmured to herself, "Breathe deep, breathe deep. Head down." And then almost as quickly as she had collapsed, she became elated - it's simply the idea for a great play that nearly knocked you out, Ellie girl.

The absurdity of it struck her as preposterous. But was it so outrageous? She could tell immediately, almost the exact moment the scheme popped up in her brain, that it had all the markings of a fine play - an audacious storyline, an intriguing plot. It had dramatic peaks with elements of humor and sadness, surprises, unexpected turns, and characters whose lives would unfold and resolve in an emotionally powerful two hours. It would be fictional, of course, but based on fact.

The saga of the Taylor family. Her story. And the insight accompanying this decision that landed straight as an arrow in her resourceful head? That she would write it herself. At first, it was an appalling notion. She had never written an essay or story, never mind a stage script. Yet she had never acted or directed before she did those things either, so why not give it a try?

The roses were forgotten as Ellie started to make a list. Where to start? A pivotal moment when Gavin left for Italy? Or another, way back, when she left for Chicago. Perhaps a moment of musing in-between when they were drifting and their marriage began to dwindle. The narrative would unwrap reminiscences and events and the repercussions from making choices. The play would end as the actors' lives continued to unfold but would remain ambivalent about the future.

Ellie pulled herself back into her chair, scribbling notes. Presenting an original piece rather than adapting an existing story was an exciting concept for their theater. The more she thought about it, the closer the scheme felt to her heart, even as she perceived it leaving her brain and floating away.

As her breathing returned, she laughed at a comparison of her situation to that of Dorothy in *The Wizard.* The young girl was earnest in following the yellow brick road all the way to the Magic Kingdom. And yet she found herself amidst an awesome ambivalence, fearful for finding a real wizard and fearful for finding a fake. Everyone in the audience knew that the story was a mere fairy tale, that no matter what Dorothy found, it was the journey to the kingdom itself that held her imagination. It was the journey that was the dream.

That's it, Ellie thought, *a story of searching for the dream. And while doing so, dropping a bit of enchantment on the world. That's what I'll write about. And the audience will come along. They will know that despite life's complications and often bitter disappointments, there can also be elements of magic. Pick up a guitar. Hover before an easel. Stand on a stage with the lights on your face, and you can make a reality that dances and sings despite the setbacks and challenges. A play of discovery - that's what I'll write. And if we can make the trek with aplomb, it will be a good voyage.*

Now that Ellie had conceived the idea, she had already moved her brain to the space that said to her, "Yes, I will do this." The enormity of it made her pulse race, her wrist veins bulge. Her mind throbbed with anticipation. She, a dramatist, an author, as well as an actor and director.

Not one speck of this risky project seemed real, yet it all seemed possible.

Ellie marveled that our best ideas can emerge in the strangest ways. Some days inspiration just appears if you find a quiet place and allow your thoughts and feelings to wander.

It might be the perfect play.

She jumped up and started pacing. What would Jeff think? She would ask.

Or Gavin? She must go to Italy and find out.

And if they were agreeable, somehow, she would learn how to write a play.

As Jeff entered the house waving a bunch of lilacs under her nose, he assumed they were having a simple dinner at home.

Then he noticed the table was set with good linens and candles. The hearty aroma of a roast drifted through the rooms. A warm peach pie still oozing its juices sat on the counter. He braced himself.

Ellie began.

"Honey, remember you said we should take a vacation? And it could be anywhere?"

Should he answer or wait?

He waited.

"Well, how would you like to go to Italy for two weeks?"

Surprised, Jeff had expected *anywhere* to be someplace like the Ahwahnee Hotel in Yosemite, California, with its views of Yosemite Falls and the famous Half Dome or perhaps Mackinac Island in Michigan. For romance and natural beauty, everyone in Iowa always talked about going to Mackinac Island or if a city, maybe St. Louis with its crowded restaurants and peppery night life. But Italy? Wasn't Gavin in Italy? Did she want to see her husband?

"Italy?" Jeff asked carefully. "That's a major trip. I'm up for it, but why Italy?"

As she sliced the roast and placed ample portions of potatoes and green beans on two plates, she presented her plan. "Everyone knows Italy is beautiful with its landscape of hills and valleys and charming villages so unlike Iowa. And we can stay in Florence, one of the most historic cities in the world. We'll travel around locally, and I can ask Gavin for a legal separation. I hate to make such a request on a long-distance phone call."

"You sure? You don't really know what's going on with him over there, but it's all right with me if that's what you want, sweet girl."

"I'll call Gavin and mention we're coming together. But no worries, I can tell by his voice if it's really okay with him. If he hesitates or sounds upset, we won't go."

"Sounds fine with me. You know the situation better than me, and we can do a nice bit of sightseeing," Jeff answered, cutting the meat and spearing the potatoes.

Just before serving the pie, Ellie started again.

"So, Jeff honey, I had another thought."

Another? He put down his fork. Should he be alarmed? Her voice quivered.

"Now listen hard before you give your opinion. What do you think about my writing a play about my family? You know, all about dreams and living in different places and those darn secrets and so many things. Of course I'd change the names and the facts and all that. A fictitious story, but based on the lives of the Taylors. What do you think?"

This was the last idea he expected. He had thought maybe she wanted to add a weekend in Paris on the way home. But all he could manage was, *This is a damn amazing woman I'm involved with.*

"Why not? he said. "But maybe the play can end before you and I meet. I could lose a lot of votes with folks giving their opinions and all."

"That's not a problem. But we're getting way ahead of ourselves. Gavin has to okay the idea first. Only the trip matters at the moment. Do you agree with that part? I'll call Gavin tomorrow, if it's okay with you."

So earnest and beautiful was Ellie, serving him a perfect rare roast with crisped potatoes, her face lit with possibility. Of course, he would say yes to any request.

But underneath his bravado, Jeff was concerned. Would she be attracted to Gavin again when she saw him in his personal circumstances - the cottage on a mountain, the quaint village, even the Brothers in the vineyards? And especially Italy, with its infinite variety of seductions.

Ellie rang Gavin's phone twice a day for three days. On the fourth day, he picked up.

"Gavin? Are you okay?" Ellie asked. "I've been trying to reach you. Jack said you just returned from Venice."

"Hi, Ellie. Yes, I'm just back," he answered, subdued.

"Venice, oh, Gavin, how marvelous! Was it amazing? Was it everything one dreams of when thinking about Venice? The gondolas and the palazzos and romance everywhere? Was it just like that?

"Yes, Ellie, it was just like that," Gavin murmured.

"Gavin, you sound a bit…tired. Are you well?"

"Well enough. Yes, tired."

"Is this a good time? I have a favor to ask, but I can call back another day," she offered.

"What is it?"

Ellie hesitated. He didn't sound like himself. In fact, he sounded halting, disengaged. Still, she was anxious, so she decided to go ahead.

"Gavin, I was thinking. My play is a hit, and I'm plumb worn-out. I haven't had a vacation since, well, I can't remember. What would you say if I came over for a short visit? I've never been to Italy. I'd come with a friend so you needn't feel obligated to tootle me around. Do you remember Mayor Jeff? There are lodgings in Florence, and we could just meet for an afternoon or so."

"Whatever you want, Ellie. I'm sort of having a bit of a rest."

"That's great, Gavin. In about three weeks?"

"All right," he replied.

When Ellie hung up, she felt uncomfortable, as if Gavin was keeping secrets again. Suddenly, she realized she could no longer guess what he was thinking by the sound of his voice.

Chapter 21

Jack and Caitlin, Ryan and his fiancée, Meghan, were celebrating with a lobster dinner at the historic Union Oyster House in downtown Boston. There were many reasons to rejoice, and not a one could they have imagined a year ago. The two couples were, this very night, dining in a restaurant opened in prerevolutionary days, the building itself famous as the oldest standing brick building in the city constructed in Georgian-style architecture. Daniel Webster, the secretary of state, was a frequent customer in the early 1800s. And just now, the waitress informed them that the booths and oyster bar themselves were still in their original positions! Jack was overcome, not only by the impressive surroundings, but also by the realization that his presence here was due to the successful artistic talents of Ryan and himself, and the thrilling but unforeseen flair for marketing by his lovely wife.

Meghan was showing off her left hand's glittering engagement ring. Caitlin bent low over her friend's fourth finger. Both girls were Irish, and when Ryan brought her home, the two became instant friends and confidantes.

Thanks to Caitlin, TheJackRyanStudios had just secured its first long-term contract, not a solitary commission, as was usual, but a contract to produce an illustration once a month for two years. It was extraordinary what his Caitlin had done, walking in the door of the drama department at a nearby college and spreading samples over the director's desk, eagerly explaining the concepts. Leaning over her display, she had the impression he was more interested in her than he was in her presentation. But no matter, he signed the papers for

TheJackRyanStudios to be the sole promoter of the school's shows and entertainments for twenty-four months.

While the girls squealed with delight, and Ryan watched affectionately, Jack was intrigued with the crammed decor of the place. Not a jot of background was visible. Boston's history was glued, drawn, sculpted in a series of tableaux that marched down the long wall. Titles over each one - *Faneuil Hall, Old Corner Bookstore*, landmarks old and new. Phrases that further celebrated the city were stenciled up high, just below the red tin ceiling: "*Freedom Trail;*" "Open to all parties but influenced by none, *The Massachusetts Spy*, 1771;" "*Midnight Ride of Paul Revere.*" Memorabilia, souvenirs, and photos were layered edge to edge like a gigantic collage around the room. An antique wagon wheel leaned against a counter. Fishermen's ropes were looped and swagged. Piles of oysters sat mounded on the counter. Towers of them, waiting for hungry customers. Although the place looked like a flea market on a Sunday afternoon, the diners ate ravenously and happily.

Suddenly, Jack conceived of a workable idea. *Yes, a good one,* he thought, mulling it over. *I'll create a series of fanciful drawings of renowned Boston restaurants, past and present. The historic ones that are recognized the world over and must be remembered. Durgin-Park, Jacob Wirth, Locke-Ober's - these iconic places about to close due to changing times. But then I'll also include a few of the newer, au courant spots. A difficult project, but which one is not? Surely Caitlin could persuade the restaurants to display copies by the register. Tourists would purchase one or a few for souvenirs and gifts, Bostonians for the nostalgia.*

Occasionally, Jack worried that his skill might one day fly off, like a gift that had been advanced but not conferred, entrusted but not permanently granted. Coming up continuously with clever and appropriate ideas was not a talent he simply assumed would always be his. With each new successful pop up, he was humbled and grateful. Each time, he whispered thank you to his father.

This new enterprise would fit perfectly into their growing portfolio. TheJackRyanStudios produced more than assignments on commission. They also self-published individual posters or folios of a certain subject, such as the boathouse series, which was selling well in bookstores. They had thought to autograph some, and these were sold at almost double the retail price. Maybe they would do the same with the restaurant grouping.

The waiter was now tying bibs around their necks for their upcoming meal. Ryan ordered four lobster dinners. He was well acquainted with these crustaceans, but Jack was not. Should he admit he had never tasted lobster, that he had no idea how to deal with the thing? Probably his best course was to ask no questions and observe how the others managed this ritual.

The waiter wove deftly between the tables and set down each dish with a great flourish. Each plate contained a bright-orange creature, lemon wedges tucked around. Next, he arranged ramekins of melted butter for dipping, a glass dish in which to toss the shells, a tiny fork, a metal instrument with which to crack the claws.

The lobsters looked alive. Jack shuddered at the sight of all those appendages. Its eyes were looking directly into his. And those frightening antennae growing from its head was a daunting sight he was expected to consume without making a fool of himself. Those at other tables were diligently slurping and guzzling, as if lobster were a delicacy.

Ryan was pointing, explaining, "Those are the legs. Those are the claws. They say the knuckle meat is the tastiest part. Right there" - Ryan indicated - "between the claw and the body itself. There's the antennae, the mouth. The claws are called pincers."

A complicated procedure, Jack mused, *this lobster dissection.*

How he longed for a crab cake or grilled salmon, a simple fish eaten with a simple fork. A thought occurred, and he turned to writing down a few words for his upcoming talk at a renowned gallery on Newbury Street. Jack found he enjoyed public speaking, a pleasant discovery unearthed when he was called upon to say a few extemporaneous words about his work at a Rotary Club meeting, the Rotarians one of his prized clients. He even tossed in a few jokes. His world was expanding beyond the studio, and he was taking the others with him.

He must remember to mention how much he owed his enthusiasm as well as his skill to his father, especially his dad's motivation in turning a chicken coop into a studio; especially when, as a boy, he sat behind the barn folding a piece of paper trying to capture the motion of a generator, and his father handed him a pencil and told him to work it out; especially the joy of him sitting at his father's side, there to learn how to *see* the shape of the hills, the shadows of the creek, the color of the leaves, and to capture those impressions on paper; especially how, ever after, he benefited from his father's most important instruction - how to refashion those impressions in his own creative vision.

While Jack was facing this unwieldy crustacean, longing for a hamburger, Danny was watching his son Ethan sit quietly in a corner examining pieces of a puzzle while his sister Emma scrambled up on the sofa, her wet diaper sagging, her fanny shaking to the rhythm of "Sunny day, sweepin' the clouds away…how to get to Sesame Street?" Then Emma was doing a somersault as Ethan picked up his beloved books, identifying letters and words, always bringing one to whoever was around to read to him. He focused intently on the story, jabbering about the action, naming the objects, turning the pages while admonishing the reader to hurry up. This was a typical scene in their household - Emma rolling or jumping or running or hopping with her brother sitting serenely beside a stack of books, picking up one, then another, the pages turning and turning.

Jeff threw a couple of pairs of pants and a few shirts into a suitcase. The navy sneakers in addition to the shoes he would wear traveling. He was ready. Ellie's clothes were tossed everywhere, over her bed, the chair, the bureau. In Boston, she had dressed either in costume or in the casual garb of a student. Caring for the twins, she wore sweats or jeans and hardly had a moment to comb her hair. But now she was about to embark on her first adult trip in years, along with a boyfriend, to visit the man to whom she was still married. And everyone told her the Italian women were stylish and chic, even when they were chasing children in the park. She decided to visit

Miss Maddie's in town and see about one or two knit dresses, dark pants, a couple of tunic tops, and a suede jacket if she got lucky. She would wait on purchasing a leather pocketbook. *I'll treat myself to one or two of those fabulous Italian leather purses when I'm there,* she promised herself.

When the couple landed at Amerigo Vespucci Airport, Ellie was grateful that Miss Maddie had come through. She found a gold paisley tunic, then another, mauve with silver threads, and black slacks that made her look thinner and younger. Miss Maddie's even had the perfect suede jacket in her size. But alas, no knit dresses. If need be, she would dash into a store in Florence, but first, she would see what the Italian women wore.

The couple headed straightaway to their small hotel in the historic center of the city. As their taxi approached the outskirts of Florence, their eyes took in similar views to Gavin's when he arrived here for the first time. Their hearts filled with awe, just as his continues to do. Slowly, as the details came clear, Ellie and Jeff's excitement grew wide and deep, as vast as the offerings that awaited.

"Gavin," Ellie cried into the phone. "We're here! The trip from the airport was unreal, like a dream. Everything's so masterful, so other-worldly, so beautifully old!"

At first, Gavin offered to meet them in the city, but after consideration, he decided she and Jeff should take the bus out and meet him at Francesco's. He promised that his friend Enzo the bus driver was a first-class tour guide and would take good care of them, telling stories about every sight they passed.

As the bus rumbled along, Ellie thought she had never before been dropped into such immediate and total serenity. The enduring landscape offered an overwhelming sense of peace, with side roads leading off to wineries and country estates. In the distance, workers toiled among the vineyards. Enzo narrated the entire way, but in truth, Ellie was so entranced with what lay outside the window, she paid little attention. It was enough for Jeff to mumble an acknowledgement in his direction now and then.

At last, Enzo cried out, "Signora, *sei qui*, you're here!" and they disembarked in the town square, right in front of Francesco's café where Gavin was waiting at a small table having a coffee.

At once, Ellie thought, *He looks tired, worn-out, just like he sounded on the phone. What could be wrong?* She hoped he wasn't ill. Despite something being off about his demeanor, his usual exuberance would surely return soon - one always tires after a trip away from home. She had heard he had achieved great success with his Venetian commission.

With great relief, Gavin observed that a nice-looking guy is holding her purse. *We'll be parents and grandparents together, but that's all,* he concluded.

Jeff looked from one to the other. *I'll just hang back,* he decided, excusing himself to find a bathroom, leaving husband and wife alone.

At one time, Gavin might have felt awkward introducing Francesco to his wife arriving with another man. But now, he merely said, "Francesco, this is Ellie."

And when Jeff returned, he said, "Francesco, this is Jeff," leaving Francesco to puzzle out the relationships.

"Would anyone care for a cappuccino?" Francesco asked.

Let him think what he will. Italians are discreet about such things, Gavin thought. *One's life is one's own business.*

"A pastry to go with it? My wife bakes them herself."

"Yes, all right, that would be lovely, whatever you choose," Ellie answered.

"*Sfogliatella,*" Gavin said to Francesco. And to Ellie, he explained, "A pastry filled with ricotta cheese and candied fruit."

That settled, Ellie looked around the intimate plaza, the stone shops, the opulent window boxes. Vendors were selling fresh produce to customers holding out their string bags. Atop their carts, resting like wagon wheels, were huge rounds of cheese. All this daily activity was set against the rolling hills, the path up the mountain, the same scene as hundreds of years ago.

Antonio joined them and then ruddy and amiable Piero. Even Gregorio, the gelato vendor, came to see what the fuss was about -

Gregorio never missed a party. Francesco's wife brought out a plate of *sfogliatella* while her husband in his long apron held onto a toddler with his left hand while pouring coffee with his right. Ellie realized she had never sat around in this manner with friends. Matt's Drugs didn't exactly elicit a similar atmosphere. And in Boston, a few colleagues would go out now and then to a diner or bar, but they hopped from one place to another, loyal to none. The only time she truly experienced such an intimate camaraderie was at the celebration after opening night of *The Secret Garden*. And then when the beer and pizza were gone, everyone went off separately, not to meet again as a group. How fortunate that Gavin experiences these wonderful moments every day. Of course, everyone had jobs, and each one eventually took off, but first, it was their habit to all have cappuccino together. And they would be here in the same way the next morning and the morning after that. Steadfast, reliable. *This is Gavin's own secret garden,* she noted ironically. *No wonder he loves it here, thrives here.*

"Gavin, I'm so happy you found this special place," she said, touching his hand.

They were both glad for this moment. Living far apart, these close occasions hardly existed anymore. Now they could relax, and all three would walk up the hill to Gavin's cottage on the mountain.

As they approached the summit, Ellie thought the scene looked like one of those pretty hill towns pictured on postcards of Italy. At its peak was a network of buildings running closely along together. Up and down the ramble went, like a toy train, rolling and rippling with the curve of the hill. But when they arrived, Ellie saw they were not separate buildings but rather one elongated structure stretched out like a series of stones threaded onto a string - the monastery - and nothing higher than its presence but God and the heavens.

Ellie lingered over the views of the lovely valley below. There were paths of cypress trees around the monastery as well as long rows along the roads below trailing off into the distance. She recalled that on the bus, Enzo told Jeff about those trees.

"They are a symbol of immortality and signify sacred space. That is why they're planted around cemeteries, convents, and monasteries. But also, they represent a detachment from the everyday mortal world, an enduring spirit of detachment or escapism that makes the landscape so enchanting, leading you off to unknown places."

The poetry of the information had disarmed Ellie. Without knowing why, she had felt sad, almost tearful. She shook it off and turned to step inside Gavin's dwelling, taken aback at its resemblance to her own - the quaint charm, the snug setting. Yet there were considerable differences. Here, the climate was temperate year-round, and nature kept growing and spreading, always green, always blossoming. If one weren't mindful, the house would be buried in roses; whereas, Iowa knew relentless months of an all-white winter when there was no green anywhere, and the roses were mere sticks, the clematis, asleep.

Ellie found it hard to believe that Gavin lived here, that he had found this place from the back of a magazine in their town library back in Iowa. *If anything made a great movie or play,* she thought, *it would be Gavin's adventure of seek and find and his extraordinary success.*

As Jeff bent his head to clear the low entry, he gave a long whistle.

"Gavin, wow! This room feels like some of the old farmhouses back home. You know, those from the early settlers. Look at these wide-planked chestnut floors, the wood-beamed ceiling."

Solid and compact, *A house for the munchkins from the* Oz *story,* Ellie thought fondly. There was a small kitchen area here, painting alcove there, daybed pushed to the side. One could stand in the middle of the room, hold out your arms, and almost touch the three solid walls. She turned toward the mullioned windows with garden views and glimpsed a stone path leading to a glass structure that stood alone - a twinkling jewel, its sides sending back points of light from the sun - Gavin's studio.

She wasn't aware she had spoken out loud until Gavin murmured, "Only me," to her comment, "Who wouldn't want to stay here forever?"

They sat in the garden listening to the bees and watching tiny hummingbirds peck at the feeder dangling from the big leaf maple. Butterflies gently beat their wings. Gavin put out a pitcher of *limoncello*, icy cold and delicious. They drank and drowsed, drifted and dreamed until Gavin closed his eyes.

Jeff eventually pulled himself from his chair for a long walk.

Oh, a good time to talk to Gavin, Ellie decided. *Or is it?* She planned to ease into it in a few days, but she had expected him to be euphoric, upbeat. Right now he seemed preoccupied and lethargic. So unlike him. Still, they were alone. The moment seemed timely.

"Gavin?" she asked.

"Gavin?" she called again.

He jerked awake, startled, as if a strange animal was licking his bare toes.

"Did everything go all right in Venice? You seem a bit down, not buoyant as one would expect."

He felt as if he were injured, pushing through a scrim of inertia. The opening of his eyes, the sluggish lift of his head an almost unthinkable task.

"Are you well?" she repeated.

"I'm fine, Ellie. Just knocked out by the drama of all things Venetian," he answered, recalling how the moonlight through his window colored Cecilia's skin like the sheen on a pearl, a singular vision impossible to paint.

"Gavin, I've been thinking about our living apart and all."

Gavin remained slouched in his chair.

"Would you be amenable to getting a legal separation? Not a divorce, but Jeff and I *are* seeing each other, and you know how kids wonder and folks gossip. People dating without being married is acceptable these days, but not if one is married, at least not in Iowa. And a separation could be dissolved or advanced at any point.

"Gavin?"

"Whatever you like," he said as he relived how ravishing Cecilia looked flinging the robe from her body, how his own rose through the exquisite pain of longing.

He struggled to keep his gaze directed somewhere near Ellie's voice.

"All right, Gavin, that's great. I'll get it started as soon as I get home. Now, um, er, can I ask you one more thing?" she said, her voice tentative.

"Okay," he mumbled.

Gavin's eyes were again about to close. Had he slipped back into his reverie? Was it the effect of the *limoncello* or this peculiar lethargy he's having? Unsure, nevertheless she proceeded.

"Well, you know our family has lived through substantial transitions and adjustments, changes, choices. Almost everyone has had experiences of their own dislocations and accommodations, and folks love to talk and complain about them. Well, I'm always on the lookout for good scripts. So I had an interesting idea."

She stopped, looked over. He hadn't moved.

"What if I write a play about a family that resembles ours? The basic facts would be different. I would change Iowa to someplace else. Maybe Ohio. And instead of two boys, the protagonist might have three daughters to make the story unrecognizable as ours. What do you think? I might even try writing it myself."

"Sure, okay."

"Sure? Just like that?"

"Whatever you want, Ellie." Spasms of loss felt like a heart attack. *Did Cecilia lay awake nights, her body aching?*

"Okay, Gavin. Thank you. Of course I'll send you the finished script for your approval."

"Sure, okay."

He mulled over the possibility that Cecilia returned to her husband's bed as if nothing had happened. Perhaps he had been an idle distraction.

Ellie took a sip of the *limoncello.* Gavin had mentioned it was produced along the Amalfi coast. Refreshing, sweet, and tart together, like sucking sour candy. She wondered if the Amalfi coast was near enough to visit.

Gavin was sure he had managed to take Cecilia's breath away. What he didn't know was whether or not she had taken away his ability to paint.

Back from his hike, Jeff chatted with Ellie while Gavin continued to doze. Slowly, the pitcher emptied, and the sun set behind the hills. And just as Ellie asked Gavin how far away was the Amalfi coast, Gavin heard Cecilia's tears falling on his shoulder.

They all wandered down the mountain to Francesco's for a delectable dinner of fresh trout rubbed with garlic and lemon and fresh herbs. Sitting in a rear booth, the mood was romantic and mirrored, leathery and dusky. No one brought up Sofia's Place, and Ellie didn't press it, sensing the time was not right. Besides, she had the vital information she needed about the separation and the play. In truth, she thought Gavin had forgotten about accompanying her to Sofia's gallery, about anything connected to her and Jeff or their trip. She barely mentioned her new position other than informing him briefly that she was directing plays in Tylersville and that she decided to move back home for good.

"Nice, Ellie. Good for you. I hope you're happy."

Just then, he felt the piercing anguish of stepping into a gilded gondola and staring up at a darkened window.

The afternoon before they returned to Iowa, she and Jeff wandered down the small street to *Sofia's Place*. Among the surrounding antiquity, it was a shock to come upon a glass exterior lit up like sparklers, reflecting the brilliant canvases that hung on the inside walls, vibrating with color and energy.

"Jeff, is this some sort of cave?" Ellie asked. "Look how these shops fit into one rocky shell. Marvelous, don't you think? How old must this be? Ancient, I bet. Oh, and look! *Sofia's Annex*. I didn't know there was a shop as well as a gallery."

A young man named Tommaso inquired of them, "May I help you?"

"Is Sofia here?" Ellie asked.

"Signora, so sorry. She is away for the day. May I convey who asked for her?"

"No, thank you. We'll look in again."

As they turned away, Ellie thought to look for one of Gavin's paintings. *Yes! There, surely one of his.*

"This was the last piece Mr. Taylor painted before his trip to Venice," Tommaso told them.

"It's on reserve. Intriguing, is it not?"

Ellie was looking at a substantial canvas portraying what could be a forest. There were greens of every hue in nature. At its core was the ominous darkness of the woods from which small animals would seek to escape, fanning out to what looked like morning sun dappling through the trees. Before this Tommaso fellow told her it belonged to Gavin, she already knew. She was sure he had painted it after their phone conversation in which she told him she was confused about her future, after her day on the bench at the Emerald Necklace, those hours in which she speculated that he might be able to paint her mood in a modernist style, then swiftly, the awareness that he could absolutely capture her depression, her melancholy, her hope. And he did so, here. She was astounded at the heartfelt connection she felt simply by his dramatic brushstrokes of a seemingly infinite variety of one color - although she did catch glimpses of red and orange and purple specks. But that a few brief murmurings over the phone should come to *this*?

Ellie turned to Jeff, who was studying the canvas with skepticism, looking in vain for a price tag.

"Jeff, I know what he is trying to get at here, but it's personal. Someday I'll tell you about it. I guess folks buy this kind of art even though it's difficult to understand, but maybe the buyer sees something in it that raises an important feeling. Gavin has stood alone in his art for a long time, and I'm thrilled that he now has a few colleagues who are *simpatico*. I'm sorry we missed this Sofia gal. I wonder if Gavin's somber mood has anything to do with her."

They then left the gallery, Ellie stunned with discovery.

His visitors gone, Gavin lay stretched out on the lounge chair between the cottage and his studio. He hardly noticed Ellie's appearance nor her departure. Barely had he paid attention to her queries. But no matter. He trusted her not to harm him or the family. Besides, he was overcome with an unknown languor that felt like an illness. Only visions of enchanting Venice; only his vast mural, a technicolor dream that provided the ordinary senses with an astonishing new world; only his own breathtaking moment when Cecilia pattered onto the terrace in her expensive black shoes - and he forgot how to breathe - lured him.

In middle age, Gavin had awakened a union of body and soul to which he had given little notice most of his adult life. Surely there would be a reckoning for the weeks of flirtatious dinners, for their dazzling night together.

And it was now upon him. He had no desire to pick up a brush. His mind lay dormant. His fingers were calm, indifferent. Would the great mural in Signor Carraro's house be the last thing he would ever paint? If so, it would be a fitting finale to his life as an artist - the woman Cecilia, integral to the magnificent city of Venice, two beauties like none other, comprising a perfect whole.

He toyed idly with the thought of moving there, just to know she was nearby. But certain elements kept him rooted on his mountain. Venice could not afford him the space and isolation he found essential. Water was everywhere. The city was flat. Here, his dominion was endless, ranging over untold hills and valleys. Here, he had friends. Here, he had the Brothers. Here, he had *Sofia's Place.* There, he had a woman who belonged to another man.

Gavin could not guess how long he remained in his garden. But for the first time in his life, he did not think of his paints a few feet away. He simply lay still, a heat burning in his body that he was powerless to snuff out. Still, he knew that if he didn't move soon, the flame would scorch his fingers and toes, brains and heart.

So finally, Gavin got up, threw a few items in his backpack, locked the doors, and began to wander.

Instinctively, he retraced the paths he had taken with Jack. In his art, he followed no tracks, but here, he was glad to take a familiar way. Just to go along, without making decisions, left or right. He hiked up mountains and slept on beaches. He walked through farms and villages, passing churches and nuns working in the fields, vintners directing their crews. He had left his journal and pen on the kitchen table and didn't even once reach in his pocket for them. His feet moved him forward through the landscape, lovely as always, but he was impervious to its charms.

One afternoon, was it in the far south, in Maremma, the land of the sunflowers, between the soft white beach and the pine forests that he saw a majestic grey heron? Gavin sat very still and watched this large wading bird feed for fish in the Tyrrhenian Sea. It was a proud creature with its white head and neck and broad black stripe from eye to crown. Its body and wings were colored in varying shades of gray, but underneath, there was only black and white. Gavin imagined it as birthed pure white until some itinerant artist painted in the dramatic contrast of blacks and grays. So beautiful and noble it was, enjoying the sea, all alone there as he himself now was, unsure of his future lot, if it included even a small portion of joyful invention.

That night, as he was about to fall asleep at the spot where forest met sand, he looked up at the stars and behold! The grey heron was asleep on a branch above his head. Its positioning was likely part of its usual habitat to avoid predators, but also, perhaps, perhaps, it was so composed to watch over Gavin, resting directly below. Gavin attributed a spiritual connection to coincidences like this. He would give this event serious consideration, coming as it did at the crossroads of memory and loss.

The sighting inveigled itself into his mind, managing to cause a small breach in his malaise.

Determined, he continued on, but he had lost his ambition to wander. Feeling the need to return home, he turned back, trying to measure the time he was gone by how long a beard he had grown, whether his hair fell below his neck. Was he away a week or two? A month? As he strolled down through the vineyards and saw the roses on the roof of the cottage, his heart felt a surge of...what? Elation, sadness, return? He found the garden neat and tended. Weeds had been pulled; the soil turned over. Apparently, the Brothers were paying attention. He lay down on his lounge chair and called to a few sparrows, just to hear the sound of his own voice. When the group chirruped back, he recalled Francesco mentioning that the sparrow was the national bird of Italy. He had thought it odd at the time, such a sweet bird, but common, to represent all of exotic, ancient Italy. He would have expected something grand, like the falcon or the condor. Oh, and over there, in the corner, near his studio, rested a pair of crested larks. When he gave them a low whistle, they turned their heads toward him and whistled back.

Finally, he went inside and put a blank canvas on his easel. For a long time, he stared at the white surface. Then he gave up his vigil and returned once again to his chaise in the garden. The effort felt hopeless. It occurred to him he had forgotten to show Ellie the painting in *Sofia's Place* that he had made after one of their phone calls about her feelings of displacement.

Suddenly, he heard a slight rustling. Looking up, he caught sight of a black-tailed godwit on the roof of his studio - unmistakable for its long legs, long bill, and orange head. He and Jack had sighted many of them along the beaches, but he was surprised to see one here, there being no water features nearby - this species of godwit were shorebirds, preferring inland wetlands.

Here was another moment for Gavin, long prone to the acceptance of fortuitous circumstances, a man who saw in ordinary moments, significant omens for one thing or another. He felt his heart shift. This special encounter with the godwit surely was so odd as to be meant just for him. The huge bird flapped its wings in a solemn gesture, then folded in on itself to sleep.

Gavin once again walked back to his cottage, picked up his brush, and hoped for the best.

His style had changed.

As if he had undergone a life-altering accident and emerged a different man with the need for new tools that would help him walk again. He gave himself over to these demands and relinquished control, letting the colors take him where they wanted to go. They had now moved from his familiar strong tones to the soft underbelly of color, the pale ones a painter puts out on his palette before mixing in the dramatic reds, oranges, purples. Over and over, he dipped into the creamy whites, the unbleached titanium, the palest of gray and tan. Was he seeking the curve of the heron's breast, the pale blush of the godwit's bill, the spiky crest on the head of the lark? The beige to caramel to sand to oatmeal, were they the soft chestnut wings of the sparrow? He couldn't answer. But as he went along, the colors felt calming, serene, coaxing him out of his indifference. He kept on, scooping up the paint, moving his brush across the surface. And as the canvas began to fill up, he felt he would make a splendid painting.

Chapter 22

On their flight home, Ellie had time to think about Gavin's indifference. His somber manner was not in character but could have been for any number of reasons. Everyone gets moody now and then. As long as his health was good, and he assured her it was, she wouldn't be too concerned.

She turned to Jeff and asked if he had a favorite painting or church or food or a favorite anything from their trip. She expected him to say the shops on the Ponte Vecchio or Michelangelo's *David* or watching the crowds in the piazzas or the evening in a romantic café behind the Piazza Santa Croce where they fed each other the divine *ravioli di zucca*, tiny pasta squares stuffed with crushed amaretti biscuits, and finished two bottles of wine.

Instead, after a long pause, he said, "Gavin's garden."

Startled, Ellie thought, *Gavin's garden?* A surprising answer, but after some thought, she was inclined to agree. Lounging on his terrace in the mild Mediterranean air, sparrows twittering on the rooftops, the glass studio standing alone in regal splendor reflecting light like shards of glass, she thought the garden did indeed contain all the elements of Italy that were beautiful and timeless. However, she would never have thought of it first thing, like Jeff. Suddenly, he was no longer just the local mayor or a sweet guy in jeans but an insightful and sensuous man. Ellie leaned over and kissed his cheek.

Then she reclined her seat and tried to doze. But immediately, her mind was assaulted with all manner of doubt. Was she foolish to even consider writing a play? Why had she been so sure of herself? She turned to Jeff, asserting, "I've never written a play before. How do I do that?"

"Honey" - he smiled - "I only run city hall. I'm sure my girl will figure it out."

And then, dismayed by his answer and missing them fiercely, she turned her thoughts to Emma and Ethan.

She often had a nagging sense that in her absence, some harm might befall her grandchildren. Why, she had no idea. Maryann and Danny were wonderful, attentive parents.

This past year, she had bought each of them pencils and a pad of lined paper. At the kitchen table, she began to teach them to write their letters. Emma was easily distracted, making stick figures of kittens and dolls while Ethan remained rooted until he had fitted each letter perfectly between the black lines. His face grew radiant at the mysterious process of putting down one letter, then another, finally making a word.

Ellie enrolled them in a children's reading group once a week at the library. After each session, they would mosey over to the stacks. Ethan slowly went up and down the aisles, pulling out a book, sitting on the floor, examining its pages. Emma played hide and seek with other children, paying scant attention to the books unless Ellie held her hand and led her purposely along. Emma checked out one or two, both discovered by Ellie. Ethan chose a dozen that he studied closely and reduced to three, telling Ellie, "Three is about right for a week, Grandma. That way, I can read them carefully and remember special things."

Both children came running. Emma leapt into her embrace; Ethan loped along behind. Eagerly, she scooped them up and settled them in her lap.

Ethan handed his grandmother Hans Christian Anderson's *Nursery Rhymes*.

"Read, read!" he pleaded, opening to the first page.

Ellie obliged, reading with a rhythmic beat, like music, to which Ethan nodded his head and tapped his fingers. However, most of the rhymes had unhappy endings. *Humpty Dumpty* fell off the wall and broke into pieces. *Jack and Jill* rolled down the hill. *Three Blind Mice* had their tails cut off. At the end of each piece, Ethan clapped and shouted hurrah! But Emma would seem about to cry. She was upset Humpty fell, that the mice lost their tails. She preferred fairy tales rather than nursery rhymes. Stories like *Sleeping Beauty* or *The Little Mermaid*, which always ended happily and often involved a handsome prince who reminded her of her daddy.

Inevitably, Emma would soon wriggle out of Ellie's lap and run to the toy area, pulling out a huge red rubber ball with a handle. Wrapping her legs around it, she bounced about the room pretending to ride a "horsie," her ponytail flying while Ethan stayed put, continuing to turn the pages. When Ellie was finished, he handed her *Mother Goose* and snuggled in deeper, there to stay until she finally had to stand and stretch.

During these story times, Ellie observed that if she coughed or lost her place, Ethan kept on reading aloud without her. Although he preferred the tempo of the childish rhymes, he could read longer, more complex stories like *Snow White and the Seven Dwarfs*. His ear was tuned to the nuances of language in a way that was surprisingly advanced for his young age. Ellie caught on to this skill of his and earnestly encouraged it, specifically directing his energies toward language. Emma, on the other hand, clearly had none of Ethan's curiosity, concentration, or inclinations.

Ellie was giddy with insight. Observing Ethan's fierce labors over his letters, his zealous ability to focus and get it right, she thought that his future might possibly involve books. Teaching her grandson to write, here in her childhood home, at the table of her youth, was, without a doubt, an unforgettable triumph. Carefully, she continued to prod Ethan's precocity into the unknown.

Jack, Ryan, and their wives were seated at a corner table in the Union Oyster House. The place had become their restaurant of choice for special occasions. And tonight, they would celebrate two momentous events - Ryan and Meghan's third anniversary and Jack and Caitlin qualifying to row in the Head of the Charles Regatta.

The waiter was pouring champagne and topping off their plates with oysters while they waited for their lobsters. An older couple nearby raised their glasses, pleased to wish the young people well. On the surface, all things seemed to be holding strong.

But not in private.

Meghan was in a hurry. She wanted a baby right away, but she couldn't get pregnant. It was surprising, considering the countless times she and Ryan tried to make it happen. Meghan wanted to consult infertility specialists. Ryan, however, wasn't ready. Badgering her husband, he became inattentive to his work. His inventive instincts grew muddied, unclear. Jack began to notice changes that were concerning. TheJackRyanStudios was known for its sharp, snappy service. Apathy and disregard would devastate their brand.

It was the first time TheJackRyanStudios was faced with a complaint. A prep school in Wellesley had commissioned a poster for parents' weekend. Ryan was in charge, and Jack was surprised at the messy result dropped on this desk for final approval. He looked in vain for meaning in the work, a clear announcement of the upcoming event. However, there was no design or plan, just a chaotic jumble of lines. It was difficult to imagine Ryan submitting such an inferior product. With their written objection in hand, Jack walked over to Ryan's desk, the sheepish look on his face giving away the knowledge he had botched the assignment.

"Perhaps you should stay home with Meghan for two weeks," Jack suggested. "Give her some personal attention. Consult with the doctors. Or take her away to a small inn in the mountains."

"Yes"—Ryan sighed—"I'll give it a try."

With Ryan gone, the office was humming and buzzing. Jack found there was no problem managing the schedule alone for a couple of weeks. He paced back and forth in front of the big window thinking through an idea, then capturing the impression right there at his drafting table. He produced a surprising amount of good, original work and didn't really miss Ryan's participation. When his partner walked in the door after his time away, Jack was almost surprised to see him.

Cordial but subdued, Ryan prepared his desk for work.

"Glad to be back," he offered.

"Hope things are going okay."

"Good to see you."

"Give my love to Meghan," the others said.

But apparently, nothing had changed.

Finally, Ryan told Jack the unfortunate story. Three months ago, Meghan became pregnant. Fearful of jinxing it, they told no one, but between the two, there was elation and hope. And then sadly, she had a miscarriage.

"She's having a hard go of it, Jack, and she's not making it easy for me. Sorry, I know I'm not pulling my weight around here."

"Give her a little time," Jack replied with a thumbs-up and a wan smile.

"We've decided to start with the doctors," Ryan said.

Soon, Ryan had additional news.

"We're going full on into the actual course of treatment starting with testing both our bloods, sperm, the *in vitro* business. It's challenging. Those hormones play havoc with your emotions, you know."

Ryan continued to share with Jack snippets of what was occurring, but it was a complex process. Meghan was often waiting for a test result or about to undergo a procedure. It was easy to lose track of what was happening at any given time. Besides, Jack felt helpless, an emotion he had not known since the Julia incident in Chicago. He offered Ryan his sincere concern and support, but it felt gratuitous. What should he say? And he was so busy managing the office alone.

Caitlin often had coffee with Meghan, but she was similarly powerless. She could hold her friend's hand. She could offer sympathy, but she too was overworked while also trying to allay Jack's concerns. Unable to ease the troubles of a couple they both loved left Caitlin and Jack adrift. In the air hovered discontent and inadequacy.

Contracts continued to come in. Every project had a deadline with designated progress dates marked on a large bulletin board. Caitlin was always busy pushing pins in, taking others out. And yet

Ryan continued to sit at his desk making useless lines on paper, balling them up, and playing basketball with the trash can. Jack strove for empathy but found it onerous to pull images of fantasy out of his head with Ryan's dark mood hovering. The sense of wasteful lingering was one neither man had ever known.

One day, as Jack entered the office, he had an odd insight. When Ryan was gone, he had managed quite well on his own. Now that they were together, every effort seemed a tedious burden.

After their Saturday rowing session, Jack took Caitlin for a late lunch to a pub in Cambridge. It had been two months since Ryan's return, and he had not yet begun producing acceptable work.

Jack would now bring up the issue hovering over the office. Ryan was her brother, and Jack might well pay a price for simply raising the subject. He had postponed this moment of confrontation, thinking the situation would mend itself. But it hadn't. There could be emotional fallout for Caitlin. She might be forced to make choices. It *had* crossed Jack's mind but only briefly that if it were ever necessary, the issue of possible severance would cause painful, perhaps irreparable, rifts in the family.

He's my brother-in-law, thought Jack, *and I love the guy. He's been my best friend all these years. When we were starting out, his father gave us cheap rent. His mother still knits me sweaters for every birthday and St. Patty's Day. But this can't continue.*

As well, who could replace Ryan's weird, off-the-wall vibe we share?

Caitlin waited, watching her husband's face as he struggled to find the precise words.

"I want to talk about Ryan and Meghan," Jack started. "At the first round of *in vitro*, there was trouble with her eggs. I think they'll try again as soon as they can. But Meghan's issues are damaging the workplace. For the first time ever, we lost a job because we couldn't meet the deadline, and other projects have been delayed. You know that better than anyone. We're heavy on referrals, and word gets around. What do you think? How can I get Ryan back on track?" he asked, keeping his voice steady.

When Caitlin didn't look surprised, it occurred to Jack that she had similar thoughts. His wife was as ambitious as he. Under her oversight, the office gears turned without mishap, no breakdowns, no needed repairs. Every glitch was taken care of without the others hardly knowing about it.

Privately, she had already spoken to Ryan.

"Have you thought of adopting?" she had asked her brother. "Infertility issues are often resolved when one already has a child. Something about relaxing and not being tense."

"Meghan's not keen to adopt," he answered. "But even if she were willing, which she is not right now, she would insist on an Irish child. Slim chance of that in this town. We'd have to go to Ireland. Anyway, it's way too soon. I might have a word with our local priest who knows things going on in the parish. I just haven't done it yet. Next up is a second round of *in vitro*."

Jack called Ryan for a meeting.

As Ryan walked toward him, Jack noted an expression of defeat. Or was it misgiving? Ryan immediately put up his hand. "I know. Look, Jack, this has been a tough period for all of us. If it's okay with you, I'm going to take another leave for a few weeks. Can you get along without me again for a while?"

"Sure," Jack said, relieved Ryan had made the proposal, not himself. But not as relieved as he had expected. He felt melancholy at the loss of Ryan's ebullient spirit firing up the rooms with an occasional "hey, guys, listen to this one!" For all Jack's bravado, this had been a two-man effort from the beginning. Without Ryan's intervention, there would be no constraints on his own occasionally impetuous and untenable proposals.

Ryan was silent.

Jack looked down at his desk.

Ellie couldn't sleep.

She was having an edgy night. Why had she thought that because she was an actress, and now a director, she could also write a screenplay? Foolish woman! Writing required entirely different skills.

It was utter folly to think she could cross that line simply because she wanted to. She thought of the characters in *The Secret Garden* and how for the Tylersville show, she had merely changed the locale and a few basic facts, staying close to the original novel. But when it went to Broadway, it was adapted as a musical. She had seen clips and was astonished at the skills involved in the new version - a musical score, choreography. It was as if the show were being written from scratch. She could never have conceived the nuances of the characters' personalities or the complex plot, the interweaving of effective dialogue. Thrashing about, alone in her bed, she had no comforting answers.

This work was not a narrative or a short story but a play comprised only of dialogue. She would have to reconstruct not only the words of others, but their subtleties, intonations, accents. It had to be clear enough so someone in the audience with a ten-year-old could say to herself, "Right on, that's just how my child sounds."

Ellie left her bed for the dark kitchen, a cup of tea, some paper, and a pen. First, above all, she needed a plot. The story itself, from beginning to end. She would place the geography in the northwest. She would have girls rather than boys. She supposed that the grandmother could be a widow. But then she would have to solve the technical problem of an older woman alone trying to run a farm. Or she could have the grandmother be deceased, but then who would babysit and bake cookies?

Perhaps she should start with the female lead joining a theater company in Los Angeles. Or the father's heroic move to France. Or an opening involving the entire family with characters of various ages, personalities, and needs. A dramatic launch was needed, one with bite, with grit. However, the more options she conceived, the more confused the project became. A blank page, and the writer can put down any words in the English language. But Ellie was intimidated by the complexities involved, the endless logistical decisions to be made. Rather than present as an exciting prospect, the project loomed as a hopeless endeavor. She returned to bed, worrying and wondering how she could possibly pull this off.

As the morning sun hit the windows, the solution suddenly came to her. As often happened in their family, someone had an insight or an awakening when he or she wasn't looking for one.

It was so obvious. Why had it seemed so elusive? Of course!

Abruptly, she jumped out of bed. This change would require a total adjustment of her entire scheme.

Forgoing its fictional aspect, she would make the play nonfiction and tell the true story of her family.

Writing fiction was confusing. Family experiences kept intruding. She was ignorant about what and what not to include, what was real, what was not. But writing the true story of the Taylors was not the proposal she had presented to Gavin. She would need to call again and get a second approval. Her concerns about him returned. Since he returned from Venice, they had hardly talked. Meanwhile, she would continue to think about her approach, starting at the perfect, logical place - the chicken coop. Gavin sitting at his easel. This opening time frame would include all the required theatrical elements - Gavin's determination, the children's interests, the tug between husband and wife, and the element of surprise. Wouldn't the audience be shocked to see the curtain rise on a shack in Iowa?

And right then, her scheme fell apart for the second time.

It was her intent to tell the story from an older folks' point of view, a sort of memoir, events unfolding through the characters' reminiscences. In a play employing this technique, the first scene shown was actually the conclusion to the plot. But in Ellie's thinking, Gavin was just starting his career. He was not yet old enough to look back. The story would have to be told chronologically, not in reverse. *Well, I'll pull back from thinking about this for a few days,* she decided. *Maybe all will become apparent after a rest. One way or another, the story is there. I only have to put it down in an imaginative, clever way. But how?*

Suddenly, Ellie was exhausted and frustrated.

I should give it up, walk away.

But she had told Jeff. She had told Gavin. There was no turning back, not for Ms. Ellie Taylor. She tossed her old jottings aside and dressed to go out for a walk.

What have I taken on? Perhaps the fresh air and the smell of roses will make me forget all about this darn play.

For two days, she rang Gavin. *He'll pick up eventually,* she thought. And while she waited, she reverted to the comfort of her fallback position - her friend, the dentist Peter Lyman. She called him Doc Pete. If asked, he would assist. From time to time, he had sent a short story over to the company in Tylersville.

She must invite him out to dinner at *Pepe's*. She always discussed important issues at *Pepe's* over margaritas. Doc Pete would help her.

"How does one learn to write?" she asked him, even before he had settled into his chair.

"My dear, I've been writing plays for over a dozen years, and I'm still trying to figure that out," he said, smiling. His eyebrows had turned prematurely white to match his hair, yet he was still youthful, still a charmer.

"You write a few lines over and over a dozen times until one sounds right. Then you read it out loud for the rhythm, the pulse. Keep working it until the cadence feels right. Then put it away for two weeks. After that time, bring it out again and repeat the process."

"But I can't even get started," Ellie cried.

"Ah, there you have it," he answered, "the nub, the heart. The story."

"Do you know what Eleanor Roosevelt once said?" Ellie asked. "Do one scary thing every day. And if writing a play isn't scary, what is?"

"I should think if you've raised two boys, you might know the answer to that," he answered, slapping his knee, pleased with himself.

He was a kind man, a generous man, but of no use at all. He had said nothing that would help her find the perfect plot, the perfect words. She was in a dark place, swimming in a dark sea.

They each had two margaritas, and although they met at her invitation, Doc Pete picked up the check.

Ellie sat upright at her dressing table. She just had an idea that might clarify her dilemma.

She would illustrate the story with a graph to portray the sequence of events. A plot outline. First, she wrote down certain names at various angle points. Then she drew a straight line from the point of the old farmhouse, for example, to one in Chicago. Another from Chicago to Boston. She made another point and a new line from the shack to the mountains of Italy and another from the farm to Cedar Rapids.

The result was fragmented lines that crossed over each other in all directions.

Where would she put Jack? And Danny?

She had hoped to design a road map, an easy path. She had hoped the chart would make sense, a neat journey from one spot to the other, guiding her somehow. But it was an absurd exercise.

Still, with Ellie, an idea that arose was an idea that could be realized. Carrying her notes downstairs where the natural light was bright, she sat in front of a window and placed another call to Gavin. She hoped he would answer this time.

If he said go ahead, she would somehow begin to teach herself how to write a play.

Chapter 23

The painting Gavin was finally able to complete upon his return from trekking was propped against the back door. He wanted to see it from his chair in the garden.

The muted colors reminded him of the canvas bought by Elena Ricci. He had painted his direct impression of clouds and sky seen at an exact moment. He remembered his mood then - ebullient, happy. This time, it was different. He painted almost aimlessly, without conscious intent, and the pale outcome was not attributable to anything specific though if he had thought about it, his life had been stripped of color.

A whooshing sound came from the roof. The venerable godwit was perched, rising to a formidable height. Their eyes met, held briefly, then the great bird flapped its wings, turned around twice, and settled down with its legs folded beneath him. With his head tucked into his chest, he promptly fell asleep. Gavin wondered if it was watching over him like the grey heron did at the beach as if birds possessed a mystical power to ensure a man's safety and well-being. Or to prove by its presence man's eternal connection to all living creatures. Was he trying to keep Gavin from feeling lonely?

Gavin hardly knew anything personal about Cecilia except that she lived in a grand villa. Their conversations consisted primarily of questions regarding his work. He asked nothing in return for fear of being misinterpreted or accused of being too inquisitive. But it didn't matter what he said or didn't say or what she asked or didn't ask.

She came to his room. And in his bones, she would remain. Because lust is a fever you relive over and over, an emotion you will move heaven and earth to recapture.

Like the godwit, Gavin was about to doze off, a nap to avoid thinking about Cecilia, about the depths to which a mature man can be irrevocably bound to a woman, no matter the brevity of association.

He could say his obsession was due to her being an integral part of Venezia's mesmerizing powers or because he was grateful to the Carraros for commissioning the spectacular mural that garnered him popular acclaim. Yes, those aspects counted but not nearly. Cecilia was simply a gorgeous, erotic potion of irresistible elements.

The painting before him turned out brilliantly, but as Gavin reflected, he thought it a mere anomalous spurt of energy, a mis-step in his indifference. Once again, he felt aimless and undirected. He wondered about the godwit asleep on his roof. If it flew off to its watery home, how would its disappearance impact his life? His lifelong sense of omens and circumstance was full upon him. This bird, this particular godwit - he was convinced - would determine his future. Why else was he here?

He would give it a name - Ulysses, a hero, a wanderer.

When Gavin endowed Ulysses with human powers and designs, he knew he was having a personal crisis. Turning fitfully in in his chair, he worried how he would get on. *I suppose I'll have to wait and see where my body and mind take me,* he thought. *Life isn't idle, and eventually, somehow, I won't be either.*

He didn't lift a brush for another week, and Ulysses remained on the roof until one sparkling morning after a serious rainstorm. Ulysses was gone. Gavin checked the roof, the trees. He walked around the perimeter of the house. He walked to the edge of the hill and scanned the valley below. A bird of that size couldn't hide easily. Not even the remains of a feather was found on the ground.

He didn't know what to do. Something had happened. Something had called the godwit away. There was a significance to its departure that Gavin must uncover. But at this moment, even while fearing the dissolution of their mystical linkage, even suffering a profound sadness, Gavin at the same time experienced a powerful urge to act. Almost like a sleepwalker, he left his garden and stepped into his glass studio.

Some time ago, he had prepared an enormous canvas with no plans for its use. Now he pulled it out from the back of his supplies and propped it against the wall. He found a low platform and placed the canvas atop its surface to raise it to a comfortable painting level. The size of it gave him pause. For a single canvas, this would be the largest he had ever taken on. He then began to mix his paints until he found the perfect shade of bright red, vivid like the San Marzano pomodoro or tomato. He then squeezed out a discreet dollop of black and his preparations were done. His palette looked almost bare. In the time it took for him to mount his canvas, the entire project appeared in his mind, whole and complete - how lust feels from desire to consummation.

A spirit was guiding his hands, moving his arms.

He would paint a series of five canvases that would tell the story. Why five? Because there were five steps from beginning to end. He'd start with line drawings of Cecilia's body - spare, pure. There would be no details of face or feature, just a black line against a flaming red background. Never before had he attempted anything like this, to paint an idea or object the viewer could clearly identify.

Over the surface, he laid down an even coat of red paint, then another. After the paint dried, he picked up a thin brush with a long handle, about to dip it in pure black straight from the tube. Briefly, differing opinions among painters crossed his mind - whether or not black required a touch of sienna to bring up some warmth. He thought of Henri Matisse, Mark Rothko, and Pierre Soulages, all of whom used black brilliantly as living lines and spaces, even as dancing light. He lowered his brush into the paint, wiped off the excess, then brought it up directly to the canvas, and made a mark.

Canvas Number 1

Cecilia standing in the doorway, just the curves and shape of her with a sweep of hair gone wild. A swipe for each breast, a line parting her legs. No details or color within the lines. After a time, he stepped back and looked. Not a single line needed to be redone. In a dozen strokes, there it was, the perception of Cecilia as she appeared that night. There was the excitement of anticipation, her body leaning into the room, head turned expectantly.

Gavin prepared four more canvases of the same size, laying cloth over the stretcher bars, then pulling, folding, stapling.

Canvas Number 2

Again, he covered the entire surface with the gorgeous tomato red. Again, he dropped his brush into the black paint. Her head fell; her hair covered her face. Her arms reached out into space. Leaning forward, she appeared about to fall. He drew no other shape or form. Neither man nor bed.

Canvas Number 3

Cecilia stretched out on her back, her legs raised, head turned to the side, arms enclosing an imaginary form.

Canvas Number 4

Cecilia sleeping on her side, her hands beneath her chin.

While Gavin worked, he kept saying her name, bringing her into the space. Cecilia. Her name was like an incantation, a spell to which he succumbed. Cecilia. And soon he could see that his lines depicted the essence of sensuous reality - grace, provocation, generosity.

Canvas Number 5

Cecilia readying to leave, her robe flowing as she turned.

Gavin finished just as the dawn was about to show its light. He had told his story without interruption or hesitation, the unfolding of a single encounter. It was done, five paintings of desire, anticipation, approach, consummation, departure. It was all there.

He carefully placed the five canvases around the garden. Among the roses and camellias, they seemed just another flower, like the scarlet geraniums, the coral begonias. Drawn to their flashy red luster, common sparrows, those little Italian birds, flew in close and fluttered around like butterflies. Again Gavin looked in vain to the roof, the trees. It was to the godwit that he owed his dramatic return. He longed to offer him a prayer for his reprieve from the void, for the mercies so bestowed.

Gavin studied the paintings. *These are gorgeous,* he thought, *brilliant, unique*, a sacred vision of God's precious creation - man and woman. Although only the woman was drawn, man's presence was felt through the artist's elegant brushstrokes. The majesty of active love conveyed in the most spare way possible. In fact, Gavin's face flushed as he continued to stare.

As night fell, he brought the canvases into the cottage as if they were his guests, to protect them from weather and small creatures, the pecking of birds. He fell asleep on the cot, reluctant to leave their company for his proper bed in the other room.

When he awoke, he knew exactly how he would proceed. The five paintings must remain together and precious to the buyer. Selling them to a rich Italian to hang in his fancy salon would be blasphemous, not to be considered merely as any other piece of art. No, he would somehow get them to Cecilia, and she could do whatever she wished with them. They were rightfully hers. He had borrowed her body to paint for his own purpose, and now he would return her to herself.

He imagined the paintings arriving at the palazzo in multiple crates. He imagined the butler painstakingly unwrapping them. He imagined him carrying them one at a time up to Signor Carraro's study and arranging them around the room just as Gavin had arranged them around the garden. He imagined the weighty heft of Signor Carraro's sudden frown. He imagined the butler stealing glances at the artworks *could it possibly be?* He imagined various options the signor might take out of spite - destroy them? Desecrate his spectacular mural?

Reconsidering, Gavin thought, *perhaps not.* Perhaps he would not ship them to Cecilia after all.

Still, he could not resist an artist's inclination to publicly show off his work. But how, where? Not in Florence, not in Venice. Some venue far distant so the Carraros would be unaware. The miles between Venice and Rome were considerable. Should the Carraros by chance hear of a viewing, they likely would not undertake the lengthy trip. Besides, Gavin had heard they were busy displaying his Venetian mural to visitors and critics from all over the world. Just last week, so the newspapers said, they had welcomed twenty-five art professors from American universities for a viewing.

Sofia had contacts in Rome. He would ask her to arrange an exhibit in an intimate space. No need for pomp or fancy surroundings. In fact, the simpler the better so as not to distract from the artwork.

Gavin took photos and boarded the bus in front of Francesco's café, greeting Enzo in a weary voice.

"Gavin, *mio amico*, my friend! Where have you been?" Enzo asked enthusiastically, as the bus rumbled along the bumpy road, making its way through the fields of wildflowers.

Sofia looked closely at the photographs spread over the table, blushing despite herself. Even in this flat, reduced form, the images popped right off the paper. *Bold and visionary,* she thought, *a profound emotion conveyed in its simplest form. Really quite extraordinary, and these are only photos, not original paintings. A bit like Matisse, per-*

haps, but so unlike Gavin. They would fetch an enormous sum, especially since they were different from anything he had done before.

She continued to study the pictures. Gavin continued to wait. Finally, Sofia looked up at him with a thousand questions in her eyes. *A woman in Venice, surely.* But as he remained moody and detached, she dare not ask. In previous days, they would have been jubilant together, already out the door on their way to celebrate at Matteo's.

Both sat quietly, each considering various components of managing this artistic bombshell. She knew his past patrons would vie for ownership. And there were new clients as well who, on her recommendation, would buy the whole lot at first sight.

But Gavin had expressed certain conditions. Selling these paintings at a good price did not interest him. He merely wanted them seen, and if someone wanted to purchase the whole lot, Sofia must first obtain his permission. He would assess a potential buyer, but for what, he wasn't sure. He only knew all five must remain together and be displayed as he directed. He wanted this story told as if the observer himself was in the throes of the experience.

"Gavin, I know the perfect place. Hopefully, I can arrange to rent it for three weeks. It would be absolutely breathtaking."

"Did you ever hear of the Palazzo Venezia? The American painter, the modernist Julian Schnabel, had an exhibit there. It proved a stunning venue for his abstract pieces. Let me tell you about it.

"Although the palazzo began as a modest medieval house in 1469, it was massively enlarged by Pope Pius IV in 1564. As the Venetian embassy in Rome promised to pay for maintenance and improvements, the pope gave them the entire complex, extracting a promise they would keep a particular wing, the Appartamento Cybo, as a residence for their cardinals. It's a gorgeous place with the finest of Italian ornamentation covering every surface."

"I recall seeing reports of that exhibit at the time," Gavin replied. "A sensational event for the likes of Schnabel to be displayed in such stately rooms. But I don't need that kind of space. Perhaps something more intimate? Especially since they will hang one next to the other. I had thought a gallery like *Sofia's Place* - modern, unadorned white walls, bright lights. But a renowned historical venue? A palazzo for cardinals, a home to Venetian legates? Why have the art compete with the setting?"

"Either would work," said Sofia, "but if you want to appeal to wealthy Italians, the Palazzo Venezia would be ideal. Also, the National Museum is now in that building. Visitors and tourists would be on the premises. Your paintings would have maximum exposure."

Sofia would see to it that everyone who had ever stepped into her gallery or had visited the villas housing his murals, every venue at which she had ever spoken, would receive notification of the opening. *And what an unexpected coup for me,* she thought, *to collect a commission on these pieces.* For a while, she had been thinking of opening a gallery in Rome; now might be a good time to take a serious look.

"Gavin, this show will be a big hit. I promise you. Are you feeling well?" she asked, missing his usual enthusiasm. "You look a bit tired, a bit…disengaged. Do you need anything?"

"I'm fine." He stood up to leave, kissed her on both cheeks, and murmured quietly to himself, "The godwit left. Its name was Ulysses," and walked out the door, leaving Sofia to wonder who he was talking about. *Ulysses who? Is that the name of a friend, a colleague?*

Gavin remained secluded on his mountain until the launch was imminent. When it was time, he packed a few things for a week's stay at lodgings Sofia had arranged. At the Santa Maria Novella station, he stumbled on the stairs, dropped his ticket. He was jumpy, keyed up. This show was unlike any of his others. A young boy seated opposite in his compartment held out a shiny green yo-yo, his eyes, pleading. He was having trouble getting the string to snap back around the spool. Gavin took the toy and flicked his wrist over and over, showing him the best way to get a successful return. Laughing and fumbling, the young boy finally did it correctly, jumping into Gavin's lap and giving him a hug. Gavin was grateful for the distraction, and in ninety minutes, they were in Roma Termini Station.

He walked to his lodgings, marveling that Florence, predominantly a product of the Renaissance, looked so different from Rome. Only an hour and a half distant, yet it felt like another country.

Rome's origins extended much further back - to Christ, to Julius Caesar, the Roman Empire, Byzantine Rome, the Etruscans, layer upon layer of history, all visible to any visitor. Ruins and monuments were preserved everywhere.

His charming *albergo*, similar to a *pensione* but somewhat larger, was a few blocks from the area of the Capitoline Hill, the noble ruins of the Roman Forum. The magnificent Colosseum, circular and arched, sat upon the earth like a glorious relic that refused to disappear. A few blocks off, atop a monumental stone staircase was the memorial to Italy's first king, Victor Emmanuel II, easily recognizable by the chariots at its apex. Sofia placed Gavin in the center of Rome's most spectacular sites, hoping that by strolling among Rome's remarkable antiquity, he would recapture his old joy.

Gavin Taylor

Oh my! A red banner with black lettering of his name was displayed at least two stories high across the front of the Palazzo Venezia. Gazing at the spectacular block-long building, Gavin immediately had qualms. Surely five paintings were not nearly enough for a single show. Surely, he did not merit this spectacular welcome. He hoped Sofia knew what she was doing.

Unusual for a celebrated artist, he was reluctant to preview the show, fearful of his desire to alter any details or find fault. He was delighted to see a substantial line waiting for the main doors to open and walked a half block around the building to a discreet side entrance. After he presented his papers, the guard let him pass, surprised at the modesty of the artist himself. Such personages were known to assume an entitled demeanor, accompanied by a doting entourage.

It was the reds he saw first. Reds with a thousand disparate meanings - the color of Valentines, of the devil's cape, of hot-blooded anger, of scarlet-letter shame. In China, red is for luck, the bride's choice, but in Africa, red is for mourning. In the Palazzo Venezia, red is for Cecilia.

When the paintings were propped in his garden, the greenery had mitigated the intensity of the reds. But not here. Despite the heavily embellished surfaces, the elaborate setting only enhanced the starkness of the art. It was the specialized lighting aimed directly at the display, Gavin realized, that gave it a sultry yet ethereal quality. But there was no doubt the five were a palpable portrayal of obsession, rendered with clarity and honesty. The marrow of lust's hungers, its progression and realization. It had also been a fine idea to hang them only a few inches apart as the viewers waited, breathless with anticipation, for the story before them to rush to its finish.

Sofia had been right, about everything.

The crowds came. The critics showed up. Wearing a cap low over his brow, Gavin wandered unnoticed. A group of American tourists chatted in front of number 3.

"Who thought sex would look like that?"

"That guy Taylor must have had some amazing affair."

"Isn't it fabulous how you can actually feel what he's showing?"

"Lucky you. I can only dream."

"How will we ever describe this back home?"

Gavin slipped out of the building and walked down to the Roman Forum. Parts of ancient buildings still stood, enough for him to imagine how the city might have looked in those long-ago times - the Curia Julia, the Roman Senate, the Arch of Titus, Temple of Romulus, Temple of Vesta. Gavin kept walking and reading small signs - Arch of Septimius Severus, Basilica of Constantine…

Most of these buildings - it was noted on a plaque - were destroyed in AD 410, around the time that the entire Roman Empire began to fall. During the Middle Ages, the land that was once the great Roman Forum was reduced to a pasture for grazing animals. *AD 410,* Gavin thought, *and all through the centuries, enough fragments of beauty remained for humanity to cherish!* He felt incidental in the landscape of time, hardly a blot in the pantheon of centuries. And yet amidst this glory, his five paintings were being exhibited just down the road in one of Rome's most distinguished structures.

He was almost taken down by the gorgeous irony of his life - the drama of his red paintings in the Palazzo Venezia ballroom and, nearby, the splendor of the ruins. They were beautiful and overwhelming, both together, like Cecilia, like Venice.

He met Sofia for dinner at a quiet trattoria. She was pleased to see him smile, his voice perky. She too was buoyant. They had barely taken their seats when she took his hand and cried, "Gavin, all five paintings were sold immediately! And you'll never guess who bought them!

"Do you want to guess? No?

"Oh, all right," Sofia teased. "I wonder if you will still want to vet these folks, considering how well you know them."

Gavin waited, an unease beginning to roil his gut.

"Signor and Signora Carraro from Venice! Can you believe they came all the way down specially? They heard about the show and had to see what you were up to!"

Her eyes were flashing, exultant.

"Gavin, I never expected this, not so quickly, not before the paying guests made it into the rotunda. Apparently, the guard at the side door let them in early. Perhaps a monetary bribe. At any rate, they're sold. But they can't take possession until the exhibition closes, pending your approval, as you wished. I told them you wanted to meet potential buyers."

Gavin's eyes blurred. A drone buzzed in his ears.

They must have been admitted to the building even before he himself had entered. At the exact moment he was listening to the comments of the Americans, Signor Carraro was purchasing his paintings in another room, missing each other by a beat or two of the pulse.

"Gavin, did you hear? Gavin?"

What were their first thoughts upon expecting an explosion of abstract images and finding proof of an illicit affair that likely occurred in their own house? Somewhere in his deepest of hearts, Gavin wondered if he had hoped for this - a way of getting them to Cecilia without sending them directly to her.

"Did Signor and Signora Carraro ask about me?"

"Honestly, Gavin, it was the strangest transaction I've ever had. As I said, they came in before the crowds. Both of them just stood before the paintings as if in a daze. Signor walked back and forth, left to right, looking and looking, whispering to his wife. I presume the lady was his wife. Of course, no price was listed, so he called over my assistant and requested the numbers. Then straightaway, the man scurried into the adjoining room to sign a preliminary agreement, subject to your approval, of course. The signora lingered, staring at the paintings. When I asked if I could be of help, she shook her head no, no, and walked away to join her husband. I heard her mutter, 'took my breath away.' Her eyes lit up like those of a startled animal. She may have whispered it twice, if I even heard it correctly at all. Do you know what she meant?"

Gavin didn't answer.

Would Signor Carraro show the paintings privately, accompanied by an amusing story? Store them in a vault, to live out of the light? Gavin imagined all five paintings fiercely burning in a small brazier dead center of his precious glass lobby.

Red flames. Red ashes.

Chapter 24

The Roman art world was stunned at Gavin's sensational show - the subject of the paintings, the drama of its presentation. The city had never seen anything quite like it.

Who was this Gavin Taylor? Have you seen pictures of him? folks asked each other. Young girls imagined his looks - bearded, scruffy, exotic. Mature women daydreamed about bedroom encounters.

But in his usual style, Gavin shunned celebrity status. The desire for glory was not in him. He was content to be a silent witness in the room, then quietly return to his mountain. *You've become a bit of a recluse, old boy,* he said to himself with some amusement. *What a pity - you could just as easily have gone the other way, become a roving party boy.* Still, he was pleased that he did what he felt he must - describe Cecilia's impact on him the only way he knew how.

He never thought she would know, that news of the show would reach the distant villa of Signor and Signora Carraro. But, of course, he was ridiculously naive or, more likely, simply lying to himself. With his great mural adorning their own house, surely they would be following his appearances forever, especially one in the renowned Palazzo Venezia. But he didn't want notification to come from himself directly, and so it worked out well, after all. *And yet,* he thought wryly, *despite our manipulations and obfuscations, life often plays jokes with the elements of fate and irony. The Carraros had purchased the entire series, and that, Gavin did not expect.*

If her husband even considered the paintings might be of his wife, Cecilia could face serious repercussions. Signor may have bought them just for that reason, to take them off the market. On the other hand, Gavin was ignorant of the intricate codes of conduct observed by wealthy Venetians. This marital behavior might be acceptable in their social milieu. Signor Carraro could think the paintings beautiful and intriguing, a tribute to his wife. He and Cecilia might even laugh together and hang them prominently. Who knows what is acceptable between a husband and wife?

But art, once produced, exists outside its creator and lives in the eyes of its viewers. A work may engage the hearts of many or only a few. It could end up homeless or in a happy space, a temporary venue or one lasting centuries. It might be bought and resold, donated, destroyed by wind or fire. But again, that was not his business. His business was painting. Sofia's business was mating buyer and seller. And ever after, the fate of the painting was left to the individual owner.

In any case, he had painted the truth. The matter was now out of his hands.

Gavin was sitting on a stone wall marveling at the remains of the Roman Forum. But even more, marveling at himself. Almost immediately after the sale of the Cecilia series, he experienced a rare and welcome calm. And now he was speculating at the beneficence of this occurrence. It was as if the godwit had followed him from the mountain to Rome, hovering over the train all the way, and then, the sale complete and Gavin at rest, flew back to its wetlands. Somehow, the heat of Cecilia's being had been doused with Gavin's sweat. Perhaps painting his emotions as he did weakened his intractable bond with her. And Gavin knew that if there was even a slight release, a mere loosening of the link, one could get over such a profound romance. When he met Sofia for breakfast the day after the show closed, he was already beginning to feel once again actively involved in his own life. How this recent peace had shown up, he didn't know. But he was grateful and wouldn't analyze it.

On the train home, Gavin sat alone. He never tired of absorbing the details of the landscape. On this trip, there was something new - a special breed of grazing sheep, furry white bodies with black noses called the Valais Blacknose breed. He was surprised at their presence, more commonly found in the frosty air of the Swiss Alps. A brief spotting, and they were gone. The farms were back, and he was then enjoying the precise manner in which the vineyards were marked off one from another by tidy borders of stones or trees, creating a patchwork of greens. The train turned around a bend, and there was a village and local station stop. A pretty young girl reached through his open window and smiled coyly as she handed over two ripe peaches for a few coins. The village disappeared as the train started up, chugging along its familiar route once more. Now there were allées of cypress trees edging the winding roads like sentries guiding one's way to an unknown destination.

Gavin had no idea about his next painting, but it was no longer concerning. He was actually wearied, just plain done in and could use a short rest. He wanted to enjoy this new contentment, to dwell in its aura. He had done extraordinary work, and his inner compulsions were no longer driving him. As long as he kept reminding himself that though he might feel steady and sure at this moment, it was his flings into the brambles that spurred him to make his most original and unforgettable paintings.

"Gavin, hi! How are things?" Ellie asked. "A show in *Rome*? You sold *everything*? How fabulous! Did you visit the famous tourist sites? Yes? I think I've seen the Colosseum on a hundred postcards!

"Uh-oh, why did I call? Well, Gavin, I was thinking. Remember that play you agreed I could write? The one about our life and family but written as fiction?

"You do remember? Oh, good.

"Well, I started to write it. Can you believe it? Old Ellie writing a stage play. Uh, Gavin, there's only one catch. It isn't working. It's difficult for me to distinguish the pretend family from the real one. So - what do you think of my writing about the *real* us? Maybe I'd change our name, but I haven't really thought it out yet. Anyone we care about knows about our life anyway.

"Gavin?"

"I'm here, Ellie. As you say, everyone knows about our life, and no one has yet called the cops. I guess it would be okay. Shouldn't you check with Jack and Danny?"

"I never thought of asking them, but I'll give them a call. So it's okay with you? Gavin?"

"Yes, Ellie, it's okay with me."

"Jack? Hi, it's Mom. I hope all is going well with you in Boston.

"Oh no! Problems with Meghan and Ryan? She's depressed because she can't get pregnant? Ryan's taking a brief leave? That certainly *is* news, but I'm sorry to hear it.

"Yes, honey, I know you'll figure it out, but it must still be a shock. Well, now that I know about your problem, this may not be the best time to ask you something, but I kind of need to know. I'm thinking of writing a play about our family.

"Yes, our real family, not a fictitious one.

"What will I say about you? Why, nothing that isn't amazing - what a talented little boy you were and how you made a successful business as an adult. Certainly nothing about Julia! Unless you wouldn't mind my mentioning her in the background, just casually, incidentally. A very small mention.

"Okay, I won't.

"Yes, of course I'll show the manuscript to you first.

"You're doing this series on Boston restaurants? It sounds thrilling! You have to go now?

"I understand you're busy. Love you, will send you a look when I'm well along.

"What? Jack, honey, you don't have to tell me. No one knows better than I that I've never done this before! But you never had your own business before, either, and look at you!"

"Danny, how's the father of my two gorgeous grandchildren?

"Of course, I'll come over for dinner Sunday. Of course, I'll bring Jeff. I have to see if my darling Ethan has started reading *War and Peace* yet! And if my beautiful Emma has learned any new gymnastics tricks.

"Do I have a special reason for calling?

"As a matter of fact, I do. What would you think if I said I wanted to write a play about our family?

"What will I have to say that's special? Why, everything about us is special! Will we be famous? Hardly, honey! I don't even know yet if I can pull it off. I'm not really a writer.

"You think I can do anything I set my mind to? Aren't you sweet? It's comforting to know you have that much faith in your mother. So you do think it's okay?

"Of course, we'll speak about it as I go along. See you Sunday. Tell the children Grandma will be there soon!"

The words flew out of Ellie's head onto the page. She was putting down sentences as quickly as if speaking into a tape recorder. By the time she needed to stretch, she had been at her desk for several hours. A dozen pages were a good beginning, and she was proud of herself.

She poured a glass of wine, shuffled the papers, and sat by the light. As Doc Pete had advised, she began to read aloud. "An essential element for gauging rhythm and pace," he had said. "Any jarring word jumps out." But before she finished the first page, she abruptly stopped. The dialogue was forced, inauthentic. It seemed impossible to recall how her family spoke thirty years ago. At best, she was guessing, putting her own spin on others' conversations. She was sure her children's words were more charming than she had written - Danny's more humorous, Jack's more earnest. And in hindsight, the intonations were troublesome and stilted. Wasn't she curt when Jack thrust his first drawing before her, interrupting her chat with Gavin? And Danny with his first fall in the creek? She was so relieved he hadn't drowned that she scolded him mercilessly while he laughed the whole time. The words Gavin spoke when he courted her in New York, when he first sighted the family farm, when he quit his job as a bus supervisor. What were they? In truth, even the twins' words from last week were veiled in shadow.

Fiction might be easier after all. She needn't search for truth, just make it up. She sighed, poured another glass of wine, and decided she wasn't ready to give up yet on her true-story concept. It was foolish to think that after one try, she would discard the whole project.

As Ellie drove to dinner at her son's house, she thought of Ethan's failure regarding the finger-painting project. For Christmas, she bought the twins a painting set.

"Dip your finger into the paint and make a design or image right on the paper. This way." She showed them, drawing a sun, a ball, with the forefinger she had immersed in yellow paint. Or they could use several fingers, even their whole hand.

"Use your fingers and hands like a brush," she said. Emma had vigorously gotten into the blue while Ethan, fastidious about his hands, kept them in his lap, scrunching his face with displeasure.

"I love the squishy feel," Emma cried, quickly plunging in five fingers, covering them with multiple colors. "Grandma, look! Rainbows on all my fingers, kinda!"

She smeared the paper with random blotches and scribbles, pages that were soon strewn everywhere and stuck with it for almost an hour. Ellie would have to wait and see whether or not Emma's zeal would amount to more than a momentary amusement. Finally, Ethan cautiously dipped in one finger, then immediately reached for a paper towel to wipe off the paint.

"Is there a brush I could use?" he whispered to Ellie.

She found one of Gavin's old brushes, but Ethan even held that tool gingerly. While his sister was cooing with delight, daubing the nose of their dog Laddie with a spot of green, Ethan was deliberate and tentative, almost worried. He had no idea how to simply play with paint. Only the printed word was concrete to him, something he could control, a page with lines and black ink, not an abstract pattern or spatter but a specific way to move himself into a world of fanciful invention.

Meanwhile, Ellie was relieved to know that Gavin would not have to worry about Ethan requiring the proper nurture to become a painter.

When Ellie entered the house, Maryann was stirring a pot of stew while the two children jabbered at her feet, building a mazelike structure out of Legos.

"A castle, Grandma," cried Ethan, "with a turret, like the one in King Arthur."

"What's a turret? Who's King Arthur?" asked Emma.

Ethan rolled his eyes at his sister, then picked up his comic-strip version of *King Arthur and the Knights of the Round Table* and held it in front of her face.

He then turned to Ellie.

"Grandma, I have a surprise. I'm going to read *you* a story."

And he began reading about the magician Merlin, and the good deeds of Sirs Lancelot and Galahad while his sister continued to fiddle with the Legos.

"Grandma, how's that? Isn't that a wonderful story?" And then, puffed up and content, he added, "I can do it all by myself now."

Ellie kissed his forehead. "Far better than I can, Ethan, honey," she answered.

The next morning, she called Doc Pete and asked him if he would come over on Saturday afternoons and teach a small child how to write a story.

Watching Ethan and Doc Pete together reminded Ellie of an odd word she heard long ago from one of her Jewish college friends. Ellie had just introduced Judith to Gavin, and the three were drinking Cokes together at the diner.

"You guys are *beshert*," Judith said.

They looked up. "Huh? What's that?" Gavin asked.

"It's a Jewish expression, meaning 'something is meant to be.' It's destined you two be together."

When Doc Pete sat on the floor finishing the gate on Ethan's castle, that word came back to her. They were *beshert* those two, the young boy and the elderly dentist.

Ellie was grateful for Ethan's opportunity, but likewise pleased for Doc Pete's sake. He had been lonely these past five years since his Gladys died and his daughter, Florence, moved to Florida with the three grandchildren. His young patients loved when he made funny voices imitating cartoon characters, and especially the bowl of tiny toys waiting for a small hand when their checkup was over; but still,

Ellie knew he missed his family. Perhaps she could bring him into hers. For a start, he was here in the living room, ripe for loving and teaching.

Ethan looked up at Doc Pete and asked, "Are you a writer? A *real* writer? I didn't know you could be a dentist *and* a writer."

"Sure," Doc answered. "Why not? We can be anything we want to be if we work hard enough. You could be a writer and paint with finger paints too if you wanted."

"Well, I want to be a writer but not a painter, not a dentist either. I haven't told my mommy or daddy yet, not even my grandma," he whispered, looking around, shy to meet Doc Pete's gaze.

And that's how it started.

Whenever Doc Pete came over, there was a dramatic change in both Danny and Maryann's demeanor. Relief and gratitude thick as smoke flowed from their bodies as Ethan ran enthusiastically toward his tutor. As if a mountain of worry had been removed and the gaping hole filled with anticipation. They now held hands and giggled watching TV. And later, in bed, they cuddled facing each other, not back to back. Danny no longer needed to lay a comforting hand on Maryann's heart to stop the sadness.

After three weeks, Doc Pete asked if he could come over on Wednesday afternoons as well as on Saturday. He had the time, and well, he'd rather be with Ethan than anywhere else. He bought Ethan a blue leather notebook. On the cover was printed "Ethan's Stories." When it was placed in the little boy's hands, Ethan cried joyfully, without shame. Whenever he finished a piece of writing, he copied it neatly into the notebook. A few times, Doc tried to entice Emma to join their writing and storytelling sessions, but she preferred to put her doll, Soft Baby, in a stroller and walk her around the yard singing songs.

Ethan was sure he could do it - make up stories filled with dreams and fantasies and write them down in a compelling manner.

After six months, his notebook was thick with words.

"Ethan," Doc Pete said. "Let's have a reading. A soiree with invited guests - the whole family and your friends, Jonas and Lem. Afterward, your mom can put out some of her chocolate brownies. What do you say?"

"Really?" Ethan said. "A reading from stuff in my notebook? Just me?"

Maryann sent out invitations, and the guests were soon assembled. Ethan wore a new red shirt and navy shorts and sat on one of the straight dining room chairs brought in specially. His hair was seriously slicked down as if he were meeting the school principal. Danny and Maryann, Ellie and Jeff, Jonas and Lem, and Doc Pete's daughter and three granddaughters, who were visiting from Florida, made themselves comfortable in the living room.

Doc Pete introduced his young student.

"Tonight, folks, we have a very special program. Ethan will do a reading of his own work. Most of the pieces are short stories. Two rhymes are also included. Ethan loves his rhymes, don't you Ethan?" He cast a loving look at the boy in the red shirt, then turned back to the group. "You're all in for a special treat. And after Ethan is done, we'll enjoy a dessert from Maryann."

Sitting in front, Jonas caught a quick glimpse of Ethan's notebook, open on his lap - neat letters marching like perfect soldiers between the black lines.

Little Ethan, eight years old then, Ellie later remembered, was relaxed, self-assured, showing no unease, only eagerness in his restless shoulders and shining eyes. He opened his blue notebook to the first page and remembered to smile at the audience, giving a little nod of his head, as Doc Pete had instructed him.

The strong young voice began.

"My first piece is called 'My New Friend.' The day my grandma introduced me to Doc Pete was the day that changed my life."

The small group shouted, "Hurrah!" and Doc Pete took a small bow.

Ethan continued.

"What I wanted more than anything was to write stories - adventures of places we had never seen and people who aren't like us - like the story of *King Arthur and the Knights of the Round Table.* Doc Pete told me to search around in my mind until I find the exact right way to say what I'm thinking. Sometimes it takes a long time. Then he makes me read it out loud to myself. That's because he says words sound different when you hear them from when you see them. So thank you, Grandma, for *bringing* me a new friend. And thank you, Doc Pete, for *being* a new friend."

The little group stood and cheered, not only for the mature sentiments, but for Ethan's skill in composition. And while the guests were gathering round, Ellie realized right then that she could write a play if she set her mind to it.

Maryann and Danny were crying and hugging their son. Of course, they knew Ethan had learned his letters and loved to read. But to craft a whole finished piece with logic and imagination and heart? *Why, he could be a child prodigy,* they thought, *someone with exceptional talent.*

Danny whispered to his wife, "Let's take a couple of these to Dr. Matthews in Cedar Rapids and see what she says. Our Ethan is showing some special ability."

And then their little boy, the frail one, the fragile one, now boldly asked his audience, "Would you like to hear my story about the Viking who crossed an ocean and discovered a new continent called Candyland? Or the one about my dog Laddie who is touched by an angel and flies to the moon?"

"Yes!" they all shouted. "Of course!"

And they all sat down again, hands in their laps, waiting to be carried away by Ethan's sugarcoated dreams and visions of faraway places.

Chapter 25

On an early fall day, Jack was rowing alone on the river when he thought he recognized her. But he couldn't be sure. Her hair was now short, and she was wearing a baseball cap; however, her body, the sense of her, looked familiar. *It was ridiculous. Impossible.* She wasn't working the oars hard, merely dipping them into the water and pulling now and then to keep up. Although he varied his pace, she was always behind him, never coming in close, but never out of sight, like the stalker she was.

On the third day, he finally decided for sure.

Hell, are you kidding me? he asked himself. *It's Julia.*

What was she doing here? He had never told Caitlin about this unsavory past event - was she now in danger? He needed to confide in someone, but Ryan was on leave, and both Ellie and Gavin would worry and offer advice from a distance.

No. He was on his own.

He stopped rowing for a few days and brought lunch to the office or had it delivered. After a week, he went out on the river again. There she was, patiently marking time a quarter of a mile from the boathouse, oars across her knees. When he started paddling briskly in the opposite direction, she followed.

Is she crazy? wondered Jack. They had a simple affair without violence or promises. It had ended - was it seven or eight years ago? - and he had almost forgotten about her. Surely, she had moved on in her life all this time. She looked hardened, mean, and the hair under her cap was showing threads of gray. What would Caitlin think? Sooner or later, she would notice Julia on his trail. She would notice a strange woman trailing them. Caitlin registered irregularities and deviations, and Julia's presence would not escape her. Maybe not on their first outing, but surely, she would on the second or, heaven help us, the third.

However, when they rowed together on Saturday, there was no sign of Julia. It was only when he was alone that she showed up. He could not figure out how she knew his schedule, or the changes he effected without advance notice. It was as if she lived on the water. One weekday morning, he rowed very early, six o'clock, just as a red sun was rising. And there she sat, oars locked, waiting.

As he walked from his home to the office, he couldn't be sure if she was following him. Now and then, he pivoted quickly as if to trap her, dodging into doorways, scanning reflections in store windows. It was so long ago, but he tried to remember what the cops in Chicago had told him, that certain mentally ill people exhibited this type of strange, aberrant behavior. But he refused to believe that someone this disturbed had remained latched onto him for these several years.

Psychopath? Sociopath? What had the cops called her? At the time, Gavin looked up the two terms, but the information was fuzzy now. Both were personality disorders. Both showed a lack of moral responsibility, an absence of social conscience. But there were differences. Was it the psychopath or sociopath who showed lack of empathy, exhibited impulsive behavior? The one who attempted to control others with threats or aggression using intelligence, charm, or manipulation? One more than the other showed a limited, weak ability to feel compassion or remorse. But he recalled that the psychologist at the police station also explained that to different degrees, both often manifested criminal behavior.

Jack's fear settled into his days and nights, but still, he couldn't call the police. She had done nothing wrong, and they wouldn't act on the basis of premonition alone. Also, they might check her past and find they had been together. What would they make of that? Blame, fault, revenge, who knew? On the other hand, perhaps he *should* tell the cops. If there was any trouble, at least a complaint would be on the record. He'd give it another few days. Then he'd decide.

His work began to morph from edgy to trite. *This must be how Ryan feels,* he thought. *Helpless. Should I give up rowing? Hell, no. Who is she to determine the events in my life? Besides, she'd find me wherever I am. At least sculling is a public sport. I'll make sure to be out only when others are rowing nearby. And folks are always watching from shore. Life on the river is constantly busy.*

I'll have to confront her.

Every day, she followed him. Her stalking was intolerable.

One morning, Jack carried his boat down the ramp and placed it in the water. As usual, she waited in the shadow of an oak tree overhanging the water. He beckoned her to come, but she didn't move. He raised his oar again. Finally, she paddled along, slowly, as if she had all the time in the world, allowing his anxiety to grow, torturing him with her delay. When she finally arrived and banked her oars, he saw her face up close - calm but with a feral glow in her eyes and lines of suffering around those eyes.

He knew immediately that words would be useless. She wanted *something*. Was it revenge? Blackmail? A perverted sort of validation of their brief affair?

"Hello, Julia," he said, their boats rocking in the wake of a passing craft.

"You got me fired," she started, her voice low, but in there a snarl, a growl. "After you left, the cops kept an eye on me. When the company was short big bucks, they called me in. They had the report you had filed. I got locked up for a year, probation for three. Did you think you would ruin my life and just walk away? I have a police record now."

Jack was stunned. She had probably rehearsed those words for years. How could he have known? They both sat in the middle of the river, fear and revenge charging the air between their two boats.

"Personality disorder," the cop had said. "You can't reach these folks without serious medical help. And even then…a long-term, rigid, and unhealthy pattern of inner experiences and behavior that affects normal thinking and functioning. An inflated sense of self-importance, an excessive need for admiration, disregard for others' feelings, a sense of entitlement…"

Jack sensed fumes of peril. Better stay agreeable, passive.

"I'm sorry," he muttered.

"You're sorry? You'll soon know what sorry is," she answered, her eyes afire with blame and vengeance. With a few backward strokes, she turned around and rowed away, leaving him powerless and exposed in his open boat. What should he do? His mind was feverish, frantic.

He had no choice. Caitlin must know.

They returned to their familiar pub. Jack felt less vulnerable in a dark corner that provided a pretense of anonymity under which he could hide from his alarm. An outside meeting, or any place like their apartment with walls of glass, was a terrifying possibility.

Caitlin had suspicions. She took his hand.

"Jack, honey," she said with an awkward smile, "should I expect difficult news every time we come to this pub? Being here reminds me of our friend Stephen who brings flowers to his wife every time someone they know dies."

He wished he had sat beside her, not across, to lay his arm on her shoulder, but he needed to see her face, to know the immediate truth of her first reaction.

"Caitlin, I have something to tell you. It began with an innocent first date," he started. "An affair lasting some weeks, then a breakup back in Chicago many years ago. I was just a kid. Nothing serious, just a flirtation."

Caitlin was quiet. So far, he had said nothing untoward, just a common, ordinary accounting. But then he almost grew tearful as he told her the full story of Julia - the stalking, the police, getting fired, hiding out in his apartment, eventually traveling to his father in Italy, there to birth the idea of starting a business with Ryan. He admitted he never knew or cared about the fallout that happened to Julia after he moved to Boston.

"But a few weeks ago, she showed up on the river, started following me in a boat."

He described his fears and concerns, his confusion. On his wife's face, he didn't see shock or judgment. There was no trace of blame or surprise, only concern.

"You must tell the police," she said. "At least file a report. Have something on record."

"Maybe, but I don't want them to go way back and investigate Chicago. It'll turn into a huge ordeal. Maybe go public. And although I was the victim, I also got fired."

Caitlin hesitated, an uneasy situation for a competent manager always in control of her circumstances. Julia was a dark and unknown entity, nothing she could direct or influence. The more they talked, the more complicated the matter became. So they sat, and eventually, they agreed to leave the matter unresolved for the moment.

But whenever they rowed together, Jack saw Caitlin looking around, checking along the edges of the river, beyond the trees. If no one appeared, she seemed to relax and focused on her workout. But Jack knew it was a pretense, an act of courage. Useless, however, since Julia only showed up when he was alone. No sighting of Julia somehow made the tension worse, as if he were making things up.

This game of hers was like a slow poisoning of the mind, a deliberate drip into Jack's brain, attacking its well-being, shredding its candor and integrity. Not understanding such perversity, he was an ineffective adversary. If she kept up this shadowing, his thinking would surely be altered. Sometimes he felt as if she were luring him into her ungodly soul. Sometimes he felt he might develop degenerate tendencies like hers. Is that what she wanted? Mind-altering revenge that, in some manner, would make him belong to her?

Julia grew bolder.

She took her stalking beyond the river and began to appear at unexpected land venues. The first, a Sunday when he and Caitlin went to the Cambridge pub for their customary lobster rolls. It was only when Jack reached up with his napkin to blot a dot of mayonnaise on Caitlin's lip that he saw Julia in the mirror behind her, holding up her fork as if in greeting, at a table not ten feet from theirs.

Another night, he and Caitlin attended a film festival, a variety of animated shorts from France. Their colleagues had been talking about it for weeks.

"You must go. It can't be missed. Go see and come back with a dozen ideas."

A client handed Jack two free tickets.

"Enjoy. This show has been sold out for months."

As they walked into the Brattle Theatre in Harvard Square, there was Julia walking just ahead, handing her ticket to the usher, sitting two rows in front of them. He thought to somehow move their seats or leave the theater, but Caitlin would want an explanation. Besides, she had no idea what Julia looked like, so why bother? Jack wondered how Julia knew he'd be there for this particular performance and from whom she obtained a ticket. *A sorcerer, a witch,* Jack thought, *a creature with the powers of the devil to intuit, to foresee, to ordain.* He stared at the back of Julia's head, but never once did she turn around. Later, when Caitlin wanted to discuss a few details of the film, he had no idea what she was talking about.

Later that week, he stopped in at the order desk of the Harvard Coop Bookstore to pick up a photography book of the Charles River that he had bought Caitlin for her birthday. The clerk had excused himself to retrieve it from the back when Julia suddenly stepped up behind him, tapping him on the shoulder and holding aloft the very book he had ordered, asking innocently, "Is this what you're looking for?"

Jack erupted with rage. His instinct was to wipe the smirk off her face. But he kept his hands down. Grasping her elbow, he pulled her outside the store, hissing, "What the hell do you want?"

"Isn't it obvious? To ruin you and your business, just as you did to me."

Off she walked, serene and steady, while Jack smoldered, terrified to guess how she might destroy him.

He found out soon enough when a formal note arrived from the committee chair at MIT's prestigious school of engineering. "We are sorry to cancel our mutual project for the upcoming spring symposium."

Two days later, the Harvard School of Design indefinitely postponed a collaborative talk on future innovations with 3D printing.

When he phoned, the secretaries were evasive. They promised someone would return his call, but no one did. He was afraid of confrontation, especially without knowing what Julia had told them. Distraught, he checked his roster of programs and commissions. How did she know what they were? Her intent might be to cancel him out, one by one. He well knew that rumor, once launched, could ruin lives and professions. He thought about warning the committed venues, but that seemed, at best, tricky, even inappropriate. His instinct was to speak of his distress with Caitlin, but he feared for her alarm, knowing her disdain for being helpless. So he held back for now. First, he would find a remedy, make a plan.

But he couldn't think clearly. He had no ideas at all for redress or repair. Nightmares of dire outcomes invaded his broken sleep. His work took on gloomy aspects and became sinister rather than playful. Turning suspicious, his anger flared in sudden spurts. He needlessly lost patience with Caitlin. One day, he even scolded the bookkeeper for a mistake he himself had made. *If a change in perspective, in his personality, was what Julia wanted,* he thought sourly, *she was succeeding.*

It was a dreary, dismal fall morning, the day after the School of Design canceled his appearance. Even the most zealous scullers were spending an extra half hour in bed. In the murky darkness, Jack was rowing so strenuously he thought he might injure his shoulder. He would throttle Julia's neck if only he could. Anger made his eyes blur, his head throb, as if he were observing a pack of jackals attacking a litter of puppies.

Suddenly, out of the fog and drizzle, a powerful force battered him from behind like a truck ramming a concrete barrier. Jack's body jerked forward. He dropped an oar. His head slammed against the frame of his boat. Stunned, he tried to shake off the blurry haze of impact, his skull a heavy lift, the mist an unrelenting blindfold.

At his rear, Julia tried to stand. Her boat swayed wildly, water sloshing over the sides. In a half crouch, she tried to sit down again but lost her balance. As swift and silent as a comet streaking across the sky, she fell, striking her head, toppling overboard. All Jack heard was a soft scuffle, a thud, and then silence.

Bubbles floated on the water's surface. A single oar was floating downstream. Where was the other? Shuddering violently, he leaned over and vomited into the current. She probably didn't realize how swiftly the winds can change on the river early in the morning. If they were blowing in your direction, how easily they could propel a boat forward. If you were not careful, these lightweight shells could set you up for harm before you could put forth a hand of restraint.

Was it too soon for a body to be carried away? Or to sink, if one were wearing clothes suddenly made sodden and heavy?

Did Julia know how to swim? She had teased him once, but he didn't know if she was serious or not. "Oh, Jack, honey, I'm a city girl. Swimming isn't my thing."

Jack cursed himself for wearing a fleece sweatshirt under a wool sweater, so many layers to peel off. Sneakers. He couldn't manage to undo the laces. His head felt like a melon dropped on the ground. He heard no sounds at all but for a lone bird crying in the night, the gentle sloshing of water, like a child playing in a bathtub. Dive in, he must. If it were Julia, and he saved her life, perhaps she would be grateful and leave him alone.

He hesitated, his cloudy eyes still unclear. He had already delayed too long. Barely could he hurl himself over the side. The water was black, the air, dark, and he flailed helplessly. Nothing touched his fingers but broken twigs and passing debris. The pungent musk of weeds smelled acrid and stung his nose.

Despairing, he somehow swam to shore right to an emergency phone that connected to first responders. In no time, the Harvard police were on site, lifting him off the ground and swarming over the land and water. A dozen officers patrolled the area with dogs and high beams, sweeping the terrain and the buildings, which sat silently, ghoulishly, stolid and uncaring. A female officer wrapped Jack in Harvard's crimson blankets.

"There!" a cop suddenly shouted, pointing to a clump of bushes along the shore, shining his spotlights. Its thorny branches held fast a limp woman's body. Julia lay twisted and tangled in the prickly shrub. Her hair was matted with blood that dripped down her face and smeared the oar she clutched in one hand. Both were knotted with burrs and grasses.

"Blood spots inside the boat," the policeman later said. "Instant death when she hit her head. A sorry accident, poor thing. She never had a chance."

An office secretary, gasping and stuttering, ran to Caitlin, pointing to the television. Seeing the mayhem, Caitlin drove right over. An army of police cars with flashing red lights made grotesque masks of innocent faces. Through the surging officers, the gathering crowds, the curious joggers, she pushed her way. The female cop was still massaging Jack's hands. Shivering, shaking with full realization now, Jack thought that not filing a police report was a good thing. That way, it was a simple case, an accident that often happens on rivers and oceans and lakes. Mishaps, calamities occurring on water swiftly and mysteriously.

"A boat could just come upon someone by mistake, especially in the dark, especially with the strong wind, especially if one is not an expert rower," said one of the policemen.

"Yeah, and all those hotshot college kids thinking they know what they're doing or showing off," remarked another.

"The poor girl probably didn't even notice that the guy had paused for a moment, and there you have it," a third officer said. "People do a lot of thinking on this river, especially so early, the quiet and all. Pausing is not an uncommon thing. But you have to be alert. With the dark and the mist, looks like she failed to give the river her full attention."

"Yeah," the female officer agreed, flexing her cold fingers. "It's certainly not the first time we've had trouble on this river."

Jack worried about Caitlin. Foolish thoughts he couldn't erase appeared like black dots fluttering under his eyelids. She might be confused or angry or think that this disastrous event might lead to the demise of TheJackRyanStudios. She might leave him. Ryan and Meghan would disappear. He, Jack Taylor, good boy from Iowa who loved birds and dogs and all small creatures, would be tried for manslaughter in the Boston courts, either in Pemberton Square or Courthouse Way, at whatever location juries heard such cases.

And just then, just as he imagined these possible fates, Caitlin whispered, her breath warm in his cold ear, "Honey, it's okay, an accident. You're safe now. We're both safe now."

The police were reassuring.

"Sorry, sir, that this happened to you. We'll take care of it. If you don't want to be checked out at the emergency room, go on home and rest."

Caitlin took her husband back to their generous apartment. After a hot shower, he collapsed in bed wearing thick socks and a sweatshirt, a knit cap. Their bedroom was pleasant, but even with Jack tucked under the wool blanket, the tall windows that looked out on the heavy sky made it feel chilly inside. He lay still, dazed by the speed with which the morning's events had unfolded. Caitlin placed a heating pad under his feet, but as his body warmed, his mind remained cold, restless with issues of guilt and remorse: whether he dived in as quickly as he could have, whether a quicker response would have saved her even with the police saying the initial injury to her head led to her immediate death. Had his cynical thinking cast a deadly karma over the situation? An inevitability? His obsession for Julia to be gone made him fear culpability or blame.

In truth, in what possible way could this entire dilemma have ended positively?

Would the police examine her past and find him there?

Jack's thoughts returned to the days before Julia showed up, those days in which he had spent every waking hour bringing laughter to others, a noble trade, exposing life's capricious, outlandish aspects with humor, with kindness.

"Jack Taylor?" everyone said. "Our lovable, outré eccentric!"

His mind thrived in innocence and joy, but now it had become tainted. He was a different man today than he was yesterday. *But what kind of a man am I now?* he wondered as his wife pattered into the room and sat quietly, taking his hand to calm its trembling.

Chapter 26

It had been six months since Julia died, and Jack was not doing well.

His nights continued to be plagued by demons - a misty morning, a bump, a splash. Did he hear Julia murmur, "Oh"? The office suffered. His work output was mediocre. Caitlin tried to be supportive, but her patience was becoming brittle. It was time to get back to work. TheJackRyanStudios was not meeting its obligations. Contracts had been canceled. Jack withdrew from participating in the Regatta, but she had not. She wondered if she were sensitive enough to his feelings by staying in the race. *But if things had happened in reverse,* she thought, *would Jack have given up his plan to row just because she had?*

His fears lingered. He quivered at dawn, at twilight. Their relationship wobbled. Resentments festered. "No," he said, to her suggestion of seeing a therapist, "just give me some time." Maintaining a helpful and sensitive attitude was oozing out of her. Alarm and concern slowly turned into powerlessness, then annoyance and an inexplicable languor, and lastly, brewing at present, anger.

Caitlin herself was floundering. She found it difficult to imagine Julia as a real person. This grievous period seemed almost a phantom occurrence. She had never witnessed Julia stalking either Jack or herself and had arrived at the river only to find Julia's body concealed under a thick covering and in the dark, at some distance.

On weekends, Caitlin continued to go down to the river and take out her boat. She returned home to find her husband slouched in a chair, idly browsing through a magazine or watching television. He never picked up a pen and paper, never showed enthusiasm for even the slightest distraction. His face was blank, with an indifferent affect.

In the office, their purposeful life dwindled. The studio was taking a downward turn. For the moment, Jack's old clients held fast, but he failed to attract new business. He barely eked out acceptable work, and none with his usual flair that drew outsiders with gusto. Essentially, he was marking time. Two major contracts were coming up for review; would they renew?

Difficult news from the Ryans only worsened the situation. Meghan failed to carry three pregnancies to term, and at last, they were planning a visit to Ireland's adoption agencies. Letters had been written, appointments booked, and Ryan's presence at work was on hold for the near future. Phone calls between the two women were perfunctory, Meghan dejected, Caitlin, helpless. In addition, Caitlin was increasingly resentful that the Julia episode remained on the fringes. Distracted, Meghan hardly ever inquired after Jack's well-being. Ryan was listless in calling Jack, busy as he was doing domestic chores and working part-time for his father, collecting rents, supervising the ledgers. It appeared that four lives had simply been outdone by life's thrusts and jabs.

One day, when Ryan and his dad were having a beer at Bailey's Pub across the street from the office, his father made an offer.

"Hey, Ryan, why don't you come work for me full-time? You can make some real money. I'll pay you double what you were getting in Boston. What do you say?"

Ryan lifted his mug and drank deeply as images of him and Jack several years ago popped up real as anything real could be, the two of them determined to make a unique mark in their particular field.

"Why not?" he answered. Just like that.

Did Ryan feel regret? Nostalgia? Did he even hesitate in the slightest? Did he give consideration to how Jack would receive this news?

"Why did you accept his offer so quickly?" Meghan later asked. "Are you sure? Do you miss working at the studio? Do you miss Jack's company?"

Ryan was the boss's son, a position of some considerable cachet and no work of a creative nature was sought or expected. But surprisingly, he enjoyed driving around the different neighborhoods to the various sites, solving problems, checking things out. He could more than hold his own managing the properties involved. And besides, he could fix anything, and there were always repairs. The guys in the office thought him a competent bloke who earned his pay.

I'm maturing, Ryan told himself. "In the beginning, Jack and I had great fun," he reminisced to Meghan. "We were young, single, out and about in Boston and had never seen so many smart and pretty girls. Most were intrigued by our particular skills. But things are different now. If we have a child, a steady job might be more suitable. No pressure, more time at home. Anyway, could Jack and I have gone on making those kinds of drawings forever? I had always felt a bit awkward, even childish, when strangers asked, 'What do you do for a living?' and I answered, 'I draw pictures.'"

Ellie thought it might be a perfect summer afternoon - a mild day, rare for Iowa in August - low humidity, dry air absent flies and mosquitoes. Her husband, Jeff, was in the garden gathering tomatoes and green beans for dinner.

Two years ago, she and Gavin received their final divorce papers. *Laziness and inertia, that's what had kept them together so long,* thought Ellie. Their marriage had begun to feel like a game. With that final decree, they both felt untethered, no longer half children, half grown-ups picking and choosing what suited at the moment. Still, there might have been a slight shiver of trepidation as to what would happen next. In Ellie's case, that concern did not linger long. Once she was divorced, Jeff immediately proposed, and they drove straightaway to the town hall with Emma and Ethan, Danny and Maryann whooping and hollering. And now here was Jeff, her new husband, the two of them making a life together, deciding what they would have for supper.

At sixteen, Ethan still regularly saw Dr. Matthews in Cedar Rapids. On his latest visit, she had said he would likely live a normal life with this caveat - if he did so quietly, with little stress and little exertion. The entire family, now including Doc Pete, cheered at her pronouncement. It was good enough for Ethan. All he wanted was a desk in a room with a window, a supply of pens and paper. His mind was constantly buzzing with creative schemes that he wanted to see come to fruition.

Eagerly, he shared the news with Ms. Thelma Dowd, the high school teacher who came every Friday afternoon to review his weekly assignments. Of all his work, she especially coveted his short essays. *If only all my students would apply themselves as diligently as Ethan,* she sighed, *they might be a crop of well-behaved geniuses rather than a mischievous, rollicking bunch of rascals.*

Doc Pete tutored Ethan closely not only in the mechanics of writing, but in its art, its mystique. And now, Ethan had confidently surged into lofty territory by writing a stage play, *The Gallant Invaders*. A gift to his grandmother, it was a work of capricious, fanciful wit, loving thanks for her lifelong attentions, her bringing Doc Pete into the family.

But no one had expected Ethan to become a local celebrity. No one had expected that impressive surprises would erupt from this singular achievement.

The Gallant Invaders was a play about an adventuresome fantasy about fearsome warriors from another planet disguised as friendly puppets. Their primary intent was to win friends by putting on puppet shows around the world, thereby revealing a kindly nature under their warlike exterior.

Ethan gathered Doc Pete and the immediate family. He was used to reading his work to them, his trial audience, and watched closely for their immediate reaction. He was becoming quite adept at knowing if their faces showed curiosity or indifference, acceptance or, hopefully, enthusiasm. When Ethan began to read aloud and everyone leaned in to catch every word, he knew the play would be a success. When he was done, the men whistled and the women embraced him. "To think of Ethan slowly scrambling after his sister, and now this spectacular blossoming!" they said to each other.

Before Ethan was even finished, Ellie decided she would present it at the theater in Tylersville as a matinee on Saturdays and Sundays for children and young adults, enlisting her best publicist.

And so Ethan began spending days at the theater, watching from the tenth row, which someone had mentioned was the lucky one. It only took a few weeks to get the show ready. The script was nearly perfect right from the beginning.

Ethan had invited Dr. Matthews to opening night. She showed up and brought along a half dozen guests. They sat in the front row, and he in the tenth, thrilled at her presence. This night was as much a victory for her as for him. In truth, no one was sure he would live to this day. He must remember not to get too carried away.

The audience's cheers thundered like waves. There was a crescendo, then a winding down and starting up again. Children stood on their seats clapping their little hands. When it became known that Ethan Taylor was the playwright, folks were shocked. Yes, it was a youthful fantasy, but nevertheless, what kid could write such a clever and sophisticated play? There was nothing amateurish or childlike about a single word of it. And by the way, didn't adults write all the children's stories?

After *The Gallant Invaders*, he felt ready to take on a serious novel, the kind he always wanted to write - horsemen and swords, noblemen and dragons, and a poor little boy named Milo who dreamed of becoming a knight. He smiled to himself, thinking that the influence of his first King Arthur book would stay with him forever.

He wrote at his desk beneath a window with bright light. Now and then, he would lift his head to watch the robins and sparrows. Then he bent his head again, and the pages piled up on the side table.

One weekend, a man from Chicago came to visit his niece, Sally Paine, a junior in high school. She and Ethan were pals. Sally waitressed on holidays at Matt's Diner, a spot Ethan often frequented. It was Ethan's luck that she took her Uncle George to see *The Galaxy Invaders*. And it was also his luck that Uncle George was a literary agent with a Chicago publisher and wanted to meet the talented new playwright.

"So, young man," George began, after they ordered ice cream sodas. "We loved your play. A kid loaded with talent doesn't come along every day. I hear you've been writing since you were a boy. What are you going to do next?

"You say you're working on your first novel? What is it about?"

And Ethan was off to the land of knights and dragons. At last, Milo had completed his journey.

"How would you like to sign a contract to be published?" George immediately offered.

Ethan stood up, jumpy with excitement. Then he realized he must remain calm so he sat down again. In those few minutes, George was already silently putting his advocacy skills to work - how best to craft this young writer into a popular success. A unique talent for his age, he was, in fact, a phenomenon. Uncle George couldn't think of a single instance of a teenager writing a story of this significance, this complexity, with mature insights in such a creative context. The publicity department at his firm would be fired up.

The path leading to the house was lit with candles in bags weighted with sand. Inside, the rooms were adorned with colorful paper chains draped across fireplace and staircase. Emma had drawn stick-figure pictures of Ethan at his desk, of Ethan taking a bow on stage, Ethan sorting his papers, taping them over the walls, the fridge, the doors. The kitchen table was heavy with fresh corn, fried chicken and biscuits. Bowls of bread pudding waited. Four kinds of pie sat patiently on the counters.

Danny and Maryann were giving a party. After so many years of unease, the family was at last going to celebrate Ethan. *At sixteen, he is handsome like his grandfather,* Ellie thought, *a young Gavin sitting eagerly in the diner, ordering pecan brownie pie and waiting until she got off shift.* And here was his Ethan, similarly tall and slim, with curly brown hair and intense dark eyes fixed in a dreamy, brooding gaze that was sexy and mysterious. Girls loved that kind of look.

Ellie never did get to write her own play. Somehow, she couldn't make it work on her own, and Doc Pete's free time was taken up with Ethan. Lou, the production manager in Tylersville, suggested she find another writer to work with.

"Doc Pete isn't the only one out there," he urged.

But the truth was, she had lost heart. With Doc Pete, the effort would have been a work of deep affection. Working with a stranger, explaining the details of a life in Iowa, would have taken the familial connection out of the effort. Besides, with all the extra work of staging Ethan's play, plus her usual theater productions, the writing project just got by her. *Either there is a fire burning, or not,* she thought. *Either it goes out suddenly or slowly, but in any case, in the end, it becomes ash.* The urgency was gone. Her joy at watching Ethan thrive under Doc Pete's instruction was satisfaction enough. After all, she didn't have to do everything in the theater, did she?

And Emma? At sixteen, she was a star. As the gymnastic champion in Iowa in her age class, she had a fan club of adoring adolescent girls. Always moving with a restless aspect, there was about her an aura of resolve and purpose as she focused on the situation at hand, assessing, calculating. She was now preparing to compete in the national finals in North Carolina. When she wasn't in the gym, she was practicing her stretches on the lawn while Ethan sat at his desk and watched her from the window, both of them stopping now and then to give a head's up or throw a kiss. As they grew older, they looked more alike, their expressions and mannerisms reacting similarly to various situations. The difference between them resided in their energy, in their ever-present duality on the emotional spectrum - her vigor and Ethan's restraint.

When Maryann had taken her to her first gymnastics class at age five, right then, first day on the mat, Emma had fallen in love with the sport. Within weeks, she was doing somersaults and handstands in the cornfields. Occasionally, Ethan was seen at one of her events. He usually wore a baseball cap and sat high up in the bleachers, leaving immediately after the game was over. No one knew him very well, although there were girls who wanted to grab that cap off his head when they caught a glimpse of those brooding eyes beneath the brim.

Danny and Maryann had a rough half dozen years with the farm. There were successive summers of drought, and other seasons with an abundance of rain that flooded the crops. Sometimes there was a surfeit of cloudy days, a twister that passed through, a sudden hailstorm that destroyed a year's profit from corn. To provide, Danny closed off most of his acreage, worked only a small portion of it, and took a job in town at the hardware store.

Farmers being fiercely independent, at first it had been tough on his sense of self-worth. The problems were nature's doings, not his, still, part of him felt like a failure. Ethan's play had helped with the household finances, but taking money from his son would take getting used to for Danny.

However, after some weeks, Danny began to enjoy his new job. Sleeping till eight, no laboring in the scorching fields, hanging around in the air-conditioning and talking with other folks. Steady pay, week in, week out. No worries about the price of corn, of rain or drought, blight or any of a hundred other calamities. No getting up in the dark. *Come spring*, Danny thought, *I'll plant corn or soybeans in those couple of acres near the house. I can handle that and still keep my job in town. Maybe work part-time. I'll see how it goes. When you live your whole life where everyone knows you, shopkeepers are willing to cut you some slack.* Maryann found a job as a teacher's aide in the middle school. After eating breakfast together and leaving lunch for Ethan, they were off for the day. They often fretted that the only company Ethan would have would be Doc Pete and Ms. Dowd, and those two only occasionally. But to Ethan, the quiet house felt privileged and sacred. He read half the day and wrote the other half, no one poking a head in to check on him as if he were a child, one with limitations.

Ellie was troubled. Jack told her about Julia's death a few hours after it happened, just as it hit the national news. But other than a few brief calls from Caitlin, she had heard little since. Was he recovering from the trauma?

She would call, choosing to keep the conversation light, newsy.

"Hi, Jack honey, it's Mom. Happy Easter! Do you have any special plans for the day? No? Nothing special? Jack, you know Ethan wrote a stage play. It's called *The Galaxy Invaders*. Can you imagine? Isn't it simply marvelous? So cute, about warriors coming to earth as puppets. It's a huge hit. Sold-out matinees Saturday and Sunday. No one can believe a young teen wrote it.

"And guess what? Some literary agent from Chicago was down for the weekend to visit family, and his niece dragged him to see the show. He found out Ethan was almost finished with his first novel!"

"A novel? What's his book about?" Jack asked.

"Knights and dragons, I think. A boy named Milo. You know, one of his fanciful capers, someone always searching for a human insight or divine meaning and getting into conflicts while doing so. Honestly, that boy reminds me of you. And this agent fellow actually bought the rights to his book!"

Jack hung up and returned to the sofa, musing, dozing. Shocking that he and Ethan had similar artistic inclinations toward similar subjects. Only he made drawings, and Ethan told stories. He wondered if his mother made that deep and strange connection between them. And further, didn't such oddball creativity in one family merit special attention?

Suddenly, he jumped up. Magazines scattered. The television remote dropped between the cushions. His head came as clear as it had ever been. Yes! An astonishing notion - the two of them, he and Ethan, working together. Anyone could see that destiny was at play. Nothing less than that. So what if Jack was twenty years older?

A pile of considerations followed. He started to pace from kitchen to study to living room to window, then back through living room to study to kitchen, more activity than he had done in weeks. First, how would this arrangement actually work? Ethan would have to come live with them in Boston, wouldn't he? Would his parents object? Would Ethan? Would he want to work at TheJackRyanStudios?

Boston was not a quiet place no matter how you tried to accommodate that need, but Jack told himself there were an infinite number of great doctors here. Surely we could work something out. Or maybe I could move out of the city, live in a place like Salem or Cohasset where it's lovely and quiet. True, he argued, but not quiet enough, not like the farm.

Ethan himself might want to stay home. He couldn't know what the boy would prefer. He couldn't know if Danny and Maryann would approve. And he didn't even know if he himself could manage a daily commute to Cambridge working his usual long hours. His mind played with guesses and concerns, but all his deliberations were speculative.

Still, Jack wouldn't let go of the impulse to work with his nephew. He went into the kitchen and made a pot of coffee. Caitlin was out rowing. He realized that this act of making coffee was the first time in months he had gotten off the sofa and done something useful for himself.

Under different circumstances, Caitlin thought Jack's prospect of a collaboration between him and Ethan might be something to consider, but in terms of their reality, his ideas were ridiculous, preposterous. Ethan living with them?

"Living with us?" she repeated. "So we would be responsible for his well-being? Jack, we never wanted children for that reason, among others. Our plan was to be free, without constraints. Remember? And Ethan has a serious heart condition, something to be monitored, supervised.

"Yes, I know life changes," she persisted. "I know we never expected a fallout with Ryan. You may be right that with Ethan, he could present a new angle on how we pitch products to clients or maybe not. I just refuse to be part of it."

Suddenly, Jack's fury broke through her argument. He sat in a living room chair and swiveled toward the window, brooding, his head down, as she voiced her objections. While she was speaking, his mind was in turmoil. *To hell with my present life,* he thought, *to hell with all of it. I'm sinking under many ships - Caitlin, Ryan, the business falling off, Julia, Grim memories everywhere. Maybe I should chuck the whole thing and go back to Iowa. Refurbish the cottage where I grew up.*

Be with my family again. Ethan could write his adventure stories, and I'd illustrate them. We could be successful, even famous.

Thinking on such far-fetched prospects gave him no peace if Caitlin was opposed.

"But I'm happy to see that you have renewed interest in things again," she said, breaking into his reverie. She spoke hesitantly, carefully, still reticent to walk over and touch his shoulder or sit in his lap.

"Okay, Caitlin. Let's leave it for now," Jack ended.

And there, the argument remained for the moment.

But his thinking forward had flipped into gear. In his head, an exhilarating idea was born, and there it would stay until it was resolved.

He went back into the office every day with stamina and a smile that pleased the bookkeeper. Clients called; the Regatta drew closer; and Ethan finished his book. But Jack had come to this - no matter what Ethan said, he was done with Boston and the Charles River. He could start up a new office anywhere. There was too much heartache on the streets he walked in this city.

What to do about Caitlin? She had made it clear that she wanted no part of Ethan living with them. How could he have a working association with his nephew and keep Caitlin happy? And keep her happy in Iowa? First, he had to find out how Ethan felt about this. And then, if Ethan were willing, somehow, he would find a solution or compromise for the rest.

Since Gavin's legendary show in Rome, he had retreated to his mountain, painting single canvases for which Sophia had eager buyers. Now that he was a celebrated artist, Gavin preferred the old days when he didn't know if anyone would be interested in his work. Somehow, his successes were sweeter for the battles he fought. He refused offers for special commissions in order to stay put, and a mystique grew around his seclusion that only made his paintings more desirable and valuable.

His chats with Jack broke his solitude.

On one such call, Jack shared his desire to work with Ethan, and how it would change his life and the way he worked. But there were so many problems involved.

It is an unexpected proposal, thought Gavin, *but not surprising.* In fact, he thought it might be exceedingly clever.

"But I've not yet spoken with Danny and Maryann," Jack explained, "nor with Ethan. And there is Caitlin, of course. A primary consideration. We had agreed not to have children. Now I'd be reneging on my part of the deal. On the other hand, at the very least, I want to get out of Boston. The town drags me down with damaging memories."

Gavin understood Jack's conflict. He too had sporadic longings for home. It would be a relief not to struggle with a foreign language, not to pause before he spoke. He missed seeing the corn silks flying on a summer day. He also wanted to share in his grandchildren's lives and to spend more time with Danny and Jack, both nearing middle age yet occasionally still in need of parental support.

He missed the company of those who had known him his entire life, from when he was a young man, just married, sailing into Pat and Sam's front yard with Ellie, to the present, these many years later, when he was slowly beginning to realize just how lonely he really was.

But alas, he could not imagine leaving Italy. Like Jack, he was a man betwixt and between. He would remain in a country he loved but with a heart missing its true measure.

Chapter 27

Caitlin had seen him around.

How could she not? He was one of those guys who seems to have been born beautiful and grown up untouched by acne or bad haircuts, at ease wherever he found himself. He had cornflower blue eyes and shiny blond hair that flopped over his forehead and a nonchalant way of tossing it back with a flip of his head, a gesture of breeding common to prep schoolers. Surely, he was once a member of the socially elite clubs popular at Harvard. On weekends, when the river was at its busiest, he was always there, his eyes pinned to her boat as she came down the river on her final sprint, pulling with the wind and skimming along at an even clip, the sun rising at her back.

The Regatta was less than a month away, and Caitlin was putting in long hours of practice. The leaves on the great oaks and elms along the shore were beginning their annual turn from green to crimson and gold. Picnickers lounged along the banks, grateful for a splendid day. The sun was dazzling as she stood on the ramp and readied her scull. Suddenly, the man with the cornflower-blue eyes came from behind and raised the end of her boat, easing her lift. Surprised, she turned.

"Hi," he said, "my name is Preston."

"I'm Caitlin," she answered.

He watched her settle in and arrange her oars. Then he gently pushed her boat into the river.

As it turned out, he had indeed been a member of Porcellian before he resigned over the no-women-allowed flap. Would he be about thirty?

"Caitlin?" he began one afternoon when she was resting on the dock letting the sweat dry and drinking Gatorade.

"Hi. Preston, as I recall?"

"Good girl, yes, that's right. May I join you?" sitting down before she said yes. "You have great technique. Where did you learn to row like that? You're a newcomer? Looks like you were born in a boat. I manage the Newell boathouse," he said, nodding over his shoulder.

"It's a big job. Maintaining the facilities, arbitrating disputes. And you know Harvard, everyone has an opinion on how things should be done. These boathouses are very personal to the rowers. Long history and traditions."

Caitlin laughed. "True, but it's Harvard, after all," she answered.

"I've been watching you row for weeks," Preston continued. "You always come alone and take good care of your equipment. You seem to have a special attachment to this place, never rushing in and out. I don't know if you have a job or are a student, but I might like to make you an offer."

Surprised, Caitlin looked up. The only proposition she had ever received was Jack asking her to manage the office. She was a kid then whose experience had consisted of a few undergraduate economics courses.

"Think you'd like to come work for me? It's pretty exciting around here. I need someone reliable to help manage things. Are you a competent manager, Caitlin?" he asked.

Is he naturally playful? she wondered. This could be a serious proposal or merely a flirtation.

"Meet me here Thursday at four, and we'll have a talk, okay?" he said, rising from the bench and handily hoisting a clutch of oars over his shoulder. As he strode smoothly into the building, she noticed his long, tan legs and wondered if he was married.

This is how Ryan must have felt when his father offered him a job, Caitlin thought, torn between his allegiance to Jack and his desire to escape a situation that wasn't working to his benefit. She blamed others for her dilemma - Julia, Meghan, and most of all, Jack, for the loss of intimacy between them. She had offered solace and advice, and he had dismissed her, making no attempt to share his sorrows. For months, they had not had a real dinner together nor a serious conversation nor made love even once. That kind of rejection would make tiny incursions into your heart until exclusion would feel like the accepted condition. And while this brush-off was occurring, Caitlin had begun to put her emotions into other pockets of interest - longer rowing times, two courses at Cambridge's Continuing Ed program, "Your Body and Sports" and "How to Improve Your Management Skills." There she met friends with similar interests who were eager to have a coffee after class. Only for her to return home and find Jack glum and silent on the sofa.

She began to dream of Preston, not as someone she desired personally, but as one who represented an available world, easily accessible, and willing to take her in. From her dreams rose crucial questions. Was she cowardly to long for acceptance into a different life? Would she be judged weak and indulgent by walking away from her marriage, as Ryan had done with the studio? Did she still love Jack?

This day, the river mirrored her mood perfectly - fast-running waters that were always on the way to someplace else. As a rower, you had to go with the current, battling for control over the wind above and the resistance below. Caught between these two opposing forces - that's where Caitlin now found herself. She feared that if she were unable to succeed in her marriage, she would fail to master the river. *That's absurd and untrue,* she said to herself. *One has nothing to do with the other.*

Why didn't she immediately refuse Preston or say to him flat out "no, I have a position managing a company that belongs to my husband." Did he know that? Had he checked her out?

Slowly, she packed her duffel - sneakers, towel, wrist bands - and began the trek back to her apartment. Today, she chose an alternate route from the usual - the river path rather than the tumult of Harvard Square with its boutiques and cafés, which she usually loved for its frenzied activity. Benches were scattered along its quiet banks inviting her to sit and enjoy lovely views across the Charles to the elegant Georgian Revival architecture of the business school.

She put her face to the sun and let her mind drift, thinking of life's ironic turns, the often uncanny choices they exact, their inescapable consequences. And isn't it the darndest thing? Your mood can be dark and deep, a feeling of helplessness moving in, as if you are doomed to remain in that bleak and murky place. Then a surprising situation unexpectedly pops up. One's mind begins to jump and shift. It begins to consider outlandish propositions. And those outlandish propositions begin to feel like real options. Shocking how the brain and the heart conspire to present fresh possibilities even amidst despair.

Would making a change be a foolish leap? Or a fortuitous one?

She almost fell asleep there on the bench in the warmth of the sun, but a cockswain shouting orders to his crew startled her. Gathering her things, she stood up and prepared to go home. By the time she turned from the river onto the block leading to the apartment, she decided to leave TheJackRyanStudios. Working with Preston in Newell in the company of other scullers was a thrilling prospect. She would accept his offer. She would take a chance. It was only when she put her key in the lock of her front door that she had a revealing insight - was she feeling the same exhilaration that Jack experienced about possibly collaborating with Ethan?

As she entered the foyer, Jack was drinking coffee, his face tired but composed. Caitlin was astonished by the dramatic shift in his body language. He was standing, not reclining. His posture was straight, not slouching. He had put on a clean shirt. For a moment, she had forgotten that ever since his mother's call about Ethan, he had perked up a bit and started going into the office.

"I'm going to give Ethan a call now," he said.

She knew that after this call, their lives would be forever reshaped.

"Do you have anything further to say before I do?" Jack asked.

Caitlin took her time, unwinding her scarf, hanging up her jacket while Jack waited for any word that would be conclusive, forever determinative.

"Jack, honey," she said, facing him, "I don't see a way out. I don't want to be responsible for Ethan, and I don't want to live in Iowa."

"This opportunity may be the only way of saving my career," he answered. "I love what I do, and I want to make it viable again. I need a partner, but it won't happen with Ryan. Maybe it would with Ethan on a whole new level of output, he being a writer, not an illustrator," Jack replied.

Caitlin's resentments from the past months gripped her throat. She hesitated to speak. *I've been shut out and lonely,* she silently accused him. *You haven't shown much consideration in that regard. Look how easily you perked up at the idea of working with Ethan though you knew it was something in which I would not be included.*

"Do what's best for you. I'll find my own way," she answered.

Jack glanced at the clock. It was dinnertime in Iowa. He dialed the number.

"Hey, Emma, my beauty! How's the champion gymnast? Been scouted for the Olympics yet? Silly? Me? No, I'm just a proud uncle. Keep turning and spinning, kiddo. We're rooting for you. Is your brother around?

"Hey, Ethan! How's it going? Your grandmother told me you have a hit on your hands! Yes, she told me that too. A book sale at your age! What can I say? It turns out we have creative geniuses in the family. So what are your plans now? Oh, you're already planning your next book?

"Well, I have another idea I want you to think about. It might be an interesting project for you."

Jack was breathing erratically. He avoided looking at Caitlin. He stood by the swivel chair, spinning it around and around.

"How about coming out to Boston and working in the company? You can live with me. We'll be a team - the two Taylors, uncle and nephew. You write, I draw. What do you think of that?"

The phone was silent.

"Ethan?" Jack asked tentatively.

"Yes, Uncle Jack, I'm here. Just stunned, that's all. I'll have to think about this, talk to Mom and Dad. As you know, there are issues. Plus, I'm pretty tied to this area. I can't even imagine how far away Boston is."

"I know. But you're young and talented, and there's a whole world out there beyond the farm."

"Do you want to talk to my dad now? And, Uncle Jack, I'm very flattered, no matter what happens."

"Hi, Jack. I heard," Danny said. "Are you crazy? Send him off to Boston to live with you? What does Caitlin think of all this? She never wanted kids, right? Never mind, it's out of the question. And by the way, you might have called me before speaking with him. Yes, I know he may want to go. That's why you should have talked to me first. But the answer is no. Actually, a clever notion, Jack. An amazing proposal if Ethan didn't need careful tending. Sorry that you're having some troubles out there with Ryan, but Ethan isn't your solution. And besides, you know how he loves to work alone."

What had he expected? He must think about his next step, what he must do if he wanted to even consider a professional partnership with Ethan. Close his Cambridge office, convince his nephew a partner would be to his benefit, and move into his old house. And then give up his wife.

That evening, Danny, Maryann, Ellie and Jeff, Ethan and Emma sat at the dinner table talking over each other about Jack's extraordinary call. The whole family was shocked. Jack should have known better. And what about Caitlin? Maryann forgot to bring out the mashed potatoes. Ethan forgot to ask for seconds of fried chicken.

Then Ethan spoke.

"It must be wonderful living in Boston. They have a ton of colleges and museums. And isn't MIT there? The place that has the amazing exhibits and classes about space and robots and telescopes?"

Everyone looked up. Ethan had never expressed a desire to mingle socially with others, never spoke of longings for distant places.

There were tears in Maryann's eyes. Ellie's head hung low. Emma placed her hand over her brother's. No one could bear Ethan's possible disappointment. Most boys his age were preparing to enter a world away from home as it would happen for Emma. The enormity of his condition saddened them all - life's favors that Ethan would miss, that he might write about but never experience. Each person at the table imagined him strolling a campus green with trees, exalted by knowledge, attending a school devoted to extraterrestrial studies and physics labs and displays of real planets and galaxies.

No one spoke. Only the clatter of knives and forks was heard and small sniffles from Maryann.

Darn Jack, Danny thought. *Why did he have to put such thoughts into my son's head?* He lifted his eyes and asked his wife if there was pie for dessert.

Jack drank pots of coffee and slept little.

Danny called his brother back, just to make sure things were set right.

"Impossible, Jack."

Phone to his ear, Jack looked out the window. A plane was circling low. In the distance, he could see the John Hancock Tower, New England's tallest building. Its windows were famous for their blue tint, presenting only a slight contrast with the sky on a clear day. He remembered something the American author, John Updike, had written about that unique building, so innovative at the time:

> *Changeably blue, taking upon itself the insubstantial shape of clouds, their porcelain gauze, their adamant dreaming. I reflect that all art, all beauty, is reflection.*

Those poetic words of a creative life gave Jack the courage to go ahead, inspiring words that urged him forward.

"What if I come back to the farm, live in our old house and work with Ethan at home? What do you think of that?" he asked.

Danny sputtered in surprise.

Jack paused while Danny's brain worked through the issues. Would Ethan welcome such a momentous commitment? Would they get along working together every day? What about those fancy people Jack knew in Boston? The glamorous places in which he had lived or visited? Back to Iowa? Was Jack serious? And what about Caitlin?

Danny had heard his stories about the Union Oyster House. Would Matt's Diner be a satisfactory substitute? Perhaps this was simply about wanting to get away from those terrible aspects surrounding that Julia woman. Perhaps after he was restored to good mental health, he would leave, stranding Ethan.

On the other hand, if Jack was suffering, perhaps he *should* come back. It was safe here. It was home.

Finally, the phone crackled.

"Okay, Jack," Danny finally answered. "I'll talk to Ethan. See if he wants to give this arrangement a try. At his age, we were all good at changing our minds, right?"

Two of Jack's posters hung in the farmhouse kitchen - one of crossover shapes and forms created for a math competition and another of ghouls and ghosts done for a Halloween fete. Several others were taped to the walls of Ethan's bedroom. His favorite, the Vikings as munchkins in rowboats rather than ships. His uncle was a towering artist with an original imagination he could only hope to emulate in words. Sometimes an idea for a story occurred to him as he looked at one of Jack's images. Every so often, Maryann hung a new one that arrived in the mail. And now, his uncle wanted to work with *him* here in Iowa?

Overwhelmed with the honor and the possibilities, he hardly thought of the practical aspects involved unlike his father. *But I'd be a fool not to give this a try,* Ethan decided. His excitement lifted and swelled. Who knew what adventure awaited in his own house?

Ethan called Boston.

"Uncle Jack? I'll try whatever you have in mind. Come home. Let's see how it works out."

Jack took a seat in the swivel chair and gazed out again at Hancock Tower, reflecting on the unpredictability and resilience of the human mind, an expansive and miraculous organ with an amazing ability to pivot, even in the midst of sorrow. Given the chance, rather than dwell in remorse, it begins to plan. Rather than nurse regret, it harbors hope.

And so, Jack began the process of dismantling his present life.

Caitlin kept her appointment with Preston. His proposition to make her assistant manager of the Newell's various components suited her perfectly. He was especially pleased to learn that she was adept with finances and figures, a chore he would gladly relinquish.

Chapter 28

The sun rose, and the birds sang, but Gavin did not pick up his brush. Neither did he bother to prepare his coffee. Rather, he walked outside barefooted, through his garden, past his studio to the flat boulder on which he sat to look over the valley and watch the morning unfold. The haze had lifted. The colors of the landscape sprung up pure and fresh. He could almost feel the dew on the grassy farmland below.

He came outside to think. The low, constant turmoil in his gut warned both of impending need and of inevitable change. It was a sensation that clearly required attention, like a beggar who came to the door bleeding from his eyes and would not be gone until Gavin bandaged his wounds.

Returning to Iowa for an extended stay was a notion he dismissed as soon as it arose. His life on the mountain was unspoiled and peaceful, and yet thoughts of Iowa kept intruding. Likely it was a sentiment that arose from growing older, from days that disappeared without a fuss or even a small footnote. In this climate, there were no storms or blizzards to celebrate seasonal changes, which brought about a spiritual awakening every few months. And in balmy, temperate Italy, life's significant movements were measured in centuries. In the States, the years advance in fleeting and ephemeral spurts. He was curious about what had changed in Iowa and what had not, such as Danny and Maryann leaving the farm and working in town, a momentous trade. But even beyond family, he missed the indelible impressions of place: Lou making up his ice cream sodas at Matt's Drugs, the *shack* (had the wisp of a breeze finally blown it over?), the dazzling yellow forsythia along the path from the house (did it still know spring's glory, or had it been dug up, replaced with asphalt?).

And those living persons he had created and raised, those who knew the answers, those who had seen the shifts and sway as the days silently disappeared and had made their own lives without him - what about them? How many holidays and celebrations had Gavin spent on the telephone or through the mails? He visited briefly every few years, but they were an inadequate substitute for one's enduring presence. Drifting in and out like an estranged uncle melted no one's heart nor his own conscience.

Gavin once thought that only by living in Italy could he find his best creative self. But after many years, he now felt he could paint anywhere. It was a good feeling, a sure feeling, even if it did not dispel what he now sensed acutely - the loss of time, irretrievably gone. Time that had vanished into his canvases. Time that accorded him fame but whose mantle he wore only sporadically and reluctantly. His finished works, now dispersed, lived in museums, in the houses of strangers. And even after he distributed generous financial gifts, money remained in the bank. Moreover, his curly hair was thinning. His knees occasionally ached. He was only - fifty-five, was it? - but he felt intimations of aging. Feeling confident now that he could paint anywhere, even on a farm, he came to believe that no one thing was the only choice.

So he would succumb to an abiding desire, long suppressed beneath the cover of perfecting his craft. He would pivot. He would explore the significance of his life's journey beyond prominence. Yes, he would do this, go back to the farm for a lengthy visit, and see if anything of himself remained to be discovered.

Such a consideration didn't feel momentous or unexpected, but rather a yearning set in the natural order of things - a time to leave, a time to return. Between those two markers was a lifetime of missing his family for the sake of his need to unearth his talent. He had left as a man with fierce inner ambitions and would return a man whose name was prominently written in the histories of great artistic movements.

Gavin now craved his coffee. He rose from the rock and went inside to start grinding the beans.

Where would he live? Jack and Ethan had taken over his abandoned house. Pegboards, desks, shelves, and cabinets were bought in pairs and set up throughout the first floor. The dining room was now their principal workplace. The pantry, repurposed for Ethan's dreaming, contained a table and recliner. A window had been punched into its wall. Upstairs, there was an extra bedroom. Would it be feasible for him to stay there briefly while he considered other potential living conditions? Options swarmed through Gavin's head. None, settled.

Until one morning, as he lingered over a second coffee and a second *maritozzo*, a breakfast brioche, at Francesco's. As his friend put down the sweet butter and jam, a possible scheme suddenly took shape. The more Gavin thought about it, the more assured he felt. Examining it for flaws, he found none of any consequence.

He would build his own small house and studio. This would not be for a permanent resettling but a house for occasional visits. A couple of sunlit rooms were all he needed. He would place it within view of the shack. Close to the family but not too close. He began doodling ideas of shape and structure on a napkin. Instinctively, he drew something very close to his present living quarters. Yes, that was it. He would erect in Iowa a near duplicate of his dwelling on the mountain. This would enable him to easily paint in both places without the need for any emotional adjustment regarding familiar surroundings. Anticipation coiled around his excitement.

What he didn't realize or even consider - what was furthest from his mind, in fact - was that a lone, self-absorbed artist might not fit into the busy, hectic life on a farm. But Gavin had a dream, a dream like a thread that had kept unspooling silently throughout his lifetime. And despite setbacks and detours, Gavin's dreams were usually attainable. He had the money to do this. He would give it a try.

Family.

He anticipated unforeseen events that would require adjustment and accommodation. Could he incorporate them into his solitary needs without resentment? Would proximity to people and their needs, their demands, extract his reluctant time and energy? He had eluded those elements by living across an ocean. Not intentionally at first, but a reality which eventually became essential. Or it might be the flat Iowa land that would prove unnerving and send him scurrying back to his mountain. Undergoing the great nomadic shift of emotional upheaval would not be taken without serious consideration, but meanwhile, he would give this plan a chance. He would embark on this journey with a full heart. After all, it was only to be considered as a long visit. No matter that during that time, he would build a house.

The week before departure, he made a final jaunt to Florence to visit Sofia. Then he had a final farewell gathering with his friends at Francesco's, a final meal with the Brothers, and a robust hug with Enzo, the bus driver.

Gavin planned to arrive quietly, driving by the glorious sunflower fields at midday and cruising without fuss into the worn spot used as a driveway. He told everyone to expect him during a certain week but gave no specific date or time. His modest arrival occurred just as he had hoped. He had a smooth enough flight, landing at the round terminal, which had been new when Ellie first flew to Chicago but was now in need of a touch-up, made apparent by the recent glass-clad addition on its right flank. Gavin found the car rental and took off for the sunflower fields.

They didn't disappoint. Not even after he had seen the majestic sunflower fields at Maremma, which meandered through neighboring inland towns and along coastal villages. Not even by their meager few acres, the farmer selling his blossoms by the road. Memory was what mattered here. His first sight of these heroic, long-stemmed yellow beauties with their golden faces seeking the sun was the spur that had set him on his lifelong painting style. He remembered the moment as if it had just happened, when he parked by the side of the highway twenty years before, overcome with insight and purpose that had risen to become his destiny.

Could one replicate our firsts - he wondered - *my first falling in love with Ellie; my first abstract canvas of* roiling reds; *my first thrill of cradling Jack at the hospital window, imagining his own possible future in the fluttering of his fingers? My first meeting with the woman Cecilia in all its mystery?*

Life offers one dramatic experience after the other for our whole lives, but it is often the one that appears first that remains embedded in our soul, pure and untouchable.

The car rolled into the farm. With relief, he saw that the scruffy parking spot remained. The shack, though somewhat more dilapidated, still stood. The grand forsythia still managed to hang on boldly after its initial spring bloom.

But then he turned from the car and faced the land. Danny warned him, but nevertheless, the utter desolation of that vast space was a shocking sight. Abandoned, the fields had gone entirely to seed. Water hemp, giant foxtail, and mare's tail - all weeds grew randomly among wildflowers of asters, coreopsis, bee balm. He had the urge to take a bushwhacker to the whole thing, scooping up the dead leavings and turning over the rich soil underneath. Eyeing the dry, idle land was a forlorn and sad thing. Danny hoped a son would eventually take it over, but Ethan would never be a farmer. Untended, it took only one season for the kind of untamed disorder Gavin was witnessing to spring up. A dozen more years, this farmland would revert to the beginning of a forest.

"Shouldn't you sell off some of the unused land?" Gavin asked when Danny told him about the situation a couple of years before.

"No," Danny answered. "I'll keep it for now. Don't want other folks living too close."

I guess our dreams are buried deep, and we don't abandon them easily, Gavin now thought. "Well, I sure know about that," he sighed. Suddenly, the mournful sight before him faded into the brilliance of Italy's verdant hills and valleys - always a fertile landscape, a castle or manor, a farmhouse or barn springing into view now and then only to disappear as the road curved.

Where is *home?* he wondered. *Here or there? What makes a place home? Is it simply the spot where you were born - that patch of domestic land that belonged to your family or the place in which you became your true self.* He had certainly become himself on the farm with a marriage of his youth, the birth of his two sons, the accidental discovery of a brochure at Haley's Dry Goods. Yet it was in Italy that his self blossomed into its full value. And it was in Italy that his eyes were opened to the gorgeous sights of a world almost as old as the human spirit. *The idea of home is constantly evolving,* he decided, *and may reside wherever your gut feels you belong. And one must have the courage to swivel and adapt and to find the good.*

"Grandpa!" a lissome young lady cried, Emma racing toward Gavin with her arms extended and her hair flying. She almost knocked him over with her exuberance. Ethan slowly ambled along behind as he had done all their lives. Emma folded her body into Gavin's arms while Ethan offered a grown-up handshake. Gavin thought that as they grew older, they looked more alike than they had as youngsters, both with eyes mischievous and earnest, broad grins, and straight teeth. And their unspoken reactions of mutual perceptions and opinions that arose from the twinning of their hearts made them of one mind, giving their faces a similar affect. They smiled together, frowned together, yet each in his own superb way was a unique and mindful human being.

The three of them walked laughing and jabbering into the house. The path was clear and short, and Gavin decided to leave his walking stick in the car. Not that it kept him from his long jaunts up and down the mountain. Nor did it hinder his small treks into the valley. No, it was only a "just in case measure," he said to himself, his balance not one hundred percent. Besides, on his excursions, he noticed even younger folks used such a prop, hand carved in a variety of beautiful organic shapes.

Bedlam erupted as the family came running. A couple of golden retrievers barked and drooled and scrambled underfoot. Gavin noticed that none of the familiar objects or furniture had been removed or altered. Pat's needlepoint sampler still hung on the wall. Sam's photo of Blackie still hung beside it. The same kitchen table and blue pottery dishes centered with yellow sunflowers and the geraniums on the windowsill. The row of four was now bright pink. Several years ago on his last visit, he tried to recall, weren't they red? Or were they purple African violets? Ah, no. The violets centered the tables at Francesco's café. Only a couple of Jack's posters had been added, and these tacked to the doors leading out of the kitchen.

But it was the shifts in his family that pulled like magnets at Gavin's emotions. His sons were entering middle age, a fact written on their faces, across their hairline, their girth. Danny still commanded a farmer's muscular heft, but he was losing his thick hair. His posture was more bent than straight. Maryann seemed unchanged until you looked closer and found the small spidery lines accruing around her nose, mouth, and eyes. *A timely moment to be here,* Gavin thought. *When one is absent at life's essential passages, one doesn't follow their stealthy advance. But advance they do whether or not you are present.* Thankfully, before Gavin could touch the sadness more deeply, he was taken over by the noise of loving greetings and concerns for his comfort. Amidst the tumult, he didn't fail to notice that Jack stood with a protective arm around Ethan.

Gavin was Jack's guest for almost a month. His son didn't speak of the past, neither of Julia nor Caitlin, so neither did he. But it was good for Gavin to see that Jack had acquired a robust demeanor and was smiling without effort. He and Ethan spent every morning together in the study Jack had fashioned. There was a constant buzz interrupted by an occasional shout of "Yes! that's it. Great idea, Ethan!" and "Love that image, Uncle Jack!" Clearly, their arrangement was working.

Gavin stopped by Ellie and Jeff's house near Tylersville. *A sweet place,* Gavin thought, *and homey. Reminds me of my own cottage - wide floorboards, cozy rooms, ceiling beams.* He was glad to see Jeff paid her small attentions such as clearing the dishes, opening the car door. After a late lunch, they drove to the theater.

"Gavin, I have a surprise!" Ellie cried. "I've put Ethan's show on the docket just for you - Saturday and Sunday matinees for a month."

The theater was full. Gavin noted the details - modern chandeliers with their pendants hanging like rotating globes, the purple-and-gray plaid velvet curtain covering the stage like a Mondrian painting. The family had already assembled, occupying the seats front row center and across the aisles. First and second cousins showed up. Gavin found his place, waving to old friends - former teachers, neighbors, old Haley from the dry goods store, hobbling in on a cane. Even old man Lou from Matt's Drugs holding onto the arm of a young man who looked like the younger Lou he remembered. And Lucy! Dressed in blue with a purple shawl, waiting for him to catch her eye so she could throw kisses.

Gavin sat between Ethan and Ellie. He kept glancing back and forth from the stage to his grandson, who was whispering every word of the script to himself as it went along. He squeezed Ellie's hand and whispered, "Oh, my girl. Look at what we've wrought."

At the end, as always, cheers echoed across the hall; the chandelier's sparkling crystals trembled. Ethan was coaxed onstage, along with Ellie. The audience wouldn't let them go.

"Ethan, Ethan!" they shouted.

This was his grandson's moment, just as surely as his had been when those doors opened onto his mural in the glass addition to Signor and Signora Carraro's palazzo.

Gavin was pleased for Ellie and pleased for himself. He was now free of the guilt that had hovered over his decamping to Italy. There would be no more remorse. At last, Ellie had valuables of her own - Mayor Jeff and the magical, wonderful parade of live theater.

Driving over to check out Matt's Drugs, Gavin noticed very few differences in the landscape or the town. Maybe a neighbor added a few acres; another sold off a parcel, but as long as the large tractor firms and Doyle's canning factory stayed intact, the town would remain steady. In this way, memories filtered down through the generations. Bittersweet but not sorrowful.

Had the soda fountain remained? Many of these old fountains were being replaced by five-and ten-cent stores. "Too much profitable real estate to be tied up by a few stools," the papers said.

Yes, Matt's was still here! The stools were still lined up in the back with the same red plastic seats with silver metal trim. A young face was behind the counter, the same fellow accompanying old Lou to the theater. *But not someone who would yet have many stories,* Gavin thought.

"I'm Brock, Lou's grandson," the boy said.

"So happy to know you," Gavin cried with delight.

And then he proceeded to tell Brock about the good old days when his grandfather put extra strawberry ice cream in his sodas and asked for stories about Italy and the pretty Italian women. Brock stood at attention, fascinated, wiping down the counter over and over, around and around.

"So, Mr. Taylor, what's your pleasure? An ice cream soda with extra strawberry ice cream?" As soon as the soda was set down, Brock asked, "What are the Italian girls like, Mr. Taylor? I sure would love to go there someday," he kept saying.

But meeting Brock started Gavin worrying about the farm. After Danny, who would take over the land?

Most days, Gavin took short walks, circling the desolate area, leaning on his stick and thinking about building a house. He mourned the empty paddock, recalling the days when Blackie was the only creature he talked to all day. He carried a small folding stool and sat for hours with paper and pencil in the middle of an empty field, birds and mice and rabbits his only companions. Yet his enthusiasm grew as he anticipated a structure in this very place, a new home in which he might live and work. The grandchildren would stop in with their friends. He calculated sight lines to the shack and scribbled out various designs. Which way would his bed face to view the sunrise? What sight would he see from his kitchen sink? Did he need an extra half bath? And made a note to himself not to forget to make wide windowsills that would accommodate potted geraniums - red, pink and white.

It was now a few weeks after Gavin arrived, and he was resting in the fields. As he sat very still, a pair of wild turkeys followed by their seven baby chicks waddled by. A rabbit darting alongside sent them scurrying. Gavin was about to fold his stool, just as the daylight was drawing down, just as he was staring at the same scene as the day before. And suddenly, he was gripped with an unexpected melancholy, a slow slide into sorrow just as the sun slid quietly into the horizon. And right then, familiar things began to feel wrong.

His stool was too low, too flimsy. A few stalks of the weedy foxtail that had matted under his feet reached under his pant cuffs and started to itch and scratch. The point of his pencil snapped, and he had forgotten to bring an extra. The lines on his paper designating walls and floors appeared misplaced. His eyes were blurry with dust. The sight before him failed to excite. How could it not, the same one day after day? And just like that, his interest in the project seemed to fade away, all in a few moments while he was thinking it was time for supper.

He sat quietly, trying to understand this change of attitude, of perception. And thinking of this, that he would never build his house, he had even more alarming notions. The eyes that saw his family with perfect love now sunk lower, deeper into that place where flaws could not be denied, where small irritants settled, and insights came to roost - an occasional expression of failure by Danny regarding the farm, the loneliness he intuited from Jack not having a female companion, the weariness that time can impose despite Danny and Maryann's affection for each other, Gavin's money for repairs unable to stave off either the reality of aging or the exacting price of habit.

Was he his family's mirror image? A life on the rise, a life dangling midway, and intimations now beginning to appear, of certain decline.

Why, here, among his own, did he actually feel lonelier than among his Italian friends? It could be that these many weeks, he had no desire to paint. There was simply no beauty in the fields. All was brown, scrub, weeds, almost nothing on which even small animals could feed. The sunflowers were finished for the season. There was no mysterious allure that he felt during mornings on top of his mountain, as if the world were unfurling on yet another blessed day.

And ultimately, through these small happenings and others of which he was hardly aware and which often surprise us by their unexpected appearance, Gavin simply lost interest in Iowa. The fire for return dwindled like water pouring from a bottle that had fallen on its side. First, gushing out with a rush, then, drip by drip, emptying out until the bottle was empty. Gone.

Feeling nonessential, a fringe personality, he had outgrown his life here. He had been fooling himself. Everyone was taken up with their own lives. He had thought that he could paint anywhere. But he was wrong. It had been a false assumption, a concocted fantasy. The idea of return had surely been advanced by sentiment, but he had overlooked the many truths before him. Now he must choose - family or Italy? In Italy, he would paint and thrive, but he would die without family. It was a destiny fated only in this way.

Another week passed. The chill of early fall appeared suddenly, as it often did in the Midwest. Cold air found its way beneath his sweater. He looked for gloves, longing for the incandescent Italian light and the mild air that stayed all year. He missed the roses and peonies along the stone path to Francesco's and the aroma of freshly baked bread luring him into the warmth of fellowship. He craved the charm of his little village, the fellowship of the Brothers. He missed tending the garden between his cottage and studio. He longed to visit the sea and marshes where the godwits and grey herons lived.

He told them at dinner.

When everyone was passing around meat loaf and late summer corn, he tapped on a glass with his spoon, as one did at a wedding before making a toast.

"Hear, hear!" he cried, his eyes smiling, his heart leaden. "You know how I've loved being here."

The table grew silent, surely a preamble to a troublesome announcement.

"I am thrilled to see every one of you happy and working productively. But as you might have suspected, painting is not happening for me here. I guess I'm an old codger who needs his familiar cave, after all."

He looked around at the somber faces.

"I'm going back to Italy. You're probably not surprised," he said. "I expect visits from you all. No excuses. It's an easy trip."

"Won't you reconsider?" pleaded Maryann.

"Are you sure?" Danny and Jack asked together. "Is there anything we can do to change your mind?"

Emma and Ethan whispered to each other, "Don't make him feel guilty. Grandpa really wants to go back. Anyway, it would be a keen place to visit!"

"At least for you," Ethan added.

Gavin wondered if anyone was relieved. Perhaps building a house would interfere with Danny's plans if he should choose to sell the land. Perhaps the process would be too much of a nuisance in their quiet life, cranes and bulldozers kicking up a noisy storm for a year, equipment strewn around, perhaps crushing the forsythia.

The next morning, Gavin made three quick sketches each of the chicken coop, the house, the empty paddock, the distant hills. He hung one set in Danny's house and another in Jack's study. The third he would take back to Italy and mount on his timbered walls in full sight of where he brewed his morning coffee.

Once again, Gavin was settled into his mountain retreat, breathing the pure air of the high altitude. He had been welcomed back with great joy and fussing about. His friends had worried he might not return, knowing he had sealed his windows, pulled the shades, and stashed his paints in a locked closet. Brothers Silvio and Antonio were now retired and spent hours puttering in the herb garden or stocking shelves in the shop. Brother Bianchi now oversaw the well-being of the monastery and its residents. Gavin smiled to himself as he recalled that as a young monk, Brother Bianchi had always been particularly intrigued by his art while the older monks kept their eyes averted. He remembered the day his five Cecilia paintings were drying in the garden, and Brother Bianchi had unexpectedly stopped by. Looking directly and thoughtfully at the canvases lined up one after the other, he asked, "Was this something you simply imagined, Signor Gavin?" Gavin wasn't sure whether the question was a good or bad thing for the guidance of the monks under his stewardship.

Gavin was reassured by positive news from the farm.

Ethan and Jack had published their first book, *The Noble Pioneers*, a work in the genre of young adult. Ethan's story was about two young friends from Nebraska, Nellie and Tom, who were enlisted by a heavenly spirit to fly off to a distant planet in a spaceship composed of half a moon, half a sun. Exploring mysterious caves and rivers of gold, they discovered that while adventures were exciting, they missed their home back on earth. Should they return in a spaceship warmed by the sun, perhaps to melt, or chilled by the moon, too dark to steer? Readers adored Jack's offbeat illustrations, fanciful enough for a child's eye yet fitting for young adults coming into their own. Their devoted readers begged for a sequel. Already known from his play *The Galaxy Invaders*, Ethan was now acclaimed as part of a team, a success, he acknowledged, achieved solely on his uncle's initiative. And Jack, feeling renewed, proud of their first venture together, lay in bed next to the window watching the stars, thinking he had made the right decision to come home.

Ethan and Jack were eagerly sought out as speakers by dozens of disparate groups. Jack usually went alone, these events tiring for Ethan, fans pushing in close, waving the book in his face for a signature. Ellie arranged to send her cameraman along with Jack and contacted a publicist who would promote them nationally. As their reputations grew, Ethan and Jack remained in their study, already immersed in their next project.

Emma placed in the top three at the nationals in North Carolina. The prizes were announced as the local college band played "Don't Stop Believin'," and "Ain't No Stopping Us Now." For Emma and the two others, it meant a week's trip to Italy!

She immediately called Gavin.

"Grandpa, can I stay a week or so longer with you after everyone returns home?"

So Emma, a teenager, came to Italy. Just as Ethan had predicted, only much sooner than he had imagined.

Emma appeared like an explosion of confetti that drifted over everyone in her presence. Her talk never ceased; her enthusiasm never dimmed. Whatever she saw thrilled and intrigued her, from the beauty of the landscape to the charm of Gavin's studio, every inch of which she examined before taking off her coat. A whirlwind of youth and energy about to pounce on a fabulous world, Gavin insisted she sit and have a cup of tea before he took her to meet the Brothers.

He was eager to see how Sofia and Emma would get along - two firebirds soaring into the heat of life, each confident of their particular universes. They would go to Florence straightaway. Emma scampered down the hill like a young deer, prancing by every stone and flower, insisting that she had never seen such a lovely flower, such an unusual stone. The folks she passed could not pull their eyes away from her. Gavin marveled at this sprite who entered his world and set it afire with her fresh, virtuous beauty.

Eventually, they caught the bus to Florence. Emma had only to smile at Enzo for him to become her devoted minion. He had her sit in the front next to him while he pointed and chatted in Italian. She didn't understand a word, but it didn't matter. She was in full thrall, nodding her head, rapturously crying "ooh" and "aah" wherever he directed. When the bus arrived at the station in Florence, she gave him a big kiss on each cheek as he stood at his post, taking off his cap and placing it over his heart, bowing his head.

After strolling through the city that was birthed, then molded, and carved during the High Renaissance, a vision never diminished for Gavin by endless viewings, they reached Sofia's charming enclave. Emma stood outside *Sofia's Place*, entranced by the juxtaposition of the ancient outside with the cutting edge within. Just then, she understood why her grandfather had chosen to live in Italy. She would have made the same choice. While gazing through the glass at the radiant art, she recalled Gavin's stories of Sofia's role in his success, of his colorful patrons throughout the years. Imagine! Her very own grandfather painting a mural on the walls of a wine cellar in one of these splendid palazzi! It was fitting and right that he be here. Now having a sense of this renowned, historic city where every sight was a noble work of art, inspecting his home, his studio, and now Sofia's gallery, Emma felt almost grown-up, with a strong sense of her grandfather's life coming full circle. She could only hope that she would possess a spark of the qualities that enabled him to make such a pilgrimage - audacity and courage, tenacity and valor. *Qualities Ethan also had in full measure living in a modest farmhouse far distant from this exotic place*, she reflected. She hugged her grandfather while he smoothed her hair, murmuring, "You're the best, Emma. A winner. Now let's go in and meet a very special lady."

When they entered the gallery, elegant Sofia emerged from behind the curtain. It suddenly occurred to Emma that her grandfather, for all his dazzling elements, might actually be lonely.

Chapter 29

Fresh young Emma practically fell into Sofia's arms. There was no shyness in her as she bounced from one painting to the next, making comments in her teen slang. "Far out. Cool. What does that line right there mean? I love it, whatever it is. Hmm, I'm not so sure about that one though."

Sofia, still glamorous in middle age, was amused at the reactions of this young girl to her first exposure to contemporary art and pleased as well with Emma's apparent eagerness to be in her company. Sofia was also a bit more mellow these days, flirtations a dubious venture for a woman whose face showed signs of wear. Watching Emma eagerly dart about the room, Sofia sighed at the apparencies of time's harsh reality. *Aging is a relentless predator,* she thought, *slowly but inevitably, a droopy eyelid appears or a wrinkle on the arm or a raised vein on the leg.*

Emma continued to circle the room, inspecting, assessing. The works before her did not intimidate but fascinated without leaving an indelible imprint. She was like a moth, alighting briefly here and there but then flying off. Nor did Sofia's splendid dress of silk and lace arouse envy, merely curiosity as to what she herself would look like in a similar outfit, not having any notion that such a garment was custom-made.

All this Gavin instinctively saw and understood as did Sofia.

And Emma? She was oblivious to the impression she made, oblivious to the valuable presence of the surrounding objects. It was people who drew her interest.

Gavin smiled fondly at Sofia. For years, she had welcomed folks with those same chairs and table. Only the wines varied. Today, she had set down a bottle of Vermentino, a local white that Gavin loved.

Why not mix it up a bit? Gavin thought. *A new table, square, perhaps. Stools rather than chairs. Or why not commission Tommaso to design a set of whimsical furniture and leave it permanently on display? Its charm might lead to the creation of functional objects she could sell next door.*

Emma besieged the poor woman.

"Do these artists live here in Florence? Are you the only contemporary gallery in the city?

"Oh, you lived in New York? My grandparents met in New York. Did you know that?

"Everything in your country is so exciting and beautiful. I could stay here forever."

Sofia and Gavin smiled at each other, both thinking, *Sweet child, isn't she having a lovely time*?

Emma looked from one to the other. Had they sent each other some sort of signal? After a short pause, she cried out, "Grandpa, I don't want to leave. Can I stay and live here with you?" She fidgeted in her chair, embarrassed at the urgency of her request.

No one responded.

Sofia finally asked, "Would anyone like more wine?"

On the bus home, Gavin asked his granddaughter, "Emma, are you serious about wanting to stay here? You're headed to college in a few months. You have a scholarship."

"Grandpa, I can get a deferment for a year. How can anyone leave this dreamy place and go back to Iowa? You couldn't. Chicago might be better than Iowa, but it's still not Italy."

Gavin hesitated. What would she do with a year's free time? And with his canvases and paint solvents crowding the rooms, there was no space in his quarters. He would speak with Sofia.

Enzo, seeing them both so quiet, whistled them home without saying a word.

Sofia sent Emma a note:

> Would you like to have lunch with me tomorrow at nearby Matteo's and sample your grandpa's favorite dish?

Gavin was not included. His stubborn granddaughter stood before him, feet apart, face flushed. They were arguing about her going to Florence by herself.

"Nothing to worry about, Grandpa. You can put me on the bus. I remember the way to Sofia's gallery. Besides, I'm eighteen years old!" She was petulant, insistent.

Is it safe for her to be on her own? Should I call her parents? No, I'll let her go. Let's see if there's anything to talk about after her day with Sofia. As he watched Emma find a seat on the bus, he noted that she was as excited as he had ever seen her. He waved goodbye, threw kisses, then turned to his friend Antonio for a long chat over their morning pastries. Afterward, he took a short walk in the hills, then returned to the cottage and organized his painting supplies. He stopped by to see his friend Piero and volunteered for an hour in the monastery's wineshop, but still, no matter how he tried to find diversions, the day seemed infinitely long.

When the sun set and her bus pulled into the village square, Emma hopped off, beaming and exuberant, and Gavin knew that her day with Sofia was just the beginning.

"Grandpa! Let's sit. I have so much to tell you. Would you like a dessert?

"No? Some fruit? Okay, good," she said, when he ordered a dish of fresh figs and apricots.

Then Gavin said, "Okay, Emma, stop fussing and talk."

She leaned toward him and placed her hand under her chin to look thoughtful and mature.

"You'll never guess. Sofia said that if I stay - if you let me - I could work with her in the gallery! She said she could use some help. She said I would meet some of the artists! Imagine, one or two might even be famous, like you!"

Gavin knew instantly that he was defeated. He remembered his own feelings when for the first time he had stepped off the bus in Florence into an enchanting city and his resolve to wander for days before attending to business. How could he refuse Emma? No one would leave Florence by choice after just a week.

He called Sofia again.

In a few minutes, all was decided. "There is a small apartment above the former candle store next door, furnished and unoccupied. Emma can stay there," Sofia said. "It's really too far for her to go back and forth every day on the bus. Here, on the premises, I can keep a close eye on her."

The next morning, even before he made his coffee, Emma sat primly on a bench in the living room. Hands together, fingers crossed, she waited quietly for him to call her parents in Iowa. The early sun poured through the window like a swarm of lacewing butterflies, reflecting reddish tints on her dark-brown hair. *Oh,* Gavin thought, *I want to paint her, just like that.*

"Hi, Maryann," Gavin began. "Hope all is well with everyone over there. Can you ask Danny to get on the other line?"

"Hi, Dad. We're both here. What's up? Are you enjoying our beautiful daughter? Showing her a good time?"

"Yes, Danny, I sure am. We have a favor to ask." Gavin cleared his throat. "Emma just met Sofia, and they hit it off big time."

In Iowa, they waited.

"Sofia offered Emma a job in her gallery earning decent money with a free apartment next door." He paused. The phone line remained silent. "Emma wants to defer college for a year. I would, of course, be responsible for her well-being. It would be quite the extraordinary experience for her," Gavin added.

After a pause, Danny asked his wife, "What do you think, honey?"

They began having a conversation as if Gavin were not on the line.

"Would it matter if she deferred Chicago for a year? How many kids get such an opportunity?" Danny persisted.

"Danny, think about it. Her safety. There are pickpockets in the cities. And you know about those Italian men. She wouldn't actually be staying with her grandfather. What do we know about this Sofia gal? And what about her gymnastics scholarship? What about that?"

Danny sighed. Gavin waited patiently, thinking, *Danny always thinks big. Maryann worries. Perhaps I should have spoken with my son alone first.*

"Sleep on it, you two. We'll talk tomorrow," Gavin said.

Early the next morning, as the Italians began to start their day - a farmer putting his cows to pasture, a vinter inspecting his grapes, carts carrying fresh vegetables to the piazzas for early shoppers - he took Emma for a walk to meet his friend Mario DiGiornio and his eleven children. *A pleasant way to distract her, hopefully to discourage her,* he thought. But it had just the opposite effect. She became even more enamored with the landscape and the people.

"Look, Grandpa" - she pointed - "these children playing games in the vineyards and calling to each other in Italian is the most enchanting thing I've ever seen."

That afternoon, Gavin called Maryann. Somehow, Danny had convinced her to change her mind. He then placed a call to the admissions department at a Chicago university. In less than ten minutes, the deferment was official. In less than a week, Emma's life had been transformed.

Packing few clothes, mostly sports outfits and sneakers, Emma was unprepared for a long stay.

"We'll go shopping," Sofia declared.

Not to the silk factory where she had her own dresses made but to funky shops such as Luisaviaroma and La Rinascente where the clothes were young and chic. Then to the Piazza del Duomo area and the Miss Trench shop. Emma tried on whatever Sofia thrust her way, disarmed by the hustle of the scene, the charm of it. Salesgirls were elegantly dressed. The simplest goods were cleverly presented to entice the most innocent shopper. Signs were in Italian, and Emma, knowing nothing about foreign sizes or prices, decided to trust Sofia and fall into an impulsive adventure.

Sofia was a determined shopper, a woman on a mission. Yet she took time to occasionally pause and reassure her young charge, "You look beautiful, Emma. *Una bella signorina!*" Staring in the mirror, Emma agreed. When in her life had she worn garments sewn with such finesse and dexterity? Certainly not anything from Miss Maddie's. Definitely not anything from the Sears, Roebuck catalog. As her parcels were sent off to her address, and the shopkeepers began to shutter their doors, she and Sofia had a cup of tea and headed home. Emma opened the door to her cozy *appartamento* and collapsed on the sofa, crying her heart out, knowing she was the luckiest girl in the world yet more homesick for her parents than she had ever been before.

The next morning, Emma was dressed in her new pale-green knit dress with lavender ribbon edging the neckline. Twirling in front of the mirror, she thought for the first time, *I'm all grown-up. Sofia was right. Una bella signorina. Even Mom would approve of this dress. And Dad, casting a long look, the more sentimental of the two, would have tears in his eyes.* Emma checked the clock and called Iowa.

Ethan answered.

Hooray, she thought.

Whenever she had news or erratic moods or fears or dreams, it was Ethan with whom she wanted to speak. There was nothing he failed to understand. Listen he did, without judgment, and offered advice only when asked. Maybe it was his quiet life with its encompassing calm. His restful moments for noticing things, especially facial expressions and nuanced body movements. He always said that if he were deaf, he would still know how people felt about something by the slightest twitch of their cheek or roll of an eye.

"Ethan, have you heard?" she asked.

"Hey, Em, sure did. Was going to call you later, but you beat me to it. So? Tell all!"

"Ethan, I can hardly describe what's happening. I had expected to stay with Grandpa for only a week, and now I have a free apartment, a job for a year, and beautiful new clothes! I may even get to meet some of the artists!

"And all because of Sofia. She's amazing, gorgeous, friendly, and generous. You should see the two huge paintings by Grandpa hanging in her gallery. I'll take pictures of both and mail them to you.

"You don't think she's doing all this for me simply to please Grandpa, do you?" Emma asked hesitantly. "That I might actually be in her way?"

"Naw. She's been representing him almost since he got over there. No need for her to do extra to get on his good side now. Besides, you're a pretty likable kid all on your own, you know."

"Ethan, it'd be so awesome if you were here."

"It's pretty cool here too, Em. Uncle Jack and I are local celebrities. Some kid I didn't even know wanted my autograph in Matt's the other day. When I asked him how he knew me, he said, 'Doesn't everyone?'"

"That's great, but don't let it go to your head. Anyway, gotta go, or I'll be late."

"Em, don't worry about anything. You're a champ. The best, and don't forget it. And Grandpa's nearby."

Emma wondered if Ethan would miss her. She wondered if someone with a heart condition could fly a long distance on a plane. But she didn't worry or doubt that even with a weak heart, Ethan had a braver soul than any champion gymnast who could jump and spin and do triple somersaults.

"How lovely you look, Emma," Sofia said as she walked into the gallery and found Sofia studying a new acquisition. "What do you think of this?" she asked, as Emma turned to look at a mass of jumbled squiggles, wavy lines, and random dots. And in such ugly colors - dark purple, black, brown.

"Hmm, I'm not sure what he or she is trying to say or, rather, do," Emma answered warily. Did Sofia expect a specific response?

"This woman artist was once attacked in her home. Does that make the painting more understandable?" Sofia asked.

Emma nodded yes, but was afraid to say, "It's still ugly, and who would buy it?"

Sofia rubbed her hands together and said, "Let's get started. It will be a busy day. We have a reception here tonight. I'm showing three works by this woman I just discovered. An unknown female artist in her sixties."

After the evening's gathering had progressed well into its second hour, there was a sudden stir among the guests. As if a door were opened and the Wizard of Oz stood on the threshold. Everyone looked around expecting a surprise or some other sensational act of Sofia's. However, it was simply Gianni Amatucci who stood there, Sofia's long-time client and old friend. But enough of a reason to cause a commotion among those present with his gorgeous dark Italian looks and his usual swagger. *He looks wonderfully rested,* Sofia observed. Likely he had spent the winter at his favorite Swiss spa. When she had a moment, she would introduce him to Emma as the man who bought Gavin's sunflower painting and helped make her grandfather famous. She turned to see if Emma noticed the effusive welcome Gianni received but grew uneasy as Emma's gaze lingered not on Gianni but on the striking young man at his side - Mattia, Gianni's son, now fully grown and dangerously handsome. Sofia sighed, just her luck that the first young Italian man Emma would meet had eyes both tender and playful. Sofia hoped she wouldn't regret getting involved in Gavin's personal affairs.

When two svelte women finally left Gianni's side, one with her hand to her throat, another patting her hair, Sofia took her hand and guided Emma over to her star client.

This older man is positively regal, Emma thought, *like a prince.*

"Gianni, Mattia, let me have the pleasure of introducing you to Emma, Gavin's granddaughter," she said.

Emma's ringing ears took in not a word. *Both men are stunning,* Emma thought. *One is like an adventure at its beginning; the other, with knowledge of a completed journey.*

"What a great pleasure, my dear," Gianni offered with a smile and a twitch of his perfectly groomed mustache. Holding her shoulders with both hands, he bent down and kissed her first on one cheek, then the other. Emma smelled something spicy and woodsy, felt the feather touch of his lips.

"Welcome to Florence," he said, his voice operatic, deep. "I hope we have a chance to get to know you while you're here."

Interrupting, a call from the other side of the room.

"Yoo-hoo, Gianni! Darling!"

"*Mi scusi,* excuse me," he said to Emma as he turned and walked toward the slim, blond-haired woman with eyes like magnetic beams. Emma felt cheated but relieved, as she wiped the sweat off her hands. She thought this man and his son were the sexiest men she had ever seen. But what did she know? She only knew boys from her hometown and a few on the gymnastic team. Hardly a match, her classmates in high school and this boy named Mattia who moved around the room with the confidence that his dashing style would not go unnoticed.

Only after she returned to her tasks did she realize that in their brief encounter, Gianni had not referred to her grandfather.

Emma dusted the artwork, ran errands, polished the jewelry cases and answered the phones. And when one of the gallery's artists stopped by, also acted as hostess, putting out the wine. The stunning discovery that a single painting could cost more than her father made in a year sparked her interest in the gallery's finances. She didn't have a hand in the management of its figures and numbers, but she was acquiring a good sense of how business dealings were carried out. Particularly notable were the small favors and charms required to influence positively the artist's attitude in his negotiations as well as the client's into raising his final offer.

During her free time, Emma meandered around the winding streets, poking into corners, unearthing the city's engaging cafés and shops. She quickly picked up Italian words and phrases which gave her confidence to talk to shopkeepers and passersby. Most of all, she loved sitting on the grassy banks of the Arno watching the scullers elegantly move their boats forward. It reminded her of Uncle Jack's stories about his former rowing days in Cambridge. Emma often took her lunch there, gazing dreamily at the magnificent views to the other side of the water where the grand palazzi sat solidly on the land. Beyond them rose the domes and carillons of the renowned cathedrals, as if it were all a mirage rising from the watery depths. *I wonder what Ethan would write about this view,* she reflected. *How can he make it any more magical than it is?*

Bless Sofia.

She had found Emma an outstanding gymnastic team at the local university. The coach was agreeable to her working out with them as a guest athlete. Every other Sunday, when she met Gavin for lunch, she told him stories of the young people she met there with whom she was becoming friendly and how they were slowly teaching her the language. Now she knew a few Italian boys to whom she could compare Mattia. However, she chose not to share those particular observations with her grandfather. What would she say? That when she first saw Pietro Perugino's painting, P*ortrait of a Young Man i*n the Uffizi Gallery, she thought it the most breathtaking face she had ever seen? And that Mattia had similar eyes and a similar mouth, the latter ripe and full with a deep dip in the center of the upper lip?

A thick white envelope arrived at the gallery addressed to Sofia and Emma.

Serata at the home of Signor Gianni
Amatucci. Celebrate the acquisition
of *Youth*, a painting by Mr. Gavin Taylor.

Sofia had discreetly remarked to Gianni that publicity around this purchase might be a good excuse for a gathering of clients, a push for both their businesses during the usual summer slowdown. She was pleased that he had followed her advice.

"What will I wear?" asked Emma.

"Darling, you have the gift of youth," Sofia answered. "You could go in rags, and you would be radiant."

"Sofia, stop kidding. Really."

"Not to worry, *la mia bella ragazza,* my beautiful girl."

On Wednesday afternoon, they made their way to Sofia's dressmakers in the heart of Florence. Emma would have her first custom garment sewn directly onto her slender body. Through the archway carved with stone cherubs and vines they marched, into the cavernous heart of the workshop itself, past the bolts of fabric from floor to ceiling, past the busy phalanx of workers set to their task with heads down and pincushions on their wrists.

Emma was asked to remove her jeans and shirt and given a silky undergarment. Standing on a low pedestal, she was cosseted and examined as if being fitted for her wedding gown. Two women and a man hovered around the astonished young girl, speaking rapidly in Italian, their fluttering hands alighting on her waist, back, shoulders. A plain white piece of cotton appeared that they gently laid over her body. The dressmakers then got busy draping, cutting, and gathering. Pins flew while they chattered in Italian, appraising her legs, breasts, hips. As they worked, one of the women slowly turned the pedestal until, after a couple of hours, the man finally cried out, "Aaah! *Si! Questo è tutto,* that's it! *Fatta!* Done!" The small group applauded while Emma dared not utter a word. Carefully, they unwound the sample from Emma's body.

A gorgeous bolt of peach silk chiffon was then brought forth and held in front of the assembled group. Everyone agreed. "*Si, si, si,*" they chorused, as the seamstresses lay the pattern out on a table and started to cut.

The next day, the three workers fitted the silk to Emma's shape and began anew to snip and clip, starting at the neck and working their way down toward Emma's ankles. At last, the final pin was pushed through the hem of the fabric. Emma had no idea of the style of dress nor any of its details. She only knew she felt like a princess, and like royalty, she stood tall and allowed others to do their job.

She couldn't wait to call Ethan.

Having a dress custom made was a difficult business. Two more fittings. Each time, the peach silk was wrapped around her body. Each time, more precise stitching was performed. After the third appointment, the man - "Call me Alessandro," he had told her - put out his hand and guided her across the vast space to a full-length mirror. She stared at the reflection of a stylish, sophisticated young woman whom she hardly recognized - a dream of a girl in a floating chiffon dress of palest apricot crowned by the burnished glints in her lustrous hair.

Chapter 29

At the magnificent entrance to Gianni's palatial villa stood a butler in formal clothes wearing white gloves. Ripe as a summer peach and just as luscious, Emma stepped with Gavin and Sofia into a splendid atrium of marble and gilt. Far down a long passageway, Emma thought she caught a glimpse of brilliant yellows she was sure were sunflowers.

Chapter 30

Sofia and Gavin underplayed Gianni's event so as not to alarm her. It was the right thing to do. If Emma had known of the splendor awaiting, she would have been far more nervous.

But as it happened, it was worse not being prepared. *How is a kid like me supposed to manage socially in this place?* she wondered. *Hopefully, I won't make a fool of myself by acting awkward or making inappropriate social gestures. Furthermore, even though we are here to celebrate Grandpa's painting, art is the last thing about which I have any knowledge. But Sofia had reported that Signor Amatucci asked especially that I attend.*

"It would be my honor," he had said. "Gavin's only granddaughter, after all!"

And another thing - although Sofia had said almost everyone present could speak English, right now Emma's ears heard only Italian. Unsure, she stood at the open door as Sofia and Gavin swept into the space, greeting everyone, most of whom they knew and Gavin speaking the language as if born to it. When Sofia and Gavin had spoken of a big house with wealthy people dressed in fancy clothes, they added she was not to worry. Emma would be a ravishing rose among the gasping, aging bouquets.

With a reassuring hug, Sofia said, "Just be yourself, and all will be fine."

But all was not fine. When they mentioned Signor Amatucci lived in a grand house, they did not say in a splendid, stately palazzo, like a nobleman. Emma's idea of rich and fancy was the home of Mrs. Molly Donovan that sat high on a hill outside town, a sprawling farmhouse of ten rooms on three floors with two barns in the northeast corner, smack in the middle of one hundred twenty acres of fertile farmland.

She felt herself getting blisters from new shoes. When was the last time she wore high heels? Her feet were accustomed to soft, ballet-type slippers specifically made for sprinting, jumping, and tumbling. And even then, her feet required constant tending and massaging. Now here they were, cramped and poky, stuffed into stiff linen footwear dyed to match her silk dress.

Ethan won't believe me when I describe this place, she thought.

Waiters in gray velvet tunics with brass buttons moved smoothly among the fashionable crowd, proffering champagne in fluted glasses perched on round gold trays or canapés of *Grana Padano* cheese puffs with prosciutto or chickpea bruschetta served on tiny silver spoons. Emma paid special attention to the savory Tuscan truffles made of goat cheese, mascarpone, parmesan. And another favorite, the s*piedinis*, small kebabs of meat marinated in onion and currant.

Suddenly, in the posh surroundings, she understood in a real way that this extravagant evening was held solely to celebrate a new painting by her grandfather. So taken was she with the fittings for her new dress, she failed to focus on the worldwide renown he enjoyed. In Iowa, he was always dressed modestly in old jeans, sitting by the shack all day. She always thought of him simply as her grandpa who painted. But now Emma realized that although the names of rock stars might be more quickly recognized, the name of Gavin Taylor was historically significant, integral to a great cultural movement. And tonight, she would be an intimate part of her grandfather's latest triumph. Emma shivered, feeling awed by her own kin but also alienated as celebrants descended and swept Gavin away.

She watched her grandfather from afar, standing tall above others. *He really is good-looking,* she thought, *not handsome like a movie star but attractive in a rangy, loose way, at ease with himself, not looking around for a better place to be, or someone of importance with whom to engage.* He was in possession of something uniquely great, which others could only imagine. Talent. It was a phenomenon similar to her own situation. When she stood on the winner's podium, boys fluttered and hovered, gripped by her achievements. Talent was sexy, any talent.

"You're amazing, Emma. Sensational!" her followers reverently cried as she claimed yet another medal. The words were not those of love, but they were inching their way toward lust, envy, or longing to be a part of what she was.

If those guys had thought about it, she reflected, *they would realize I spend at least six hours a day practicing, working out, same as Gavin, forsaking other activities, denying pleasures of food and play.* How often had she heard, "Oh, I wish…if only," as if her accomplishments were made of wishes, not grueling, relentless work. No one focused on the long, arduous journey required. Same with Gavin, as if he hadn't spent a couple of decades in a chicken coop painting the same hills, fields, trees until he at last discovered his personal style and forged his true path.

She hardly felt the soft touch on her elbow until he whispered, "*Ciao*, Emma," and she turned to face Mattia, dressed in a dark striped suit, an expensive silk shirt of the softest violet and a ruby-red tie. *Oh, he's gorgeous,* she thought, taking a step back and wobbling on her heels, feeling clumsy and gauche before his easy, self-assured elegance.

"Have you ever seen the sunflower painting?" he asked, the words rising from his throat in a dusky Italian accent.

She faltered, shaking her head no, not wishing to sound like an Iowa schoolgirl or a farmer's daughter, a drab contrast to the language Mattia spoke, that Sofia spoke, every word like a song, the pitch high, then low, dipping like a gull on the tip of a wave. He guided her down a long corridor with walls of carved paneling rubbed with silver leaf and planted her at the open arch for her to better absorb the remarkable scene about to leave her breathless.

A ravishing, glorious conservatory lay open before her.

Its towering glass ceiling was so high as to seem part of the sky on a clear day. The shape was a soaring, perfect six-sided hexagon.

Two solid walls and three of faceted glass magnified themselves dozens of times. The sixth wall, an open expanse in which she was standing. Emma paused, blinking in wonder, not knowing where her eyes should rest - on the radiant colors of the spectacular art, the exotic flowers, a thousand greens of the landscape beyond? The setting sun cast red and orange streaks of dappled light into the room. Even as she watched, their radiance slowly faded until they melted into the smoky night. With a last gasp, like the sinking of the *Titanic*, its mighty aft reaching for the sky, then upended, silently sinking into the sea, so, too, the entire outside scene disappeared beyond the distant hills. And Emma remained inside a glittering crystal prism that comprised an entire world created from the owner's fearless taste.

And on the walls, Gavin's paintings.

Facing each other across the room, as if they were two Michelangelo sculptures having a conversation, were sunflowers and roiling reds. Between them, in a low round arrangement, rested a dozen rare orchids in weathered stone pots. Here were the paintings that launched Gavin's career, come to life on the grass beside an abandoned chicken coop, Blackie pawing the ground nearby. The breathtaking surprise of it all was about to make her cry. But just as her tears were about to fall, a handkerchief was thrust into her hands. As she stifled sobs into Mattia's linen offering, she asked herself how Gavin managed to convey such emotion without presenting a concrete subject. Simply by color, texture, movement? And then, once again, and always, she thought, *I wish Ethan were here.*

If she didn't know, she might wonder what she was looking at. But she did know. The family had talked for years about sunflowers being the catalyst for Gavin's success. She herself had traveled that highway many times in summer when the sunflowers were in bloom. But she wondered if the experience would be more meaningful to a viewer if he knew that the yellows and greens referred to a specific subject. Probably not, she decided. The public had always been thrilled by Gavin's brilliant canvases without them being named as any particular thing. In any case, they apparently did evoke various realities or particular emotions. When she overheard Gianni tell a colleague the painting reminded him of the sunflowers in Maremma, his friend remarked that for him it evoked memories of an unusually hot but happy summer of his childhood. A different perception, another memory retrieved. And wasn't it a wondrous process for each person to find his own personal meaning?

Mattia turned her around and placed her six feet from roiling reds.

Of course, she knew the story behind this piece, Gavin's picking up a pamphlet on abstract expressionism at Haley's store and racing home to paint this, his first abstract painting. A not-so-young man who suddenly discovered a style that released him from painting nature as its own apparent truth. Overcome by the demon red, he expressed it in as many hues as he could devise. Yet when Signor Amatucci looked at this painting, he saw poppy fields wrapping the hills of Tuscany. And in this room, he had arranged his vision of that particular landscape in spring.

"Any painting this size has to be viewed a bit farther back," Mattia explained.

Although Emma was sure he meant it innocently, the offhand remark made her feel as if he didn't expect her to know that. It was so obvious. When you stood back, you felt in the heart of the painting's dramatic center, grasped the entirety of the work. Up close, the paint was merely a meaningless blur.

Her head ached.

After these initial two works created in his unique style, Gavin evermore painted impressions that flitted across his brain, reconfiguring them into images set down however he saw his dreams.

In this way, Emma was beginning to learn about art.

At the end of the grand corridor, the crowd had clustered around Gavin's recent work, propped against the wall on a high, wide wooden stand. With Mattia at her side, she walked over to join the guests. Gavin doesn't usually title his paintings, she recalled. However, it seems he did so in this particular case. Curious. He must have had a specific reason.

Youth, he called it. Like all his paintings, it was a study in movement.

A background of creams with splotches of dark reds and browns in the center. Moving toward the top, umbers and siennas becoming lighter as the strokes twisted and turned over each other, almost like a woman pinning up her hair. Dots of metallic bronze scattered about. Suddenly, a peculiar insight popped up. She remembered that one morning in his cottage when he had murmured, "Those reddish tints from the sun…" When she asked him what he meant, he replied, "Nothing, not important." It was her! A type of symbolic portrait; her grandfather's *sense* of her. She was sure of it.

Here it was, in Gavin's inimitably inscrutable manner, the feeling of sunlight drifting over her dark hair. And those coils of energy reaching upward. Gavin surely had painted his granddaughter as a tireless force spinning and twirling and jumping off the edge of the canvas.

Stunned, she leaned in and focused on the way he had captured her spirit, struck by the originality of his concept, the skill of its execution, and especially his ability to elicit profound emotion from a formless subject. Mattia sat beside her, puzzled by her singular attention. There were voices in the background. Signor Amatucci was extolling the new painting. Gavin rose briefly and offered a small wave. Sofia threw kisses to the guests. The room erupted in applause. Signor Amatucci invited his guests to have more champagne and to visit Gavin's other works in the conservatory.

And still Emma sat, overcome with understanding.

She remained longer in the shadows as her awareness evolved. She now perceived her life and that of her grandfather in a way that excited, soothed, and reassured all at once, that resolved her baffling emotions these many months. Now she understood that her life would be as different from her grandfather's in style and geography as she could imagine, yet both would be sterling examples of grit and spirited effort. Hopefully, of excellence. And further, immersed as she had been in this glamorous world, she had come to the same conclusion as did her Uncle Jack years earlier, that here in this splendid land, she would be an enthralled visitor but not a permanent resident.

She looked around for Sofia and Gavin, anxious to say good night and find her way home. Distracted by her reveries, she did not feel Mattia behind her until he took her hand and asked with those compelling eyes if she would have dinner with him the following evening.

Emma spent a fretful night. She knew she should have told Sofia or Gavin.

But she hadn't. Would they consider Mattia, at twenty-four, too old for her? And with his devastatingly good looks, an area of concern? She had never had a secret before. At least not one this dramatic. She wanted to hold it close, to polish its surface with possibilities, to relive undisturbed the look of him in the violet shirt, the red tie.

She asked Mattia to pick her up at seven on Wednesday evening. The gallery would close early, and she could dress slowly.

What shall I wear? Emma wondered.

Thanks to Sofia, she had many lovely, very stylish, very Italian choices. But they were all dresses. Is that what a young Italian girl would wear on a casual date?

In the end, she opted for a touch of Iowa enhanced by a taste of Italy.

Her good black jeans with a long pullover sweater of a lovely garnet and green weave, a recent purchase from a neighborhood shop, echoes of her grandmother's outfit at her interview with the theater company.

When she answered the doorbell, her first thought was that the black pants were perfect. There Mattia stood, handsome in pressed navy jeans, a white linen shirt with the sleeves rolled up. His throat tan, his hair wet from the bath, holding out a bunch of daisies.

They sat outside under the stars at a cozy trattoria on a quiet side street. Despite its relaxing aura, Emma felt ill at ease. She had no idea what to say, how to act, even where to look, Mattia's chestnut brown eyes aglow with curiosity. This was her first real date. Until now, her life had been devoted to gymnastics, and the boy gymnasts were her pals, like brothers. Girlfriends at school gossiped about going to parties or dances, but she had given such activities little consideration. Every motion her body made, every morsel of food she consumed, was carefully monitored and scrutinized to further her skills. But she hadn't minded. She had made a choice. Her goal was to win competitions. But now Mattia was an intimidating prospect, not only handsome and older, but also rich as a prince.

The candle between them cast shadows on the faces of other diners who were laughing and murmuring but seemed as distant as characters in a play. Mattia tried to remember if he had ever gone out with a girl who was not Italian. And an American! There was a grace to Emma's simplicity, an honest, intelligent mindfulness that he found enticing. She had none of the posturing of girls he had dated. *Those I have known are of a different order,* he reflected, *born of an ancient culture. But Emma was fresh, grown, and bred from a brand-new country. Besides, she was gorgeous and had no inkling of it. As an athlete, her body was superbly toned. And her skin so fair, and those reddish-golds in her hair so thickly falling around her face.* To him, she was one of God's perfectly formed creatures.

"May I explain the menu?" he asked. "A traditional Italian meal has seven courses, each consisting of small portions."

"All those courses for one meal?" she asked, astonished.

"Yes, we linger over our food. We can spend the entire evening at the table. An *antipasto* to start - cheese, sausage, olives. Then *primo piatto*, or first course, usually pasta or soup or a risotto."

"What is risotto?" she asked.

"A creamy rice dish, which can be flavored in various ways - often with porcini or mushrooms, as you call them. Then the *secondo piatto*, or second course," he continued. "Veal or lamp, chicken or meat. A protein of some kind. As I said before, small servings."

Emma listened to the explanations, his lovely voice melodious, seductive.

"Then a side dish, *contorno*, served with the *secondo piatto*. Often, potato or broccoli romano, or chicory."

"Ah, then *insalata*, salad. I think Americans serve the salad *before* the main course?"

"Finally, *formaggio e frutta*. Cheese and fruit. And, at last, dessert, or *dolce*."

After each sentence, Mattia asked Emma to pronounce the Italian words, smiling as she tried her best, curling her tongue, crimping her lips. All the while, they sipped red wine from Chianti, a drink not allowed on her regimen. And suddenly, they were laughing and flirting, and she couldn't pull away from his eyes. He let his hand gently graze hers, and in an explosion of astonishing discovery, her body burst with desire.

"May I order for you?" he asked.

"Please," she managed, her voice thick with new hungers, quickening impulses.

"*Tagliatelle* with *pesto alla Siciliana, per favore,* if you please," he said to the waiter. "And for the *secondo piatto*, the *peposo*," he ordered. "A delicious Tuscan peppery beef stew," he explained, turning to Emma. "And of course, the *insalata* next, and then the *formaggio e frutta*. We'll see later about dessert."

Far too much food, Emma thought. "And you eat like this every day?" she asked Mattia. "I would never be able to do a single lift after such a meal."

But tonight, she wasn't competing.

Despite her practical upbringing and her athleticism, Emma was a dreamer, like all young girls. She often found herself lost in various fantasies - such as, living on her own or daring to drink wine that was not good for her or wondering why she had been thrust into this time and place, speculating if this man in front of her lived in spacious rooms above that splendid conservatory. When Mattia pushed the candle aside and leaned toward her to point something out on the menu, she felt as if the heat of the flame was burning her skin.

The tagliatelle arrived, long flat noodles steaming with savory red sauce.

"May I show you?" Mattia asked. "Unless you already know how we Italians eat pasta."

Relieved, Emma said, "Yes, please."

Mattia deftly held a large spoon in one hand, scooped up the pasta with a fork, and with the grace of a gourmand, twirled the fork within the spoon until the noodles were a neat, tight bundle. Then he placed it carefully into his mouth.

"How amazing," she said, impressed with the elegance of the gesture.

Recalling the endless pasta dinners when she and Ethan had long strings of spaghetti hanging from their forks, making slurping noises competing to see who could suck the noodles into their mouths the fastest. Dollops of sauce dotting their lips, the tips of their noses, the front of their shirts.

Feeling inept, in which hand did he hold the fork, the spoon, she tried to follow Mattia's example. Unfortunately, continuing to think of Ethan, her attention wavered, and the noodles slipped off the fork, dropping a hefty spoonful of sauce on the front of her garnet and green sweater. Aghast, she looked down at her chest and began to stammer an apology. Before Mattia could stop her, rather than blot lightly, she was wiping forcefully, smearing the nasty red stain over the garment's delicate threads.

"Don't be sorry. This is your first time eating pasta our way," Mattia said.

True, but it didn't lessen her humiliation. She refused to cry.

Conversation became strained. A pall was thrown over the meal. *How will I carry on with this mess sprawled across my chest?* she wondered. It was a warm night, and she had not brought a sweater as a coverup, nor did Mattia have a jacket she could borrow.

Mattia was annoyed with himself.

"*Chiedo scusa.* I apologize," he said. "I should have ordered the penne or rigatoni, easy to pick up with a fork. But no, I wanted to show off winding the noodles," he sheepishly admitted.

He tried but failed to change the mood.

"Eating Italian food is dangerous until you get the hang of it," he said, still attempting to console. "Most people need several tries to manage the noodles." But her shame did not diminish.

"Tiramisu, *per favore*," he ordered.

An elegant, richly layered concoction of ladyfingers, coffee, and mascarpone on a white china plate. *Maybe this will serve to loosen things up. I'll tell her a story about sticking my fingers in a large bowl of tiramisu when I was a boy, thereby spoiling dessert for my parents' dinner party. Perhaps she'll smile again.*

Mattia hoped but failed to recapture their flirtation. Emma was dawdling.

"Is there a problem?" he asked. "We can get some *tartufo*, a gelato and chocolate dessert, or a *panna cotta*, a creamy vanilla pudding. Would you prefer that?"

The tiramisu sat before her, beautifully prepared, artistically presented. She hadn't realized that it contained coffee. How could she say that she had always hated coffee? That the offensive odor was wafting right now up into her nostrils?

"We Italians are too smug about our cuisine," Mattia said, trying for humility. "I shouldn't have made assumptions."

It was useless to prolong the evening. He signaled for *il conto*, the bill. When it was paid, he walked Emma home under the chill of estrangement. For once in his life, the "Mighty Mattia," as his friends called him, was powerless.

The next morning, in a long box of gold foil wrapped with silver ribbons, Emma received a delivery of white roses. She could almost touch the droplets of moisture on their petals. On the enclosure card, he wrote with a flourish:

Second dates are always better.

She smiled, feeling her mortification begin to fade.

He waited two days, then sent over a courier with a note:

> *There's a concert, violin and cello, Wednesday evening in the Boboli Gardens. I'll pack a light supper of mortadella on focaccia, some slices of melon. Are you interested?*

How could she say no to a violin concert in the Boboli Gardens? And Mattia was so sweet for thinking to bring sandwiches rather than a noodle dish. Still, she would bring a sweater to throw over her blouse should the need arise.

Chapter 31

Jack decided to celebrate his and Ethan's recent good fortune by getting himself down to Matt's for an ice cream soda. He had been using the excuse of the book's success for at least four sodas now. This day, while Brock made him his favorite, chocolate syrup with chocolate ice cream, Jack's head was rolling over ideas for Ethan's most recent scheme. He had doodled on both sides of two paper napkins before Brock even spritzed in the club soda. It was neither in Ethan nor Jack's nature to welcome idle time. They both knew that a substantial lapse between their current book and the next one might invite a fickle public to seek other authors.

But just as he was mulling this over, he was struck with an intense ache beneath his ribs. It had happened before, and always at unexpected moments, like right now finishing up his soda. An awareness of the other truth of his new reality - the sad part, that in his manhood, he was a lonely soul. He craved female companionship, and not Ethan or ice cream sodas or being back home would fill him up.

Rummaging around in the bottom of his glass for the few extra drops of syrup, he didn't notice someone quietly slide onto the stool beside him until a voice with a melodic lilt asked, "Well, Jack Taylor! I'll be darned. It *is* Jack Taylor, isn't it?"

He turned to look into the lovely face of a woman with eyes tender and amused. Her short curly crop of blond tangles bobbed about as she swiveled on her seat. *Who is she?* he wondered. He hated when folks you don't recognize assumed you knew their names. Fortunately, she quickly relieved him of a possible blunder.

"You wouldn't know me, but I'm Susan's younger sister, Addie."

"Uh, er, Susan?" he asked.

"Susan, or I should say Susan Larson, my older sister. She helped your brother out when the twins were little," she said, smiling impishly.

"I must confess," Addie continued, "I didn't know what you looked like until I saw the cover of your book. I read it at least once a month to my kids."

Jack wondered who in town had the honor of putting a wedding ring on this young woman's finger.

Seeing his brows tighten, she added, "Oh, not my own children. I'm a teacher. My class loves your book. We're all fans."

Jack relaxed, appraising anew this charming woman with the merry eyes, pleased to notice there was no ring on her left hand.

At seventeen, Ethan's body had grown gracefully into manhood. He had whiskers on his face and hair on his chest, and despite living a sedentary life, his limbs displayed the attractive hardiness of youth. He might be a young man with limitations, but he was not without needs and appetites. Now suddenly in his late teens, he was taken with a surge toward lust. His family, even Emma, never referred to this inevitable phenomenon. Although they were farm people familiar with the sexual natures of all living things, teenagers' coming of age was an awkward subject. Besides, how could they help Ethan in this regard? Could he even have an intimate relationship with a woman without endangering his life? He would never run, ride a horse, or climb hills. Was making love similarly restrictive? Until now, Emma was always at hand. Her dramatic presence precluded the need for another woman, Ethan's constraints being minor and manageable. But now he was eighteen, and his body longed and yearned and desired.

As he rose from his desk, Ethan's head fell heavy onto his chest. Taking in large gulps of air and coughing phlegm, his eyes watered; his heartbeat was erratic. He sat very still, waiting for the attack to lift. And while he waited, he felt in the deepest part of his soul that no matter how many stories he wrote, how well-known he became, he would likely live alone for the rest of his life. Alone, without the privileges and intimacies of married life.

He couldn't bear it.

And as if nothing could be more unfair, just as the sweat was drying on his face, his Uncle Jack came through the back door, whistling, "Oh, What a Beautiful Morning."

As Emma and Mattia were finishing their caprese sandwiches in front of the Palazzo Pitti, they watched the last tourist leave the building, the guards close the ornate gates. Mattia had allowed an hour's free time before the concert to stroll the fabulous paths of the renowned gardens behind the palazzo. This was, after all, the spectacular garden that was copied by the grandest courts of Europe - a vast, one hundred eleven acres. Tonight, Mattia and Emma could only hope to see edges and corners of the whole.

"The Palazzo was built by the banker Luca Pitti in the fifteenth century," Mattia began as they walked along. "Soon after he started construction of the gardens, the Medicis took ownership and continued to work on the gardens, as well as enlarge the palazzo, during their entire reign. Hundreds of years."

The pair meandered among priceless works of art, sculptures and fountains from the fifteenth to seventeenth centuries. Vast lawns were defined by immaculately trimmed low yew hedges. Paths were lined by high hedges of holm oaks. Towering cypress trees stood in rigid patterns. All was meticulously designed in the most formal manner. Not a leaf or branch was untended. Clever garden "follies," or small buildings, were scattered over the scene, built purely for aesthetic pleasure. Bacchus riding a turtle presided over an entrance as the obese, naked dwarf Morgante, the most popular of the dwarfs of the court of Cosimo de Medici. Built in 1550, an amphitheater for theatrical productions, the Anfiteatro di Boboli. An Egyptian obelisk soared skyward at the end of a long open walkway. The Casino del Cavaliere, now the Museum of Porcelain, stood on the grounds. As well, the famous Kaffeehaus, an eighteenth-century pavilion, a rare example of Rococo architecture in Tuscany. All of it conveying the feel of an open-air museum. As they strolled along the walkways, scenes of heroic Renaissance architecture and landscape unfolded.

Emma was quiet. Mattia kept glancing over; was she pleased? In truth, Emma was astounded. But what would she say? That it was pretty? Or fascinating? Or almost too much of a spectacle for her to take in?

Eventually, they found their seats for the concert, metal chairs set up in a grove edged with rows of pink camellias. Thick shade trees with trunks six feet wide shaded the area. Slivers of daylight from the waning sun threw spotty shadows over what comprised the backyard splendor of the colossal Palazzo Pitti.

Waiting in the scented air, Mattia began to describe the Buontalenti Grotto, the garden's most famous masterpiece.

"The most curious place you will see in all of Florence, one of the city's dazzling glories. Three magical rooms of allegories, frescoes, statuary, and fanciful images creating the impression of being in the midst of an eccentric, bizarre fairy tale."

Emma was barely able to make out the grotto a short distance off with its exotic stone stalagmites and stalactites cascading over the entrance, framing the opening into a mysterious cave.

"The viewer is transported, transformed," Mattia continued.

Just then, tiny lights like holiday sparklers popped up out of the darkness. An elegant duo appeared, lightly adjusting their chairs and the music stands. The man in a tuxedo cradled a cello; the woman in a black dress, a violin. Their dark clothes melted into the background, leaving illuminated only their faces, hands, and instruments. The audience fell silent, as reverent as if at mass in the great Il Duomo. Tenderly, the musicians placed their fingers on the strings. And then, out of the night, the glory of Pachelbel's "Canon in D" rose like a heavenly spirit. With the first lift of the notes, Emma felt tears beginning to form. Even the birds were silent, listening. The plaintive sounds drifted through the night until, after a while, they finally wound down, as gently as love can appear from behind a cloud. The pair of musicians paused, shifted, then again lifted their bows, and dipped into Haydn's "String Duo in D Major."

Mattia reached for Emma's hand.

The palace garden was designed for kings, fitted out for Florentine royalty. There was music to summon the angels. Mattia sensed Emma's awe, lightly squeezed her fingers. It was a night for the beginnings of a romance. But, in fact, Emma was thinking of Ethan. She envisioned his innocent face transformed into disbelief as she described this scene. If she spoke further of grottos and caves, he would likely be fashioning her accounts into stories.

"Ingenious," the critics would say of work he would produce from her descriptions. "Inspired. Visionary."

But how could she share experiences with her brother that held possibilities for her but not for him? Dr. Matthews had long ago laid out the rules, prescribed a restricted activity diet. What did that mean for his future? The family would never know for sure. Ethan just had to live carefully and mindfully. Fate would take care of the rest.

Oh my god, Ethan, she thought.

Jack was arranging his papers and smiling happily. It was about a woman, of that, Ethan was sure. What else would account for his ebullience?

"Ethan, my boy," Jack started. "I met this gal named Addie Jenkins over at Matt's. She's a teacher. Do you know her?"

Ethan did not. But he knew a Susan Jenkins, who helped in the house when he was a little boy.

"I think her name was Susie."

"That's her older sister," Jack said. "She's married now. Addie and I are going to the movies on Saturday night. Would you like to come?"

And Ethan knew then as sure as he had ever known anything, that this was Uncle Jack's arising, and that every day of his own life from now on would be no better than the one he lived today. He felt the sting of dislocation, of loss. It didn't matter that he was a compelling storyteller or that he had special gifts. He was sick of living in his head. He was tired of describing exploits of worlds beyond earth. His body was now telling its own stories, and no conclusion he could imagine would end well.

A dim glow lit the path as the ushers stood ready to lead out the guests, but Emma stayed seated. Mattia waited, allowing her time to linger. He tried to see the scene through her eyes, naive and unschooled, but it was difficult. He had practically grown up in the Boboli Gardens. The grounds were as familiar as those of his own father's estate. He and his friend Nicolo used to play hide-and-seek among its splendidly clipped mazes. So he simply sat quietly. When the last of the stragglers were gone from the aisle, Emma stood, and Mattia followed.

Sofia gave Emma time off, and Mattia was quick to scoop her up on his silver Vespa and spin her around the Italian landscape. From the craggy Apennine Mountains to the coastal beaches, they wound through country roads, skimmed along the sea, not to the usual touristy places but to those that revealed the spirit of Italy's daily life - lunch in a farmhouse where the owner built his ovens outside, the better to see his vineyards. Then a climb to the roofs of the medieval castles in Siena and San Gimignano; an afternoon on the beach at Viareggio during *Carnival* with its papier-mâché floats and parade known as the *Passeggiata a Mare* along the Promenade; sea coves of Portovenere on the Ligurian Coast at the base of spectacular, craggy headlands, and on the cliff's stony hilltop, a fortress with a view of the brilliant aquamarine Gulf of Poets far below.

Astonished, Emma gushed, "A body of water named the Gulf of Poets? Could anything be more romantic?"

A speedboat brought them to nearby Cinque Terre, five idyllic fishing villages set into the rocks edging the Mediterranean Sea. The inhabitants had built terraced landscapes, steep and rugged plantings, to cultivate their grapes and olives. Emma and Mattia climbed the cliffs like the wild ibex. They hiked past two, in fact, standing tall and proud on a narrow ledge. Their long curved horns were framed against the rocks like a still life painting. As they pushed on ever higher, Mattia held tightly onto Emma's hand, the paths and steps often intricate or unreliable. The sea became part of the sky, a glorious sight Emma had never seen growing up in landlocked Iowa.

But Emma grew edgy at the throngs of visitors nearby who filled every empty space and corner. Strangers often so close they could hear her whispers to Mattia. Thoughts of unspoiled Iowa farmland pierced her heart, but immediately flew off as she scrambled to keep her footing.

In the hills of Cinque Terre, they found a small, flat plot of land and spread out a blanket for lunch.

And here, it happened.

Mattia edged over and lightly put his fingertips under Emma's chin, gently guiding her face toward his. Before he kissed her, he looked long into her eyes until he could sense her heart yearning for him. And finally, his kiss, mixed with the sea air and the bleating of the wild goats and the earthy, citrus scent of the grapes, Emma lost in the taste of his mouth.

All at once, leaves rustled, stones scattered. Hikers. The disturbance gave her a necessary pause. She pulled back, trying to catch her breath, placing a hand on Mattia's chest. Wait. She pulled away, lightly resting in the curve of Mattia's shoulder. There she remained until she stood up and began to fold the blanket. She both cursed and blessed the distraction of hikers. Pulling away from Mattia's arms required an extreme effort of mind and limb, but the affection of a companion that would stretch out into the future was what she wanted, not a momentary indiscretion.

And it was just then that she knew she would cut short her stay and leave Italy. Mattia's attentions and the country's charms would go on forever, but she could no longer wait to see what was happening at home. Was her grandmother's latest production a success? Were her folks still pleased with their jobs? Her coach sent a note that the team wasn't the same without her. But, most of all, she missed her twin.

Several months earlier, Maryann had observed that Ethan suffered an episode of some kind. She wasn't sure what had happened. Neither was Jack. Only Ethan had turned moody and withdrawn.

"For a few weeks, Ethan didn't want to work and stayed in his room," Maryann told Emma on the phone. "But then he had his yearly visit with Dr. Matthews. That seemed to cheer him up, thank goodness. Not that he was entirely his old self, but he would laugh at dinner and showed an interest in writing again."

Emma was happy to know that Ethan was back on track. It made her feel less dejected that she hadn't been around when he needed her. When they would finally take a walk around the farm, Ethan would tell her what had been going on.

"Just one touristy spot before you leave," Mattia announced, "an unforgettable sight." They entered through an unmarked side entrance of the magnificent domed building, guarded by a lone sentry who tipped his hat at recognizing Mattia.

The Medici Chapels - a complex of buildings, its two main structures built within the Basilica of San Lorenzo.

Although the Medici family was associated with other churches, this was considered the official Medici church, their famed mausoleum, a tribute to the dynastic power that lasted centuries. The singular chapel Mattia led her to specifically was the *Sagrestia Nuova,* housing the renowned sculptural cycle of statuary by Michelangelo called *Twilight, Dawn, Day, Night.* Furthermore, the four reclining figures, the room, and all its embellishments comprised the sculptor's first foray into architecture. The entire world considered this chapel one of the finest examples of the Renaissance period. The monumental allegorical figures were set high up on marble pedestals beneath niches containing statues of Lorenzo, duke di Urbino, and Giuliano, duke de Nemours. Marble, gilt, and precious gems were put together with unequalled mastery to form a majestic space. All of it rare and dazzling.

Emma pivoted in wonder.

"Michelangelo's intent was to portray a complex symbolism of human life where its active and contemplative aspects would interact to free the soul after death," Mattia explained.

Mighty, Emma thought, *everything - the figures, the decoration, everything is mighty.*

She didn't know how to begin thinking about such grandeur and about Michelangelo's philosophy of life and death, here creatively rendered. She felt utterly lost yet utterly exalted.

As she looked more closely, she was taken with an outlandish impression of the four sculptures. She may not have been used to viewing artistic masterpieces, but she *was* used to noticing every detail of the human body, a condition of gymnasts who analyzed every inch of their flesh for any performance advantage. *Why,* she wondered, *were the lower limbs of these marble figures heavy and muscular, like a man's, and the torsos and heads of two, graceful and feminine?* It seemed a peculiar portrayal. She dared not ask Mattia and reveal her ignorance, but Gavin would surely have an explanation.

Outside once again, Mattia waved and shouted *ciao* to many passersby. When they arrived at his silver Vespa parked near the Basilica's entrance, Emma swung her long legs over the back seat and thought, *If only my folks could see me now, my arms around this handsome young man, my hair lifting on the breeze as the engine revs up and takes off with a lurch and a flourish.*

On their last afternoon together, Emma turned nineteen. Mattia planned a quiet day, wine tasting in the Tuscan countryside. They whipped along winding deserted roads on his Vespa, stopping every few miles at an ancient stone winery, the vintners welcoming Mattia as if he were family.

Emma knew that Mattia was seducing her with the people and the country. However, despite his wooing and their feverish kisses, despite her pleasure in the sublime surroundings, she was reluctant to abandon herself altogether. Mattia would always be part of a fantasy in this fantastical place. But she belonged elsewhere. The peace, the serenity back home - she had never fully appreciated the value of an unhurried life, of open spaces that never filled up. Whenever she drove by the sunflowers or the cornfields, there was rarely another car in sight and, only occasionally, a farmer in the fields. She wanted to spend time with Ethan before fall term. With her folks, her friends, strolling around the farm. Here, the magnificence of the culture overwhelmed. It might make you dream, but it failed to present what would be real for her.

Gavin was, of course, exempt from such considerations. His was a different kind of love as he contentedly lived a singular life alone on the top of a mountain.

Emma and Mattia finished their day with a ride at dusk along the Arno River. A kind of review and summing up of the beautiful, ancient city with its old lamplights casting threads of silver on the water, stone walls, grand palazzos, and overall, the splendid golden light that united the whole in an ancient harmony. No aberrant architectural feature or tourist or colorful happening disturbed the peace. A turn away from the river and Mattia shut down his scooter in front of *Sofia's Place*. He placed both hands on Emma's shoulders and gave her a sweet kiss on each cheek. His thoughtful eyes glistened, his throat felt thick. He looked long into her eyes, then whispered, "*Fino a che non ci vediamo di nuovo*." Until we meet again. As sad as she was, Emma smiled to herself, thinking his words sounded straight out of an American movie. And surely Mattia represented the perfect script for a romantic fling in Italy. Returning to his vehicle, Mattia threw his leg over the seat and pressed a button, the engine thundering and growling. Without looking back, he raised his hand high, his fist giving a shake. Emma watched him go. She would describe all this to Ethan and eagerly wait to hear what he would say.

Emma began to straighten her few rooms above the old candle shop. She returned items to their proper shelves and bought a new duvet for the bed. Then she took down her suitcase and began to fold in her pretty new clothes. Every gesture was bittersweet. Who would not bemoan leaving such a place and the wonderful folks who gave freely of their friendship?

Sofia's artists wandered in to say goodbye. Tommaso clasped a thin gold thread of a bracelet around her slender wrist. Benito, a sculptor from Naples, handed her a small marble carving of her likeness. Gastone from Sicily painted her portrait with a watercolor wash over a few lines of ink and placed the tiny work in a locket of rose-colored enamel.

She and Sofia stood in the center of the living room.

"Sofia," she cried, hugging this spirited woman who she thought belonged with her grandfather.

"I don't know what to say - your many kindnesses, your generosity. You've been wonderful to me."

"I've loved every minute," Sofia replied. "I expect you back here for another long visit," both of them wondering if that would ever occur.

How lovely, Sofia thought, *to be a young and beautiful Emma with unlimited choices and only for you to pick and choose.* She could already feel the quivers of loss as Emma waved goodbye and walked out the door.

Before leaving, Emma wanted to move up to the mountain and spend time with her grandfather. She loved to observe how he got into his work, propping a blank canvas on his easel, then gazing contemplatively out to the garden. A turn back to the canvas and more reflection. Finally, having reached a decision, he put aside his calm demeanor and squeezed tubes of color onto his palette. Coating his brush with paint, he at last approached the blank surface. And then, as if he were perched on the tailwind of a tornado, he raced to the finish day after day until the storm wore itself out. Only occasionally did he pause to stand back and assess. Emma tried to imagine what he was thinking, to anticipate his next move, but she never could. When she was sure he would add a specific daub here or there, he would make an entirely different choice. Over and over until the surface of his canvas was throbbing with energy.

Gavin's palette. Was it his fifth? His tenth? The wood was no longer visible. Stained with traces of a hundred colors, its layered shadows symbolized a lifelong journey of serious effort. She thought the item itself was a work of art and should hang on a wall. Or perhaps be sold to a collector for a substantial price.

It was not unlike her own process in the gym as she hovered on the fringes, coiled to spring. But only after dismissing the possible dangers of injury, of misstep, was she ready. And only after a final assessment of her body, of the pommel horse, the rings, the far corner of the mat, the dozen elements that would thrust her forward and keep her straight, all the way to that podium and a bow of her head as a judge placed a medal around her neck.

Was it like that with Ethan when he started to write a story? A blank page. What will be his first word? A spark, an opening flutter skitters across the brain, and the pen goes to the paper. The energy begins to run. The mind travels and wanders, and he makes choices - one phrase or word is better than another. He deletes, replaces, reworks, and suddenly the story is starting to shape up. He does this repeatedly, and he now knows he is in the heart of the vortex. It is exactly where he wants to be. As he takes something out and puts something in, it is just like Gavin painting over his existing work. And he simply keeps going until he's ready to clean his brushes. And Ethan until the words feel right and his pen comes to rest. And Emma raises her arms at the end of her performance.

Perhaps for anyone striving for excellence, Emma considered, it is the same process. Take hold of a dream, master the required discipline, and do your best.

Grandfather and granddaughter sat together in the garden while Emma asked questions.

"Grandpa, did you want to paint when you were my age?

"What made you leave the farm?

"How did you meet Grandma?

"Why did you get divorced?

"How did you come to settle here on this mountain?"

Their talk was an unraveling of factual memories that she was gathering for an understanding of his life. Almost as an afterthought did he offer a slight mention of a mural he did for a museum in Venice.

"Venice! How thrilling," Emma said. But then Gavin's voice trailed off, and Emma was reluctant to make further inquiries. She was developing a sure sense of when, or not, Gavin was willing to engage. Every now and then, their talk was interrupted by a great grey heron flapping its wings on the roof of the studio. At these times, they honored its call for attention by sitting silently and gazing up respectfully at the giant bird.

Emma was anxious to ask more personal questions. Are you happy? Are you lonely? Did you ever want to remarry? Have more children? Were you ever attracted to Sofia? Would you have stayed in Iowa if Grandma had encouraged your work?

But such questions would intrude on his private life. She couldn't bring herself to ask them. After her days with Mattia, she knew there were personal sentiments one doesn't share with another.

Still, she wondered about the unanswered questions. *Only between Ethan and myself,* she reflected, *is there no inclination to hold back.*

Emma was now making her final farewells. Brother Bianchi invited her and Gavin to dinner in the grand medieval hall where the monks in their humble robes of burlap were lined up behind their chairs for the traditional blessing before the meal. After dessert, Brother Bianchi said a few words about the gift of talent bestowed and how the rest of us must be grateful and beholden. Then a toast to the virtues of family.

"Gavin, thank you for letting us know your lovely daughter. If she follows in your generous and mindful footsteps, surely you will have achieved the reward of fatherhood.

"Emma, my dear child," he concluded, "may God bless you, and may you return to visit us again one day."

There was no need to send out invitations. Word had passed throughout the village that Francesco was planning a farewell gathering for Emma. All the shopkeepers left their doors open and strolled on over - the gelato vendor and the art supply owner, the flower lady and the baker, Mario and Piero, the vintners from the mountain whose sons were now running the businesses while their fathers sat in the village square and played cards, *Scopa* or *Briscola*. In truth, the party merely represented the Italians' everyday celebration of life, which its people observe keenly on any day, for any reason.

As she rode the bus to Francesco's, Sofia fingered the weighty, hand-forged chunks of gold links around her neck, grateful she had decided to sell Tommaso's jewelry in the Annex. It had turned out to be a profitable endeavor for them both. She wore a splendid tunic in sapphire blue over black silk pants and should have felt the beauty she was, but rather, she felt oddly nervous. This was the first time she had traveled to the top of this mountain.

When the bus finally rumbled into the village, Gavin was waiting. As the doors opened, he held out his hand to help her down the steps. Just at that moment, Emma noticed his eyes crinkle with smiles. As if he had known Sofia from long ago but was just now meeting her for the first time. Sofia's eyes too were tender and yearning. As she reached the lowest step, her hand in his, neither pulled away, and there her hand lingered.

When his guests had gathered, Francesco spoke.

"Dear Emma," beaming at her with proprietary fondness. "You brought the spirit of youth into our lives, reminding us of our own younger days but also bringing in the new. That is what you gave us, the old and the new together, *il vecchio e il nuovo insieme*, in your beautiful soul. And for that, we thank you. But we also pay a special tribute to your grandfather. We have known him so long, it is as if he was born in our village. He taught us how to *see* and *understand* a new kind of art, an art of the present, not of the past. And yet, like you Emma, somehow combining the beauty of both together. And now, my dear people, *vino* for all!"

Francesco laid out a sumptuous spread. Sofia stood next to Emma, explaining the table.

"That one is called *culadur*," she said, pointing, "shad, fried with onions, lemon, white wine, grated cheese. And here we have *crema del Gerre,* which is pecorino, milk, grappa, olive oil, and herbs. And this in the blue bowl is called *cibreo*, chicken giblets, tomato paste, garlic, onion, and a single anchovy. To the pot you add egg yolks, flour, lemon juice."

Emma grimaced at the mention of chicken giblets.

"Oh, try it, silly! *È delizioso*! Francesco's *specialità.* And the last, *friggione*, an onion and tomato dip, slowly cooked, not bruschetta but similar. Don't mix these dishes together. Try one at a time on the bread and toasts."

A wreath of rose petals was placed on Emma's hair by Francesco's youngest daughter, Amalia.

"We made it ourselves, especially for you."

Three of her sisters held hands and sang, "*Con Te Partirò*," in Italian, then in English, "*Time to Say Goodbye*," weaving in and out of the chairs while their brother Sandro strummed the guitar.

Next, Francesco and Antonio stood, hands over their hearts, and belted out "Arrivederci Roma" until everyone had tears in their eyes. Emma, weeping with love and affection, knew this moment was as precious as any she would ever know. Furthermore, she would have no need for Ethan to explain any of its truth.

Emma fondly watched the villagers feasting and laughing together. No one had given a second thought to leaving their shops for the festivities. Mario and Piero had halted their game. Francesco's wife had come out from the kitchen to watch her children dance. Gavin had discreetly held on to Sofia's hand. After all, life was to be honored and praised, and there was not a moment to squander.

Emma was enchanted by the exuberant mood, the spontaneity of emotion. Right before her eyes was a template of incalculable worth - that beauty and glory are not restricted by time or place or by age. Neither are they restricted by wealth or fame. *We young folks tend to think that only the young experience beauty and glory,* Emma reflected. But that is not so. Just look around. Those glorious elements do not end, not ever. They appear again and again in a thousand ways, to people everywhere. Although it could be said that maturity is likewise something to be celebrated, the appearance of beauty and glory is perhaps never quite as pure as that first time, when one is young and innocent.

About the Author

Formerly an interior designer and painter, Pamela Hull wrote her first book, *Where's My Bride?* at age sixty. This venture was to be a one-time effort, a tribute to a remarkable husband and marriage. However, as the endeavor unfurled, she unearthed a keen love for writing narratives.

Her second book, *SAY YES! Flying Solo After Sixty*, a memoir, asserts that neither age nor being single is an impediment to living a rich life, a subject relevant for all ages and genders.

Moments that Mattered, nonfiction, followed *SAY YES!* and examined how ordinary, everyday experiences, could prove to be life-altering.

And then, for the first time, a work of fiction. *What Love Looks Like* is a complex, often bittersweet collection of unforgettable short stories exploring utterly dissimilar relationships.

Her current book and first novel, *The Lives We Were Meant to Live*, follows the personal journeys of the Taylor family. Individual ambitions and longings are slowly revealed, or not, which move each of the characters toward their respective futures.

Ms. Hull's essays and poetry have been widely published in select journals such as the *Bellevue Literary Review*, *Ars Medica*, *Lumina*, *North Dakota Quarterly*, and others.

Her two children were born on the East Coast and raised on the West. Despite bicoastal lures, the author has chosen to reside in Manhattan for the grand adventure of flying solo in a great city.

Printed in the USA
CPSIA information can be obtained
at www.ICGtesting.com
LVHW041340110124
768547LV00063B/1569

9 798887 936666